MW01128257

THE PROMISED PRINCE

KORTNEY KEISEL

First edition November 2020

Cover design by Seventh Star Art

Map design by Foreign Worlds Cartography

www.kortneykeisel.com

To my angel mother

I wish you could have been here for the writing process. You would've loved this book. I hope you're smiling down on me from heaven

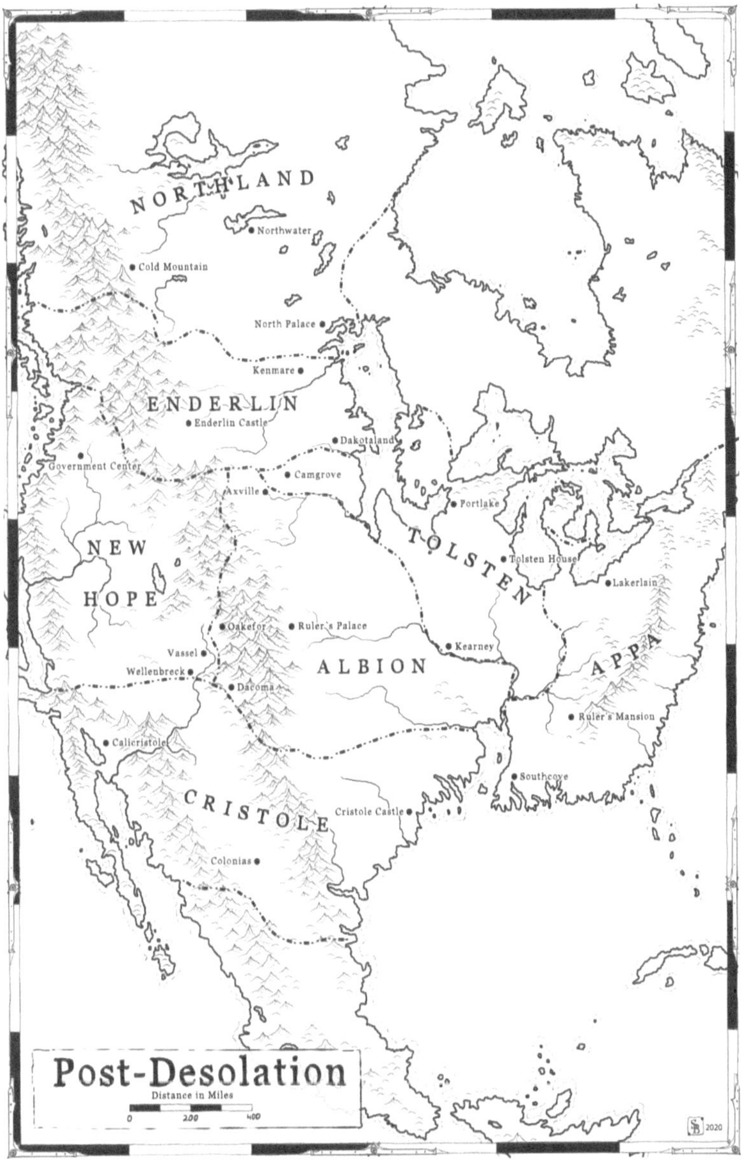
NORTHLAND
Northwater
Cold Mountain
North Palace
Kenmare
ENDERLIN
Enderlin Castle
Dakotaland
Government Center
Camgrove
Axville
Portlake
TOLSTEN
Tolsten House
Lakerlain
NEW
HOPE
Oakefor
Ruler's Palace
Kearney
Vassel
Wellenbreck
Dacoma
ALBION
APPA
Ruler's Mansion
Calicristole
Southcove
CRISTOLE
Cristole Castle
Colonias
Post-Desolation
Distance in Miles
0
200
400
SB
2020

1

Renna

The Kingdom of New Hope
The Year 2259 - 200 Years After Desolation

R*oad trip.*

Renna had once seen an old photograph in the artifact room back at the Government Center. The picture was a pre-Desolation advertisement for the Tetons, some mountain range that was probably destroyed two hundred years ago in an earthquake or by an atomic bomb. In the photo, a group of girls stood with arms around each other in front of the mountain, smiling like they were having the time of their lives. The blonde in the middle wore a shirt that said, *This is my road trip shirt.* Renna wished she could wear a comfortable road trip shirt instead of the tight-fitting travel dress that currently rode up on her waist.

She tugged at the dress—*again*—and stared out the window as the transporter drove along. Over the past few days, she had watched the coastal land of New Hope melt away into a sunbaked desert as they traveled southeast across the kingdom. Now, the arid landscape brightened to green plains, letting Renna know they were almost to their kingdom's border. *And closer to Wellenbreck Farm.*

A knot pulled tightly in her stomach. She couldn't travel this far and not stop at Wellenbreck. But the last time Renna had suggested they visit their old home, her mother had refused.

"We're not staying at Wellenbreck," her mother had said. "Can you imagine a princess sleeping there?" Her mother had wrung her hands as she shook her head. "No. No, we don't want to give Seran any reason to think I wasn't worthy of marrying her father." Renna knew better than to challenge her mother when she was nervous—queen or not. She'd relented, even while determining to pick up the fight later.

Renna's eyes darted to her mother in the seat across from her. This would be her last chance to convince her. The queen's head leaned against the transporter's door, smashing her brown hair and the regal twist it was tied in. Even while sleeping, her mother looked elegant. Next to Renna's mother was her dark-haired stepsister, Seran. She read a book, clearly unphased by their travels.

Renna sighed loudly, hoping the sound would wake her mother.

It didn't.

She tried shuffling her legs, knocking her mother's feet slightly as she stretched and yawned in a high shrill.

Nothing.

The woman was out.

Frustrated, Renna leaned back into the seat, not missing Seran's smirk from behind her book.

I'm going to miss my chance, Renna thought, shaking her head.

Suddenly, as if from heaven above, the transporter hit an unexpected bump. Probably the cement corner of a pre-Desolation house or part of a steel beam from a bridge or something. Whatever it was, it was too much for the transporter's thick tires and built-in suspension. It threw Renna's mother into the air, jolting her out of her coma; she gripped the door handle, glaring over her shoulder at the closed panel that hid the transporter's driver from her wrath.

Her free hand covered her heart. "I swear, King Bryant will hear about how bumpy this ride to Albion has been. It's time the Council of Essentials starts paving roads. Then travel between kingdoms would be easier and more comfortable." She looked to Seran for support. "Don't you agree?"

Seran paused her reading, giving her stepmother a sweet smile. "I agree that paved roads would make for a more comfortable ride."

Queen Mariele seemed satisfied with the response, easing her hands to her lap.

Seran had a diplomatic answer for everything. Maybe that's why Renna's mother preferred Seran over her. But Renna couldn't worry about that now. A stop to Wellenbreck Farm was a much more critical issue.

It was now or never. Renna straightened as she spoke. "Mom, I know you said the caravan was going to stay the night in the city of Vassel, but I think Seran would get more rest at Wellenbreck Farm."

Seran eyed her curiously over the edge of her book.

"Oh, Renna. Not this again." Her mother's shoulders sank with an exasperated breath. "I already made my decision. We are not stopping at Wellenbreck. Seran isn't interested in staying at our old home. Besides, it's completely unsuitable for a princess."

Renna was desperate to visit her old home; she hated to resort to manipulation, but desperate people did desperate things. "You're probably right. The inn at Vassel, while old, would be better. And I'm sure it's much cleaner than when we stayed there with Dad. When was that? Five? Six years ago?"

She could almost see the memory play back in her mother's mind.

Renna turned to Seran who had put her book down, no doubt interested in Renna's performance. "We only stayed there one night, so how could we really judge the cleanliness of the entire inn? I'm sure we just got a bad room." Renna shrugged. "Or they just forgot to wash the sheets."

Across the transporter, her mother's body tensed with concern.

So close.

What else could she say to tip the decision in her favor?

"I don't mind staying at Wellenbreck Farm," Seran cut in. "It was your home before you married my father. It might be nice to see where you both come from."

Renna shot a grateful look to her stepsister. How could her mother refuse Seran? She would never.

Queen Mariele scoffed. "There isn't much to see. It's just a simple house and farm. The Vassel inn will be much more comfortable for you, I'm sure."

"No, really. I want to see Renna's beloved Wellenbreck."

Renna could see her mother weigh Seran's words in her mind, but it wasn't enough to make her shift her decision.

"Besides," Seran added, "if the inn at Vassel has a history of being dirty, I could never be comfortable there. Cleanliness is crucial."

Seran for the win!

The queen was silent for a moment. Finally, she let out a defeated huff. It was amazing the power Seran had over her. "Perhaps we *should* stay at Wellenbreck Farm. Nellie runs the house, and I know she keeps everything spotless." She looked at Seran hesitantly. "It's not a nice place, though. Nothing like what you're used to."

"It sounds perfect." Seran smiled then raised her book again.

"But we'll only stay at Wellenbreck Farm one night," her mother stated, giving Renna a pointed look. Her gaze shifted to Seran and she softened, placing a gentle hand on her knee.

"You can rest before our final descent into Albion so you'll look fresh when we arrive at the palace. You don't want Prince Ezra thinking you don't travel well."

Renna glanced around the vehicle to Seran and her mother, doubting that Seran's mysterious fiancé would even think to notice whether she traveled well or not.

Queen Mariele pushed a button, rolling down the panel between her and the driver. "Mangum, send a guard on a personal transporter ahead to Wellenbreck Farm to inform Nellie and Preetis they need to prep the house for guests tonight . . ."

As her mother continued to rattle off instructions, Renna glanced at Seran and silently mouthed, "Thank you." She couldn't have convinced her mother without Seran's help.

Seran dipped her chin in a nod then turned her attention back to her book.

Sometimes the princess surprised Renna. Seran was usually so proper and in control, but there were moments when her serenity slipped, and she seemed almost like a regular girl. Today was one of those days.

Usually, Renna didn't know what to say to Seran. They were so different. Renna was free-spirited and out of control—most of the time, anyway—while Seran was calm and composed. Compared to Seran, Renna often felt immature, even though Seran was only a year and a half older. Plus, Seran was a princess. A *gorgeous* princess.

Not that I'm ugly. Renna caught a reflection of herself in the window, tucking a piece of her hair behind her ear. She liked her blonde wavy hair that refused to lay straight, her sun-kissed complexion from hours spent at the beach, and her green eyes. Her father always said they were the greenest eyes he'd ever seen, but he'd also said she was the most beautiful girl in the world, so how could she really trust him? Especially when the most beautiful girl in the world currently sat across from Renna, wearing an expensive, purple pleated dress.

Though, it wasn't the elaborate dress that made Seran look exquisite. No, she would look equally beautiful in a neutral, working-class dress.

Seran's beauty was a once-in-a-lifetime kind of beauty. She was thin, with natural curves in all the right places. Her endless lashes complemented her dark eyes and flawlessly curved eyebrows; she wore her black tresses swept back in a classic, restrained up-do, accentuating her high cheekbones. She was exotic, sweet, and wise for her twenty years. Her fashion choices were bold in color, yet still tasteful. Seran was the ideal combination of everything proper, lovely, and royal.

The prince of Albion is going to love her.

Seran was definitely worth the wait of a ten-year betrothal, and probably the best thing the prince, and Albion, would gain out of the marriage alliance.

The surrounding small towns started to feel familiar as they neared Wellenbreck Farm. Renna soaked it all in, feeling as though the lost pieces of her heart were finally clicking back into place. Fourteen years of memories flooded her mind as she thought back to a life different than the one she lived now. The happy memories centered around her father—working the alfalfa fields, dancing in the kitchen, climbing the grassy hill behind the house, swimming at Wellenbreck Pond.

The pond had been her favorite place of all. On weekend nights, her father would load Renna on his shoulders and trek up the hill, singing songs she was sure he had made up. They spent warm summer evenings swimming together in the pond, tucked into the lush meadow surrounded by thick trees, hidden from the world. They even devoted an entire summer to building a wooden dock to fish from. Renna had been too young to help, but she'd tried to be his assistant anyway, bringing whatever tools and measuring boards he'd needed. Most days, she'd skipped rocks while her father hammered away, but he'd given her all the credit in the end. Back then, it had been just the two of them and their laughter.

Renna's heart raced when she saw the small stone cottage Nellie and Preetis lived in next to Wellenbreck Farm. They had been there since before Renna was born, keeping the farm running, helping with the house. When Renna and her mother moved to the Government Center, Nellie and Preetis stayed behind to take care of everything.

The alfalfa fields stretched from the roadside to the tree-lined hill where Wellenbreck Pond waited. The crops were full and green, and Renna breathed a sigh of relief; Preetis had done an excellent job maintaining them.

She strained her neck, trying to get a view of the farm-house. The two-story home wasn't large or elegantly adorned. It was shaped more like a rectangular box with a triangular, pitched roof. Three gabled windows jutted out from the roof, matching the windows below. In a few places, the cream plaster had peeled off from the house and the stone wall surrounding the front yard had crumbled away. She wished her father was alive to fix things. The years of absence and neglect had obviously taken their toll, despite Nellie and Preetis's best efforts.

Renna blinked back a tear, refusing to be sad. Her mother had gifted her a few short hours at Wellenbreck Farm, and she needed to use that time wisely. She wanted to explore every-thing, but she would need to escape the caravan first. Other-wise, her mother would rope her into some random assignment, like showing Seran's friends around. Seran's friends were the last people Renna wanted to spend time with while at Wellenbreck. She scanned the area for the best escape route.

The transporter's rubber tires crunched over small pebbles as the vehicle rolled to a stop. A few moments later, the door flung open, and a guard's outstretched arm helped her mother and Seran out of the vehicle. The arm reached for Renna as well, but she bounced past it, twirling around to get a better look at the place. Two other large transporters parked behind them, carrying Seran's friends, a few royal advisors, and their three maids. A dozen guards on personal transporters dismounted and started unloading bags from the backs of the vehicles. Her mother's maid, Cypress, shouted orders to the rest of the staff.

It was time to get lost.

Becoming invisible in the mayhem of guards and maids was easy. No one in the royal caravan was worried about the queen's tag-along daughter.

Dodging several guards with luggage in their hands, Renna ran into the small, wood stable along the side of the main house. Her head popped into a few stalls, looking for her old horse, Canyon Ann, but none of the horses were there. The stable was empty. Preetis must have them in the fields; they would have to reunite later. Renna scanned the stable, finding what she was looking for on a rusted hook next to some rakes.

Thank you, Preetis. Renna unfastened her pink travel dress and pulled the farmhand's work pants on, throwing his gray shirt over her head. The best part of moving to the Government Center had been the upgrade to vibrantly colored clothing. One minute at Wellenbreck Farm, and she was already back to wearing muted colors. She turned her head as she ran out the stable's back door, giving the bustling front yard one last look. Nobody seemed to notice her sprinting for the hill.

Renna smirked. Dressing as a man had likely helped her cause.

The mile-long path to the water was overgrown with abandonment, but as Renna approached the pond, everything else around the water remained the same. In a way, it was comforting how time had left this place behind, yet it was still here when Renna needed it.

She walked across the splintered dock, knowing from memory which boards to avoid stubbing her toes on. The smell of aspen trees filled her nose as she breathed in. She thought about testing the water's temperature first, but her father's voice sounded in her thoughts. *"Don't think. Just jump."*

So she did—letting out a scream as she plugged her nose.

The chilly water covered her, reviving her senses. She let out another yelp when she came up for air—not because of the cold, but because she was elated to be home. She drifted on her back, letting the water lap around her.

The cold pond tugged at her memories, bringing them to the front of her mind. She could picture her father with her, see flashes of his facial expressions, his silvery beard, his broad shoulders, his playful eyes. It felt so real. Vivid memories had been hard to come by as time passed, but memories were effortless at the pond.

The buzz of a personal transporter scattered Renna's thoughts away. She groaned, lifting her head. It had to be Mangum, her mother's guard, coming to take her back to Wellenbreck Farm. Was she missed already? She slapped the water in front of her.

I just got here.

Couldn't her mother give her one afternoon? It had been *four years* since Renna had been there. Four years since she had left her comfortable home at Wellenbreck Farm for a fast-paced life at the New Hope Government Center. Four years since her mother had married the king of New Hope.

The PT's hum grew louder, echoing off the thick trees. Renna had seconds before Mangum would arrive. She couldn't really blame him. He was following the queen's orders.

She blew out a breath in frustration and began swimming toward the dock when a sudden idea made her stop. If she was going to be dragged back to her mother, she might as well do it in style.

Renna grinned. She flipped onto her stomach, waiting until the PT's sound was upon her, and then immersed her head underwater. She floated, careful not to move a muscle.

She didn't know how long it would take for Mangum to find her, but for the sake of a joke, she was willing to hold her breath as long as she could. After all, when faking her death by drowning, appearance was everything.

Poor Mangum. He'll probably have a heart attack when he finds me.

2

Trev

Trev slowed his machine to a stop, his muscles relieved to have a break from driving. He had started the day in Dacoma. His father didn't see any use in visiting the small, far-away cities in the outskirts of Albion borders. But Trev wanted to show every citizen that he cared for them. If Trev had to be forced onto a campaign tour, he would do it his own way. The tour was supposed to help him in the King Ruler election at the end of the year, but it was more than that to Trev. He wanted to get to know the people—their needs and struggles. How could he lead them, be their king, if he didn't know them?

Trev kicked out the stand at the bottom of his PT, letting the weight of the motorized bike rest against it. He pulled his helmet off, hanging it on the machine's handlebars. His body ached everywhere from straddling the leather seat for so many miles. Even his fingers hurt from grasping the handlebars and pushing the lever forward with his thumb.

He turned to the water, hoping its coolness would soothe his tired muscles. Soft ripples rolled lazily along, begging him to dive through their perfection. His eyes followed the hypnotizing movement until he noticed something gray bobbing in the water a few yards away. Squinting against the warm sunlight, he stepped to the pond's edge for a closer look.

Was that a body?

Alarm took over.

He sprang into action, removing his boots and weapons belt. With one swift motion, he dove into the water, the sting of cold pricking his skin. His focus was on getting to the lifeless body's side, and in three strokes, he was there. He pushed the body over, recognizing the curves of a young woman. Massive amounts of wet hair covered her face, tangling between his fingers.

Heart pounding, Trev wrapped his arm under her shoulder and dragged her limp body to the dock's ladder. It was a bit awkward, but he managed to hoist her up and spread her out on the decaying wood. Had he found her too late? He leaned over, checking her neck for a pulse.

That's when the dead girl gave him a heart attack.

"Save me, Mangum!" she shouted, jerking dramatically.

The sudden burst of life from the drowning victim startled Trev, causing him to jump back, but there was nowhere for him to go. He was going to fall, and there was nothing he could do about it. Everything seemed to be in slow motion—arms and legs flailing in the air as he dropped back. For a split second, his eyes locked with the woman, who looked as surprised as he felt. Then his back slapped against the water, and he fell under.

He emerged with an alarming amount of spits and coughs.

"You're not Mangum," the girl gasped, leaning over the dock's edge, eyes wide. She reached her hand out to help pull him up.

"And you're not dead," he grumbled, purposefully avoiding her proffered hand. He swam to the ladder instead.

"No." She winced. "I'm not dead." She watched him struggle, her expression confessing her guilt. "I . . . was faking it."

"I can see that." He climbed up the ladder and collapsed on the dock, hands resting limply on his heaving chest as he stared at the blue sky above him.

She was quiet for a moment until, suddenly, her body shook with an inexplicable spasm. Trev sat up, his brows folding together in confusion. Then she spasmed again and again until she obviously couldn't keep it in, and she doubled over.

"Are you *laughing*?"

His question only made it worse. She wrapped her arms around her stomach, trying to hold it in, but the laughter continued to roar out of her. Her face dropped into her hands as she shook her head back and forth. She tried deep breaths, but then she peeked at Trev through her fingers and came completely undone.

He was irritated at first, but the longer Trev watched her shaking form, the harder it became to stay mad. Despite his best efforts, laughter escaped his lips too. It was strange, the two of them sitting in a puddle on the dock, laughing like children. Trev couldn't remember the last time he had laughed so hard.

It felt good.

Trev gasped through a laugh, "Why . . . why would you fake drowning?"

"It was meant to be a joke," she defended.

"For this Mangum person?" Trev cringed. "I feel sorry for the guy."

Sucking in, she slowed the momentum of her giggles. "You're right. It's not funny," she said. "I'm sorry . . . for it all."

Trev was curious. He scooted his body so he could sit on

the edge of the dock, swinging his legs over the side. "So who's this Mangum guy, and why did you get us confused?"

"Well, I wasn't expecting anyone else." She rolled over to the edge copying the way he sat. "I've been coming to this pond my whole life, and I've never seen a single person here. How did you find this place?"

"My friend and I stumbled upon it a year or two ago. I haven't been back since, but I needed a break today." He kicked his legs back and forth over the water. "Do you live around here?"

She hesitated.

"What?" He pulled his head back. "It's not like I'm going to come knocking on your door."

"I grew up not far from here," she hedged, her gaze falling to the water below. "What about you?"

"I come and go as I please," he said mischievously.

She raised her eyebrows, likely curious about his vague answer, so he opted for changing the subject. "What's your name?"

"Why? Do you keep a record of all the girls you save?"

"Only the pretty ones," he joked, thinking he would add her name if such a list existed. She *was* pretty. Water dripped down from the top of her forehead and the ends of her blonde hair, making tiny splashes all around her on the dock and prompting Trev to push his hands through his own dripping hair. Her wet clothes accentuated the curves of her body and Trev looked away. She must have noticed his sudden avoidance because she self-consciously pulled at her gray shirt so the damp fabric didn't cling to her chest.

He tried again. "Are you going to tell me your name? If I did have a list, I'd want you on it."

"You're a complete stranger," she deflected, bestowing a small smile.

Trev raised his hands. "All right, fine. Then I won't tell you my name either, and we'll be strangers forever." He looked her over again. "But at least answer me this. Do you always wear boys' clothes?" he asked, nodding toward her gray pants.

She laughed. "Have *you* ever tried swimming in a dress? It doesn't work very well."

"This may surprise you, but I've never gone swimming in a dress," he said, his tone serious.

"Then you have no room to judge." She smirked.

Trev smiled, wondering why this girl was so easy to talk to.

"You know," he leaned back against his hands, "there are better ways than pretending to drown to get a man's attention. I can talk to Mangum for you. Let him know you're interested."

"What?"

"Mangum." Trev reminded her. "You know, get his attention for you."

Her nose wrinkled. "I don't want Mangum's attention."

She deserved payback for the fake drowning. "So then you wanted mine?" Trev grinned as her jaw dropped in surprise.

He probably shouldn't be flirting with a random country girl. He was engaged, after all. But this was more talking than flirting. Surely there was no harm in that.

"I did *not* do this to get your attention," she objected. "I already told you I wasn't expecting anyone else."

"It's fine. You can admit it." He gave her a sly smile.

"First of all, I don't know you. Second, even if I did know you, and I was purposely trying to get your attention, I would have done it so much better."

"Is there a better way to pretend to drown?" He smiled, unable to hide his amusement.

"Well, if I had been trying to be appealing I would have worn a dress, not a man's oversized shirt—"

"I agree. It's painful to look at you." That wasn't true. She was very attractive.

"And not just any dress," she continued, pointedly ignoring

his comment. "I would have done some investigating and found out what your favorite color was—"

"Blue," he interrupted.

"What?"

"My favorite color is blue." Then he gestured for her to continue.

She rolled her eyes, but Trev saw her smile. "All right, I would have worn a blue dress—"

"A colored dress? That's expensive. You'd do that for me?" He raised an eyebrow.

"I would have worn a blue dress"—her eyes warned him not to interrupt—"that hugged my body, leaving little to the imagination."

Trev didn't feel the need to add anything. He liked what he heard.

"Then I wouldn't have floated there lifeless." She threw her arms in the air, making waves with her hands. Trev leaned away to avoid being hit. "I would have splashed around, wailing and crying, to make sure that you stopped and rescued me." She dropped her hands into her lap. "Then you would have heard my cries for help and dove into the water—"

"Like I did today?" he deadpanned.

"Yes. Apparently, you have *some* redeeming qualities." She took a breath before jumping back into her reverie. "Once I was safe on shore, I would have looked up at you, held your gaze, and waited." She paused and turned her head to look at him.

"Waited for what?" he asked, amused and absorbed by her story.

"For you to kiss me, of course," she said matter-of-factly like it was the only obvious outcome.

"You kiss people you don't even know? Right after you've met?"

"No!" She shook her head with an edge of annoyance. "It's just a pretend scenario. We already know each other in the story. That's why we kiss. Why would I want your attention if we don't already know each other?"

Trev raised the corner of his mouth into a slight smile. "Because I'm so good looking?"

She turned and looked him over, pretending to consider. "No," she decided, her expression impassive. "You're not that good looking."

Ouch. Trev's ego was wounded, but her answer came too quickly for him to really believe she didn't find him *somewhat* attractive.

"Well, I'm afraid it would take more than a pretty, colored dress and some eye contact to get me to kiss you." He folded his arms across his chest. "You'd have to be interesting and confident too."

"Which I am," she added.

"No, I don't think so," he maintained. "You're clingy and desperate for my affection. That's why you pretended to drown."

She frowned and Trev knew a brief moment of victory. It was her turn to have her ego wounded.

"No, that's not it at all," she said again, this time with more passion. "Perhaps I'm poor . . . maybe even your servant, and I have to pretend to drown because you are too arrogant to see the love right in front of you."

"No." He kept his tone even. "You're deranged and controlling. I've been kind to you, and you've taken that kindness as something more. You devised this drowning scheme as a way to—"

"This is my pretend story. You have no say in it," she snapped playfully, cutting him off.

"Okay, then how does it end?" He sighed, surrendering control of the plot. "After you gaze up at me, what happens?"

She peered over the pond, caught up in her fairytale. "You look into my eyes, and you finally see me, not as your poor servant girl, but as the woman you were meant to spend the rest of your life with." A smile grew across her lips. "You kiss me, and then we live happily ever after."

If the fake drowning hadn't convinced him the girl was crazy, this did. "Happily ever after is an ancient concept."

"What do you mean?" she asked defensively.

"You know. Love. That one-and-only person you're supposed to spend your life with. Happy endings. All that. It doesn't exist." He rolled his eyes just thinking of it.

"Of course it does." She sounded astonished, as if his objections were absurd.

Something twisted inside him, but his voice remained impartial. "There's nothing in my life that proves true love exists."

She looked away for a moment, and Trev internally kicked himself. He hadn't meant to get personal with her. He didn't usually get personal with anyone, besides his friend, Drake. Now her silence was starting to make him uncomfortable.

"I understand what you're saying," she said finally. "There isn't much in my life either to prove that love and happy endings exist." Her voice was quieter as she spoke, and her eyes no longer held the twinkle that had been there moments ago. Trev shifted, feeling remorseful. It was like he had popped her make-believe love bubble.

"I can tell you more about what *isn't* love than what *is*," she continued. "But I know what kind of love I want in my future, and it's not the kind I've witnessed."

"What if you never find the love you're looking for?"

"I'll create it," she replied with certainty.

Trev grinned, bemused by her funny ideas about love. He'd never heard anyone talk about love like that. In fact, hardly anyone in his life talked about love at all. In his circle, there was no such thing as love—only negotiations.

He cleared his throat, not liking the serious direction of their conversation and the earnest way she looked at him, like she expected him to respond with his own views on love. She wasn't going to get that from him today.

He didn't know what else to say, so he did what his royal advisors told him to do in unknown situations—he flashed a brilliant smile. They told him smiling made him look confident. Smiling won the people over. It was all part of Trev's charm. It usually came naturally, and he relied on it in situations like these. Sometimes he didn't even know he was doing it. Today though, he knew. For reasons he couldn't explain, he wanted the unusual woman to like him.

His flashy smile appeared to surprise her, and she looked at him in obvious confusion, until a huge smile of her own spread across her mouth. He was winning her over.

"What are you doing?" she asked.

He answered without moving his lips. "I'm smiling."

She laughed. "But why is it so creepy?"

"I didn't know it was." Then they both burst into laughter.

She leaned in closer, touching her shoulder to his playfully. "Thank you for saving me."

She was teasing, but the warmth in her smile was sincere. Strangely, it made his heart lurch.

"You're welcome." His voice came out raspier than he intended, but her sudden nearness caught him off-guard. It had been a long time since he'd used his charms on a woman. They worked better than he remembered.

When Trev had first pulled her out of the water, he'd noticed her beauty but only in passing. Now, conversing with her, he was wholly captivated. Golden waves of wet hair tumbled around her shoulders down to her chest, framing her expressive green eyes—eyes that told an animated story every time she spoke. Her skin glowed with the tint of a summer tan that complemented her pink lips. And her smile—it was the biggest prize of all, making him somehow feel a surge of happiness every time she bestowed it on him. His attraction to her seemed to grow exponentially, with an intensity he couldn't deny.

"You know, I should probably give you a reward for saving me."

Was she batting her eyes at him? He couldn't account for this flirtatious change in her behavior. All he knew was that her face and, more importantly, her lips were getting closer to his. It was weird. He didn't even know her name, and here she was, acting like she was going to kiss him.

This was moving fast.

She was moving fast.

He parted his lips in anticipation. She paused, her green eyes holding his gaze. He didn't dare look away, or he might miss her next move.

Or was it supposed to be his move?

In her pretend story, she held her rescuer's gaze and waited. He was supposed to kiss her. That's what she wanted, right?

But could he do it? In a way, it was wrong. What about the princess of New Hope?

I haven't even met her yet.

This would be his last kiss with another woman. The last kiss he chose for himself. Maybe he owed it to himself to have one last kiss.

He closed his eyes and leaned in, ready to give her what she wanted, when suddenly her satisfied voice snapped him back to reality.

"Thanks for the help, stranger." Her smile radiated with playfulness as she spoke. She tousled his hair like he was a schoolboy and hopped to her feet. He didn't realize that he'd been holding his breath until the air escaped his chest in a mixture of relief and disappointment.

"And by the way," she paused for a moment, eyebrows raised, taunting him, "we were both wrong. I *don't* need a pretty, blue dress to get you to kiss me. Just some eye contact will do." She pursed her lips together in the most adorable way and then ran off into the trees.

No. She *frolicked* into the trees—like she didn't have a care in the world.

Trev sat there, stunned, trying to figure out what had just happened.

Then he knew.

That was *her* charm kicking in, and she had won.

3

Renna

A laugh escaped Renna's lips as she made her way to her father's grave. Her dad would have loved her interaction with the stranger. She had inherited her mischievousness from him. When he was alive, he used to prank absolute strangers, making big scenes. She'd loved that about him.

Renna approached the meadow, noticing the puffy, white dandelion heads scattered throughout the deep grass. She picked one up, holding it to her mouth as she blew the seeds into the air. A light breeze carried them into the middle of the small field where her father's grave lay. The sun shone on his headstone, casting an angelic glow on the ground surrounding the grave. Preetis and Nellie had kept the wild grass from overtaking the monument, maintaining a clear path to and around it. Trees circled Renna, closing her in, keeping her safe from the bustle at the house down below. She was happy knowing her father was above Wellenbreck Farm, not far from their pond and everything he had loved.

"Hi, Dad," Renna whispered, kneeling over the marble headstone to trace the letters of his name. KIMBALL DEGRAY. Only his body rested there. His soul was somewhere else—maybe with her always. At least that's what she told herself, so she didn't feel stupid when she carried on conversations with him.

"I'm sorry it's been so long. You know I would come every day if I could." Her voice was low.

She wiped away a stray tear trickling down her cheek, unsurprised to find it there. She was used to the ups and downs of her grief. One minute she'd be laughing, and the next she'd be curled up on the bathroom floor, praying the hurt and tears would subside. Today though, she was here with him.

"You would have loved the ride here," she said cheerfully, laughing to herself as she swiped another tear off her cheek. "Actually, you would have hated it. Mom complained the whole time about how bumpy it was."

She picked at a few blades of grass in front of her. "But you would have loved the government transporter we rode in. We covered more miles in an hour than we ever covered in a day with Canyon Ann pulling the wagon. I wish everybody was allowed to have one. It would change regular people's lives." She sighed. "But only fancy people get fancy things, and Mom's fancy now."

Renna's smile faded. "I would give it all up, all the nice things, just to have you back." She could feel the emotion creeping into her voice. "I miss you so much, Dad. It still doesn't seem real—you gone, Mom marrying Bryant, moving to the Government Center. None of it feels like my life. I should be used to it after four years, but I'm not."

She looked around at the trees and bushes lining the edges of the meadow. Everything seemed bigger; time had matured the trees just as it had her.

"I'm sorry Mom didn't come say hi." Renna let out a slow breath. "I suppose we both know why. It's probably for the best, though. I went swimming in the pond, and we all know Mom hates that. I also pretended to drown and made some guy dive in and rescue me." She chuckled, the man's wide grin flashing in her mind.

Renna lay on her side, propping her head up with her hand. "It's been rough at the Government Center. It seems like no matter what I do, I can't please anybody, especially Mom." Renna's voice got quiet again. "I wish you were here. You would know what to say or do."

The leaves clapped against each other in the breeze. Time slowed as Renna stared at her father's headstone. She had longed for moments like this, moments where she could lay beside him and feel content. The sun broke through a cloud and touched her face, warming her soul, and suddenly her father was there with her.

Renna didn't know how long she rested there with him, but too soon, it was time to go. She kissed the tips of her fingers, pressing them against his headstone. "Love you, Dad."

She stood up and brushed off the clumps of grass and dirt that clung to her damp clothes and left the sanctuary of the meadow, promising to return again tomorrow.

The farmhouse came into view as Renna began her trek down the steep hill. Orange sun rays scattered across the skyline, colliding with miles of open fields. It was hard to imagine this land as anything other than farmland. She had been told by her father that it was once covered with roads, buildings, and homes. Growing up, she'd found pieces and artifacts of what used to exist there, before Desolation happened. There were even a few structural remains left, where concrete foundations jutted out of the ground, but grass and weeds covered them now as if the earth had simply adopted them as her own.

She ran toward the stone house, wishing she could stay at Wellenbreck Farm, but tomorrow they would continue to the kingdom of Albion. Outside the house, soldiers worked to set up tents. There wasn't enough room inside for the entire caravan. Soldiers and maids needed to sleep outside.

Renna accidentally slammed the back door behind her, her eyes adjusting to the dimly lit kitchen when she suddenly realized she wasn't alone.

"Nice outfit," Jenica sneered, making the other girls surrounding the kitchen table look up at her and snicker. Renna sighed. She still didn't understand why Seran's friends were part of the caravan to Albion, but apparently, Seran needed to have her support group with her at all times. So here they were.

At least they had ridden in a separate transporter. Renna wasn't sure she could handle a week of travel confined in a small space with them. Airplanes would have made the journey so much faster, but those had been deemed unessential from the very first Council.

"Thanks." Renna smiled at Jenica. "I found it in your closet." She sauntered into the room and opened a few cupboards, looking for something to eat.

"I think everyone knows I would never be caught dead with a pair of pants in my closet. Especially colorless ones."

Renna rolled her eyes. "You should try pants sometime. They're comfortable." Finding a bushel of grapes in one of the cupboards, she plopped a few into her mouth and leaned back against the kitchen counter to face the girls. Everything about them in Wellenbreck, in her kitchen, felt wrong.

Jenica's light blue eyes glared back at her. "Why can't you be civilized for once? Women don't wear pants."

"They wore pants before Desolation," Sheridan chimed in. She was a bit of a know-it-all, always ready with information.

"That's probably one of the reasons civilization got destroyed—ridiculous clothing choices." Jenica's attention went back to the small bottles of colorful liquid laid out between them. She leaned her head down over her hand, forming a pile of straight blonde hair on the table. Slowly she painted the red liquid over her fingernails.

"Where did you get that paint?" Renna asked, her curiosity getting the best of her.

"It's called nail polish," Sheridan replied, not even looking up from painting Lizanne's nails.

"My mom got it from the under-counter market," Jenica bragged.

"So, it's not essential?" Renna asked.

"Of course it's essential!" Jenica sneered. "My hands need it. Besides," she paused to blow on the wet polish covering her nails, "the next Council of Essentials is in January, and my father promised to lobby for nail polish. I'm sure it will be approved."

Of course Jenica believed she had that kind of power over the Council of Essentials. Had she forgotten that during the rebuild two hundred years ago resources had been scarce? The seven leaders couldn't just deem something like nail polish essential because *their hands needed it.* Renna had a hard time believing nail polish would ever be deemed essential to survival, but lately, the Council seemed to approve luxuries for the ruling class that weren't essential at all.

It was a strange sight—a group of women who had nothing better to do than paint their nails. Most girls their age had to work. That used to be Renna's life. She had spent exhausting days beside her father in the fields. Now, as a member of the ruling class, she had nothing to do. Guilt spread through her like fire. She hated how unfair it was—how some people lived lives of luxury while others worked hard to survive. Something was wrong with the Council of Essentials, and nobody seemed to care.

Lizanne spoke up. She hardly ever spoke, so Renna liked her best, and she had the most amazing red hair that lit up against her pale skin. "I can't believe you grew up here. It's in the middle of nowhere."

"I like the seclusion," Renna replied. "It's peaceful. But

really it's not that isolated. Vassel is only thirty miles north of here."

Jenica looked around at the house. "This explains a lot about why you act the way you do. You don't know any better." She was a master at making her words sound kind while insulting a person at the same time.

Renna pushed away from the counter. She'd had enough girl talk for one afternoon. "Where are Seran and my mother?"

Sheridan pointed upstairs. "Seran is napping, and your mother is in the front room, I believe."

Renna headed toward the narrow stairs at the back of the kitchen. Better to change *before* her mother saw her in pants.

On her way up, she almost bumped into a plump body coming out of the bathroom.

"Nellie!" Renna grabbed the woman into a tight hug. Nellie's head landed just below her chin. There had been a time when the two of them had been the same height, but that was when Renna was thirteen. "I've missed you so much!"

Nellie pulled back, looking around. "Shhhh, child. There is royalty sleeping in this house."

Renna grimaced, as she followed Nellie into her old room and shut the door behind them, surveying the room. It seemed smaller than she remembered, especially the bed. Besides the size, the most significant difference was how colorless everything was—the curtains, bedding, and walls—they were all muted in grays and creams, a stark contrast to the colorful world at the Government Center.

Nellie spun around to look at Renna and put her hands on her hips. "Child, I have been waiting all afternoon to see how fancy you've become in the last four years in your colored clothing, and look at you. You're dressed like Preetis!"

Renna smiled. "I may have borrowed your husband's clothes to go swimming."

Nellie let a laugh escape as she shook her head. Her brown hair was slicked into a bun, a cream apron pulled tight around her chest. She looked exactly like Renna remembered.

"Stealing Preetis's clothes and sneaking off." Nellie laughed. "I'm glad to see you haven't lost all your spunk."

"I may live at the New Hope Government Center, but I'm still Kimball Degray's daughter," she said with a sly smile, sitting down on the bed. "Where's Preetis anyway?"

"Oh, you know Preetis." Nellie sat beside her, the weight of her body sinking the mattress and sending Renna up like a teeter-totter. "He's always about some task. Now let me look at you, child." Nellie's eyes scanned over Renna. "You look so beautiful. Your father would be so proud." She placed her hand on Renna's cheek. "I see him in your eyes and your smile. You went to see him, didn't you?"

Renna nodded. She didn't dare speak, or else her emotion would escape, spilling out like water from a broken dam.

"Good." She sniffed and looked away but not before Renna saw tears brimming in her eyes. "Now that's enough of that." Nellie stood up like she was too busy to sit still another moment. "I would unpack your things, but you have some fancy maid to do that for you now."

"Nora? You'd like her. She's very chatty."

"I don't have time for chitchat. I've got a princess to feed and must make sure she's *comfortable.* Not to mention all my regular tasks." Nellie shook her head as she spoke. "And don't even get me started on the hoity-toity, good-for-nothing girls taking over my kitchen downstairs."

Renna laughed.

Nellie's eyes turned serious. "Have they been good to you, child?"

"The girls downstairs? Not a bit."

"Not just the girls, but everyone. Are you happy there?"

Renna forced a smile. "It's been okay. I wouldn't say I fit in. But most days, I'm happy."

"And your mom . . . is she happy?" It was a delicate question that required a delicate answer.

"She's doing better than I've ever seen her do." There was a sadness in Renna's voice that she couldn't hide—a longing for her childhood.

"It's all that expensive stuff. That'd make any of us happier." Nellie smoothed her apron. "Well, I best be getting back to work before your mother notices dinner isn't ready."

"I'll come help after I change."

Nellie smiled back at her, reaching for the doorknob.

"Hey, Nellie?"

"Yes, child?" She turned back to Renna.

"I ran into a man at the pond today. He looked only a little older than me. He had dark curly hair and . . ." A handsome face, easy smile, vibrant blue eyes. "He was on a PT. Is he local?"

"Not that I reckon. Nobody around here is allowed to have a PT," Nellie answered before shuffling out the door.

Nellie was right, of course. Only someone working in a government position had access to a PT. Ordinary people didn't have clearance to drive machines like that. Renna remembered seeing the man's weapons belt tossed at the pond's edge with the rest of his things. A soldier, then, most likely. Not from New Hope, though—she would have remembered seeing a man that attractive walking the halls of the Government Center. She wouldn't have forgotten a face like his.

4

Trev

Daylight faded, shining its last light on the cement buildings of Vassel. The small New Hope city was the only town for miles with an inn. One dirt road split a row of cream plastered shops. Trev parked his PT for the night and gathered his things from inside the bike's seat compartment. Lights emanated from the inn's windows, the glow inviting him in. Sounds of laughter and casual talk grew as he approached and swung the door open.

The front room was lined with brown tables and booths where several guests ate dinner. Trev's stomach growled with hunger as a wave of delicious smells overtook him; the scent of fresh bread was the strongest. Drake sat alone at a booth in the corner, his tall body towering inches above the other guests, though he was seated, and his broad shoulders almost spanning the width of the bench. A plate of meat had already been brought out to him.

"You couldn't wait to eat until I arrived?" Trev threw his bag down on the opposite bench before sitting.

"Well, I didn't know when you were going to appear again since you snuck off this afternoon," Drake said coolly, hardly greeting him with a glance. His shaggy brown hair fell over his forehead, and he whipped his head to the side to shake it away from his brown eyes. "Where have you been?"

"Sorry. I visited that pond we found by the border." Trev leaned forward to survey the array of chicken and pork on Drake's platter before selecting a chunk.

Drake finally looked up at him, exasperation on his face. "Trev, I am the head of your security. How can I protect you if I don't even know where you are?"

"Protect me from what?" Trev looked around as he tore the piece of chicken between his fingers, the smaller bite ending up in his mouth. "Vassel is small, remote, and friendly to Albion."

"It's *my* job to assess threats to your safety."

"And what's the risk level here in Vassel?"

Drake was stone-faced until a small smile cracked the surface. "Extremely low."

Trev grinned, popping another piece of chicken into his mouth.

Drake softened. "Next time, just tell me where you're going, okay? The king will have my head if anything happens to you on my watch."

Trev nodded, knowing his friend was right. He should have told him where he was.

"Did you enjoy your swim?" Drake asked sardonically.

The girl's face flickered through Trev's mind. "It was interesting."

Who was this Mangum guy? Trev decided he didn't like him, whoever he was.

"I met a girl," Trev said, unable to keep the excitement out of his voice.

Drake paused mid-bite. "And?"

"And, I don't know." Trev shrugged. "She was really fun."

Drake was silent for a moment. "May I remind you that we're meeting your fiancée in two days?"

"I know that," Trev said with a touch of irritation.

"Then you're also aware that it's in poor taste to flirt with some New Hope country girl."

"I never said we flirted."

Drake leaned back and folded his arms over his chest. "It was implied."

Trev rolled his eyes, hating the fact that Drake knew him so well.

"You haven't noticed a girl in years," Drake continued. "As your friend, I'm happy for you. But as your head of security, it's my responsibility to tell you—"

"Drake," Trev interrupted. "I know my duty. You don't have to tell me anything."

Drake's stare was heavy. "You're lucky you didn't see the New Hope caravan when you were at the pond. The innkeeper said they're staying at the farmhouse down in the valley."

Trev took a breath. He hadn't realized the New Hope royalty was so close. But of course they were. They were expected at the ruler's palace in a few days. "I didn't see anyone but the girl."

Drake kept going. "And it's a good thing since you were with a woman other than your fiancée."

Trev sighed, regretting telling his friend about the girl. "It was nothing. I'll never see her again, and I didn't even get her name."

Drake paused for a moment longer, then nodded. "As long as you understand that it's far too late for a fling."

"It wasn't a fling." Trev motioned to the waitress to bring another plate of food.

Hoping to dislodge the skeptical look from Drake's face, he changed the subject. "What did I miss while I was gone?"

"The rest of the men traveled ahead north to Oakefor. The mayor is expecting us tomorrow afternoon and promises a crowd of people to greet you."

"I hate the big production. I just want to see the town,

shake a few business owners' hands, and meet the people. Nothing too structured."

"I know that's what you want, but that's not what your father wants."

"My father isn't here." And thank goodness for that. The trip would have been miserable with his father in tow, criticizing him the entire time.

"I know, but he's right. You need to win over these small towns. The election is in a few months, and Joniss Doman grows more popular every day." Drake shoved a massive piece of chicken into his mouth.

Trev scoffed. "I can't imagine how."

He watched as Drake chewed the meat down enough to speak. "Joniss is schmoozing people all over Albion. Flattery is his strong point. I know you don't like it, but you have to play the game. You have to be just as appealing as he is."

"And fake?" Trev asked bitterly.

"But that's just it. You're not fake. You really want what's best for the people of Albion." Drake stopped talking as a waitress approached their table, balancing a tray in one hand.

"Thank you," Trev said as she set a platter in front of him, his eyes focused on the food.

Drake dabbed his mouth with a napkin. "We still haven't received word from Hoskins and Brey. Hopefully, they're only a few days behind us."

Trev took a bite of his meat, savoring the salty taste, and sat back against the bench. He had dispatched the two spies three weeks ago to gather intel on the kingdom of Tolsten. There were rumors that the neighboring kingdom was creating more sophisticated weapons—weapons like the ones before Desolation. Weapons of mass destruction were against the Treaty of Essentials. During the rebuild, all seven leaders from each of the new countries had signed the treaty. If Tolsten went against the agreement and built sophisticated weapons, it could lead to war, something that Albion and the surrounding kingdoms were desperate to avoid. No one wanted to ignite another Desolation-style conflict.

Trev swallowed. "We'll just have to get their information back in Albion. Whenever they arrive."

"What time do you want to leave for Oakefor in the morning?" Drake asked.

Anxiousness settled deep in Trev's stomach. Traveling to Oakefor only brought him closer to the Albion Ruler's Palace; these were his last few days of freedom. You would think a man in his position had anything he wanted, including freedom, but freedom was the one thing he didn't seem to have. What little freedom he had now would soon be smothered by an arranged marriage and government duties that kept him at the ruler's palace. He was desperate for a few more hours to himself before that happened.

"Later rather than earlier. I'm in no rush to get to Oakefor," he answered.

Drake nodded. "All right. We need to make sure we're there by midafternoon. That's when the meeting with the mayor is."

"Don't worry. We'll be there." Trev wanted to meet with the mayor. He just wasn't in a rush to leave this place.

Thankfully, Drake seemed to understand what he needed. Understand how everything in his life was about to change and that he just needed a little more time. Maybe that's why his friend pretended not to notice the next morning when Trev awoke early and left on his PT. At least this time, Trev left a note.

He headed south thirty miles, back to the pond by Wellenbreck. He tried to convince himself that it wasn't to see the girl again, but there wasn't any other plausible reason to go back. Still, she likely wouldn't be there. Trev didn't have much experience with fake drowning, but he was pretty sure it didn't happen often.

He slowed his PT to a stop, searching the area for any sign

of her. The pond was quiet and still. Trev exhaled, disappointment knocking the wind out of him. He stood there for a moment, surprised by how letdown he was. He didn't even know her and now, he would never get the chance. The realization left him feeling unsettled and full of regret.

Still, it was for the best. Nothing could happen with her anyway.

But even that knowledge didn't ease his disappointment.

5

Renna

The sun broke through the window in Renna's room early that morning, spoiling her sleep. She wanted to stay in bed, but escaping would be much harder later on. She needed to leave before Seran woke up, and Renna's duty to the princess began. All of Seran's friends were here to see to Seran's every whim. Surely she didn't need Renna, too.

Slowly, she lifted her legs out from under the covers and pulled herself out of bed. She scanned the room for one of her suitcases but didn't see anything. She supposed they were with her maid, Nora, but she didn't want to wake her. She didn't want to wake anybody.

Renna's eyes fell on an old, gray day dress hanging in the closet across from her. She remembered sneaking into her mother's room years ago and snatching it away to play dress-up. It was a typical day dress for a working-class woman, cut straight and loose with a high, square neck. Two oversized, rectangular pockets rested just below the hips, good for shoving your hands into, but not great for carrying things.

Clothing hadn't changed much over the years, especially for the working class. Day dresses were long, covering the legs and arms and were always in neutral colors. Renna hated how hot they were, but they were practical, designed to protect her from the sun and elements when she worked in the fields.

On her tiptoes, Renna crossed the room, examining the dress before throwing it over her head and undergarments. She let out a deep sigh. The fit wasn't great, now that she was grown. The sleeves were three-quarter length instead of long, and the dress ended mid-calf, but it would have to work for today. She had forgotten how unflattering these dresses were. When Renna had moved to the Government Center, the first thing she had welcomed wholeheartedly was the upgrade in clothing.

Renna opened the door to her room and peered out. She looked down the hall to the master bedroom where her mother slept. The door was closed.

Thank you, she whispered to herself.

Seran's door was cracked open, but if Renna was quiet, she might make it past undetected. She crept down the hallway, each step deliberate until she reached the top of the stairs. She took each stair slowly, knowing exactly how to dodge the creaks in the old wood. Reaching the bottom of the stairs safely, she quickly glanced into the front room where Seran's friends were sprawled out, still sleeping. That wasn't a surprise. They'd sleep all day if they could.

Renna headed to a closet nearby, quietly opening the door. She pulled out a satchel and a blanket and stuffed it in the bag. Next, she went to the kitchen for bread, granola, and cheese. If she had her way, she would stay at the pond until the caravan was leaving. Packed with provisions, she sidled over to the back door and pushed it open. The cool morning air filled her lungs with happiness. Eyes closed, she sucked in as if it was her first time ever breathing fresh air.

Everything felt different at Wellenbreck. It felt better.

Male voices startled her. She pressed her back against the stone wall and tiptoed to the corner of the house to get a better look at who was there.

Guards.

There were always guards in her way. The four men were supposed to be on patrol outside the house. Instead, they stood chatting in a semi-circle.

The last thing Renna wanted was to be funneled back inside by one of her mother's co-conspirators, but these men weren't expecting Renna. She was confident she could slip out unnoticed.

Renna waited until the guards' heads were turned, then she scurried to the long rows of corn stalks fifteen feet away. Without thinking, she dove to her knees as if her escape was a matter of life or death. She swung her shoulder bag onto her back and started crawling, immediately feeling the damp mud between her fingers and seeping through the bottom of her dress.

Ugh! Why didn't I just bend down?

She was a mess, but she convinced herself that it would be fine. She could wash up at the pond and then have breakfast at her father's grave.

Halfway through the row of corn, Renna decided it was safe to stand. She sighed when she saw the mess she had made out of her dress. She lifted up the bottom of the skirt, picking at the mud as she walked, trying to flick it to the ground. She took a stick and worked at the dirt on the bottom of her shoes. She was so engrossed in cleaning the mud off her clothes that she hardly registered the rest of her walk to the pond.

As she approached the clearing, splashing sounds triggered the abrupt stop of her feet. Her head jerked up, but she couldn't see anything between the trees. Renna listened again. More splashing sounds. Her heart raced as the noises confirmed someone was swimming in her pond.

The soldier from yesterday flashed through her mind.

Could it be him?

It seemed unreal, but as she peered around the last tree, a head of dark curls appeared in the water. *It was him.*

And with very little clothes on.

He had left his weapons and shoes on a rock near the edge of the dock, but this time he'd also removed his shirt and pants, which meant he was swimming in nothing but his undershorts. His muscular arms pierced through the water and then out again with each stroke.

Courage swelled in Renna's chest, tempting her to continue the game they had started yesterday. Her lips crept into a devilish smile as a plan came to mind.

His clothes were only a few feet away on the rock.

Renna waited until he dove under the water again. Then, without hesitating, she made a dash for the pile. As she scrambled forward, she wondered how much a person could hear underwater. She used one hand to steady her bag against her hip so he wouldn't hear it jostling. He was more likely to hear her beating heart. It pounded loudly between her own ears. Reaching his clothes, she scooped them up against her chest and scurried back toward the tree.

She might have been caught, but luckily his eyes were closed when he came up for air. Brushing away the water threatening his eyes, he pushed his hands to his face and up through his hair. It gave her just enough time to reach the tree and hide safely behind it.

She looked down at the pile of clothes in her arms: black pants, a white shirt, and a black button-up jacket. She noted that they were surprisingly clean for a soldier, and she resisted the urge to smell them.

That would be weird.

Then she reminded herself that she had just stolen a stranger's clothing. Everything about this situation was weird.

So she smelled them.

The aroma of lemongrass-scented soap filled her nostrils.

He's a frilly soldier.

Sloshing sounds in the water startled her. Renna peeked around the edge of her hiding place to see him nearing the water's edge. She willed her breath to be quiet, guessing that he was probably looking for the heap of clothing he had left by the water. He muttered something she couldn't understand under his breath, but she clearly heard the string of profanities that came next. For a moment, she panicked.

I stole his clothes! This was a mistake.

Maybe he didn't want to play any games today. Maybe he was in a terrible mood and had just wanted a quiet swim to feel better.

But she was in too deep now. There was no way out.

With as much confidence as she could muster, Renna casually walked out from behind the tree. "It looks like it's your turn to be rescued," she said as she dangled his clothes from her finger.

He looked in her direction, and the same smile from yesterday returned.

The game was on.

He huffed. "I would hardly call this a situation where I need rescuing."

Renna stepped closer. "Is that so? I guess I'll just keep your clothes." She shrugged, an innocent look on her face. "After all, I'm always looking for more boy clothes to swim in."

He pushed his body out of the water and onto the dock, revealing muscles she had never known existed nor cared about until this moment. Feeling flustered by his bare chest and wet, clinging undershorts, she quickly walked forward and threw the clothes onto the dock, losing all her confidence from moments ago.

"Here you go!" She stumbled back onto the grass awkwardly, searching for somewhere else to look.

"Are you all right?" Amusement filled his tone.

"Yes! I'm fine! I just, um . . ." Why wasn't there anything to look at? Or anything to say that didn't make her seem like an idiot? She covered her eyes with one hand as she spoke.

"You're here, and I'm here, and you don't have your clothes on, and you need your clothes . . ."

He snickered as she rambled on.

"Pants! Pants are important to have, and most men wear them, at least in front of me. And um . . ." She glanced from under the palm of her hand.

He still wasn't dressed.

Instead, he stood on the dock, dripping wet, his blue eyes glimmering with amusement. "I had no idea my chest had such an effect on women."

"It doesn't," she lied, determined to wipe his smug smile away. She lowered her hand to her hip, trying to regain some of her pride back. She was completely horrified by how ridiculous her actions must have seemed to him. "I thought I saw a snake and . . . I hate snakes."

"It's okay if you liked what you saw." He shrugged, obviously not believing her.

She *did* like what she saw. In fact, she highly doubted there was anything much better, but she wasn't going to admit that to him. She waved her hand flippantly. "I've seen dozens of men shirtless just this week, all of them with better-defined abs than you."

There was his cute smile again, stretching from ear to ear. "Dozens of shirtless men, huh?"

Great! Now I sound sleazy!

He studied her. "What happened to you? Maybe you do need my clothes, after all."

Renna sighed as she looked down. She had forgotten about the dried mud all over her dress and sleeves. She didn't even recall smoothing her hair out this morning before she'd left her room. How she looked should have been the first thing she considered when she saw him. Instead, she stole his clothes.

She silently cursed herself for being so stupid. All she could think about now was how self-conscious she felt, no thanks to her mother's too-small gray dress covered in mud stains.

"I tripped on my way here." Another lie.

"I know how to clean your muddy dress," he said with a growing smile. "You need to get it wet. Come swim with me." He nodded to the water behind him.

"Right now?" Her eyes went wide.

"I thought you liked swimming."

"I do, but I'm not swimming with you." She shook her head. "I don't even know you."

"You can call me Trev," he said, offering his hand out to shake.

"Just Trev?" she said, raising a questioning eyebrow. Usually, men gave their entire formal name.

"Just Trev." He shrugged.

Renna slowly took his hand and immediately a surge of energy went through her. His eyes flashed to hers as if he felt the chemistry too, and something inside of Renna—something she couldn't explain—flickered alive.

"What's your name?" he asked, not dropping her hand.

Yesterday she hadn't wanted to tell him her name, but today things were different. Today she decided to match whatever game he was playing. "Renna. Just Renna."

They stood there for a moment like time had evaporated away. Her eyes blinked, remembering why they were holding hands in the first place. She gave a quick shake and pulled her hand out of his grasp.

"Now we're not strangers," he explained. "Now you can go swimming with me."

Renna looked at the water. She did want to swim, but in her mind, her mother's disapproving voice told her how inappropriate it would be. It was the only thing stopping her from running down the dock and jumping in the water.

She folded her arms over her chest. "I can't swim in a dress. I told you that yesterday."

"So take it off." He smirked.

"I thought the point of getting in the water was to clean my dress." She raised her shoulders. "If I take it off, there's no point in swimming."

"Excuses, excuses," he said, clucking at her.

Renna let out a rough laugh. "Normal people don't just strip off their clothes and go swimming in front of strangers."

"You're not normal."

Her jaw dropped. "Yes, I am."

"The moment I found you faking your own drowning, I knew you weren't normal."

Her brows furrowed. He was right.

"Still, I'm not going to take off my dress and swim with you. There are modesty rules in place to keep relationships appropriate." She held out her hands, her fingers counting as she rattled off some of the guidelines. "Women should wear dresses. They should never wear anything that reveals too much of their shoulders, chest, and back. They should wear a dress color appropriate for their station—"

"I've already seen you break one of those rules yesterday by wearing boy clothes," he said, cutting her off.

Trev was right again. Renna had never cared much about the modesty guidelines. It wasn't like violators were punished by law. It was more about social scorn than anything. But there was no one here to witness except him.

Slowly Trev began to walk toward her, and Renna recognized the mischievous look in his eyes. She backed away. "Don't even *think* about it."

"You better run," he said, getting closer.

What else could she do?

She took off running toward the trees, screaming the whole way.

It didn't help.

Trev came up behind her and grabbed her around the waist. She tried to wriggle free from his wet grasp, but he was too big, too strong. In one quick motion, he pulled her back against his chest and swung her in a circle, her feet kicking out as she spun. She could feel the moisture from his body soak through her back.

Somehow, he managed to sling her writhing body over his shoulder. She pounded on his back with clenched fists as he strode across the grass and back onto the dock.

"You know what? *You're* not normal." It wasn't normal to go from strangers to throwing a girl over your shoulder. And it definitely wasn't normal how much she secretly loved it. She hit his back again. "Put me down!"

He kept walking closer to the edge of the dock.

"No!" she screamed, but he was already moving to throw her in the water. She probably deserved it as payback for yesterday, but still, Renna tried to reason with him. "Okay! Okay! I'll get in, but on my terms."

"On your terms?"

"Yes."

"If I put you down, are you going to run?"

"No!" she groaned.

He slid her to her feet and let go, taking a few steps back. "All right." He gestured to the water. "Get in then."

She let out a breath. "Fine. Turn around so I can change."

"I promise I won't look." As he turned, the beginnings of a grin formed on his lips. "At least not more than once." He was joking, but that didn't stop the red flames from creeping up her face.

Renna pulled her dress over her head and dropped it on the dock beside her. She stood in nothing but her undergarments, feeling exposed and uncomfortable. Even if she thought the modesty rules were stupid, it was still too much to bear. She leaned over and grabbed his shirt, still resting in a clump on the dock beside them. She slipped her arms into the sleeves. It was far too big for her, with the sleeves dangling to her elbows and the hem ending mid-thigh, but it was exactly what she needed to feel comfortable. How could her mother be mad about this?

"You are so slow," Trev complained, his back still turned.

"Calm down," Renna said. Then, she took off running down the dock, leaving Trev behind her.

"Is that my shirt?" She faintly heard him yell. Then she leaped from the dock, the rush of water overhead swallowing the sound of his protests.

When she came up, he was beside her, his shoulders glistening with water. He reached out and pinched the fabric of his shirt. "Very funny," he said sarcastically.

"I wasn't trying to be funny. I was trying to be modest."

"Well, you didn't think that through very well, did you?"

"What do you mean?"

"The shirt is see-through." His eyes sparkled.

Renna looked down and grimaced. The white shirt clung to her skin, showing the exact outline of her undergarments. Luckily, if she stayed under the water, Trev still wouldn't see anything.

"Back to the modesty rules. Did you know that, before Desolation, women wore whatever they wanted, even pants?" he said, breaking into her thoughts. "They could wear any color and show as much of their skin as they wanted." His arms waved back and forth through the water, keeping his body afloat.

"Yeah, I guess they didn't care much about modesty."

"Maybe you should've been born in that era," he teased.

"Maybe I should have," she said with a sly smile.

"Okay, *just Renna*, what do I need to know about you? You know, so you stop referring to us as strangers."

"Well," her smile grew, "I like to swim. Preferably in boy clothes."

"And steal boy clothes," he cut in.

"Yes, I do that too." Her eyes glimmered as she continued.

"I really love food. Like really love it. I would lick my plate clean at every meal if it was acceptable."

"What else?" he asked, treading water.

"Ummm." Her head tilted back and forth as she thought. "I speak before thinking. My mom hates it. In fact, she hates a lot of the things I do. I think I embarrass her." She shrugged her shoulders as if admitting guilt. "I don't do anything with weapons even though my father tried tirelessly to teach me skills. I'm not the type of girl who is going to save somebody or save the day."

"Do you find yourself in a lot of situations where you need to save the day?" he asked.

She smiled. "Not really, but you never know."

"I see."

"What do I need to know about you, *just Trev*?" she asked.

His answers came easily. "I love the color blue because of my blue eyes. I hate carrots. My best friend is named Drake. He lets me win whenever we fight, and it drives me crazy. For once, I want it to be real. I like being a leader in the army. It's what I'm good at. At least I hope I'm good at it."

"Are you one of King Carver's soldiers?"

"Yes." He hesitated. "I'm an officer in the king's guard."

"The king must really trust you," Renna said, kicking her feet against the water below.

Trev laughed at this. "Actually, the king doesn't trust me at all."

"How are you an officer in the king's guard if he doesn't trust you?"

"The prince trusts me explicitly." Trev grinned like he found something humorous about their conversation.

"What's so funny?" she asked, eyeing him.

"Nothing." Then he dove under the water and out of sight.

Renna let out a squeal as his hands tugged at her calves, nearly pulling her under the surface.

He came up for air, water droplets rolling down his forehead and eyes. "Did you think I was a shark?" he asked sarcastically.

"You are worse than a shark. You're like a little boy in a man's body."

He splashed her with water, confirming what she had just said.

Renna dipped her chin into the water, scooping up a mouthful of the cold liquid. As her head came up, she spat it into Trev's face. He immediately turned his head and squeezed his eyes shut, dodging the spray.

"Thank you for that," he said dryly, turning to face her again.

"You're welcome."

Trev suddenly sprang into motion, sending a froth of water into her face as he spun and swam away. "Race you back to the dock!"

Renna barked one surprised laugh, then dove after him. With his generous head start, Trev beat her handily and reached the dock before her, climbing up the ladder to sit on the edge. She followed suit and sat beside him, their feet dangling over the side like they had yesterday. She pulled his wet shirt away from her chest, hoping to retain some shred of modesty, and tugged the hem, so it covered her thighs. But there was nothing she could do about his bare chest.

It was just bare and so very . . . there.

"Okay," he said, pushing his wet hair back from his face. It was amazing how his curls dangled perfectly, even when wet. "Ask me any question."

"All right." She thought for a moment, wanting to challenge him. "What's your biggest fear?"

His expression changed, and she wondered if he thought her question was dumb. Then, he responded simply. "Disappointing everyone."

Renna was taken aback. She hadn't expected such an

honest answer. She thought he'd say something silly, like spiders or vampires. "What do you mean?"

"There's this job that my father wants me to have—actually, a lot of people want me to have it—and I guess my biggest fear is that I'll fail them all. I might be terrible and mess everything up."

"It sounds like a pretty important job."

"It is," he said, his voice weighted with worry.

"Do you even want this job, or are you just doing it to please everyone else?"

Trev hesitated like he was really thinking about her question. "I want it. I've wanted it ever since I was a little boy, and I think I could make a difference. It's just a lot of pressure."

Despite feeling a little jealousy, Renna admired him. It was clear he had a plan for his life. Her own life was in constant limbo. She spent her days escorting Seran to events, attending social lunches or political meetings, and entertaining wealthy women at the Government Center with her mother. But things were already changing. Soon, Seran would be gone, married to the prince of Albion, and her mother would expect Renna to marry some prestigious man so that she could have a prestigious life as if that mattered to Renna. Her life was not her own. Everyone just told her who to be and how to act.

Trev spoke again, scattering her thoughts. "What about you? What's your biggest fear?"

Renna bit her bottom lip. "Ending up like my mom."

"Is your mother so bad?" He raised his eyebrows in surprise.

"No. She's a good person, but she has a hard time with life." Renna tried to find the right words. Her mother had been depressed for years, well before her father had died. Since marrying King Bryant and moving to the Government Center, she seemed happier, so Renna wouldn't describe her as depressed anymore. "She spins everything negatively, and that leads to a lot of worry in her life. She always worries about what other people think about her. About us. I don't want to be like that."

"I don't think you're like that," Trev said, his blue eyes sincere.

She rolled her eyes. "You don't even know me."

"I've seen enough of you to know that you radiate happiness. It's one of the things that makes you so attractive."

"You think I'm attractive?" She raised a questioning brow.

"What?" His face colored. "No, I just meant that . . ." He scrunched his nose as he bumped his shoulder into hers. "You're all right, I guess."

She thought the same thing about him, but she didn't dare say it out loud. Since her father's death, Renna had watched her life become an endless procession of people she didn't care about and appointments that didn't matter. She was stuck in a gray, dull life, despite all the colors surrounding her. But Trev had opened her eyes again. Nothing seemed muted anymore. Everything was bright and colorful, just the way it should be.

A summer breeze floated around them, and Renna's entire body shivered.

"We better get you dressed." Trev hopped to his feet, offering his hand to help pull her up. Her fingers touched his and her body shivered with chills. But this time, they didn't have anything to do with the breeze.

Trev

TREV DIDN'T THINK that Renna could have gotten any more interesting than the girl he'd met yesterday, but as he fastened the belt to his pants, he realized how wrong he was. Today she was adorable. At first, she'd been a nervous, self-conscious wreck. It was a completely new side of her, and he'd liked watching her squirm. Then in the pond, he found himself liking the realness of their conversation and the honest way they were able to talk to each other. She was fun and witty, bringing out the best in him.

She stepped from behind the tree, fully dressed again in her muddy clothes. Her blonde hair hung down wet and just as unruly as it had been yesterday. Water dampened her dress where her undergarments were, and a brown bag dangled from her shoulder.

"All dressed," she said, throwing him his wet shirt.

"Thanks." He wrung it out and pulled it over his head. "What's in your bag?"

She patted the satchel's soft leather and listed the contents. "Bread, granola, cheeses, and a blanket."

"Really? I'm starving!" He reached for the bag.

Renna instinctively turned away, pulling it out of his reach. "What if I don't want to share?" She smirked.

Trev reached even farther, trying to grab the handle of the bag. He missed. He raised his eyebrows, matching her playfulness. "I think you owe me. Since we met, you've pretended to drown and stolen my clothes."

"Well, you threw me in the water today," she challenged.

"You jumped in of your own free will."

She puckered her lips together. "True. I guess I have to share then." She reached into her bag, revealing a tattered brown blanket. They both took a corner of the fabric and pulled, spreading it out across the dirt and grass. She knelt down, laying out the food.

Trev lowered to the ground, ripping off a chunk of bread and throwing it into his mouth. "Tell me more about yourself," he said between bites. He didn't know why, but he wanted to know everything about this girl.

"More?" Renna put a slice of cheese in her mouth. "I can't think of anything else to tell."

"Do you sing?" he asked.

Her mouth stretched into a frown as she chewed. "Terribly."

"Do you dance?"

"Flawlessly." She sat up a little taller, an edge of pride coming through her voice.

"I'm going to need to see." He added in his most official voice, "We can't have people throughout the countryside claiming to be excellent dancers when they're not."

She brushed the crumbs off her skirt and stood up, reaching for his hand. "All right, but I need a partner. Do you think you can keep up?"

A smirk formed on his lips. "I've danced a time or two." Trev grabbed her outstretched hand, electricity sizzling between them. It had been a long time since he'd felt this way and man, it felt good. She smiled too and then pulled him to a spot away from the blanket, placing him across from her.

"We need a beat to get us started," Renna said. She stomped her foot wildly on the ground over and over, dust flying into the air. She nodded at him to see if he caught the pattern of the beat. "Recognize this?"

It was a popular folk song rhythm he'd danced to many times at parties. "Of course." He reached for her hand again, and they started to chassé to the left in rhythmic moves.

Typically, Trev was an excellent dancer, but Renna made him nervous. He had to think about every move, what step came next, and where his hands were supposed to go. As he worried about trying to impress her, she tripped on his foot, almost falling. They both laughed, neither of them sure of whose fault it was. With each step or direction change, their laughter grew louder. They no longer followed the pattern of the dance, but instead spun around faster and faster.

"I think I'm going to be sick!" Renna broke free of the circle and spun to a stop. She focused on the ground with her hands on her hips, trying to will the dizziness away. It didn't work. Losing her balance, she toppled over and landed on her back in the grass.

Trev burst into laughter. "You're right," he said, fighting

his own dizziness until he made it to the ground next to her. "You are the best dancer I've ever seen!"

By this time, Renna laughed so hard that she couldn't speak, or at least Trev couldn't make any sense out of the words she said.

"I definitely think you should teach lessons. People would come for miles to witness your graceful movements."

She hit him on the arm. "You're making fun of me!"

"Your dancing deserves it!"

"I want another chance!" She stretched out, holding her stomach where the pains of laughter still lingered. "With real music and beautiful dresses so I can prove how good I am."

"Maybe you aren't excellent after all, but no one has dared to tell you."

Renna tugged at a handful of grass and threw it at him. His eyes flickered with amusement, but he didn't move. She grabbed another handful of grass and threw it at him again. He ignored her, so naturally, she pulled out more grass and knelt in front of him, piling it on top of his head like a bird's nest.

He grabbed her arms and pushed her to her back again, the bird's nest on his head scattering down over her. She squealed as his legs straddled her torso, restraining both her wrists with his one hand while the other plucked fresh grass.

"You don't stand a chance!" He pulled at the grass around them, throwing it onto her in big mounds. Renna shook her head and her body trying to break free, laughing the entire time.

"Do you give up?" he asked.

"Yes! Yes!" she screamed, still trying to wiggle free.

Trev held a pile in his hand, ready to attack. "I'm not sure I can trust you."

"I think you got it in my mouth," she said as she spat into the air.

"You started it," he said innocently. "You're like a twelve-year-old."

She laughed and squirmed again, trying to free herself.

"How old are you anyway?" he asked, still holding her firmly to the ground.

"Eighteen." She gave one last struggle for freedom, but to no avail. "How old are you?"

"Twenty four," Trev answered. He could feel the heaviness of her breathing beneath him, and for a moment, it was like everything in his life paused. This strange girl made him feel differently than he ever had. He studied her, her flushed cheeks, her soft lips, her green eyes that always seemed alight with passion about something. She was intoxicating. There was something about Renna that connected with him—a pull toward her he couldn't deny.

But he *needed* to deny it. He was engaged.

The thought stung, and he quickly rolled his body off of hers. Trev gestured behind him to his PT. "I should probably get going." He needed to put some space between them, even if he didn't want to.

Renna

Renna let out a long breath, regret flaring inside her. She shouldn't have been with a man on the ground like that. It had been innocent fun at first. Then something had changed in Trev's expression, and suddenly their playful moment had turned intimate.

But then he'd scrambled away so quickly. Maybe she'd just imagined it?

Either way, she couldn't help but like him—at least what she knew of him.

And his looks. They couldn't be ignored. The combination of his athletic build, dark curls, severe blue eyes, and that boyish smile were proof enough that God was feeling generous the day he had created him. She twisted her hair between her fingers, willing herself to play it cool.

"Are you headed to the ruler's palace in Albion?" Renna said as he knelt back down on the blanket to help her clean up. She didn't want to sound too hopeful.

He looked away guiltily. "I am."

"I'm going there too," she said, her voice eager. So much for playing it cool. She waited for him to say they could meet again or to say anything, really, but he just sat there, shock taking over his expression. Clearly, seeing each other again hadn't been in his plans.

A pang of insecurity bounced around inside her.

"You're going to the ruler's palace?" He paused for a brief moment, then added, "To work?"

To work? *Oh. He thinks I'm a servant.*

Logically, she couldn't blame him for thinking that. The gray dress alone was a symbol of the lower class. People in the government or ruling class wore colored clothes. Then there was the mud and the free-spirited way she had acted in front of him—swimming and dancing. None of that was becoming of a woman in her position.

Still, his words cut. Renna had spent the last four years trying to prove to everybody that she belonged in high society —something she wasn't even sure of herself. In one second, he dismissed all the effort she had made.

Her hurt turned to anger. A quick temper had always been her weakness. She would prove to him just how wrong he had been.

"No. Sorry to disappoint you, but I'll be *staying* at the Albion Ruler's Palace with my mother." She stood and raised her chin. "Mariele, Queen of New Hope."

She tried to pull her blanket out from under him so she could make a dramatic exit, but the fabric wouldn't budge.

A flood of confusion splashed across Trev's face. "I didn't

know," he stammered. "I just assumed by the way you were dressed and how you acted . . ."

She glared at him, daring him to finish his sentence. Meanwhile, she kept tugging on her blanket until he finally rolled off.

"Does a woman in my position have to be perfect all of the time?" She crumpled up her blanket then struggled to shove it in her bag. "I thought for once I could just be myself, but I guess I was wrong." She turned with purpose and began heading back in the direction of Wellenbreck Farm.

Trev tried to stop her, but every time he stepped in front of her, she turned and walked in the other direction. It was actually quite immature of her, but she couldn't help it. He had embarrassed her. Or maybe she had embarrassed herself. It was always hard to tell.

"Please." Trev grabbed her shoulders, forcing her to look at him. "I don't understand. Your mother is the queen?"

Renna was disgusted with him. "Of course, that's the part you want to talk about—my mother being a queen. Maybe you should try starting with an apology!"

"I'm sorry!" He smiled a little bit, trying to charm her into forgiveness. "It's just a misunderstanding. Honestly." He shook her shoulders so that she would look at him. "I'm sorry! I really am."

"Well, you should be!" Her voice turned cold and haughty. "Prince Ezra is expecting us; I'm sure *he* wouldn't confuse me with the help." With that, she wiggled out of his grasp, spun, and walked away, head held high. She meant to prove how much of a lady she was.

She had seen Seran act this way for years; surely she could manage it now.

Trev

Prince Ezra is expecting us.

Her last words played back in his mind. Trev couldn't believe it. Renna's mother was the queen of New Hope. That meant Renna was the princess. Drake had said that the New Hope caravan was staying nearby. She was on her way to the Albion Ruler's Palace to meet *him*. But if she was on her way to meet her fiancé, why was she out here flirting with a soldier?

Probably for the same reasons he was flirting with her.

She was nothing like he'd expected. There were rumors about the New Hope princess, about her beauty and perfection, but the woman storming away from him now was a mess of a girl. He pulled himself together and ran after her.

"Renna! Wait! We'll laugh about this someday," he said as he caught up to her, matching her stride for stride.

"Laugh about the fact you thought I was a servant?" she snapped.

"About all of it!" But Trev was already starting to laugh. "You'll be the most beautiful lady in Albion, dressed in mud."

He could see that she wanted to stay mad at him as she turned her face from his laughter and bit her lip, but slowly his efforts softened her anger until she looked at him again. Still, an edge of annoyance masked her expression, and a clip of sarcasm tainted her words. "I bet you wouldn't even want to be seen with me."

He raised his eyebrows in jest. "Only stolen moments in dark corners. I have a reputation to uphold." At this, Renna scoffed and tried to turn away, but Trev grabbed her shoulders again. "However, I might be able to squeeze you in for a dance. As long as you don't embarrass me with your dance moves."

She half-smiled and half rolled her eyes at his insult.

"I can't believe you are going to Albion." He shook his

head, unable to hold back his smile. He wanted to tell her who he was but decided it would be more fun to surprise her at the palace.

"Is that going to be a problem?" Renna glared. "Do you have a girlfriend back in Albion I have to avoid or something?"

"A girlfriend? No." He cocked his eyebrow. "Is there a boyfriend somewhere waiting for you?" he asked.

Or a fiancé?

He was dying to hear her answer.

"No." She shook her head quickly as if the thought were absurd. "Most men keep their distance from me."

Good.

"But you," she continued, her voice overly dramatic, "I'm sure you're very popular among the ladies."

"Oh, that's just because I don't look down their dresses when they curtsy."

Renna threw her head back with laughter. "Wow. I can't believe you just said that."

"It's true. Other men need to hide it better."

"So you're saying you do look, but you just hide it better?"

"Absolutely not! I'm a gentleman through and through." He winked at her.

Her smile grew bigger, and he knew she wasn't mad anymore. "You're annoying," she said, eyeing him.

"And funny?" he pressed.

She bit back a smile. "No. Just annoying."

Trev couldn't believe it. He was relaxed for the first time in years; Renna had suddenly rearranged all the stresses inside him and created space for carefree moments like this.

Knowing who she was changed everything. It was fate the attraction and the inexplicable pull toward her.

They were meant for each other.

Renna

RENNA DECIDED TO forgive him for confusing her with the help. Especially since the intense look was back in his eyes. The look he'd had when they were lying in the grass. The look that made Renna feel like *something* was about to happen.

His hand swept across her hair as his fingers pushed it behind her ear. His intimate touch made her nervous in a good way. Every single nerve in her body came alive, keenly aware of his fingers on her skin. She looked up to find him already watching her, his blue eyes burning brightly. Yesterday morning, she didn't even know he existed. Today, all she could think about was how much she didn't want to lose him.

"You are quickly becoming my favorite person." He spoke quietly, his words somewhere between a normal voice and a whisper.

Renna swallowed back the butterflies rising in her stomach. "You must not know that many people."

Trev smiled—the full smile that Renna was beginning to love. He stepped closer. "What would you do if I kissed you right now?"

Her heart tripled in speed as her eyes met his. "I would probably wonder if I'm doing it right."

Oh, why do I always say the first thing that comes to my mind?

Trev laughed, the sound soft and deep. "I'll let you know if I have any complaints."

Renna's stomach turned over itself, and her breathing became heavy. Slowly, he leaned down and touched the tip of his nose to hers. She closed her eyes, anticipating his lips' soft touch when the unexpected drone of an engine interrupted them.

Renna jumped, and her sudden movement left Trev's lips to clumsily brush against her lower cheek. Or maybe it was her neck—she wasn't even sure. Flames of red embarrassment crept up her face at the awkward almost-kiss, but they flamed even hotter when she turned to see Mangum emerge from the trees on a PT and skid to a stop behind them. He jumped off the motorized bike and came toward them angrily.

How much had Mangum seen?

He stopped a few paces away, his brows pulled together in a stern frown. "Renna, your mother sent me to find you. The caravan is leaving within the hour."

"It's my fault," Trev said, stepping forward confidently. "We lost track of time."

Mangum's eyes narrowed on Trev. "I could've guessed who was to blame."

Renna cringed. Did Mangum have to play the role of father right this very second?

"Glad we're on the same page." Trev smiled, and she marveled at his ability to remain calm under Mangum's glare.

"We're leaving," Mangum said to Renna in a clipped tone, his eyes never wavering from Trev.

Renna was all too happy to oblige, unable to bear her mortification for another second. "Will I see you at the palace?" She nervously looked between Mangum and Trev. She hated that they had to have their goodbyes in front of him.

Trev winked at her. "You won't be able to miss me."

And with that, Trev climbed on his PT, started the engine, and drove off into the trees.

6

Renna

Renna sat on the PT behind Mangum; his stiff posture was proof enough that he was upset with her. She thought about keeping her mouth shut for the entire ride, but she couldn't. She needed to ask Mangum a favor before it was too late.

"Mangum?" Renna spoke into the side of his helmet. "Can we stop at my father's grave real quick?" Mangum was usually so serious that Renna wasn't entirely sure what he thought about her. She guessed that he liked her, at least a little bit. Why else would he have put up with her pranks for so long? She hoped that he would do her this one favor today.

"Your mother will be upset," he said against the wind.

"Please, Mangum." Her hands pulled tightly at the sides of his shirt. "It's on the way."

His body relaxed. "Fine. But just for a moment."

Renna smiled, hugging him to her chest.

The meadow came into view around the corner, and Renna could hardly wait for the PT to slow to a stop before she jumped off. She ran across the secluded glade to her father's graveside.

"We're leaving," she whispered under her breath, not

wanting Mangum to hear. "I couldn't leave without saying goodbye, but I promise I'll come back. I'll find a way to come back." Renna bent down, grazing her fingers over the headstone. "I love you, Dad. I'll always be your little girl."

She hesitated for a moment before running back to the waiting PT.

"Okay, we can go now," Renna said, wrapping her arms around Mangum. As they drove along, she studied Mangum's hair coming out the back of his helmet. The brown strands were heavily streaked with gray.

As they came down the hill, guards folded up tents and carried them to the waiting transporters. Everyone's heads flipped to Renna when they heard the personal transporter. Mangum parked and helped her to the ground. Her hair was still damp, and so was her dress where her undergarments had soaked through, plus all the dried mud remained. Renna sighed as Mangum escorted her past the men, knowing she was giving the guards quite the show.

"I must notify the queen of your activities." Mangum's voice was solemn as he opened the back door for her.

Renna was careful to avoid eye contact; she couldn't bear to see the disappointment in his kind eyes. "It's really not necessary," she said, hoping he would reconsider.

"I wish it wasn't, but I work for your mother." Mangum nodded then left to go report to the queen.

"That should be interesting," Renna muttered under her breath.

"There you are, child," Nellie said as Renna walked into the kitchen, closing the door softly behind her. "You missed lunch, but I saved some sandwiches for you. I'll put them in a sack, and you can eat them on the way."

"You're always so kind to me, Nellie."

"I'll put some carrots in there too. Something healthy for you."

Trev doesn't like carrots.

She smiled just thinking about him, his boyish charm, and the way he joked with her. Humor was always Renna's weakness when it came to men, so Trev and his witty personality were enough to keep her highest hopes about love alive.

Preetis came through the door behind her, carrying a bag of vegetables. He looked older than Renna remembered, with wrinkles curling around his eyes and lips. His hair was gone on the top of his head, and his tan skin looked tougher than before. But he lit up with youthful excitement when he saw Renna.

"There she is!" he exclaimed, kissing Renna on the forehead. "I was beginning to wonder if I'd ever see you this visit."

"I know, I'm sorry. I haven't been around much."

"Well, let's get a good look at you." He pulled Renna to her feet, holding out her arms. "You're all grown up and looking just like your dad."

"Nah, I'm better looking than he was."

Preetis chuckled. "It's a good thing he isn't here to hear you say that."

The sound of bustling skirts interrupted them, announcing the arrival of Cypress, the queen's maid. She strode into the room with an air of emergency, like always. Her brown hair was cut short, and her eyebrows arched high into the creases of her forehead, adding to her intensity.

"Renna, the queen requests an audience with you." She spoke with an edge of anxiousness to her voice. When Renna didn't immediately jump to her command, she snapped, "Now!"

Renna knew better than to keep Cypress waiting, let alone her mother. She gave Preetis and Nellie a frustrated look and followed Cypress up the stairs to her mother's room.

Mariele was seated on a large chair near the window. The room was bare and gloomy compared to the queen's enormous chamber at the Government Center. Two soldiers were carrying the queen's trunks from the room as they entered. She waved her hand impatiently toward the guards and Cypress. "Leave us." Cypress gave a knowing nod and closed the door behind her as everybody left.

Renna waited in silence for her mother to make the first move. Was she going to start her lecture with her sneaking out this morning, or would she lead with her being found alone with a man? Renna's bet was on the man.

"Haven't I warned you about promiscuous behavior?" her mother said, worry evident in her voice.

"Yes, you have, and that's why I continue to avoid it."

"Mangum said he found you in a questionable situation with a man." Mariele rose and paced the room, her smooth movements accentuating her slender body. "Is he lying?"

"We were just standing there. I don't think that is considered questionable."

"Mangum said you were kissing."

"I wish we'd been kissing," Renna said under her breath. She looked at her mother. "I'm sorry, but there's really nothing you need to worry about. It was all very innocent."

"I'm always worried."

That was true.

"There is a lot expected of you—of us. If something were to happen—"

"Nothing happened." And when Renna said nothing, she meant nothing. She was pretty sure the awkward neck kiss hadn't counted as a real kiss.

"Did anyone else see you?"

"No."

"Let's hope not. For your reputation and for mine."

Of course, her mother would be worried about that. Ever since King Bryant had sent for her, she seemed desperate to prove to the entire kingdom that she belonged and was worthy of her position.

"Like I said, nothing happened, so you don't need to worry."

Her mother wrung her hands. "Just promise me you'll keep it that way in Albion. Mangum said the man made plans to see you at the ruler's palace."

"The palace is a big place. I bet I won't see him again." Renna hoped that wasn't true.

"What's his family's name? Are they prominent in Albion?"

"I don't know. He never told me his last name." Renna smiled to herself, remembering the cute way he had said, *just Trev*.

The queen raised an eyebrow. "And what about his position?"

"He's an officer in the king's guard."

Her mother was silent for a moment, then sighed heavily. "Please remember that this silly flirtation comes second to the courtship between Seran and Prince Ezra. Nothing distracts from that." Mariele's brown eyes were pleading. "Seran needs us right now, more than ever."

"I know."

"And for goodness' sake, Renna! Clean yourself up for the ride. We're leaving soon."

"Okay." As she left, her mother shook her head in what could only be disappointment.

Her father used to say her mother made mountains out of molehills. Now that Renna was older, she understood what he'd meant. Her mother had always been fragile. Anxiousness ruled her emotions. Her father tried hard to make her mother happy, but nothing worked for long. She had been cold and indifferent to him, often picking fights. It was hard to watch and hard to forgive, especially since Renna adored her father.

Her mother's mood had improved since they moved to the Government Center. Renna still remembered that day four years ago when a transporter arrived at Wellenbreck Farm with a special message from the king of New Hope. Her mother had read that letter through tear-filled eyes.

"Finally!" she had said, over and over again. It was like her mother knew that one day King Bryant would come for her, which came as a complete surprise to Renna. She couldn't understand why the king of New Hope would marry her mother, the wife of a common farmer, or how he'd even known who she was. Had her mother entered some sort of contest to be the next queen of New Hope? Or did she somehow know King Bryant? None of it made sense. But a month after Queen Isadora died, King Bryant sent for Renna's mother. Almost instantly, she went from being Mariele Degray, living on the far lands of the kingdom, to being Mariele, Queen of New Hope.

Renna remembered the king's servants packing their things—touching everything. Before Renna knew it, she'd been forced to say goodbye to her home and her way of life. It had been traumatic, to say the least. Guards had pulled her from her father's grave. She'd sobbed and screamed that she didn't want to go, clinging to Prectis and Nellie until the guards pulled her away from them, too. The memory was so painful, it took her breath away. Now she was leaving Wellenbreck Farm again, except this time she had something to look forward to.

Renna made her way to her room to clean up. Thankfully, Nora had left a dry dress and undergarments on her bed. She picked up the clothes and walked to the bathroom across the hall, turning on the faucet in the tub. Renna held her hand under the running water, trying to find a reasonable temperature. She was grateful to whatever leaders after Desolation who had voted to keep running water. It seemed like an obvious thing, but after Desolation, when everything was destroyed, people wanted to go back to a simpler way of life.

Running water had been deemed essential in one of the early councils, but new things were added every time the

Council of Essentials met. Transporters had been added at the last council, but only for political leaders and soldiers.

Not wanting to delay the caravan's departure, Renna quickly bathed, threw on her pink travel dress, and headed downstairs. Nellie was in the kitchen, packing up the last of the food for travel. Renna ran to her, almost knocking her over with the force of her hug.

"I wish I had more time here with you."

"Child, we're not going to do a big sad goodbye again. You can come visit whenever you want." Nellie released the hug and put her hands on Renna's cheeks. "Promise me."

Nellie's hands on her face made it difficult to move, but she managed a stiff nod.

"Now, go outside and say goodbye to Preetis."

Renna hugged her tightly one more time. She hated saying goodbye to them and to Wellenbreck, but this time it was different. There were no tears and screams. She was older now, stronger. She had been through the worst and had come out the other side. Her future wasn't exactly bright—although Trev was a bright spot—but she could handle whatever came her way.

Renna took the back door out of the kitchen, thinking she might find Preetis working in the fields, but instead, she found Seran sitting on a bench next to the back door, her legs crossed gracefully. Long black hair poured down her shoulder, smoothly pooling in her lap. She looked beautiful with the summer sun on her—illuminating her like an angel. But when did Seran *not* look beautiful?

"Have you seen Preetis out here?" Renna squinted out toward the nearby fields, scanning for the farmhand's lanky form.

"Who?"

Renna had to remind herself that Seran didn't know this place—didn't know Preetis. "The caretaker. Tall, bald, and wears a gray farmhand uniform."

Seran answered without even glancing her way. "I think he's out front, loading the transporters."

Renna moved to go, but something about Seran's demeanor beckoned her to stay. "You okay?"

Seran's dark eyes flicked to hers. They were full of glossy moisture and a sadness that Renna had never seen there before. Seran was always so carefully in control of her emotions, but today things were different.

"I can see why you like it here so much. There's so much open space. It's refreshing." Her voice caught as she spoke.

Renna hesitated for a moment, then stepped closer.

"Is everything all right?" she asked, doubting Seran would tell her even if something *was* wrong. They didn't have a bad relationship, but they weren't close. Their conversation topics usually covered meaningless gossip, the latest fashion trends, events held at the Government Center, the king and queen, and the weather.

Seran was silent, staring out at the fields with an unmistakably sad expression. Renna pressed gently, "Are you nervous about going to Albion?"

Seran smiled lightly. "Am I nervous about going to a new kingdom, a new home, and living with a new family? Probably no more nervous than you were when you had to leave this place."

Renna hadn't thought about it that way, but it made her see her stepsister differently. Seran was the perfect princess, but for a brief moment, Renna just saw a girl carted away from her home in a negotiation.

Renna eased onto the edge of the bench next to Seran. "I was nervous about moving to the Government Center, but I still had my mom. And you have your friends."

"I'm sure they'll be a great comfort to me." Seran sighed. Renna couldn't tell if she meant the comment sarcastically or not.

"And you'll have Prince Ezra." Renna smiled with encouragement.

"Yes, I'll have Prince Ezra." Seran turned her head the other direction, discreetly wiping an errant tear. "My father's advisors tell me he's handsome, charming, and kind."

"Then it sounds like your father made a good match for you."

"Yes, I'm very fortunate." There was an edge of bitterness in her voice, but Seran quickly moved on, straightening her back and smoothing her dress as she stood. "I better go see if they're ready to go. I hope you find your friend," she said, swishing past Renna.

Renna sat on the bench a moment longer, surprised. She couldn't believe the honest moment she had just shared with Seran. It had only taken four years for her stepsister to open up to her. Now that they were finally getting closer, Seran was leaving.

Renna followed Seran around to the front of the house where maids and guards busily loaded the last few items into the transporters. The queen and Seran's friends stood around the vehicles, watching the guards load the backs with luggage.

Jenica walked to Seran, calling to Renna over her shoulder. "Where did you run off to today?"

"I had a secret rendezvous in the woods with a handsome man." As she said it, she could feel her mother's eyes cutting into her.

Jenica laughed flippantly. "Oh, Renna! At least you have a sense of humor."

"Yes. Thank goodness for that," Renna said sarcastically.

Mangum bowed before the queen. "We're ready to go, my lady." He held the door open for them.

Renna met Preetis behind the vehicle. "I'll see you in a few weeks on our way back through." She hugged him, stretching to the tips of her toes to reach around his shoulders.

"You save more time for me when you come back. I'll put you to work in those fields."

Renna laughed. "Plan on it."

She climbed into the transporter and watched as Wellenbreck faded from her view.

7

Trev

Trev skidded his PT to a stop in front of the Vassel Inn. Drake sat a few feet away at a metal table under the shade of the inn's canopy. Other than him, the patio was empty. A finished plate and cup were laid out in front of him.

"You went back to see the girl, didn't you?" Drake asked.

Trev smiled and shrugged at his friend.

"What are you thinking? You're getting married in four weeks!" There was an edge of irritation to Drake's tone. "I mean, I understand that you're being forced into a marriage with a woman you don't know, but this isn't like you. It's a little late to behave this way."

"It's never too late to go after a pretty woman." Trev's eyebrow raised up.

Drake closed his eyes and pressed his fingertips together in front of him as if praying for patience. "When the king expects you home tomorrow to meet the woman you're engaged to, then yes, it *is* too late. Nothing can happen with this girl. *Nothing*."

"Relax," Trev said with an easy smile.

"I'm not going to *relax*. You are *engaged*." Drake shook his head as he rubbed the stubble on his chin, clearly frustrated.

"She's the princess of New Hope."

Drake snapped his head up. "Who?"

"Renna." His voice deepened.

"Who's Renna?"

"The girl I met at the pond. She's the princess of New Hope."

Drake's eyebrows shot up. "I thought the princess was named Seran."

It hadn't occurred to Trev that she had changed her name, but Drake was right. The princess of New Hope *was* named Seran. She must have changed her name so he wouldn't know who she was.

That's why she didn't want to tell him her name when they first met.

It all made sense now.

It wasn't like Trev went around calling himself Ezra.

"How did you find out?" Drake asked.

"She told me."

"She told you?" Drake repeated. "Does she know who you are?"

"Not yet." Trev looked forward to her reaction when she found out.

"Why haven't you told her?"

"It didn't come up."

"It didn't come up?" Drake asked with exasperation.

"Why do you keep repeating everything I say?"

"Because I can't believe what I'm hearing." Drake was speechless for a moment, then let out a harsh breath. "I feel like the fact that she is the princess of New Hope, and you are the prince of Albion—who she is about to marry—is an important piece of information that you should have mentioned."

"What's she going to do? Go find another prince to marry?"

"You never know. If she doesn't like you, maybe she'll call

off the marriage treaty. Albion needs the alliance to work more than New Hope does."

"Why wouldn't she like me?" Trev feigned offense. "I'm a catch!"

"Do you like her?" Drake asked.

For years now, the best he had hoped for out of the New Hope princess was someone he could tolerate, maybe even respect. But Renna was more than that. She was unexpected, and so were his rapidly developing feelings.

Trev shrugged. "We get along."

Drake's jaw dropped a little. "I've never seen you like this."

"Like what?"

"You know." Drake flipped his hand over and over as he searched for the right explanation. "All *crazy* over a girl."

A puff of air vibrated through Trev's lips. "I'm not *crazy* over a girl."

"Yes, you are." Drake's eyebrows raised in amusement. "Big time."

"You're an idiot." Trev rolled his eyes, needing a way to hide his unexpected blush. "Are we leaving for Oakefor or not?"

Drake held up his hands in a gesture of defeat, then stood from the table and gathered his things. "I was just waiting for you."

"Our tests have shown contamination in our water supply for two weeks now. And each day, the contamination levels grow worse." Oakefor's Mayor Agribba pulled the test tube out of the well and held it up for Trev. There was a crowd of people gathered around them in the city square. Everyone was curious to see what Prince Ezra would say about their water problem.

Trev looked at the murky water in the glass tube. "Why haven't you petitioned for help?"

"We have. As soon as our well water tested contaminated, we wrote to King Carver asking for the proper chlorinated chemicals to flush the contamination out. A week later, when we still hadn't heard anything, we sent a few men to the ruler's palace to speak to the king personally. They haven't returned yet." The mayor pulled nervously at his thick, brown beard as he spoke.

Trev frowned. He didn't understand why his father hadn't done anything for the people of Oakefor. Water contamination was a big problem, although he had a feeling that his father didn't care much about that. Still, a king who didn't answer his people's petitions was bad optics, and his father certainly cared about that. Why hadn't he sent aid?

"What has your city done for water over the past two weeks?"

"We boil our drinking water. Even after boiling, though, a lot of folks have come down with fevers. Most still fear drinking the water. Luckily, the Domans brought huge containers of fresh water. They have been our saviors."

Trev shot a concerned look to Drake standing next to him. So Maxwell and Joniss had been here before them. For the people of Oakefor's sake, Trev was glad. The city needed that water. But this wasn't going to help Trev's election campaign. Joniss was clearly trying to gain momentum and votes any way he could.

"We're concerned about our crops. Irrigation water has been affected. Contamination levels have risen to the point that we stopped flooding our fields as a precaution. We can't afford to risk the harvest. It rained two days ago, but if this goes on much longer, we'll lose our crops for the season."

Trev nodded and motioned to one of his men standing behind him. "Zarek, take a man with you to the ruler's palace immediately. Tell my father's advisors that Prince Ezra is demanding chlorine for Oakefor's water at once. Bring the chlorine back as quick as you can." He turned to the crowd so all could hear him. "We'll have this problem fixed in two to three days at most. Do you have enough drinking water to last you until then?"

Mayor Agribba nodded. "Yes. The water the Doman's brought should last at least that long, and we still have the option of boiling if we need to."

"What if our crops don't recover?" a thin man shouted from the crowd. His skin was tanned and weathered, likely from hours of sun exposure.

"First, let's see how the crops do before we make any plans. But be assured that King Carver and I are willing to provide for your city in whatever way we can. "

Trev walked through the crowd of people that circled the city well, shaking their hands and answering any other questions they had. He was stopped by an elderly woman, her gray head barely reaching the middle of his chest.

"Bless you for coming, Prince Ezra." The old woman squeezed Trev's hand as she spoke. Her wrinkly skin was coarse against his fingers. "We've had a Trevenna king since the first Council of Essentials. I think you'll be the best king yet out of all the kings since Desolation."

Trev stared back at the woman, humbled to see how much faith she had in him. "Thank you for saying that. I hope I can live up to your expectations."

"I know you will. I can see it in your eyes."

"My eyes?"

"Yes. They're kind."

"I hope so," Trev said with a smile.

"Prince Ezra?" A little girl ducked through the crowd and tugged on his jacket. She wore a tattered cream dress and had scraggly blonde hair tied back at her neck. "Are you going to marry a princess?"

Trev thought about Renna, and, for once, he didn't hate answering the question. "Yes, I am."

"Will you bring her back to Oakefor so we can meet her? I've never seen a real princess before."

He patted the girl on the top of her head. "Well, she actually looks a lot like you."

The little girl beamed.

"We're all really excited about your upcoming marriage, Your Highness," another onlooker said.

"I am too." For the first time, Trev actually meant it.

8

Trev

Trev and Drake arrived in Albana city at the ruler's palace the next morning. Trev could see his father's watchful eye from his balcony above the courtyard. He gestured with his hand for Trev to join him upstairs. It wasn't going to be the typical father and son joyful reunion. King Carver had always shied away from emotional connection.

Trev entered his father's office to find him seated at his desk, poring over a stack of papers. The room was lavish, with stained woodwork and trim covering the walls. Rich leather couches were positioned in front of a large stone fireplace with several smaller leather chairs facing the king's mahogany desk.

"You're late," King Carver said, barely glancing up from his work. His dark hair and beard were peppered with silver, and his face held deep lines.

"Good to see you too, Father." Trev casually sat on a couch next to the fireplace, rummaging through a nearby tray of food that had been brought in for his father.

"You were supposed to be here last night."

Trev picked up a piece of fruit and put it in his mouth. "We got held up."

"A messenger sent word that the New Hope princess will arrive this afternoon." His father looked up from his desk. "Do I have to remind you how important this alliance is?"

Trev already knew, of course, but was sure his father would tell him anyway.

"You need the princess to help get you votes in the election. Some factions believe our family has ruled this country too long."

More like people think you have ruled too long.

"They want change. They want Joniss Doman, which we know is a terrible choice. He only wants power and control."

And you don't?

"It will be harder for people to vote against you once you're married to the New Hope princess. Joniss doesn't have New Hope." His father smirked. "We do."

The marriage alliance was something King Carver liked to brag about—how ten years ago he'd had the forethought to arrange a marriage alliance with New Hope and plan the ceremony just a few months before the election.

"What if people don't vote based on New Hope? What if they vote based on who is helping them right now?"

"Bah! New Hope has the strongest military in all seven kingdoms. People will vote based on the fact that New Hope's military, combined with ours, will keep them safe from Tolsten's attacks."

"Father, I've spent the last year touring the kingdom, and I can tell you that most people have more worries than just Tolsten. They also care about their livelihoods, earning enough money to survive the winter, and keeping their crops from failing. If people vote based on those things, I might not win the election. What happens to the alliance then?"

His father leaned back in his chair. "If you don't win the election, the terms of the alliance won't be honored. Albion will lose everything."

There was a lot riding on Trev—on him becoming king. If he somehow messed up the election, his kingdom would suffer. He alone held the future of Albion in his hands. When he really thought about it, the pressure suffocated him.

"Of course, if you lose the election, we wouldn't be giving up all chance at a crown. You'd have to go to New Hope and gain support there. Though, King Bryant still has thirteen more years to his reign, which isn't ideal." His father rubbed his chin. "Unless we usurped him somehow."

Trev dropped his head into his hands. "You're unbelievable! Do you even hear yourself?"

"What?" The king shrugged.

"I can't believe you would suggest usurping King Bryant just so I could become a king. It's despicable and I won't be a part of it."

"Don't lose the election and you won't have to be."

Trev gave him a pointed look. "You're not helping my chances. Did you know that Oakefor's main water source is contaminated?"

"I heard something about that."

"Why didn't you send help? They're desperate."

His father rolled his eyes. "It's good for people to feel desperate. It helps them realize how much they depend on us. Now they'll be grateful when we do help."

"No, they're grateful to Joniss Doman for personally delivering barrels of water when their *king* ignored them. If you want me to win this election, you're going to have to start listening to the people and helping them because that is exactly what Joniss is doing."

The king's face colored with sudden rage. He picked up a book on his desk and threw it at the tray of food on the table next to Trev. The plate toppled to the ground, flinging fruit and cheeses everywhere. "Don't tell me how to run my kingdom!" The king pounded his fist against the desk. "I am the one who has kept Oakefor and everywhere else safe from

Tolsten for the last thirty years. Without me, people would be under Tolsten's rule!"

"Our people need more than protection. They need a king who listens," Trev shot back.

Carver let out an exasperated sigh and calmed his voice. "You think you know it all, don't you?" His father glared at him. "That you know exactly what this kingdom needs. Did you know there was an attack on the province of Axville? On our border with Tolsten?"

"What?" A burst of air escaped Trev's chest.

Carver looked oddly pleased, as though the news of the attack cheered him. "We received reports of a group of Tolsten soldiers ransacking the city and kidnapping eight young women from the town. As far as we can tell, they took the girls back to Tolsten. There's no more information on their whereabouts, but the reports say the land on our side of the border is still overrun with Tolsten soldiers."

"When did this happen?"

"A few days ago, while you were busy shaking hands with peasants." His father leveled a condescending smile at him. "As you can see, Oakefor's water problem is the least of my worries. Right now, Tolsten is my only concern."

"When will you let go of this obsession with Tolsten?" Trev asked.

"You couldn't possibly understand." His father huffed. "They think I killed her—my own wife."

"I know." Trev's stomach tightened. He had loved Queen Avina from Tolsten. His father had married her a year after his own mother had died during childbirth. Queen Avina was the only mother he'd ever known and Trev vividly remembered the day he'd heard her ragged scream outside his window, only to look down and see her sprawled and broken on the hard ground below, her body contorted in ways that even a seven-year-old boy knew were wrong. Servants quickly ushered him away, but not before he saw his father barrel across the courtyard toward her, bellowing orders and demanding to know how this could have happened.

His father was many less-than-honorable things, but he hadn't killed his wife. Even as a boy, Trev had sensed that Avina was sad. He had often taken her poppies and roses from the palace garden to cheer her up, but it had never been enough. Now a grown man, Trev understood the signs more clearly. Avina had been fighting a battle in her mind, one he couldn't hope to understand. His father's brash and unsentimental manner likely hadn't helped, especially when partnered with Avina's inability to bear children for the king. Over time, she retreated further and further into herself. Before long, she was a shell of a person.

Tolsten used her death as a reason to start a war, blaming King Carver, saying he'd murdered her. Avina's brother, King Adler of Tolsten, wouldn't accept any other explanation.

"With New Hope's military, we will finally be able to defend our kingdom against Tolsten and win," Trev's father said, a satisfied gleam in his eye. "Joniss doesn't have that. He is nothing more than an act. The wedding will take attention away from him and put it back on you. You and the princess will visit some cities. If you want to personally address some of their needs, then fine, but let's remind them who the real enemy is. The fear of Tolsten is the surest way to make people vote for us."

Trev hated it when his father used the word *us* when talking about the election, as if he planned to run the kingdom in Trev's stead. Unfortunately for his father, his thirty years were up. His reign was over.

"Charm the princess," the king continued. "Give the people of Albion a fairytale wedding, and I'll take care of Tolsten." He swiveled in his chair, turning his back on Trev. "You are dismissed."

Trev couldn't recall a time when he had ever left his father's office not feeling frustrated. Winning the election had consumed his father for the last few years, almost as much as his obsessive rivalry with Tolsten. The people of Albion had suffered because of it.

A few more months. That's it. Then I can help the people the way they deserve with Renna by my side.

9

Renna

The nerves were really starting to get to Renna. Or maybe it was just excitement. It was hard to tell. They had been traveling for a day and a half, stopping often for bathroom breaks and to rest. They would arrive at the Albion Ruler's Palace today. For most of the ride, Renna stayed quiet as her mother and Seran chatted about government gossip back at New Hope.

She was used to the close relationship between her mother and Seran. Used to being the third wheel. Her mother and Seran just understood each other.

Rather than try to keep up with them, Renna passed the time by looking out the window and watching the scenery change. She had never been to another country before. The rolling hills of New Hope abruptly changed into rising peaks with patches of evergreen trees and rocky edges. At the summit of the tallest mountain, Renna saw the remains of clean, white snow where the summer sun hadn't yet melted it away.

The transporter rolled to a stop as a guard approached the window. "Your Majesty, Albana City has come into view."

The queen peered out the window, wanting to get a better

view. "Send a soldier ahead to the ruler's palace and let them know we are arriving soon."

The guard nodded and stepped away from the vehicle.

Her mother turned to Seran as the window rolled up. "Are you ready for this?"

Seran pulled her lips into a tight smile. "The people of Albion want protection from Tolsten. They need us." Seran hesitated a moment, then added, "They need me."

The queen tried to reassure her. "You are doing a good thing. It's an alliance that will be mutually beneficial to both parties. Albion gets the support of our superior military and the use of our ports. In return, New Hope gets access to valuable resources. Iron, silver, and gold are all items that are scarce in New Hope. The Rocky Mountains of Albion are rich with them." Her mother smiled back at Seran. "And the marriage joins two powerful, royal families together. Those connections will help keep you and your family in leadership and royalty for many years to come."

"I know." Seran nodded.

Renna was in awe at how dignified and intelligent Seran seemed while maintaining an air of gracefulness. It was clear that she had been prepping for this role her whole life. Seran was going to be a magnificent queen; still, there was something about her smile that made Renna feel sorry for her.

It was an odd thing to feel sorry for a princess.

Outside, buildings began to be more numerous. Renna pressed her face against the glass and sucked in a breath at the sight. The capital of Albion was larger than Renna expected. Cream and gray four-story buildings were sandwiched together by narrow, cobblestone roads. Windows and balconies decorated the sides of the buildings, providing a quick glimpse of the working families who lived inside. Damp laundry hung from lines, dancing in the summer breeze—in sync with other colorless shirts hung farther down the road. As they drove along, Renna could tell by the buildings they were getting closer to the ruler's palace. Apartments got a little taller, a little nicer, and more colorful. Nothing was cream anymore. Instead, buildings were plastered in yellow, blue, and green, with colorful trim around each window.

Renna's stomach flipped over in anticipation as the transporters approached the palace's perimeter wall. Large iron gates automatically opened in front of them as the sentries within saw their arrival. All three women eagerly pressed against the windows, trying to get a good look at the ruler's palace in front of them.

Renna thought the Government Center in New Hope was nice, but it was simple compared to Albion's royal residence. The level of luxury here had been kicked up a notch or two . . . or three. Large fountains lined both sides of the cobblestone drive, spaced apart every ten to twenty feet.

Since when are water features considered essential? Renna raised an eyebrow. They had nothing like that back in New Hope.

But it appeared that Albion was less concerned with essentials when it came to their royalty. Perfectly trimmed grass stretched out for hundreds of feet leading up to the palace. The drive ended in a circle with an enormous fountain in the center, dumping gallons of water into a circular stone pool.

Then there was the palace. It was enormous, with exquisite architecture that practically screamed *unessential*. Towers and gables jutted out of the roof across the entire building. The exterior was covered in balconies and windows of all sizes, facing every direction. Three grand stone staircases led up to the palace entrance, a massive archway surrounding two ornately carved wooden doors.

Renna's mouth hung open in shock. She couldn't understand it. The New Hope Government Center was a lot more practical with its flat roofline and box-like exterior. In a world of essentialism, how could the kingdom of Albion justify such luxury?

Beyond the circular drive, a crowd of people waited for

them, some of them wearing expensive colored clothes and some in working-class gray. Soldiers lined each side of the path leading to the front steps of the palace. Her heart fluttered. Was Trev among them?

Since she'd last seen him, Renna had dreamed up an entire future for the two of them. She would spend her time in Albion getting to know him. He would show her around the kingdom, and when the time was right, he would kiss her under a moonlit sky. And who knew? From there . . . maybe they would fall in love and live happily ever after. She liked those kinds of endings, even if Trev didn't believe in them.

She looked across the transporter at Seran. Would she get her own happy ending with the prince of Albion? Renna hoped so.

The transporter slowed to a stop in the circle drive.

It was time.

Renna's breaths got heavier as she looked over her reflection in the window, smoothing her blonde hair. Across from her, Queen Mariele fidgeted with Seran's updo, fixing a few stray strands of hair.

"You look lovely," her mother said to Seran.

Renna could see Seran's chest rise and fall as she nodded back to the queen.

"Everything will turn out okay," Renna said, offering Seran a small smile.

Seran bit her bottom lip. "Thanks."

The air inside the transporter was thick as a guard approached and opened the door.

10

Trev

King Carver stood just below the palace steps, ready to greet his royal guests. Trev and Drake were just a few steps behind him. The entire palace had come out to see the arrival of the New Hope royalty. A crowd of political leaders and citizens lined the pathway in anticipation, craning their necks to see over the wall of Albion soldiers separating them from the path. Trev's heart raced with excitement and nerves. He couldn't wait to see Renna's reaction when she realized that he was the prince.

"I hear the princess's beauty surpasses all others. Maybe I will keep her for myself," the king leaned over and whispered, half-jokingly.

Trev tightened his fists at the thought of his father with Renna but chose not to say anything. His father had always had a weird sense of humor.

The caravan slowly moved toward them. Dozens of New Hope soldiers on PTs flanked the three black transporters as they rolled into the circle. The transporter in the middle was reserved for the royal family and displayed the purple and yellow New Hope flag.

The crowd seemed to get louder as each transporter came

to a stop outside the courtyard wall. New Hope guards dismounted from their PTs and set a formation surrounding each side of the main transporter. Trev waited impatiently for the guard to open the door.

"Relax!" whispered Drake. "The whole city can hear you breathing."

Trev tried to slow his heavy breaths.

The guard opened the transporter door, extending his arm to help its occupants down the narrow steps. The first to emerge was undoubtedly the queen. Trev could tell even from where he stood that she was beautiful, but in a different way than Renna. She had brown hair that was swept up on the top of her head, and she wore a crimson dress made out of the finest silk. Her movements were poised and regal as she stepped down from the transporter and moved to the side to make way for the princess behind her.

The guard reached into the transporter to help the princess out next. Each movement seemed slow and drawn out. Sweat gathered on Trev's forehead. Never in his life had he been this nervous to sec a woman, especially one he had already met. But Renna was going to be his princess, *his queen*. How could he remain calm when his entire world was about to change?

But instead of seeing Renna's familiar golden waves of hair, another girl stepped out of the transporter—a girl with black hair and creamy skin in a richly adorned purple dress. The mysterious woman raised her chin proudly and took her place to the right of the queen, indicating her role as princess.

This wasn't the princess he expected. Where was Renna?

Then he saw her. The guard helped her out of the transporter last, and she moved to stand on her mother's left. She wore her hair up in loose braids around her head with a few stray pieces framing her face. She looked more timid than the others, her shoulders slightly hunched as though the hundreds of eyes on her weighed them down. But then she took a breath and threw her shoulders back as if a wave of confidence had washed over her. She stood in her pink dress—elegant in her own way—though not like the queen and the other girl.

Renna seemed distracted as she glanced down the row of soldiers lining the path. She turned her head to the side like she was looking for something.

Or someone.

Trev's heart sank. She was looking for *him.*

None of it made sense. He turned to his father's chief advisor. "Gaines, who is the girl on the queen's left?" His voice sounded harsh.

Gaines stepped forward, ready with information. "Yes, that is the daughter of the queen. Renna, I believe."

"So she's Seran's sister? Also a princess?"

Please.

"No, sire. Miss Renna is the product of the queen's first marriage. She has no birthright within the royal family."

Gaines's words hurt like a punch to the gut.

Drake put a steadying hand on Trev's shoulder as the three women started to walk toward them.

Renna

Renna sensed hundreds of eyes on the three of them as they began their procession toward the palace. There were so many people watching them, but everyone was really looking at Seran. This was a big moment for her.

She eyed Seran from the side, marveling at how calm and collected she seemed. She clearly knew her own importance, moving forward with poise and confidence.

Then Renna glanced straight ahead. A colorful group of people waited at the end of the path. Albion royalty, she assumed, mixed with advisors and political figures. She wanted to get a glimpse of Seran's prince, but it was difficult to make out who was who from this distance.

The soldiers on each side of her were much easier to see. Was Trev among them? He said that she wouldn't be able to miss him. She could picture him watching her now, ready to smirk at her surprise when she finally spotted him. As each step brought them closer to the courtyard, Renna discreetly searched the soldiers' faces for Trev's laughing blue eyes and dark curls. Instead, unfamiliar eyes stared back with serious, unblinking expressions. As far as she could see, Trev was not there.

Renna's mother slowed her pace and then stopped several feet from the king. The king stood before them in a navy suit with a pin of the blue and white Albion flag on his lapel. His features seemed hard and menacing as he waited for introductions.

The herald's voice boomed behind the king from the palace steps. "Introducing Her Royal Majesty, Queen Mariele Haslett of New Hope." The queen bowed gracefully.

"Her Royal Highness, Princess Seran Alyssa Haslett of New Hope."

Renna glanced in Seran's direction, a bit in awe as she curtseyed smoothly. How was she so good at that?

Renna hated this next part—the part where she was introduced like an afterthought.

"And Miss Renna Degray."

She did her best to curtsey the way Seran had, but she doubted it looked even close to the same.

King Carver stepped forward and took her mother's hand. "Queen Mariele, welcome to Albion. It's a pleasure to meet you. I am Carver Trevenna, King of Albion. I hope your travels weren't too tiresome."

"Not at all. Thank you," Renna's mother said with perfect grace. "King Bryant sends his regards. He wasn't able to come with us at this time, as he had to attend to some pressing business back home. He'll arrive in a couple of weeks for the wedding."

Renna couldn't help but smile. From this interaction, no one would ever guess that her mother spent most of Renna's childhood locked in her room, depressed. Today, she stood as regally as any woman ever had. Pride surged inside Renna. Her mother had come so far.

King Carver nodded. "May I present my son." The king turned to his left and gestured behind him, where a man with curly, dark hair stepped forward, his head down, and his eyes focused on the ground. As he raised his head, their gazes locked for a brief moment.

A jolt of shock shot through Renna.

Trev.

The king's next words took her breath away. "Ezra Trevenna, Prince of Albion."

The color drained from Renna's face. She had been so focused on finding Trev in the line of soldiers that she hadn't seen him standing at the king's side.

Until now.

Ezra Trevenna. Trev.

It was clearly a mistake. It had to be. But no one protested that the wrong man had been named. To everyone else, nothing was amiss.

Trev wasn't dressed in black pants and a plain white shirt like most soldiers wore—like he *had* worn with her. No, now he was dressed for the part of a prince in a pair of perfectly tailored dark blue slacks, a brown leather belt, a light blue dress shirt with navy pinstripes, and a solid yellow tie. Colored clothes or not, he looked good.

Renna watched in disbelief as Trev stepped forward and kissed her mother's hand. "Your Majesty. It's a pleasure to be in your company. Our kingdom has never beheld such beauty."

Her mother inclined her head and smiled, eating up every last word of his cheesy line.

He stepped toward Seran, and the reality of what was happening finally started to sink in.

Trev is the prince of Albion. Trev is Seran's Prince Ezra. Seran is marrying Trev.

He must have said something charming because Seran's ringing laugh brought Renna back to reality. "You're charming and good looking?" Renna heard Seran say. "That's a dangerous combination, Your Highness."

"I'm afraid my charm gets me in trouble often." His eyes darted to Renna as Seran laughed.

Renna's chest constricted, a muddle of emotions threatening to take over. Confusion. Hurt. Anger. Embarrassment. Her mind couldn't even keep up with the storm swirling inside her. Why hadn't he told her?

"Well, I hope not too much trouble." Seran's shoulder dipped closer to Trev as she spoke. "At least now that I've arrived."

"Now that you've arrived, everything will change. I can assure you of that." He glanced at Renna again.

His words were like a slap across Renna's face.

He moved in front of her. She did her best to mask everything, her face turning to stone.

He greeted her in almost a whisper. "Miss Degray."

She wondered if she could knee him in the groin but decided against it, knowing she'd probably be arrested.

He took her hand and kissed it, just as he had with her mother and Seran, but now his touch enraged her. He was the prince, and he never told her.

Everything between them had been fake.

Renna stood frozen in anger, unable to even pull off a decent curtsey. Trev didn't seem to notice, quickly turning away and resuming his position at his father's side.

That's it? He didn't have anything else to say to her?

Where was the 'I'm sorry that I never told you I was the prince of Albion'? Or, 'sorry for almost kissing you and making you fall in love with me when I am practically married to your stepsister'? Not that Renna expected him to say all those things in front of his fiancée. But his eyes could have conveyed *something*.

Anything.

The king exchanged pleasantries with her mother and Seran for a moment longer, something about getting settled before the dinner celebration, but Renna hardly listened. She was still trying to get a handle on her shock. The onlookers in the courtyard began to disperse as the king walked away.

Trev glanced in her direction before he turned to follow. Her hurt eyes met his. For the first time, they saw each other for who they really were: Trev, the prince, and Renna, the country girl playing the part of a lady. She thought he might say something—she hoped he might—but instead, he turned and left.

Renna's heart went numb.

The head maid of the ruler's palace appeared at the queen's side to escort them in. Renna followed behind, her shock preventing her from keeping up with the group. They passed through the doors under the arching entryway into a large hall, with light blue walls and a tall, coffered ceiling. In front of them, a large staircase with light green, diamond-patterned carpet curved upward.

The maid took them to their rooms, giving directions and explanations all along the way. Renna hoped that none of it was too important because she couldn't focus on a single word.

They were assigned their own rooms, each spacious and finely decorated with large windows and a balcony facing the mountains. The color schemes were colorful and bright. Renna's room had a vanity and mirror against the wall by the door to the bathroom. On the opposite side of the room, a large bed covered in a maroon comforter dominated the space, flanked by a single nightstand and lamp.

Once left alone, Renna sank onto the bed, tears already forming in her eyes.

How could this have happened? Losing her father, the one person she loved and idolized more than anyone in the world had nearly destroyed her. Then to be taken from Wellenbreck —her home—to the Government Center so soon afterward, to live among people who hardly cared that she existed, to spend the next four years of her life living as a shadow of herself, letting her mother down when she couldn't live up to her expectations, never sure where she belonged . . . it was too much.

With all the changes she had experienced in the past four years, her stolen moments with Trev had been some of her best moments. He had made her hope again, made her feel optimistic, made her believe that perhaps there was a happy future for her somewhere. Now that was taken from her too. It was more than she could stand.

She had a lot of practice not letting loss get the best of her. Things were never as bad as they felt. But the pain she felt over losing Trev—even just the possibility of Trev—drove through her so powerfully that she couldn't keep it at bay. It was a pain born from all the things she'd lost, and it threatened to carry her away now. She decided to let it.

Cradling the soft pillow below her face, she decided she would give herself one moment of sadness, one moment to surrender to her shock, her anger, her embarrassment, and her broken heart. Wet tears spilled onto the pillowcase. She had been a stupid girl thinking that she was on the verge of her own fairytale.

She wasn't a princess, and she wasn't the one Trev was going to marry.

11

Trev

Drake called after him, but Trev didn't let up his pace. His anger and frustration drove him, and he was desperate to release it somehow. He made his way to the training grounds at the side of the palace where the king's soldiers trained. Loosening his tie and rolling up his sleeves, he strode into the dirt arena where several soldiers already sparred.

"Is there a soldier willing to fight me?" he shouted above the practicing men's grunts.

Some broke off mid-spar at the prince's arrival, bowing respectfully. A few young men stepped forward, eager to show off in front of the prince.

"Whoa, whoa, whoa!" Drake gasped as he burst into the arena. "Forgive me, but you're in no mood to fight with a young soldier. You might kill one of them." He stepped in front of Trev, putting both hands on his chest to stop him.

"Drake, if you know what's good for you, you'll get out of my way."

"You're being irrational."

Trev blew out a harsh breath. "I'm not going to *kill* anyone."

“Still, don’t take your anger out on one of these boys.”

“Are you volunteering?”

Drake shook his head. “If I have to.”

“Then let’s go.”

Sighing, Drake removed his gray vest and weapons belt, then took his place across from Trev in the dirt. A small crowd of soldiers gathered around to watch, forming a wide circle around them.

Immediately, Trev swung his right arm toward Drake’s face. Drake quickly stepped to the side, leaning away from the punch.

“Are we boxing?” Drake said as he shuffled away.

“You’re the one who volunteered.” Trev spun, dust flying in the air, then sent a blow to Drake’s ribs. Drake grabbed his side for a moment but didn’t swing back.

“Fight me!” Trev yelled. He took two steps forward, throwing his arms in a sequence of jabs.

Drake ducked out of the way, calmly adding between breaths, “What do you think we are doing?”

“Fight me! That’s an order!”

Drake lunged for his waist, his arms wrapping around Trev’s body as they both toppled to the ground. Drake grunted as he used the weight of his body to pin Trev and lowered his voice so only the two could hear. “I know you’re frustrated about Renna, but I’m not going to fight you.”

Trev pushed Drake off of him roughly and sat up, breathing hard. How did everything with Renna get so messed up? He shook his head, trying to figure it out.

Seeing that Trev appeared less likely to hit him now, Drake looked up at the crowd of onlooking soldiers. “As you were, gentlemen. Back to your drills.”

The men dispersed, but not without casting a few curious looks over their shoulders.

Trev combed his hand through his hair. “She’s not the princess.”

Drake nodded but didn't say anything.

"I don't know what to do now."

"Yes, you do. You're going to forget about Renna and give all your attention to Princess Seran."

Trev looked away. He didn't like that solution.

"You're going to do this because you love Albion and because you're going to be the next king."

He sighed. Drake knew him well. Since he was a young boy, he had been motivated to become the next king of Albion. There was so much good he could do for his kingdom, for his people. He would be a good ruler—at least better than his father.

But up until a few days ago, he had always pictured himself ruling alone. His betrothed princess from New Hope had seemed almost imaginary. But then Renna came into his life, and he started to imagine a different future, one where his queen would rule by his side.

Partners.

To find out now that he had imagined the wrong girl was a blow.

"I gave in to her, Drake," he said quietly, avoiding his friend's eyes. "I let myself . . . *feel* for her. I thought she was going to be my . . ." Trev didn't allow himself to finish. What was the point? He had been wrong.

"You're going to make the best of it, Trev. Besides," Drake rested a hand on his shoulder and gave a light shove, "there are worse fates than yours. Princess Seran is . . . stunning. A ten out of ten."

He was right. Seran *was* gorgeous, polished, and confident. But none of that seemed to matter right now. She wasn't Renna.

Where was Renna now? What was she doing? Was she as upset about their situation as he was?

He *needed* to forget about Renna and move forward with

Seran. But no matter how hard he tried, his head couldn't convince his heart to let her go.

12

Renna

Renna awoke to her maid's gentle voice. "M'lady?"

Her tears had eventually given way to a deep nap, but as consciousness returned, the ache inside her throbbed to life again. Sleep hadn't smothered it away for good.

She had been careless with her heart. It wouldn't happen again.

"I'm sorry to wake you," Nora tried again, "but it's time to get you ready for the welcome feast."

A feast? Renna cracked an eye open. Now that was something she could get excited about. She hadn't had a decent meal since she'd left Wellenbreck Farm, and her stomach ached for the finer food dinner would offer.

She rolled over, sitting up at the edge of her bed. She watched as Nora shuffled around the room. Her tiny little body rushed back and forth, gathering from Renna's bags the things she needed to do Renna's hair and makeup.

"You must be tired, miss! All that traveling really takes it out of you."

Renna forced a smile as she climbed out of bed and walked to the vanity.

"Being here is so exciting! A new palace. New dresses. And

isn't Prince Ezra handsome? I never thought the princess would find someone as attractive as she was, but I was wrong."

Renna frowned as she sat down at the vanity. Nora had always been a chatty maid. They were about the same age, so usually her collected gossip was entertaining. Not today, though.

"He's okay. If you like arrogance."

"Okay? You must have had dust in your eyes because he is better than okay." Nora fussed with Renna's hair. "He looks so strong. Can you imagine what is hidden under his shirt?"

Renna *could* imagine.

"And then those curls! Don't you just want to run your fingers through them?"

She did, actually.

"I bet they're soft. Not full of hair products."

Renna grunted noncommittally. It was like she was inside Nora's personal fantasy with the prince.

"And his blue eyes! I mean, bright blue eyes are so cliché, but the prince pulls it off, don't you think?"

"I guess." Renna tried to sound uninterested.

Nora continued to ramble, and Renna listened politely as she talked about what a perfect match Seran and Ezra were and how beautiful their children would be. Renna might've tried to escape her incessant chatter earlier, but Nora had a firm grip on her hair as she twisted it into fine weaves. Besides, Renna wanted to look her best for dinner.

She convinced herself that her desire to look nice was purely for herself, not Trev. But if she was honest, she couldn't deny wanting to look beautiful to show Trev what he was missing.

She quickly chided herself, shaking her head to chase the thought away while Nora fussed at her to keep still. Renna was stupid to think that Trev would even notice her with Seran in the room. She had enjoyed his focus for a few days, but all that would change now.

But then, why had Renna had his focus at all?

He was engaged the whole time back at Wellenbreck. She even asked him if he had a girlfriend, and he had lied about it. Her lips pursed together in anger. Was she just an easy target? Someone he could flirt with and kiss and never see again? Well, now she was stuck here with him.

"All done, miss," Nora declared after a few minutes, stepping back to admire her work. "You look lovely, if I say so myself."

Renna looked in the mirror and had to agree. Despite her stern face, she looked good. Strands of hair wove in and out of each other in a braided pattern around the crown of her head, accentuating the different shades of gold throughout. It was some of Nora's best work.

Nora held up a green fitted evening gown with long sleeves. The silk fabric nipped at the waist then hung straight to the floor. She helped Renna step inside and fastened the back. Nora added a gold necklace to adorn her collar, complimenting the square, lace neckline.

Renna stepped in front of the vanity mirror and gave a low whistle. "Nora, I don't know how you did it, but now I look like I actually belong here."

"Of course you belong here, miss! Now go and find yourself a prince of your own."

Renna had already found a prince. A lying, backstabbing one that she couldn't stop thinking about.

13

Trev

Trev hid behind a stone pillar down the hall from Renna's room, feeling absolutely ridiculous. How had it come to this? To skulking about in the dark corners of his own palace? But he had to see her. He had to explain the mix-up.

Her door opened, and a tiny maid hurried out with a pile of laundry. Renna followed soon after, stepping into the hallway and closing the door behind her.

Trev had to catch his breath. She looked like a completely different person from the girl he'd met at Wellenbreck Pond. He thought about the many different versions of her he had seen—the witty comedian, the nervous Renna, the unpolished lady, the angry girl—but standing before him now was a dignified beauty. The fabric of her dress curved over her body in ways that he would never forget; the memory would likely drive him crazy all night. Her hair was pulled up, revealing the striking base of her neck and shoulders. But the worst part was how the green dress set off her eyes perfectly.

He swallowed a frustrated groan.

She headed down the hall in his direction. As she passed his hiding place, Trev grabbed her arm and pulled her into the shadows behind the pillar where they wouldn't be seen.

She almost screamed, but the alarm in her eyes softened when she recognized his face.

And then her eyes iced over.

"What are you doing?" Her voice was loud and stern.

"Shh!" Trev couldn't be discovered with her. He looked around to see if anyone was coming, then took her hand and dragged her back to her room. He shut the door behind them and shoved her farther into the room, causing her to stumble just a bit. Feeling bad, he released her and backed away. He hadn't meant to be so forceful with her.

Renna whirled around to face him. "Are you insane?"

"I'm sorry." He raised his palms, signaling he was there in peace. "I just want to explain."

"How kind of you to squeeze me in before you have dinner with your fiancée," she huffed.

"That's not fair," Trev said back to her. "You *know* I'm not that kind of guy."

"I don't know anything about you," she spat. "You lied to me."

"I did not!"

"I should have known better when you said your name was *just Trev.*"

He grimaced, hating how she made him sound like an idiot when she imitated his voice. "When I'm outside the palace walls, I *am* just Trev, the soldier. Especially when I'm in New Hope."

Her arms folded across her chest. "Playing the part of an unattached soldier is fun for you, I'm sure."

"I am unattached." He said it before thinking, then stammered through a pathetic rebuttal. "I mean, I was . . . kind of."

She laughed mockingly. "That's your explanation for flirting with me? Dancing with me? Not to mention the whole grass fight."

"Last I checked, none of that is illegal when you're

engaged to someone you haven't met before." He took a step forward. "And since we're bringing everything up, you forgot to mention swimming together in our undergarments."

She rolled her eyes. "How could I forget that?"

He scoffed. "Yes, how could you forget that?" He couldn't seem to get it out of his mind.

She glared at him, unconvinced.

"Okay." He shrugged. "I admit that I shouldn't have flirted with you when we first met. But to be fair, I later believed you were my betrothed. My actions were in earnest."

"What are you talking about?" Her brows furrowed.

"You said your mother was the queen, and the prince was expecting you. What else was I supposed to think?"

Renna went silent and looked down at the floor as if playing back the memory in her mind.

Trev continued. "I felt so comfortable around you, and we got along so well. When I thought you were the princess, I couldn't wait to surprise you in Albion as your fiancé."

Renna gave a shuddering sigh and ducked her head, hiding her expression.

"I should have told you who I was." His voice softened. "I never meant for any of this to happen."

For a few tense moments, Renna didn't move. Then, quietly, she said, "My mother *is* the queen of New Hope, and Prince Ezra *was* expecting us." She raised her head slowly. But when her eyes met his, Trev was surprised by the hardness there. "If you ever thought about anyone other than yourself, then you would have known that the princess you expected is not the *daughter* of the queen, but the *step-daughter*."

Trev flinched. She was right. He should have known that she wasn't Seran. But he let himself believe that she was because he wanted her to be. He looked to the floor, running a hand across his face.

"Did you skip your history lessons, Prince Ezra?" Her

voice was cold. "Or did you never care enough about your fiancée to actually learn anything about her?"

Trev bristled, the judgment in her tone striking a nerve. Without thinking, he snapped, "It's not my job to know the history of *your* country. I have people who do that for me."

Renna's eyebrows flew up in shock, and Trev's stomach clenched. Why on earth had he said that?

"Well, you're exactly what I expected of Prince Ezra." Her voice was harsh. "Stuck-up and arrogant."

He shook his head, and defensively shot back, "You seemed to enjoy my arrogance the other day. You practically begged me to kiss you."

Renna took a step closer, her fiery eyes burning into him. "Your memory fails you, Your Highness. *You* wanted to kiss me."

He *had* wanted to kiss her. His eyes dropped to her lips for a moment.

What was with this complete lack of self-control when it came to Renna? It was just one more thing to feel embarrassed about. He *hadn't* known she was the princess the first time they'd met. He shouldn't have flirted with her or returned to Wellenbreck the next day, hoping to see her again. He was getting married . . . and soon.

"When I did all that, I thought you were the princess," he argued even though it was a lie.

"Well, I'm not."

"Thank goodness for that." His words came out harsher than he meant. Why was he behaving so terribly? He had come to apologize. He wanted her to forgive him.

Renna closed the distance between them. "Yes. Thank goodness for that."

Heat rose in his chest. Renna was here, in Albion, inches from him, looking more irresistible than ever. He wanted to run his fingers through her hair and get lost in her lips. It was weird how much her anger made him want to kiss her even more. He hadn't kissed a woman in years, so why was that the only thing he could think about now?

They stood there, staring at each other, nothing between them but the rise and fall of their chests.

A hint of desire flickered across her face, but it was gone as quickly as it appeared.

"I wouldn't want someone like you anyway." She pushed past him, bumping his arm with her shoulder on her way out. The door slammed behind him. Trev paced back and forth before slapping his hand against the closed door.

He hadn't wanted someone like her, either.

Until now.

The great hall bustled with servants and guests ready for the feast celebrating the arrival of the New Hope royalty. Men from Albion's ruling class wore tailored suits with colorful ties, while the women on their arms showed off fancy gowns and glittering jewelry. Servants walked through the crowd with trays of drinks, keeping guests happy as they waited. Everyone stood in the center of the room around the bottom of the grand staircase, talking about the princess and the upcoming wedding to Prince Ezra. Across from the stairs, tables were arranged in a semicircle around the royals' head table. Tall, arched windows lined the walls beyond the tables, but the darkened night sky prevented anyone from seeing the view out of them.

Trev waited on the dais at the head of the room, brooding. He should be mingling with the guests like his father was, but he didn't feel like it. It wasn't like he hadn't done *anything*. He had met Seran's friends and passed them off to some soldiers who were lucky enough to have the night off.

Drake hopped up on the platform next to Trev. "Prince

Ezra! Don't you look dashing tonight in your suit. You almost look as good as me."

"Let's get this night over with," Trev growled.

"That's no way to act at your wife's welcome party."

"She's not my wife." He was starting to pace now, but paused to add, "Not yet, at least."

"And she won't ever be if you don't cheer up. You're very ugly when you're angry."

The horns sounded, signaling the entrance of the New Hope royalty. Queen Mariele stood in the center of the balcony overlooking the ballroom in a turquoise gown that bunched together on the sides. Princess Seran and Renna stood on either side of her.

The crowd hushed, and all eyes turned to them as the herald's voice reached the far corners of the hall. "Her Royal Majesty, Queen Mariele of New Hope. Her Royal Highness, Seran Alyssa Haslett, Princess of New Hope. And Miss Renna Degray." All three women made their way down the middle of the staircase, perfectly centered between the two marble banisters.

Seran wore a shimmering gold dress that trailed to the floor, and her long black hair was pulled back halfway. She looked stunning, but Trev stopped pacing when he saw Renna. He could see her indignant feelings written all over her face, from her blazing eyes to the way she tightened her lips.

"She's not making this easy," Trev muttered to himself. There was an unspoken rule now. She was off-limits. Without turning his head, Trev leaned over to Drake and whispered harshly, "She's the most infuriating woman I have ever met! Accusing me of lying! And to think, she doesn't want somebody like me." Trev let out a rough laugh. "Well, I don't want someone like her!"

Drake looked confused. "I don't know what you're talking about, but you need to escort the princess to dinner."

"Huh?"

Drake signaled with his head in Seran's direction. "The princess is waiting for you to escort her to the royal table."

"Right." Trev tugged on his suit jacket and made his way to the center of the room where the three women stood at the bottom of the stairs. He couldn't let Renna distract him. He needed to stay focused on Seran.

His father had already collected Queen Mariele and walked with her toward their table at the head of the room. Arriving before the princess, Trev bowed. "Your Highness."

He offered her his arm, and Seran glided forward, wrapping her long fingers around his forearm. He took a deep breath.

I can do this. For Albion.

"Princess Seran," he began, lightly covering her hand on his arm with his own as they walked. "Were you able to get settled?"

"Yes, thank you." Seran smiled up at him graciously. "My room is very comfortable, and your staff has taken good care of me. I already feel welcome here."

"I'm glad to hear it," Trev responded, but he was distracted. Behind him, Drake's overly pleasant greeting to Renna made it difficult to focus.

"Miss Degray, I am Officer Drake Vestry. May I escort you to dinner?" Drake asked.

"Of course, Officer Vestry," she said, sounding a little too pleased, in Trev's opinion.

"I'm so happy to finally meet you." Seran's smooth voice cut into his eavesdropping, jolting Trev's attention back to the woman beside him. "We've been engaged so long, but it hardly felt real until I saw you today."

"Yes, it definitely feels . . . surreal."

As they walked, Trev strained to hear Drake and Renna behind him. He should return Seran's polite conversation, but his curiosity was powerful.

"Do they always go to this much trouble when guests arrive?" he heard Renna ask.

"When the guests are as breathtaking as you."

I'm going to kill Drake.

"You know none of this is for me," Renna said, as if to shrug off his praise.

"Actually, it is. I spoke with the head of the royal staff and specifically told them you were coming. When they thought it was just the princess, they had leftovers planned for dinner."

Renna let out a laugh, and Trev's fists tightened.

She responded, "Well then, as the guest of honor, I demand a seat next to you at dinner."

Trev turned just in time to see Renna's full smile on Drake.

It's going to be a slow and painful death.

"Don't you agree?" Seran's voice broke into his thoughts for a second time. She looked at him expectantly, and he realized that she must have been speaking to him. He hadn't heard a single word.

"Yes, of course," Trev managed.

King Carver and Queen Mariele walked in front of them, reaching the royal table in the center of the great hall first. The queen gathered her turquoise dress in her hands, sweeping it to the side as the king helped her into her seat. Trev followed his father's lead, pulling the chair out for Seran. Trev sat to the king's right with Seran taking her place beside him. Seran's friends flanked her other side. Queen Mariele sat to the king's left. Drake pulled out the chair next to Renna's mother and gestured for Renna to sit down. Trev caught his friend's eye, giving him a warning look.

Once the head table was seated, the rest of the guests found their seats at the surrounding tables. Chairs scraped against the floor, and hushed conversations whirled around the room as everyone waited respectfully for dinner to start.

The servants appeared with the first course—chilled

strawberry bisque—and laid a bowl before each guest. Renna eagerly grabbed her spoon and dipped it into the cold liquid, bringing it up to her lips. Her eyes closed with the first taste, savoring the flavor.

"This is delicious!" she said, mostly to herself. She reached her spoon in for another bite and closed her eyes again, repeating her sounds of satisfaction.

Trev hadn't even lifted his spoon yet. All he could do was watch her.

"You seem to be enjoying it," Drake said, amused.

She smiled sheepishly. "I'm enjoying it a little too much, aren't I?"

"Not at all. Like I said, it's all for you."

"In that case, I'll make sure I enjoy every bite." She glanced pointedly at Trev before leaning her shoulder into Drake's, playfully nudging him.

Trev wanted to punch his best friend, even though Renna was the one doing the flirting. Drake must have sensed it too, because after a quick look at Trev, he turned to Seran seated across the table from him. "So, Princess Seran, how do you like Albion so far?"

The princess smiled perfectly. "Your country is beautiful. The mountains we saw along our journey were absolutely stunning. We have nothing like them in New Hope. And I am impressed with your palace. There are many . . ." She hesitated for a moment. "There are many . . . *upgrades* compared to New Hope. We don't have marble flooring or elaborate decorations." She paused and looked at Trev. "But I'm sure the prince can tell me all about the palace and the upgrades. I look forward to getting to know him and the royal family."

Trev gave a polite, albeit awkward smile in response.

King Carver interjected. "Yes, we have a few advancements in Albion. Nothing that the Council needs to concern themselves with, and certainly nothing to trouble yourself over, Princess Seran. We want you to feel comfortable here while we work through the final details of the marriage alliance. If there is anything you need, please don't hesitate to let us know. And I'm sure Ezra will be delighted to entertain you."

Renna looked up from her soup at this and chimed in, her smile as sweet as an angel. "How gracious of Prince Ezra."

The queen nodded, obviously pleased by her daughter's seemingly kind comment. But Trev wasn't fooled. He heard the thinly veiled sarcasm behind her words.

Trev smiled back at Renna, answering through his teeth, "Of course." Then he turned to Seran. "I'm looking forward to getting to know you as well, Princess. I haven't been able to think of anything else these last few weeks."

Renna's spoon paused midair as she took in his words, but she only faltered a moment before shoving the soup into her mouth.

"I suppose our advisors will convene first thing tomorrow?" Queen Mariele asked.

"Yes, I see no reason to delay," King Carver agreed.

The servants came to retrieve the bowls of soup so they could serve the next course. Renna was still sipping hers as a young girl reached between her and Drake to clear it.

"Oh, I'm not quite done!" Renna awkwardly reached for the bowl as the girl lifted it onto her tray. She managed to dip her spoon in for one last bite and carry it to her mouth, but not before a large drop fell onto Drake's shoulder. Everyone around the table held their breath at the spectacle.

A sardonic laugh escaped from Seran's blonde friend. Trev couldn't remember her name. Jen-something?

"I'm so sorry!" Renna choked through her mouthful of strawberry bisque. She grabbed the napkin in her lap with her free hand, her cheeks flushed with embarrassment, and awkwardly fumbled to wipe the stain from Drake's shoulder.

Drake batted her napkin away good-naturedly and used his own napkin to dab the stain. "Leave it. This actually couldn't have worked out better." Renna looked mortified and confused, as he continued, "You see, I love the smell of strawberries. For the rest of the night, the smell of this soup will stay with me. I can literally turn my head and smell strawberries." Drake's face remained completely serious. "In fact, people will wonder why I smell so good."

Another reason to kill Drake. The list was getting long.

Renna let out a small laugh and then looked to the king to recover. "Forgive me, Your Majesty. You have an excellent chef here."

King Carver's brow furrowed in what could only be disgust.

The young servant girl still hovered over Renna's shoulder, squirming uncomfortably.

"That will be all. Thank you," Renna said when she recovered enough from her own embarrassment.

"My lady, I need your spoon," the girl replied in a quiet voice.

"Yes! Of course!" Reaching up, she handed the girl the spoon, and the servant quickly scurried away. Trev noticed Renna's cheeks burning again.

"Renna, have a care for manners, please." Queen Mariele laughed nervously. "I shouldn't have to remind you who we are dining with." She picked up her glass and raised it toward King Carver before lifting it to her lips.

Renna's embarrassment seemed to turn to irritation. With a cautious glance at Trev first, she leaned over and whispered to her mother loud enough for Trev to hear. "Don't worry, Mother. It's not like *I'm* here to marry the prince."

Trev choked on his drink—sputtering out a series of coughs.

"Are you all right?" Seran put a concerned hand on his shoulder.

He cleared his throat. "Yes, I'm fine."

King Carver spoke. "I heard you stopped a day at the

border." He looked at Queen Mariele. "Near the city of Vassel?" His question was an obvious attempt to appear engaging.

Queen Mariele dabbed at her lips with her napkin before answering. "Yes, we stayed one night at an extensive property there."

The king continued, "And did you enjoy yourselves?" He looked at Seran for an answer.

Seran's dark eyes turned to the king. "It was nice to rest from our travels, but Wellenbreck was a bit too quiet for my tastes."

From down the table, Jen-something piped up. "Wellenbreck Farm was completely boring. There was absolutely nothing to do there."

Renna pursed her lips together.

Drake gave a quick glance at Renna, then turned to Trev. "Actually, there's quite a lot to do. Prince Ezra and I discovered a pond nearby that is excellent for swimming. When we're in the area, he visits often."

Trev's eyes widened. *Seriously? Did Drake have to bring that up right now?*

The king huffed at the mention of swimming, and Queen Mariele turned her sharp gaze to Trev. "Really? Wellenbreck Pond?"

Trev cleared his throat. "No. Drake is mistaken." He flashed an annoyed look to his friend. "It's only a pond. One of many. I find everything about that area to be completely unremarkable."

Renna stood abruptly, her chair loudly falling backward to the floor. "Your Majesty, if you will excuse me, I'm not feeling well and would like to retire to my room for the night."

Without waiting for the king's answer, she turned briskly to leave. Her skirts swooshed against the fallen chair, tripping her up slightly, but she somehow managed to escape the room without falling.

Jen-something let out a very unladylike snort at the scene, then quickly brought her hand to her mouth to hide it.

Trev felt awful. He needed to go after Renna to apologize. He didn't care what his father or anyone else thought. He scooted his chair back, but Drake's voice halted his movements.

"I better go make sure Miss Degray is taken care of," Drake interjected.

I'm sure you will.

"It has been a fascinating evening." Drake stood up and bowed toward the women. "Queen Mariele, Princess Seran, I do hope we can continue our conversations tomorrow."

The women nodded politely.

All Trev could do was watch as Drake ran after Renna.

14

Renna

Dinner had gone horribly wrong on so many different levels. For one night, couldn't Renna have been the epitome of a perfect lady? No. She had to behave like typical Renna. Her mother was going to freak out.

And then there was Trev.

His constant jabs had rattled her, each insult disguised so no one but her knew what he really meant. She hated him. Or at least, she wanted to hate him.

She didn't care about Trev. Which meant she should probably stop calling him that. Prince Ezra. His name was Prince Ezra. He was *Seran's* Prince Ezra.

Renna leaned her back against the wall in the hallway outside the great hall. Trev had looked so amazing tonight, from his perfectly tailored blue suit to his intentionally tousled hair. Everything about him exuded confidence and charm. Even when she had fought with him before dinner, she hadn't been able to stop thinking about how good he smelled and how perfect his strong features looked when he was angry.

So he was incredibly handsome. Who cared? There was more to love than physical appearance.

Love.

Why had she used that word? Attraction was more accurate.

She *was* attracted to Prince Ezra. But who wasn't? He wouldn't be a prince if he wasn't painfully attractive. Renna had never even heard of an unattractive prince. They probably didn't exist. But then, if all she liked about him was how he looked, her feelings would be easy to overcome.

Deep down, though, Renna knew it wasn't just his looks that made it impossible for her to stop thinking about Trev. She liked the easy way they had joked and conversed at the pond, and she liked the way her heart had exploded when he'd touched her or looked at her. It was electric. That's how she had always imagined love would feel.

She looked to her left and then to the right. She had no idea how to get back upstairs to her room. Where were all the servants? There was no one around. She had come down the stairs inside the great hall and could find her way back if she used those same stairs again. But that would mean re-entering the room she had just so clumsily left. She turned and stared at the door.

She took a deep breath. This was going to take courage.

The door swung open suddenly, and Drake appeared. He was taller than Trev by a few inches and slightly bigger, but he looked to be about the same age. His brown hair was shaggy on top and in the back, and it had a waviness to it that Renna assumed was from the length, not natural curl.

"What are you doing?" he asked, watching her as he closed the door behind him.

"It's not what it looks like," Renna stammered as she pushed herself away from the wall.

"It looks like you're staring at a door."

"I was staring at the door, but I wasn't waiting. I mean, I was waiting, but not waiting for someone to come after me."

"Uh-huh." He folded his arms in front of his chest. "Then what *are* you waiting for?"

"For enough courage to go back in."

He raised his eyebrows in surprise. "Why would you go back in there?"

Her shoulders sank in defeat. "I'm . . . lost."

"That *is* a problem." He looked around. "Luckily, I know my way around this place." He nodded down the hall. "I can get you safely back to your room if you'd like."

She sighed. "Officer Vestry, if you can get me back to my room without more embarrassment, you will be my favorite person in Albion."

He grinned at her slyly. "If I'm your favorite person, you should probably just call me Drake."

"The last time a man told me I could call him by his first name, he ended up being a prince." Renna shrugged. "One engaged to my stepsister."

"We should probably talk about you and the prince," he said as they walked in unison down the hall.

She cast Drake a sly look. She bet he wanted to talk about Trev, so he could run back and tell him everything she said. She appreciated Drake's kindness, but his loyalty was to the prince. She couldn't forget that.

So she lied.

"There's nothing to talk about. I met Trev at Wellenbreck." She quickly corrected herself. "I mean, Prince Ezra."

"You know, his friends all call him Trev. He didn't lie to you about that. And he *really* did think you were the princess. He was crushed when he found out you weren't."

Renna's breath caught in the back of her throat. He was crushed? "It doesn't matter. We talked a few times. It wasn't a big deal. I never expected to see him again."

More lies.

"In fact, I haven't really thought about him since Wellenbreck." Renna hoped she sounded convincing.

She couldn't tell if Drake believed her or not, but he didn't ask any more questions about Trev, so she quickly changed the subject. "Are you an officer in the king's guard?"

"Technically, I'm head of security for the royal family, but my family is also good friends with the Trevenna family." The hallway opened up into the entryway. Drake stopped in front of a large staircase. "If you take these steps to the top, you'll find your room down the hall."

Renna recognized her surroundings from when she had first arrived. The marble banister had caught her eye—the way it looked dull and unassuming until the light shone on it, then it glistened expensively. "I guess it's good I'm going to bed early. Who knows what kind of entertainment your prince has planned for Seran tomorrow."

"We're going horseback riding tomorrow."

Renna perked up. Horseback riding was definitely something to look forward to.

Drake continued, "I believe it's a tour of the countryside so the princess can see what her future lands look like."

"Oh." Renna's perkiness faded away.

Her future lands.

She started up a few steps and then turned toward Drake. "Thank you for everything tonight. I think you were the best part of my day."

His smile was genuine as he turned to walk away. "Consider me part of your personal welcoming committee."

Renna's room was dark and empty as she entered. Nora wasn't there, but that was no surprise; Nora wouldn't have expected her back so soon. Renna dressed for bed and climbed under the covers, knowing sleep wouldn't come easily. She was consumed by what Drake had told her.

Trev was crushed. *Crushed.*

Drake had no reason to lie to her. Which meant it really had been a big misunderstanding. Trev had thought she was the princess. Renna's anger had blinded her when he'd first claimed as much, preventing her from seeing Trev's side of the story. Still, he should have known that Princess Seran wasn't the daughter of the queen. Questioned her when she said her name was anything but Seran. He should have realized.

She didn't want to be angry anymore. It was exhausting fighting Trev, and right now, she needed all her strength to fight her feelings for him. But her anger made her heart feel safe, like if she stayed mad, she couldn't get hurt again.

Tomorrow was a new day—a new chance to forgive and forget the prince.

Maybe she would have better luck then.

15

Trev

Trev woke late and headed down to breakfast. He meant to talk to Renna and apologize for the way he had acted the night before. Last evening had made Trev uncomfortable. He never treated people like that, and now he regretted it. He had been the worst kind of host. He had been the worst kind of everything since he'd found out Renna wasn't the princess.

By the time he made it down to breakfast, everyone had finished eating, and the servants were cleaning up. He grabbed a croissant, hoping he would get a chance to talk to Renna before the entourage went out riding.

Trev walked to the stables. He could hear people talking outside, already gathered for the ride, waiting for horses to be brought out by the servants, but he didn't feel like mingling with anyone in the entourage, at least not yet. Instead, he ducked inside the stable before anyone saw him, stopping short when he heard a familiar sound. Renna's laughter echoed through the stalls as though it were bouncing from one barrel of hay to the next. He rounded the corner to see her talking cheerfully with a stocky young stable boy.

When the boy recognized him, he immediately bowed. "Your Highness."

Renna turned to Trev, and her smile faded. Her hair was weaved into a single braid that was flipped over one shoulder. She wore a long, burnt orange skirt with a fitted matching top. She curtsied slightly. "Prince Ezra."

Trev hated the formality of it all. He wanted to go back to when things were easy between the two of them.

"Good morning, Miss Degray."

She barely acknowledged his address, instead turning to the horse in the stall beside her.

"What brings you to the stables?" He tried to make his voice sound normal, cheerful even.

Her voice was decidedly not cheerful. "I had some extra time before the excursion. I thought I would see what kind of horses you keep here." She looked up at him pointedly. "Is there anything wrong with that, *Your Highness*?"

"You're free to do whatever you want during your visit," he said sincerely. She turned her attention back to the horse in front of her, but Trev pressed on. "Do you ride?"

She squared her shoulders. "Of course."

"Boy, fetch the lady—"

"His name is Jamison," Renna inserted, and Trev winced at the judgment in her tone. Apparently, she wasn't impressed with the fact that he didn't know his own stable hand's name.

The boy visibly beamed with appreciation. That, or he was smitten with Renna too.

"Jamison," Trev tried again. "Will you please fetch Dara for Miss Degray to ride this morning?"

Jamison's eyes went wide with surprise. "Dara? Your Highness, I thought she was promised for—"

"It's all right." Trev kept his eyes locked on her. "She's perfect for Renna."

The boy bowed and scurried off. Renna turned her attention back to the horse in front of her, stroking the mane and whispering into his ear. For a brief moment, Trev wished he was the horse. It was a laughable thought.

With each passing second of silence, his nerves grew worse.

"Are you going to talk to me?" he asked.

"That depends on whether you are going to act like a complete jerk again."

"I wanted to talk to you about that. To apologize for how I behaved last night." His voice lacked his normal confident tone.

"Which time?" She turned to face him, anger burning in her eyes. "There are so many bad moments to choose from."

"For it all. For the things I said. I don't know what came over me." He could see by her flashing eyes that he wasn't getting very far with her. "There is a lot of pressure surrounding this marriage alliance. But when I thought you were the princess, I was excited for my future. Then you weren't actually the princess, and I didn't know how to handle my frustrations, so I acted like—"

"An ass." She cut him off before he could finish, her eyes searing into him.

"Yes, an ass," he said quietly.

Her expression was still stern as her focus went back to the horse, stroking his snout evenly.

He wished she would look at him so she could see how sorry he felt. "I really did enjoy our time together."

Her hand paused its gentle movements as a new emotion swept across her face, but she quickly wiped it away. She cleared her throat and turned back to Trev. "I told myself last night that I didn't want to be angry anymore, so . . . I forgive you. I can see how it was all just a silly misunderstanding," she said, extending her hand for him to shake. "And I'm sorry for the assumptions I made about you."

Her forgiveness was guarded and judging by the formal handshake she extended to him, things weren't quite back to normal. But then, their normal had been so charged with attraction. They would have to find a new normal. Was that even possible?

He took her hand and immediately chills formed on the back of his neck, which made his heart start racing faster. He didn't let go of her hand—just kept it there—the current spreading like fire between them.

"Friends?" he managed to get out.

"What else would we be?" Her words came out in a whisper.

What else *could* they be?

Nothing.

"That is, if you can handle being friends with me." Her playful banter was coming back. That was a good sign.

He smiled with relief. "I'm sure I can handle it."

Hearing sounds of Jamison's returning, they both dropped their hands and shuffled apart from each other. The boy entered the stable with a stunning mare in tow, her coat sleek and black.

"So this is Dara?" Renna asked, admiring the beautiful dark horse.

Jamison led the black mare to where they stood. The horse seemed uneasy with her surroundings, pulling her head back against the reins.

"Hey girl," Renna calmly whispered to the horse as she leaned in closer. "I'd like to be friends with you. I just became friends with the prince." She eyed him with a whimsical gleam. "So maybe we can be friends too."

Being friends is better than nothing, Trev told himself as he watched her.

The mare settled with each of Renna's soothing words. "I think she likes me," Renna said, her smile big and animated.

It's impossible not to like you.

"My Lord, which horse should I prepare for Princess Seran now?" Jamison asked.

"This horse was meant for Seran?" Renna asked with guilt.

"Yes." Trev nodded. "But I think she prefers you. Jamison, find Princess Seran a different mount. It looks like Dara and Miss Renna are friends."

Jamison nodded and left.

Renna leaned her forehead into Dara, and Trev noticed the smile on her face. He had made her happy. Things were definitely looking up from yesterday.

"I feel bad taking Seran's horse," Renna said, still staring into Dara's eyes.

"Don't. We have plenty more." Trev admired her as she stroked the horse's thick mane. It was just another part of her that was attractive—the way she could put anyone or anything at ease.

"She's great, you know."

"Dara?"

"No. Seran," she said, finally looking at him.

Trev swallowed. "Yeah, she seems wonderful."

"Did you guys talk much at dinner?" After she asked the question, her face colored a bit like she remembered the dinner fiasco all over again.

Trev pretended not to notice. "I didn't have a lot of time alone with her to talk."

"Well then I hope you get a chance today." Renna nodded, her smile tight.

He respected the way she was trying to turn his attention to Seran, but at the same time, it hurt. Somehow her efforts at being a good sister made him feel rejected.

"So do you ride as well as you dance?" he joked, wanting to get back into their usual banter.

Renna straightened her back. "I *do* dance well, but I am even better at riding."

"Right," he teased. Without even thinking, he took a stray lock of her golden hair and tucked it behind her ear. His hand brushed down her ear and then to the side of her neck unnecessarily. Her breath caught beneath his touch.

Behind them, someone cleared their throat, startling them both. They turned, and Trev recognized the guard who had found them at Wellenbreck standing in the stable doorway. It was like an alarm went off in this guy every time Trev touched Renna. Which was good, since he shouldn't be touching her at all.

"Miss Renna, your mother requests an audience with you."

"Miss Degray is joining the entourage for a tour of the countryside this morning," Trev said to the guard with perfect timing.

The guard gave a stiff nod. "Of course, Your Highness. I will let her majesty know to expect her daughter later this afternoon."

"Thank you, Mangum," Renna said.

Trev raised his eyebrows in interest. So *this* was Mangum—the guy Renna had pretended to drown for. This made Trev like her even more. Unfortunately.

"Princess Seran is waiting just outside the stable for you, Your Highness," Mangum said with a stern, pointed look at them both. Then, with a quick bow, Mangum disappeared out the barn door.

Renna took a step back from Trev, her expression guarded again.

"I guess I'll see you out there," she said tonelessly. She pulled Dara's reins and led her out the back, leaving Trev standing in the stable alone.

King Carver's staff had planned an entire week of activities to allow Trev and Princess Seran time to court, while also showcasing the country of Albion for the New Hope visitors.

Today's horseback tour was just one of these festivities. While New Hope's and Albion's chief advisors worked out the details of the marriage treaty, Trev would host a tournament of games, a festival, a picnic with school children, a visit to market day, and a ball in honor of the New Hope royalty.

Trev led his New Hope guests and a group of Albion's most prominent men and women by horseback north of the ruler's palace. He pointed out the tallest peak of the Albion mountains, places in Albana City, the acres of farmland under the direction of King Carver, and a few pre-Desolation ruins.

Princess Seran rode next to him, their pace slow enough to allow conversation. Her hair was slicked back into a high ponytail, and she wore a light purple riding outfit that made her pale skin glow.

"Do you like your role as the prince of Albion?" Seran asked as they rode along.

"There's good and bad as I'm sure you know. I don't know life any other way, so it's hard to compare. What about you? Do you like being the princess of New Hope?"

"It comes with a lot of meetings and a rigorous education, but there is also a lot of ease and luxury, so I guess I can't complain. However, I would have been perfectly happy out of the spotlight in dull and colorless dresses."

He wasn't expecting that answer. "You don't like the spotlight?"

"It's not that I don't like it. It's part of my job—my role as princess—and I take that seriously. But if my life were different, if I had a different role that wasn't so public, I'd be fine with that too."

"Are you scared to marry me?" he asked, trying to face the awkwardness of their situation head-on.

She smirked, her dark eyes gleaming. "That's a very forward question."

Trev shook his head. "I'm sorry. You don't have to answer."

"I want you to ask me questions like that. To approach this marriage with honesty. I've been engaged to you since I was ten years old. Every time I played dolls or house, you were the prince. You were the happily-ever-after." Her dark eyes glanced away. "You ask if I am scared to marry you. My answer is yes."

It was a relief that her answer matched his own anguish. He was scared too.

She continued to speak with poise. "I'm scared for the little girl that pretended to know you, that she'll be disappointed in who you are. And, I'm scared for the woman I am today, that I won't be what *you* want."

"I'm scared of disappointing you too," Trev admitted. "Not that I'm a bad guy or anything. I plan on being a good husband and partner. I just don't know if I'm what you want."

"If it matters, each moment I spend with you, I get less scared." She half-smiled, barely showing her straight, white teeth. "So, you must be doing something right."

"I don't know about that," Trev argued.

They rode in companionable silence for a moment until Seran's expression turned grave. She lowered her voice. "I heard about the attack on Axville. Is it certain that Tolsten was involved?"

"Almost certain." Trev sighed and ran a hand through his hair. "There have been skirmishes with Tolsten soldiers on our side of the border."

Her smile was grim. "It looks like you may need my military after all."

Trev shifted in his saddle. It felt odd discussing his country's political maneuvers with Seran. But she was going to be his queen in a few weeks. He needed to get used to sharing things with her.

"I hope it won't come to that. I'd like to keep New Hope away from battle, if I can."

"But that *is* the point of our marriage, isn't it?" Seran met his eyes. "If you need our men, they're yours."

"Thank you," was all Trev could mutter in response. A marriage for a military. The thought made him sick. How could two things so starkly different from each other be tied together?

Their conversation bounced from one topic to another. Trev found that they had a lot in common. Her mother had passed away. She had no siblings and felt the pressure of being an heir to the throne. She was knowledgeable in the workings of her government and her people and seemed to have good intentions when it came to governing. His father had been right; marrying Princess Seran was a good choice for Albion.

But was she a good choice for him? Under different circumstances, Trev might have welcomed the arrangement wholeheartedly. But all he could think about now was Renna at the side of the group and the men on their horses surrounding her. They were all harmless, really. A few young, eager soldiers and young men from the city, and then Mr. Tybolt, a large, balding, married man who frequently had his last meal stuck in his hairy beard.

Trev was confident none of those men could impress Renna.

At least he hoped not.

16

Renna

The horses slowed to a stop as the company came upon white tents and buffet tables of food laid out for them by servants.

A servant helped Renna down from Dara's back and took the reins from her hands. "I'll take your horse, my lady," he said, pulling her horse over to be tied up, leaving Renna alone.

There were so many men from prominent families on the outing. Her mother would call them "potential marriage matches" and would be thrilled with the attention they were showing Renna. None of the men seemed to view her as the afterthought stepsister like the men in New Hope. Instead, they clamored to talk to her. In New Hope, she was an unfortunate reminder of the queen's former life. But here in Albion, she was part of the royal caravan and an honored guest. It was a nice change, even if it meant she had to be around Trev.

She turned and nearly bumped into him and Seran.

"Renna, I'm so glad to see you," Seran said with a genuine smile. "You seemed upset at dinner last night, and I just wanted to make sure you were okay."

Renna glanced awkwardly at Trev, then back at Seran. "I wasn't upset."

"Are you sure?" Seran pressed. "It seemed like something was bothering you."

Seran! Stop! Please!

Renna shook her head. "Nope. I'm fine."

"Have you had a chance to meet Prince Ezra?" Seran asked, switching to another equally awkward topic.

Renna cleared her throat. "Only briefly."

"Miss Degray, it's a pleasure to see you again." Trev stiffly bowed in front of her, kissing Renna's hand, sending a shot of tingles down her spine—tingles that needed to stop immediately.

Renna gave Seran a playful look. "You're right, Seran. You are much better looking than Prince Ezra."

Trev nodded dramatically. "I couldn't agree more."

Seran shook her head, smiling. "I never said that. Renna is known for pranking people."

Trev raised his eyebrows. "Is that so?"

Renna's eyes dropped to the ground as her face flushed.

"Yes," Seran said, looking between them. "I think you will get along well. You both have a playful energy."

"That's . . . uh . . ." Trev stumbled over his words. "I . . . uh . . . don't know about that," he finally managed to get out with a nervous laugh.

Renna wanted to crawl under a rock. Her joke had definitely backfired.

"In fact," Seran said, still beaming, "Renna should join us tomorrow for the tour of the palace."

Just the three of us? No, thank you.

Trev smiled at Seran, though it looked a bit strained. "I thought it was just going to be the two of us."

"Oh, but Renna would love it. You'll come, won't you?" Seran looked at her expectantly like she was secretly begging her to come. If Renna didn't know any better, she would think

Seran was trying to avoid being alone with the prince. Renna didn't understand. She would give anything to trade Seran places.

"I couldn't." Renna shook her head, looking at Trev for some help. "I don't want to intrude."

"Nonsense!" Seran stood a little taller. "It's a palace tour, not a candlelight dinner."

"Perhaps the queen would like to come too," Trev offered, obviously not thrilled at the idea of the three of them alone.

"Yes!" Seran smiled at the two of them. "It's settled then."

Lizanne walked to Seran's side, grabbing her elbow and whispering in her ear. Trev glanced at Renna. He held her stare for a moment then looked to the ground.

"Okay," Seran said to Lizanne. "I'll be right there." Seran turned back to them. "There are a few young ladies I need to meet."

"I'll go with you," Trev said a little too eagerly.

"It's all right." Seran put a hand on Trev's arm and smiled. "I know you have people to talk to as well. I'll come find you in a moment." And with that, Seran followed Lizanne away.

"You don't have to keep me company." Renna tried to release him. "You can go talk to somebody else."

"And leave you alone?" Trev smiled. "I'm too much of a gentleman to do that."

"Who says I'd be alone?" she challenged, raising her eyebrows. "Mr. Tybolt and I have struck up a romance. I'm sure he'll be along shortly to claim me."

Trev fought back his smile. "Didn't you know? He's already married."

"That is definitely a shame." Renna looked serious. "I suppose I'm destined to a life of loneliness, pining after Mr. Tybolt and all his charms."

"You'll probably love him your whole life and refuse to marry another," Trev added.

"You're right." She smiled. "I'll take up a job as a beard trimmer, hoping to see him every few months."

"You'll save clippings from his beard in a treasure box and smell them every night."

Renna gasped. "Gross!"

"Did I take the story too far?" Trev's face remained serious.

A puff of laughter escaped her nose. "A little."

"I thought I was really onto something with the beard clippings."

Renna's laughter faded when she caught a glimpse of Seran across the grass. Her dark eyes watched them, but then she nodded politely and turned toward the young women she was getting to know.

"How are things going with Seran?" Renna asked, hoping to remind Trev of her. She didn't *really* want to talk about how things were going between the two of them, but that seemed like the kind of thing a friend would ask. And they were friends now.

Trev watched Seran from the side for a moment, then spoke. "She told me a little about her childhood, growing up betrothed to me. She said she used to play with dolls, and that *I* was the prince in her happily-ever-after make-believe games."

"That's actually quite adorable," Renna said. She looked at Seran again, wishing it didn't hurt her heart so much to hear that.

"Yes, it is. It's also a lot of pressure—to live up to a figment of her imagination."

Renna's voice was light. "As if you need more pressure in your life."

Trev chuckled. "I guess I have an entire lifetime to figure out how to be the man she hoped for." His lips dropped down and his shoulders slumped, contradicting his laugh. He looked at Renna. The carefree twinkle in his eyes was gone, replaced by sadness. He smiled, but Renna saw through his mask to how unhappy he was. He bowed. "Miss Degray, I hope you enjoy the rest of your afternoon." And with that, he turned and walked away.

Renna's heart tightened uncomfortably, and she let out a deep breath. Just being friends was going to be harder than she thought.

She found a table on the opposite side of the tent from Trev and Seran, hoping to sit as far away as possible, but somehow still ended up with a perfect view of them through lunch. Renna tried not to watch their interactions, but she was keenly aware of every lean, touch, and whisper the two shared. It was torture.

She had to stop this. She didn't want to be a front-row spectator to their courtship.

"Miss Degray?"

Renna turned to see a young man towering over her, a little like he'd been sent from heaven to save her from her misery. But this guy made her worry. He was attractive, and he knew it. He was tall and muscular, his hair light brown, streaked with golden highlights from the sun. His eyes were dark with flecks of yellow, and they were mischievous like he was about to do something he shouldn't. His smile came easy and was warm, inviting, and full—a real heartbreaker.

He gestured to himself. "I'm Joniss Doman."

"Renna Degray." Renna inclined her head respectfully. "But you already knew that."

His answering grin was mildly suggestive. "I have to confess, I've been waiting patiently for a chance to meet you."

"And why is that?" She couldn't think of a single reason someone would want to meet her when Seran was nearby.

"Because you are by far the most beautiful woman here."

A skeptical laugh escaped her. He couldn't be serious, but the compliment was nice all the same. "Well, I hate waiting for anything, so that sounds awful."

"I think you are worth the wait." He took the empty chair beside her.

Recent experience had taught Renna she should be wary of men, but she was grateful for the distraction. She glanced once more toward Trev and Seran to see their heads bent together in whispered conversation.

"People like us should stick together." Joniss rested his elbow on the table casually, bringing her attention back to him.

"People like us?"

"Yes. People who are incredibly attractive and charming." He gave her a dashing smile, and she couldn't help but laugh at his arrogance. She couldn't tell yet if he was actually this conceited or if he just feigned it for humor. "You see, I can help you here in Albion, show you around, introduce you to important people." He raised his eyebrows again. "Entertain you."

Renna smirked. He was definitely entertaining. She leaned back in her chair and folded her arms across her chest. "That sounds awfully generous of you."

"I'm a generous man." He stood and motioned for her hand. "In fact, let's start getting to know each other now, on the ride back to the palace."

She stood, placing her hand in his, unsure of what she thought about him and his forwardness. As they passed the other table, her eyes met Trev's. He seemed surprised and even a little upset.

She raised her eyebrows in challenge. He didn't get to care about how, or with whom she spent her time.

THE RIDE BACK to the palace was all about Joniss Doman. He was very self-assured, and that was putting it politely. His father was the high ruler of a province in Albion, and his family was among Albion's most distinguished. Renna could tell by his fancy-cut riding suit that he came from money. For the first twenty minutes, Joniss went on and on about his wardrobe—the different colors, patterns, and textures of his suits and ties. Then for another fifteen minutes, he described —in great detail—his "rigorous exercise routine," which he rotated through weekly in various different athletics.

Somehow his in-depth description of himself came with just enough flattery to keep Renna smiling the entire ride.

Back at the palace, Joniss helped her off her horse. He was a bit too touchy, placing his hands unnecessarily on her hips as he helped her down. As soon as her feet touched the ground, she backed away from him slightly.

"Do you find weddings romantic?" His expression was overly suave. "Because I'm hoping that you'll be in the mood for a romance of your own."

Renna laughed out loud at his absurd flirtation. She handed the reins of her horse to a servant.

"I'm serious," he said. "I find you very irresistible."

"Officer Doman, you don't know anything about me." She still wasn't sure if she liked Joniss or not, but she did like his attention.

"Find me tonight at dinner. I would love to get to know you better."

Renna was sure he would since he hadn't asked a single question about *her* the entire ride back.

"Maybe you'll find me first." She gave an awkward curtsey before walking away.

Per Mangum's bidding, Renna made her way to her mother's room. She had a feeling she was in for a scolding for the scene she'd made at dinner last night. Mangum stood guard outside the queen's door, staring blankly ahead. His body stiffened when he caught sight of Renna.

Renna smiled at him. "I'll never prank you again if you tell my mother that you forgot to give me the message to meet her."

Mangum's eyes dropped and he shifted his weight nervously. "Actually, there is something I need to tell your mother."

Renna couldn't understand why he was acting so strange. "Okay."

"I need to tell her about you and Prince Ezra." He glanced up at her again. "That he was the soldier with you at the pond."

A lump formed in Renna's throat. She hadn't thought about the fact that Mangum would recognize Trev, that he would tell her mother. "No, Mangum. Please," she begged. "I didn't know he was the prince when we were back at Wellenbreck. If I had known, I wouldn't have . . ." She couldn't finish her sentence, couldn't say it out loud.

"What about in the stable this morning? I know what I saw." His incriminating eyes broke her heart a little.

"That was nothing. We were actually talking about Seran and how we were just going to be friends."

He shook his head. "Your mother needs to know. It's my job to inform her. It's my job to protect the alliance."

"No, it's your job to protect her and *this* will destroy her. Not to mention it will destroy what little relationship I have with her."

Mangum bit his lip.

"Please don't say anything. I don't think I can handle finding out that the guy I like is engaged to my stepsister AND deal with my mother's anger." Her eyes welled up with tears. "It's just too much."

The lines in his face deepened as he frowned. "Renna, this is a dangerous secret."

She blinked back her tears. "It will be fine. I know my place and it's not with Prince Ezra."

"You know your place?" he confirmed.

Renna nodded.

Mangum let out a heavy breath. "Fine."

Renna jumped into his arms.

"We'll keep this just between us," he said, patting her on the back. "But I'll be watching you closely."

"Thank you, Mangum." Renna pulled back from the hug. "Thank you for understanding."

He blushed and looked away, clearing his throat. "Your mother is waiting for you. You better go in."

Renna took one deep breath then rapped her knuckles against the wooden door.

Cypress opened the door with the same disapproving look she always wore. "Your mother has been waiting for you."

"I came as soon as I could." Renna stepped around the maid. She found her mother sitting on a red velvet chair, reading a book.

"I'm glad to see that you supported Seran on the outing today. I worried after last night that you would be uninvited."

Renna sighed. Her mother couldn't even make it through one sentence without bringing up her missteps from the night before. She couldn't even imagine what her mother would have done if Mangum had told her about Trev.

"Mom, I think you're looking at last night all wrong. My behavior only made Seran look that much better. Isn't that the point? To make Seran look good for the prince?" Renna smiled, hoping to soften her mother's mood.

"You embarrassed yourself and me. I'm concerned that if you keep behaving that way, King Carver will call off the wedding."

Renna clenched her jaw. She was pretty confident that, with everything at stake in his conflict with Tolsten, there was no way King Carver would call off the wedding. But there was also no way to convince her mother of that.

"I'm sorry. I'll try to do better."

"I would appreciate that." Mariele stood, walking to the balcony's open doors, her arms folded over her chest like she was trying to keep her emotions locked inside. Renna hoped that the scene last night hadn't spun her mother into some sort of episode.

"The soldier you met at Wellenbreck," her mother said, her face to the window. "Is he here?"

How could she answer this question without worrying her mother? She considered her words carefully, then replied, "No. The soldier I knew at Wellenbreck is definitely not here."

In a way, that was true. The man she thought she knew, the one she had dreamed up a future with, didn't exist anymore.

"How are Seran and Prince Ezra getting along?" Her mother's countenance cheered.

"Delightfully," Renna muttered.

17

Renna

Renna had successfully avoided Trev and Seran all last night at dinner—sitting across the room with Joniss, her back to them. She was proud of herself, dodging the happy couple like a soldier would his enemy during war. Not that she was at war. Well, maybe she was at war with her heart, but nevertheless, she still considered last night a success.

There was no way to avoid them the next morning during the palace tour, though. At least her mother was there as a buffer. Renna did her best to hang back with the queen as they weaved their way through the kitchen, sitting rooms, dining rooms, and offices.

Trev's palace tour included inconsequential details that no real tour of a palace would have, especially when amazing paintings and artifacts from before Desolation were displayed all over. He had this great way about him where he could keep a straight face even when he said the most ridiculous things.

"See this closet?" He opened a door in a high-ceilinged hallway, revealing cleaning supplies stacked on the shelves inside. "This closet has the sturdiest shelves in the entire palace."

Renna shook her head. She couldn't believe he was actually behaving this way in front of her mother and Seran.

"No, really. And look over here." He walked to a light switch at the end of the hall. "This light switch is the fastest switch in the entire palace." He flicked it off and then back on again, making the lights above them flash. "See. So fast, you didn't even notice a difference."

Renna choked back a giggle, cupping her hand over her mouth. Seran, at least, looked mildly amused, but her mother simply stared back at Trev with a blank face. Trev cleared his throat uncomfortably, clearly sensing that his humor wasn't appreciated. "There's one more room I want to show you all."

Trev led them into a dark room and shut the door behind them.

"Should we be worried that this is where you send the assassin in to kill us in a dark, empty room?" Renna teased.

"Renna!" Her mother exclaimed.

"No one is going to die." Trev laughed. "I promise you'll like it. Just give me a second."

Renna could see shapes all around and above her but couldn't make out what they were. She could hear Trev shuffling around the room until he threw back thick, wine-colored curtains, letting rays of sunlight illuminate the space.

Renna immediately recognized it as the palace's artifact room. The New Hope Government Center had one as well. The giant, open room had tables set up in rows with wide aisles between them, the displays making a maze to weave in and out of. Each corner had a different theme with information and artifacts that came from the Pre-Desolation world. The walls were dark mahogany, making the room feel rich and important, and the ceiling was domed in the middle with space large enough to suspend the wing of a pre-Desolation airplane down from the top.

"It's huge!" Renna exclaimed. "So much bigger than the one back home."

She marveled at the bits and pieces of what had once been life before Desolation. The first section was dedicated to artifacts that had been part of electronics. Probably things that had been collected in the rubble and donated over the years. She recognized a few items: a broken television screen, the top of a personal computer, a charred cellular phone, half of a remote control. They had a few things like that on display in New Hope as well.

Then there was the section on transportation. That was Renna's favorite—twisted pieces of automobiles, rubber tires, handlebars, and wheels of all sizes.

Mariele paused, looking at an inscription hanging on the wall. Renna read it over her shoulder. 'Handlebars of a child's bicycle.'

Trev looked at the women. "You know I've always wondered why bicycles have never been deemed essential. Maybe I will bring them up for discussion at the next Council of Essentials."

"Really?" Renna exclaimed. "That would be amazing! The only way the working class can get around is by walking or on horseback. It makes travel so much harder."

"And a lot of people can't even afford a horse," Trev said passionately. "What are those people supposed to do?"

"Exactly." Renna nodded. "It's a big problem, especially for those in rural communities."

Excitement danced in Trev's eyes. "We could take the idea of the original bicycle and build upon it. Maybe design it so more than one person can ride it at once. And we could design some kind of wagon that can attach to it, so people could pull things." His eyes went wide. "Or we could introduce cars. We already have transporters that are similar, we just need to make them smaller and more affordable so the average citizen can buy them."

"I love your enthusiasm, but there are many other factors

that need to be thought through." Seran's voice of reason broke into their conversation.

Trev and Renna turned to look at her.

"For instance, anything with tires would be difficult since our roads aren't paved. Transporters were made to travel over uneven terrain, but cars and bicycles would mean the Council would have to allocate funds toward developing new infrastructure."

"Maybe bikes could be designed with thicker tires so people can ride on uneven roads?" Renna offered.

"Perhaps." Seran shrugged. "But there's more to it than just tires and roads. If the working class is able to move around more easily, things like the economy could change and be disrupted. The Council is right. Things are much simpler when people stay in the region or area they were born in."

"Oh," Renna said, dropping her eyes to the floor. A flood of self-consciousness rushed through her. She hated how the Council always had the final word on everything.

Seran smiled in her genuine way. "It was a good thought." She clasped her hands behind her back, walking away to join the queen at another display across the room.

Renna pointed to the fragments of what was once an automobile, a crushed door, a fender, a piece of a roof. "I still think the Council should let everyone have one of these. I know the Council helped keep peace and order after Desolation, but nowadays, it seems like they just want to regulate what we can and can't do. For the working class, at least." She looked pointedly at Trev. "Your father is a part of the Council of Essentials. Is he trying to regulate his people?"

Trev stole a quick glance at Seran and the queen as if he wanted to make sure they couldn't hear his response. "Yes. Unfortunately, my father wants power. The Council of Essentials is where leaders can gain and exercise the most power over the world. I don't think he started out that way. I think in the beginning he had good intentions. Over the years, those good intentions have turned into greed."

Renna had been taught her whole life that the Council of Essentials and the leaders who were a part of it had the world's best interests in mind. But ever since she moved to the Government Center, she was beginning to see a new side of the Council, a side that was more about power than protection.

"I worry that the same thing will happen to me." Trev's words broke into her thoughts. "I worry that I will start out with all these good intentions, like the bicycle, but I'll change over time. I'll start to only worry about what's best for myself instead of what's best for my people."

His honesty tugged at her heart. He walked away, not waiting for her to answer or reassure him he wouldn't be like his father. He stopped in front of a giant 3D model of the world before Desolation. Seran and the queen were already studying it. Renna followed behind to see what they were staring at.

She ran her finger over the area on the map labeled *Indonesia.* It was hard to believe that the eruption of a supervolcano halfway around the world had set off a chain reaction that changed the world forever.

"It's amazing anybody survived those seventeen years," Renna said quietly. She already knew what events led to Desolation and the rebuild—the eruption, the natural disasters, the nuclear wars—but seeing it laid out like this tied her stomach up in knots. What if that had been her? What if she had lived when the earth swallowed itself up? The thought made her uneasy.

Next to the Pre-Desolation model was a model of the seven kingdoms built on what was left of the North and South American continent.

Seran raised her chin proudly. "The world, as we know it,

is smaller with less inhabitable land, but we will be stronger. The Council of Essentials makes us stronger."

Seran had so much confidence in the Council of Essentials, in government, while Renna's was fading. Nothing that the Council did made sense anymore. There was no equality.

They all stared at the model quietly, until Seran and her mother moved to another display about occupations. Trev nodded for Renna to join him in the opposite direction. She had some anxiety about being alone with him but followed anyway.

"Ah! This is what I wanted to show you." Trev motioned for her to come over by him. His hands rested on the sides of a glass case. Inside was a paper book with pictures of people all over it.

"It's a magazine," he said.

"No way! It's almost completely intact still! I've only ever seen a few ripped pages of one."

"I know, right?" His excitement was contagious. Then he did something crazy. He lifted the glass and gently started turning the pages of the magazine.

"What are you doing? You can't touch that!" Renna looked around in a panic. "You're going to get us in trouble."

"Who's going to yell at me? Besides, Drake and I used to sneak in here when we were boys and look through it."

She raised her eyebrow. "You don't respect the preservation of precious artifacts from history, do you?"

Trev snickered. "I do now that I'm older, but this is a special circumstance. There." He stopped at a picture of a beautiful woman in a fancy dress. Her arms and shoulders were bare. The red fabric of her dress curved perfectly around her breasts, pushing them up, spilling them over the top. The fabric continued down her body, hugging her tightly until the dress dramatically split open over one thigh, revealing one bare leg. The other leg was hidden under the red silk. The woman had her hand on her hip, posing for the picture.

"See what I was talking about? No modesty rules." He seemed pleased to show her something new.

She looked at Trev accusingly. "Now I can see why you and Drake would sneak in here."

"We were very resourceful," he said with a mischievous glimmer in his eye. "We weren't *just* looking at the pretty women. We read the articles too."Renna laughed, rolling her eyes a bit. She read the caption silently, shaking her head in amazement. 'Blake Lively brings her A-game to one of high fashion's most glamorous events in a strapless Vera Wang dress.'

"A strapless dress? How did it stay on without sleeves holding it up?" She leaned in closer to get a better look.

"It was probably too tight to go anywhere," Trev guessed.

"I suppose you're right."

Trev lifted the glass back over the magazine, leaving it on the page of the stunning young woman.

"You kind of look like her, you know?"

Renna let out a very unladylike laugh. "In your dreams."

"Maybe I will dream about it . . . you and me . . . dancing in fancy clothes. You said yourself back at Wellenbreck that you wanted another chance at dancing."

Trev shouldn't be saying things like that, but his smile was so innocent, so charming.

Renna's heart beat obnoxiously until her guilt pulled her into reality. She looked around the room for her mother and Seran, who thankfully leaned over a display of children's toys. Renna pretended to be interested in another display to distance herself from Trev, but of course, he followed her.

"I almost forgot. I brought you something." Trev pulled out a small napkin from his pocket. He gently unwrapped it and held it in front of her.

"What is it?" Her brows puckered together.

"It's called chocolate." He broke off a piece and handed it to her.

"Where did you get it?" she asked, examining it in her fingers.

"We did some trading with the kingdom of Cristole. The weather and humidity in Cristole make it the perfect place to grow cocoa beans. Now we have a whole stash of them in the basement." He plopped a piece into his own mouth.

Slowly, she raised the small piece to her lips but stopped just short of them. "Is this where you poison me?"

"Do you think *everyone* is trying to kill you or just me?"

"Just you, I guess." Renna smiled. "It smells good."

"Would you just eat it?"

She quickly placed the foreign food into her mouth. Trev watched as her expression changed from nervous anticipation to complete bliss. "You have ruined me. I don't think anything else will ever satisfy me again," she said, taking in the delicious flavor.

"I feel the exact same way." Trev stared at her intently, all hints of joking gone from his handsome face.

Renna panicked. She did the only thing she could think of; she punched him in the shoulder and then whispered. "You are the biggest flirt I have ever met. Are you practicing all these lines on me first before you use them on Seran?"

Trev's unwavering gaze broke as if the mention of Seran reminded him of who he should really be spending his time with. He looked over his shoulder at where Seran stood, her back to them. "I should go to her, but I'll see you tomorrow. It's the first day of the Tournament of Games." He began to walk away slowly, still speaking to her as he went. "You're really going to like all the competitions. I know it."

Then he was gone from her side.

18

Renna

A buzz of excitement surrounded the outside of the palace for the Tournament of Games. The grassy lawn in front of the palace had been transformed into a small arena. Booths were set up with food vendors, and a few portable toilets lined the outskirts of the grass. Young men from the army and working-class men from nearby villages eagerly waited in line to sign up for the different competitions. Winners from each day would compete on the final day in a tournament of champions.

Renna felt the energy as she strolled among the crowd. Joyful sounds of laughter rang from young children as they ran around their mothers. Groups of women chatted while their men bragged about their own skills and talents. It was a happy day in Albion.

She smiled at passersby and tried not to look for Trev. Her smile faltered a bit when she finally saw him. He was seated in the stands next to Seran, front and center where the best seats were. They leaned their heads in close together, and Seran was smiling at something he said. The carefree feeling of the morning escaped with Renna's breath.

But it was good. Good for her to remember he was Seran's.

Someone better would come along for her. She just had to make it through the wedding, and then she could go home.

Renna found an open seat next to her mother and sat down. Luckily, Trev and Seran were several seats away. It would be easier to act like she didn't care about him if she could ignore him. But then she heard Trev and Seran talking.

"Why are there so many men signing up?" Seran asked. "What kind of prize do they get if they win?"

"Well, the tradition in Albion is for the winner to receive a kiss from a woman of his choice; I'm sure most men would choose you."

Seran let out a light laugh.

"Are you comfortable with that?" Trev asked.

"I suppose there's only one man I would *want* to kiss, but I'll consider it an honor to perform the duty if called upon."

Renna leaned forward to see Trev's response to Seran's words. He looked flustered; or maybe he was thrilled. It was tough to tell. Renna slammed her back into her seat, hiding them from her view.

"Prince Ezra," her mother called. "Join me for a moment."

What? Why?

Renna's heart stumbled as Trev stood up and came their way.

"Your Majesty. Miss Degray. You both look lovely this morning." His comment was meant for her mother too, but his eyes lingered on Renna a little too long.

"Prince Ezra." Queen Mariele nodded back at him. "How kind of you to arrange such an exciting competition during our stay. Will we have the pleasure of seeing you compete in any of the games this week?"

"I'm afraid it's not customary for royalty to participate."

"Of course not. You wouldn't want to be injured," her mother replied.

"Actually, it wouldn't be fair to the other competitors. I'd most likely win every event."

Her mother laughed and Trev grinned, but Renna raised her eyebrows at his cockiness.

"Miss Degray, do you doubt it?" His smug smile challenged her.

She had hoped she wouldn't have to speak, especially not in front of her mother. But how could she ignore a direct question? She breathed in. "I doubt anyone who brags about their own talents."

Her mother's mouth dropped open.

"Even when they have the right to brag?" Trev didn't seem angry. Just amused.

She smiled coyly. "Unfortunately, we'll never know if you have that right."

"I guess you'll just have to take my word for it."

"And we will," Queen Mariele desperately added.

Trev nodded to the queen before turning his smug smile back on her. "Miss Degray, I hope you won't mind, but I took the liberty of inviting my dear friend, Mr. Tybolt, to sit with you today."

Her eyes narrowed. "Thank you, Your Highness, but that's not necessary." The last thing she wanted was to be stuck with Mr. Tybolt all day.

"Ah! Here he comes now. Tybolt!" Trev gestured to the large man. "I was just telling Miss Degray what a dear friend you are to our family and how I would like you two to be better acquainted."

Renna could not believe what was happening. The sweaty man actually sat down and, in doing so, took up half of her seat. She looked to Trev to save her, but he seemed all too pleased with himself and the situation.

"The games are about to begin." Trev backed up a few steps. "I trust you two will get along great."

"Indeed!" Mr. Tybolt yelled, deafening Renna's left ear in the process. This was going to be a long morning.

With an impish grin, Trev retreated to his seat, leaving Renna to glare at his back as he walked away. Clearly, she had underestimated how far he would go to carry out a joke.

She tried to focus on the tournament, doing her best to ignore the enormous, sweating man beside her. Archery was the first event. There were fifteen contestants in total. As each man was announced, Tybolt found something critical to say about him. They were either too poor, their clothes too gray, or they were somehow beneath him—even if they came from a respectable family. He insisted he was a far better bowman than any of the participants. Renna couldn't even imagine Tybolt having enough muscles under all his layers to hold a bow, let alone standing still long enough to hit a target.

Renna was careful not to do or say anything that encouraged more conversation, but Tybolt hardly needed encouragement. He continued to lean in closer and closer until her neck began to hurt from straining away. At one point, Tybolt became so animated that saliva flew from his sweaty mouth and landed all over her neck. She silently cursed Trev as she wiped the liquid with the sleeve of her dress.

Her eyes continued to scan the arena until they found Joniss. He stood casually against a wooden post, feet crossed, and arms folded across his broad chest. He raised his eyes toward the large man next to her, and Renna subtly shook her head, eyes wide in feigned panic. Joniss mouthed the words, "I'm sorry."

"Did you also know I am skilled in other types of weapons?" Mr. Tybolt was still talking. Would he ever stop?

Not waiting for her answer, he continued to tell her specifically what weapons he liked to use and who he had challenged. With each word, his stale breath burned her nostrils.

Turning her head away, she dared to look down the row in Trev's direction. He was smiling as Seran talked. Unbelievable! He had stuck Mr. Tybolt on her while he was enjoying Seran and the archery competition.

He was officially the worst.

Then the worst's beautiful blue eyes glanced at her. She gave Trev her most irritated glare as payback for the unpleasant situation he had placed her in. Trev held his fingers up to his chin, opening and closing them like pretend scissors to a beard.

19

Trev

"I have something planned for us after the competition," Trev said to Seran over the cheers of the crowd. "Somewhere I wanted to take you."

"That's thoughtful of you, but I'm meeting with the dressmaker to discuss plans for my wedding dress." Seran said, excitement edging her voice.

Trev forced a smile. "That sounds important." The wedding still didn't seem real to him, but this was a clear reminder that things between him and Seran were definitely real.

"Perhaps we can spend some time together later?" Seran reached out, squeezing his arm.

"Of course."

Trev tried to turn his focus back to the end of the competition, but every once in a while, his eyes drifted to Renna a few seats down. He'd hoped Tybolt's placement would come across as a joke, though after watching Renna shrink away from the man all morning, he began to wonder if it had been a little too much for him to put Renna through. The one upside was that no other man could get anywhere near her while Tybolt was there—his immense body acting as a barricade between her and any other suitor.

But that wasn't fair of him, and he knew it.

"So I'll see you later?" Seran asked when the competition was over, pulling his attention back to her.

"Sure." Trev stood.

"What are you going to do?"

Renna stood, trying to escape Tybolt. Maybe Trev should rescue her. He smiled back at Seran. "Oh, I'm sure I have some policies on my desk that need to be reviewed."

He waited until Seran had walked away and then he made his move, arriving on the scene just as Tybolt stood and asked Renna and her mother to accompany him to the lunch buffet.

"I think—" Renna began to say until Trev interrupted her.

"I think Miss Degray already has plans for lunch."

Tybolt shrunk a little in Trev's presence. Sweat trickled from his forehead down into his beard. "I see."

"My mother, however, would be thrilled to accompany you." Renna smiled warmly at the queen, who didn't know quite how to respond.

Recovering quickly, Queen Mariele said with a polite smile, "Certainly."

Tybolt shuffled his massive body around several chairs, trying to exit. The queen took his offered arm. "Well then, thank you for a most agreeable morning," he sputtered to Renna.

"Agreeable doesn't even begin to describe it." Renna smiled sweetly, and Trev laughed under his breath at her seemingly innocent remark.

Tybolt paused, looking confused, and then escorted the queen away.

"Do you want to get out of here?" Trev asked.

"Where's Seran?" Renna said, glancing over his shoulder for the princess. "Don't you need to spend time with her?"

Yes, he should be with Seran, but she was busy. "I asked

her if she wanted to come with me, and she turned me down. She has a meeting with the dressmaker." He shrugged. "Instead of canceling my plans, I thought I could take you."

"Don't you have more important things to do?" she asked.

"I wouldn't have asked if I had more important things to do. Do you want to come or not?"

She looked around them, likely checking to see who was watching or noticing them together.

"I guess it would be all right," she finally answered.

"Trev! There you are." The pair turned to see Drake coming their way. "Should we all walk to lunch together?" he asked, desperation infusing his tone. Undoubtedly, he thought it was a bad idea for Trev to be alone with Renna.

Probably because it *was* a bad idea.

But there was no harm in being around Renna, not out in public. Besides, Seran had said no. She'd probably be happy he'd taken Renna instead.

"Renna and I have other plans," Trev replied.

"Other plans besides lunch?" Drake asked, not even trying to hide his irritation.

"Yes." Before Drake could respond, Trev pulled Renna away. They walked side by side, though Trev kept his hands clasped behind his back in case he had a spontaneous urge to touch her. That seemed to keep happening.

"I hope you don't feel like you have to plan something to keep me entertained. I know you were just trying to be nice by saving me from Tybolt, even if you were the one who stuck me with him in the first place. If you want, we can turn back to lunch."

"Who says I was just being nice? I meant what I said. I have other plans for you." He pointed to the training field lined with men. "Have you been over here yet?"

Renna shook her head.

"This is where all the soldiers train. It's one of my

favorite places on the palace grounds. Men working hard to learn and improve their skills for the good of their king and country."

They walked past rows of young men lined up to receive instruction from their captains.

"Couldn't these boys have come to the tournament today?"

"No, these boys didn't have the afternoon off. Besides, a soldier never lets the appearance of peace dictate his work ethic."

"The appearance of peace?" Renna raised her eyebrows. "You don't think this is a peaceful time?"

"Things are never as peaceful as they seem."

"Your country is not at war, and nobody is rioting against the crown. The king has aligned himself with New Hope. What more could you want?"

"I just don't want to miss anything or trust the wrong person."

"What do you mean?"

"There are rumors of Tolsten spies infiltrating Albion." He probably shouldn't tell Renna all this, but he couldn't shake the urge to open up to her. "I feel this weight on my shoulders that I have to find the spies and what they want before they do something that I can't control."

"Maybe it's just a rumor." She shrugged.

"Tolsten has recently frustrated some of our military plans. Nothing big, but small things like building a military fortress on the same border location where Albion had plans to build. Things that could be dismissed as coincidence, but also could be something more."

"So, how do you know who to trust?"

"I don't trust anybody." It was true; he didn't trust anyone outside his circle of friends and family—and now, Renna.

She whirled around, smiling. "Maybe that boy is the spy." She pointed to a young boy practicing hand-to-hand combat across the field. "Or that man, or that man, or that man!" Her finger moved from one person to the next.

Trev pushed her arm down. "The spy could be *you*."

"Or you." She smiled, raising a brow in the process.

Her playful expression made his stomach flip with butterflies. "Leave the spies to me. What you need to worry about right now is your aim."

"My aim?"

Trev nodded at the shooting range, separated from the rest of the field by a fence. A young soldier working the desk bowed at Trev, handing him two small handguns. He turned to Renna. "Do you know how to shoot?" He started walking toward the line that faced the targets before she could answer.

Renna followed behind, trying to keep pace. "Of course not. It's not like we had guns just laying around at Wellenbreck Farm. Only soldiers are allowed to have guns . . ." Her words trailed off as she watched him load bullets into the small, black weapon.

Trev finished his preparations and turned to face her, gun outstretched, waiting for her to take it.

She stared back at him, unsure.

"What are you afraid of?" he asked.

Renna shuffled her feet. "Oh, I don't know. Hurting someone, hurting myself, failing, looking like a fool, embarrassing you, embarrassing myself, and possibly upsetting my mom."

"Renna, I didn't take you for a woman who cares what other people think."

She shrugged her shoulders.

"Do you want to learn how to shoot a gun or not?"

She nodded her head up and down.

"Then try it and stop worrying about what other people think."

Trev gently placed the gun in her hand and pointed to a small button on the left side above the handle. "This is the safety mechanism. Right now, the safety is on, so it won't fire even if you pull the trigger. When you push that button, the safety will release, and the gun will be ready to fire. Leave the safety on until we're ready to shoot."

"Safety first," she teased.

"Always," he said.

"Wow, it's really light." She lifted her hand up and down to feel the weight.

"Yeah, it is. The Council approved gun technology upgrades to the ones they had before Desolation to be safer and more reliable. These are also quieter, so there's no need for ear protection."

She nodded as if everything he said was deeply important.

He spread his legs shoulder-width apart, putting his arms straight out in front of him, hands clasped together with the gun in between his fingers. "This is the position your body should be in when you're ready to shoot."

Renna copied his stance.

Trev's eyes scanned slowly up and down her figure. "Your body looks *good*." He gave her a wicked smile.

Renna quickly lowered her arms. "Ezra Trevenna! Are you a gentleman or not?"

"What?" He raised his hands in innocence. "I was talking about your form. I feel completely violated now."

She gave him a warning look.

"I promise." He smiled. "I am all about business."

Her incriminating expression melted into a slow smile.

"Now, go back into your stance," he said, making some adjustments to her hand placement before he explained about sights and how to aim at the target. When he had given all the instructions, he said, "Okay. Let's see what you've got."

She released the safety and fitted her finger over the trigger. Her breath stilled as she pulled the lever, sending a bullet flying through the air. It pierced the bottom left corner of the target ten yards away—not close to the bullseye at all.

"I did it!" she squealed with delight, spinning to face him, the gun pointing in all directions as she turned.

Trev scrambled to get his hands on the weapon. "Whoa! What happened to safety first?"

"Oh! Sorry." Her eyes and mouth went wide like she was just as shocked as he was that she'd forgotten the rules. It was another adorable expression to add to his list. "I forgot."

"This time, let's see if you can hit the target."

"But I did hit the target."

Trev shook his head. "You hit the paper."

Renna lined up again and fired bullet after bullet. Some shots were way off, but some circled the center of the target. When there were no bullets left, she handed the gun back to him, this time with the safety on.

"Let's see you do it now," she challenged.

Trev reloaded the gun and fired one after another with every single shot piercing the center of the bullseye.

"Wow! You're amazing."

"I'm all right." He picked up the second gun and handed it to her. "Do you want to have a friendly competition?"

"Absolutely not! You would destroy me."

"What if I shot with only my left hand and moved my target ten yards farther?"

"What does the winner get?"

"If I win, I get to dance with you once at the tournament festival." Dancing was a normal thing. It would look bad if Trev didn't dance with his fiancée's stepsister.

She folded her arms across her chest. "You said I was a terrible dancer."

"Well, someone has to teach you."

"And if I win?" she asked, pursing her lips together.

"What do you want?"

Renna thought for a moment before deciding. "More chocolate."

Trev laughed. "I should have known it would have something to do with food. Deal."

They shook on it.

Trev turned and asked the young man behind the desk to move his target ten yards farther than Renna's. Off-duty soldiers began to notice something exciting was happening, and it didn't take long for word to spread through the training field that Prince Ezra had challenged Renna to a target shooting match. A crowd of men started to gather around to watch.

The bet was unfair, even if Trev did shoot with his left arm. He was one of the best gunmen in Albion, next to Drake. But that was the whole point. He counted on his skills to get him that dance with her. Never in his life had he been so grateful for all of the long days he had put in practicing.

She leaned in so only he could hear. "I feel nervous with all of these guys watching."

He whispered back with a smile, "You *should* feel nervous. They're not here to watch me."

"Well, in that case, I'll give them a show." Renna stepped up to fire. The bullet landed low on the target but was well within the second ring. She grinned at the crowd of men applauding behind her.

Trev raised his left arm, releasing his first bullet. Shooting with his opposite arm felt awkward, but he managed to hit the target closer than Renna had. She shot another that landed even closer than her first. The soldiers cheered even louder for her. She looked at him with raised eyebrows, daring him to match her shot. He couldn't back down from those green eyes. His bullet landed right next to hers.

"It looks like we're even. Whoever has the best shot on this next one is the winner," he said. "Don't mess up."

She pulled the trigger and was disappointed to see the mark in the upper right corner of the paper, not touching the actual target

It would be easy to finish her off now, and Trev wasn't going to hold back. He raised his arm, but just as he released the bullet, Renna's soft fingers tickled the back of his neck behind his ear, burning his skin with her simple touch. The bullet sailed through the air high, missing the paper target completely.

The men laughed and cheered as Renna raised her arms in victory.

Trev couldn't believe he had lost. He never lost unless it was on purpose.

"Poor Prince Ezra. How embarrassing to lose to a woman, and in front of so many of your comrades!" Renna said, her voice full of sarcasm.

Trev lowered to one knee in front of her. "Renna Degray, I am your humble servant of chocolate."

She threw her head back as a burst of contagious laughter bubbled out of her throat. Both her arms raised above her head in victory. He smiled, watching her until his stomach squeezed with frustration. She was not his, and she never could be.

As they strode back to the palace, Renna gloated about every detail of her win.

"Even though the gun was light, I worry my arm will be sore tomorrow from shooting so much," she said.

"I could always rub it for you," Trev joked, stepping toward her, impeding her way.

Renna's eyes dropped, and she stepped around, continuing forward. "Instead of chocolate, I should've said that you couldn't flirt with me anymore."

He shook his head. "I wasn't flirting with you."

She dipped her chin, giving him a pointed look.

Was he flirting with her? He hadn't meant to, but whenever he was around Renna, the line between friends and *more than friends* blurred.

"Okay, fine. I was flirting with you. But I didn't mean to." He matched her pace again.

"Well, stop." She looked nervous, keeping her focus straight ahead until she abruptly stopped and looked at him. "It's just . . ." She paused, indecision visible on her face.

He knew what she wasn't saying. *Who* she wasn't mentioning. Seran's kind face flashed through his mind, reminding him of her honesty, her vulnerability; he closed his eyes and tried to shake away his shame.

"You're right. I won't flirt with you anymore." They continued walking. "But can we still be friends?"

"Of course," she said too quickly.

Trev turned to face her but continued to walk backward. "Friends with no accidental flirting. I got it."

He wondered if he really did *get it.*

He stopped walking, making her nearly bump into him. "I'm glad we're still friends. I like having you as my friend."

Her breath stilled at his nearness, making him smile.

"You're still flirting with me," she said plainly. "You can't even go one second."

He raised his eyebrows. "That was not flirting. *That* was friendliness. Don't confuse friendliness for flirting, or my kindness will all go straight to your head." He shook his head as if he found her impossible.

Renna's mouth dropped open, letting out a puff of air.

He smiled back at her before leaving. "Have a wonderful day, Miss Degray."

20

Renna

A fire burned in the palace fireplace, which seemed odd to Renna, considering that it was the beginning of September, and the temperature outside was still warm. Somebody at the palace must have thought it would make the large room where the women gathered after dinner seem cozier. Seran and her friends assembled around a circular table playing cards while Queen Mariele sat at a desk nearby. She had received a letter from King Bryant earlier in the day and now worked a pen furiously over her response. Renna sat, her back pressed against the soft velvet sofa as her eyes scanned the words of a book. Despite her effort, it was hard to concentrate with the mindless chatter of Seran's followers filling the room around her.

"Seran, I don't know how you are going to kiss the sweaty guy who wins the tournament. It's going to be disgusting," Jenica scoffed.

Lizanne mused, "Too bad Prince Ezra can't enter the competition. Then you could kiss him instead."

"Seran doesn't need a tournament to kiss the prince," Sheridan snapped at Lizanne, and Renna wondered again why they all talked down to Lizanne so much.

"Maybe they've already kissed." Jenica raised her dark eyebrows questioningly.

All women, including Renna, looked to Seran for the answer.

With a shy smirk, she placed a stack of cards on the table. "A lady never tells."

The other women laughed.

Renna sucked in all the air around her and tried to focus on her book.

Jenica added to the pile of cards on the table. "I think Albion is treating us all very well. There are so many good-looking men to choose from."

"Have you met Officer Vestry? He's so dreamy!" Lizanne said.

Sheridan kept her eyes on her cards as she spoke. "Yes, very handsome!"

"Or what about Officer Doman?" Lizanne paused to speak before picking up a card from the pile.

"Lizanne." Jenica looked as if she were disgusted. "You're just naming every man you've met."

"I would stay away from Officer Doman. Ezra said he's trouble." Seran placed another card on the table.

Ezra said?

Trev hadn't told Renna that.

"Officer Doman is challenging him for the crown." Seran pushed a loose strand of hair away from her face. "I didn't think much about it, but Ezra said he has a lot of followers. Definitely stay away from him, or else it might look like we're favoring the competition."

Jenica snickered. "Maybe we should send him back to New Hope with Renna then."

The women giggled.

"You'd do that for Seran, wouldn't you, Renna?" Jenica laughed over her shoulder.

Renna kept her eyes down on her book, pretending she hadn't heard them.

Seran spoke over her cards. "That's not necessary. Renna is free to marry whomever she wants."

Not true at all.

Renna kept her face expressionless as she stared at her book but was grateful for Seran's defense.

Sheridan turned toward Queen Mariele. "May I ask how the negotiations are going with the marriage treaty?"

The queen looked up from her letter. "There are a few details left to sort out about trade. Once those issues are agreed upon, the document will be drawn up for review by King Carver, myself, and King Bryant's advisors."

Renna had heard about these negotiations for years. The vital New Hope military, access to New Hope ports, trade considerations in Albion, and the exchange of votes at the Council of Essentials, promises that if someone voted for this, someone else would vote for that.

Whatever happened to voting for something not because you were in an alliance, but because it was the right thing to do?

Her mother continued, "I imagine we're only a few days away from signing."

Sheridan nodded in an official way as if she understood all the ins and outs of the agreement. "It's good to have those things taken care of before the ceremony."

"Seran, let's talk about your wedding," Lizanne said with excitement. "I want to hear every detail of the plans so far."

Renna definitely didn't want to hear every detail. She stood to leave.

"Leaving so early, Renna?" Jenica smiled wide and Renna's stomach soured.

"It looks like it." She wanted to say something catty but managed to suppress the urge.

Renna left the ladies behind, taking the side stairs up to

her room. She was finally getting the layout of this enormous place. She pushed the door open to her room to see Nora's small frame standing there all giddy.

"Miss Renna, a secret admirer came to visit." She walked over to the bed and pointed at a small box on top of her pillow.

"A secret admirer?" Butterflies fluttered in her stomach. "Who?"

"I don't know. I was getting fresh towels. I'm sure it says on the note."

Renna reached for the paper and unfolded it.

Renna,

Normally, I would compliment you on how beautiful you looked tonight at dinner. I would tell you how I wished you were sitting next to me, conjuring up one of your pretend stories, or how I wish I could spend time with you again just to see what crazy thing you'll do or say next. Normally, I would say those things to you, but I'm not going to do that. I'm not going to flirt with you—I promised I wouldn't.

Tybolt

Renna laughed as she reached for the box and opened it. Inside were four individually wrapped squares of chocolate.

21

Trev

Trev waited at the large circular table in the high ruler's room for his weekly meeting to start. The meeting consisted of the king and the six high rulers from each province in Albion, and the commander of the army, Fenton Pryer. Trev and Drake attended whenever possible, preparing for their future roles if the upcoming election went according to plan.

Alba Folly and Levi Karda, the two longest-ruling high rulers, sat across the table from Trev, whispering. Their heads bent together like they were talking about something serious, but whatever it was, they clearly didn't feel inclined to include Trev.

Trev studied the dark stain of the table in front of him. He thought about getting himself a cup of water, but the pitcher was on a side table across the room, closer to the two men. He didn't want it to look like he was eavesdropping on their conversation.

"Tell me it isn't true," Drake said in a hushed voice, lowering his body down in the seat next to Trev.

"I'm assuming you heard about the shooting competition between Renna and me," Trev responded coolly.

"Yes!" Drake snarled. "And I can't believe it."

"Which part?" Trev asked. "The part where she beat me or—"

"All of it!" Drake eyed the two men across from them, whispering so only Trev could hear. "You're supposed to spend time with Seran, *your fiancée.* Not her sister." Drake rubbed his forehead in disgust. "It doesn't make Renna look good either."

Trev leaned back in his chair, folding his arms. "I disagree. She looked very good."

Renna had a way of looking good no matter what she was doing.

"But that's exactly my point. You can't have everyone see you alone with Renna. You're terrible at hiding your feelings for her."

Maxwell Doman entered, followed by the king and Fenton Pryer, forcing Drake to pause their conversation. "Never mind," he hissed. "We'll talk about this later."

"Our men still haven't located the missing girls from Axville, and my patience is growing thin. King Adler must be stopped!" King Carver barked, opening the meeting.

"With all due respect, sir, we are unsure if King Adler had any knowledge of the Axville attack," Commander Pryer said.

"His hands are in everything!" his father yelled as he stood abruptly and paced back and forth. Everyone watched in silence as he picked up the pitcher of water and slammed it against the wall.

"Let's strike back," Levi Karda interjected. He was the high ruler over Axville and had an additional reason to be upset by the attack. "When word gets out all over Albion about what happened, the people will want justice for the taken daughters of Axville."

"I'm afraid it's more complicated than that," the commander said. "During the election tour, Prince Ezra and Officer Vestry sent two men undercover to Tolsten to gather intel specifically on weapons. Those two men returned yesterday."

Trev sat up. "Why wasn't I told? This was my mission."

His father waved him off. "You have more important things to worry about with the princess. Your men gave Fenton and me a full report."

Trev exchanged an irritated look with Drake. He should have known his father would take over.

"Were they successful?" Drake pressed.

"Unfortunately, yes." Commander Pryer gave the king a sharp look before continuing. "It's exactly as we feared. Tolsten has been manufacturing sophisticated weapons. Our spies aren't exactly sure what the weapons are designed to do. They appear to be some sort of air missile."

"What is King Adler thinking? Did he really think all the other countries wouldn't find out? Wouldn't try to stop him? He's directly violating the Essentials treaty," Levi Karda said.

"I don't think any other country could stop Adler at this point. His missiles give him the upper hand," Niles Ticking added. He was a newer high ruler, only ten or so years older than Trev.

Maxwell Doman lowered his voice, adding, "Maybe it's time we take more drastic measures."

"What do you have in mind?" King Carver asked.

Maxwell looked at the other men around the table. "We should attack when they least expect. Like during the wedding."

Trev laughed incredulously. "You can't be serious. We haven't even signed the marriage treaty yet, and you want to pull New Hope into an armed conflict on the wedding day? Use *their* military without even bothering to ask for their consent?"

"Besides," Alba Folly added, "according to the marriage treaty, New Hope has pledged their military backing for defense purposes only. Taking this step makes us the aggressors."

"This *is* defense," Levi Karda insisted. "It's a justified reaction to Tolsten's aggression. They crossed our borders and took our people hostage. Hitting them back now will deter future harassment."

"A full-on military engagement is not deterrence, Levi," Alba said, his face red. "That's called war, and we need New Hope's consent to even think of declaring it. Without their support, Tolsten will crush us."

"And, if our spies are correct, Tolsten could simply use their cache of illegal weapons to blow us off the map," another high ruler, Joss Oviatt, inserted. "Even with New Hope's support, declaring outright war would be suicide."

King Carver gave a short, frustrated sigh and glanced around the table. "Do we have any better ideas?"

Suddenly, a voice said simply, "Kill King Adler."

The room went silent as each high ruler turned to stare at Maxwell Doman, who stared back with serene calmness.

Trev broke the stunned silence first, enunciating slowly. "Are you out of your mind?"

"Assassination!" Alba choked. "And just how do you expect us to do that?"

"Impossible!" Niles huffed across the room.

"Do you want to start another Desolation?" Sebban Challis spoke up. He was the one high ruler that usually kept to himself.

Maxwell answered plainly. "We can stage it to look like an assassination from agitators within Tolsten—an inside job that can't be traced back to Albion."

The hungry gleam in his father's eyes knotted Trev's stomach.

King Carver sat back down in his chair and gestured to

the commander. "Fenton? What do you think? Could we pull this off?"

Trev had to shut this down immediately. "We can't just kill the leader of another kingdom. It doesn't reflect what our country believes in. What *we* believe in."

"Albion believes what I tell them to believe," the king snapped back.

Trev shook his head. It wasn't the first time he doubted whether his father had the people of Albion's best interests at heart. Increasingly, it seemed like winning this twisted game against the king of Tolsten was all his father cared about. Trev tried again. "Father, this could set a terrifying precedent. If we assassinate a world leader, what's to stop others from doing the same thing to us?"

"To Maxwell's point, though," Commander Pryer interrupted, his eyes thoughtful, "no one will see our hand in it if we can frame local insurgents. Albion will be safe."

Trev's eyes widened in disbelief. "Commander, are you *honestly* suggesting that we commit a murder and then allow innocent men and women to take the fall for it?"

"They're hardly innocent if they're rebelling against their king." Pryer sniffed. He turned to King Carver and continued. "To answer your question, Your Majesty, I believe it could be done with careful planning."

"You're wrong if you believe no one will ever find out," Niles Ticking scoffed.

"Father, this is madness." Trev looked around the table at the other high rulers, hoping to find other allies. "Do you all agree with this?"

"No," Alba said firmly, taking off his glasses and setting them on the papers in front of him. "Prince Ezra is right. This is not a can of worms we want to open. Even if we assassinate Adler, it solves nothing concerning the illegal weapons. There is still the possibility that the assassination starts a war."

"You act like we're the ones starting a war. Have you

forgotten Tolsten's attacks on us year after year?" The king's anger was starting to rise again. "Tolsten's attack on Axville! I will no longer stand by and watch Adler have his way with our country. This war between us has been ongoing, and we will finish it."

"Perhaps I spoke too hastily," Maxwell said, back-peddling. "My anger got the better of me. Of course, we all want justice for Axville, but this isn't the way." He looked at Trev. "I think the boy is right; there are consequences to this plan that I didn't think about."

King Carver couldn't do anything unless he had the majority vote in the room, and he clearly wasn't going to get that.

"Fine. We'll pretend this idea never existed. King Adler is not to be touched," his father said to the group of men, but Trev didn't miss the intense look his father gave Fenton Pryer. "For now, we have sent a large number of men to Axville to assess the situation. We have also sent an official statement to King Adler demanding the hostages be returned."

"We will wait for Adler's response before we make any further moves," Commander Pryer said as he looked at the men around the table.

THE MEETING WAS finished. Trev cursed under his breath when he saw Joniss coming down the hall. He was the last person he wanted to speak to right now.

"Ezra." Joniss always purposefully left out the *prince* part.

"What do you want?" Trev said, unable to hide his dislike for the man.

"We missed you at the tournament events today."

"I had meetings."

"That's a shame." Joniss faked sadness. "I spent the day with Renna. She's such a lovely girl, don't you think?"

Trev's face turned to stone despite his best efforts.

"How are things going with Seran?" Joniss asked.

"Excellent." Trev responded too quickly for it to be believable. "What's not to like about the princess?"

"She's a little too uptight for my taste, but as far as arranged marriages go, I guess it's an okay choice for you. I myself like my women a little wilder. Renna, for example." Joniss smirked. "She's exactly my type."

Great. Joniss suspected something between him and Renna.

"Who knows, maybe we'll end up being brothers-in-law." Joniss's expression was smug.

"I doubt Miss Degray would agree to marry you."

"Perhaps not." Joniss laughed. "But at least she has a choice in who she marries, as do I."

22

Trev

The next morning, Trev leaned against the arena fence, watching crowds of people file into the stands. Conversation and laughter filled the yard while spectators waited for the final day of the Tournament of Games to begin.

Trev looked up and his heart stumbled. Renna walked toward him, her arms swinging casually at her sides. Her hair was spun around the top of her head in a bun, and she wore a pale pink day dress that complimented her golden complexion. Was there any color that didn't look good on her?

He glanced at Drake and Joniss across the arena from him, talking with a group of soldiers. They both watched Trev as if somehow they knew how much his heart raced because of her.

Trev wanted nothing more than to smile back at her—to comment on her wispy gracefulness, but Drake's words still hung in the back of his mind. *You are terrible at hiding your feelings for her.*

"Good morning, Prince Ezra," Renna said as she stopped in front of him.

His eyes stayed focused on the crowd of people in front of him. If he didn't look at Renna, maybe his heart rate would go back to normal. And maybe he could hide—correction —*get over* his feelings for her.

"I wanted to thank you for the chocolates you left the other night, but I couldn't find you yesterday."

A smile tugged at the corner of his mouth, and he let his eyes meet hers. "You don't have to thank me. You won them fair enough."

"Yes, I guess I did." She rested her hands on the fence post that lined the arena and leaned in closer. Trev could smell the citrus scent of her hair, but he tried to ignore it. "I also received a note with the chocolates. Something very flirtatious from a man who promised not to flirt."

From the corner of his eye, he could see Joniss walking toward them. "I don't believe the note was from me."

"Right." The side of her mouth raised into a slight smile. "How foolish of me."

"I hope I'm not interrupting anything." Joniss obnoxiously slung his arm around Renna's shoulder.

"Not at all." Renna shifted under his weight. "I was just telling Prince Ezra that I can't believe the tournament is almost over. He missed some exciting competitions yesterday. Don't you think, Officer Doman?"

"Yes, Ezra missed out on a lot yesterday," Joniss said, pulling Renna into him.

Trev narrowed his gaze. The man was such a snake. He resisted the urge to punch him in the gut right then and there and watch him topple over to the ground. He could almost imagine how good it would feel.

Renna looked uncomfortably between the two men.

She started talking fast. "Well, we're down to just sword fighting and then the championship. Then some guy gets a kiss from Seran."

Trev opened his mouth to speak, but Joniss cut in. "Who says the winner will choose Seran?"

Renna scoffed. "Everyone."

Joniss turned his face toward her, so his lips were by her ear. "I would choose you."

Renna dropped her head nervously. "Oh."

"It doesn't matter who you would choose," Trev said bitterly. "You're not competing, remember?"

"I'm always competing. You, of all people, should know that." Joniss shot a flinty smile at Trev, then grabbed his sword. "I think I'll go enter right now." His mouth twisted downward in mocking pity. "It's a shame they don't allow royalty to compete. I would've enjoyed beating you."

Joniss winked at Renna before walking toward the fighting arena.

Trev forced out a breath.

Somehow he had just unwittingly goaded Joniss into entering the competition.

Renna

Renna couldn't believe Joniss had entered the competition. He walked into the ring like a warrior, unsheathed his sword, and crouched low, ready to fight. With each clash and clang of swords, her nerves worsened. She had seen sword fights like this in New Hope, but she had never cared about who won or lost before. Now, a part of her hoped Joniss would win. She found herself flinching and ducking right along with the competitors in the ring. She pressed her hand over her chest as if she could still her beating heart and watched as Joniss defeated opponent after opponent until his arm was raised as the champion. He looked at Renna, his mouth lifted into a half-smile while his chest panted up and down with fatigue.

It was flattering that Joniss was doing this for her, and the jealousy burning in Trev's eyes gave her more satisfaction than she dared to admit. It seemed like there was some sort of lover's triangle happening now that she hadn't even known existed.

The crowd dispersed for lunch while the obstacle course was being set up. Renna found Joniss under a canopy just outside the arena. He rested on a bucket, drinking water as passersby congratulated him on his wins.

"Nice work out there," Renna said.

"Did I impress you?"

"I think you impressed everybody." She glanced in the direction of a group of girls gawking at him.

"But I only wanted to impress *you*."

Renna bit back her smile. Joniss didn't need any more encouragement.

"Officer Doman!" a group of young soldiers called as they walked by. "Which girl are you going to kiss after you win?"

He looked to Renna. "Isn't it obvious?"

The boys looked her up and down, whistling.

She looked away, trying to hide the red flames creeping up her face. "You might not win, you know."

"I don't plan on losing." Joniss stood, raising his eyebrows in a way she was sure he had practiced in the mirror a hundred times. He took a step toward her, making her body shiver with nerves.

"I'm looking forward to that kiss." He moved closer until his face was only inches from hers. His eyes swept across her face and down to her lips. Her breathing picked up dramatically, causing Joniss to smirk. "And I can tell you're looking forward to it too."

He stepped back and walked away without another glance. Renna let out a breath and rolled her eyes. But as she watched his retreating back, she wondered if he was right. Did she actually want Joniss to kiss her?

She followed Joniss to the obstacle course, and her mouth gaped open at its massive size. She hadn't expected anything like this. She had heard the obstacle course was another Albion tradition—they had been doing the same obstacle course for more than fifty years. Still, she had expected something ancient-looking, not a large, sophisticated sequence of events.

The course began with a steep wooden wall with four ropes to climb up it. Then there were nets made out of rope to crawl through high in the air that led to a thin beam for balance. Large crates filled with hay were positioned below in case a competitor fell. Across the beam were swinging sacks at different speeds meant to knock a person off. If they made it past all of that, they had to slide down a wall to a landing where suspended wooden logs hung above them. Competitors needed to use their bodies to swing and grab the next log until they made it to the other end. The final obstacle was a large rolling log with a pool of mud below it. Contestants had to make it across the unstable log to the finish line without falling in the mud. If they fell off at any point in the course, they would have to start over. The obstacle course was a race—whoever finished first would be deemed the tournament champion.

The crowd cheered as the first three contestants were announced, but when Joniss stepped out onto the sand, they erupted in a roar. It seemed as though the entire stadium was cheering for Joniss to win.

Everyone except Trev.

Renna glanced down the row at him. He leaned forward and rested his elbows on his knees, his expression as hard as iron.

The starting horn bellowed, sending each man leaping toward his rope, and Renna's heart to her throat. Joniss's upper strength gave him an early lead as he powerfully hoisted himself up the wall, but the other men weren't far behind. He reached the top first, hurling his body into the nets below. The next man over the wall dove into the nets just behind him, catching Joniss's leg to pull him back and tangle him up in a struggle. The audience booed as another contestant behind them took the lead.

Renna found herself yelling out in a very unladylike way, booing in her deepest voice at the man, but her mouth snapped shut when her mother's nails dug into the side of her arm.

Joniss untangled himself from the man and shoved away from him roughly, reaching the beam in second place. He walked quickly across the shaft but had no chance to overthrow the leader yet. The crowd cheered as a swinging sack hit the leader's shoulder, knocking him enough that he lost his balance and fell off the course. Joniss paused, studying the swinging bags and their timing. He sprinted past the first three then paused in a safe pocket, waiting to get the timing of the next three. After a few tense moments, Joniss found the rhythm and easily made it across as another contestant was knocked to the ground.

The crowd roared, and Joniss raised his arms in triumph, flashing a winning smile. He turned to where Renna sat and winked before grabbing the ladder. Renna's face flushed a hot red, and she had to look down for a quick second to gain her composure.

Joniss leaped toward the first log. She couldn't help but notice how his biceps bulged and twisted under his sleeves as he dangled from the wood and swung his legs to propel him to the next log.

Of course, she made the terrible decision to look in Trev's direction and instantly regretted it. By the glaring way his eyes met hers, he could probably read her lustful thoughts.

Joniss arrived at the final obstacle. The only thing standing between him and winning the tournament was the rolling log suspended over the mud. A few long, quick strides and he was at the other end, arms raised in victory. It was unbelievable how he made the entire course look easy. Cheers rippled through the stadium. People were on their feet, clapping and yelling. Renna slowly stood, biting her lip out of anxiousness.

This was bad.

Or maybe it was good. After all, Renna needed something to help her get over Trev.

"How interesting that Officer Doman has won." Her mother studied Trev. "Jealousy is a powerful emotion."

Panic started to rise in Renna's chest. "What do you mean?" She tried to act unfazed by the whole event.

"Only that Officer Doman and the prince are not close. I assume his winning will cause an even bigger rift between them when he kisses Seran."

"Maybe Joniss doesn't plan on choosing Seran." Her words came out sharper than she had wanted.

"Then why does Prince Ezra seem upset?" Her mother nodded in the prince's direction.

Renna looked down the row to see that Trev had called his assistant, Crosby, over and whispered something in his ear. Crosby nodded and delivered a message to the head of the tournament, a pudgy man with a beard, standing next to Joniss at the end of the course. Joniss shook his head back and forth with intense laughter as he listened to Crosby deliver his message.

"Ladies and gentlemen," the head of the games yelled. "There has been a change to the tournament rules. This year the winner of the obstacle course must face one last challenge before claiming the title of Tournament Champion."

Confusion weaved through the rows of spectators, some calling out angrily.

But the man continued, "For the last challenge, Officer Doman must defeat Prince Ezra in a wrestling match."

The crowd went wild.

The color drained from Renna's face. "I thought it wasn't customary for royalty to participate in the tournament."

Her mother leaned in. "Like I said, jealousy is a powerful emotion."

Trev

"WHAT'S THIS ABOUT?" Joniss spat over the yelling crowd.

"Nothing. I just felt like changing things up this year," Trev said as he climbed the last step onto the platform and stood next to Joniss. He unbuttoned his shirt and kicked off his boots. "Are you scared of losing?"

"This wouldn't have anything to do with the tournament prize, would it?" Joniss smiled knowingly as his eyes slid across the arena to where Renna sat in the stands.

Trev gave him a steely glare but didn't answer.

Joniss chuckled. "You better be careful, Ezra. I won't let you win like Drake always does."

Joniss pulled off his shirt and climbed up onto the log suspended over the mud, walking carefully to the far side so Trev could climb up. Trev handed his shirt to Crosby and clambered up behind him, the log swaying dangerously with his added weight. Joniss crouched down and laid a hand on the rough surface to steady himself. Then, he straightened slowly as Trev gained his balance on the opposite end.

I'm probably going crazy. He and Joniss were about to wrestle on an unstable, rolling log hanging over a crate of mud, and it had been *his* idea.

Every wink and flashy smile from Joniss to Renna had led him to this moment. Then thinking about Joniss choosing Renna for the kiss had pushed him over the edge. Trev couldn't let that happen. In a way, he was helping Renna—saving her from Joniss's games. At least that's what he tried to tell himself.

Both stood there, knees bent, waiting for the other to make

his move. Joniss was bigger, but Trev had seen him fight before and knew himself to be faster. Joniss swiped a hand toward him, upsetting the log's balance, but Trev batted his hand away. Both men adjusted their weight to find balance again on the moving log.

Joniss shuffled toward him, locking his hands on Trev's shoulders. Trev tried to wiggle free but ended up with his hands on Joniss's arms. The pair twisted and pulled, bent and strained, but neither fell. The log began to roll faster, and both men fought to keep their footing. Their arms dropped as they struggled to regain their balance. Then the battle started again.

Joniss lunged low toward Trev's legs. He was more aggressive than usual, and the element of surprise almost knocked Trev completely off the log. He fell to his stomach, his arms wrapping around the wood to hold himself above the ground. His feet dangled dangerously close to the mud.

So this was how it would end. Trev would look like an idiot in front of everyone, and Joniss would kiss Renna. At that moment, his pride hurt more than his jealousy.

He looked up at Joniss, his cocky smile giving him a new burst of determination.

Trev couldn't let Joniss win.

Without even thinking, Trev swung his leg up over the log, hitting Joniss hard in the shins and knocking him off balance. He waved his arms in quick circular motions, trying desperately not to fall. The log slowly shifted with Joniss's panicked movements. Trev clung to the log, muscles tired. He couldn't hang on much longer. Finally, the log spun just enough, causing Joniss to lose his footing. He dramatically fell back into the mud, sending splashes of the brown substance flying onto Trev's arms and face. The crowd jumped to their feet, cheering loudly for him.

When the announcer called his name as the winner, Trev figured it was safe to let go. He slipped into the mud next to

Joniss. The two men sat there in silence for a moment, flinging the sticky substance off their arms and hands.

"I guess you won," Joniss reached out to shake Trev's hand. The gesture was more about saving face with the onlookers than about being a good sport.

Still, it felt good. "Like you said, Joniss," Trev said, with narrowed eyes. "*I won.*"

23

Trev

Bonfires lit the square in front of the palace that night for the Tournament of Champions celebration. The palace gates were opened wide to invite the entire city, from the lowest worker to the king himself. Rows of tables sat at the center of the square, each lined with platters of fruit, sweet bread, and cheeses. At the end of each table were barrels full of red punch. The steady beat from the musicians swirled through the courtyard, mixing with laughter.

Trev hid at the edge of the party and watched the crowd, safely wrapped in shadows as he leaned against a stone pillar of the palace wall. Citizens danced, ate, and drank—appearing, at least for the moment, content with their king and country. Seran mingled through the guests, smiling at young children, shaking hands with their parents. She was the perfect hostess—working the crowd like a queen.

Even though the people were clearly enjoying the festivities, the entire event was just political posturing on King Carver's part. It was all part of his master plan to impress the queen and princess, to show them how generously he treated his people and how much they loved him for it in return. Trev scoffed as he thought back to the conversation he'd had with his father earlier when he'd emerged from the mud as Tournament Champion.

"That was brilliant!" his father had said, actually clapping him on the shoulder as Crosby pulled him up and handed him a clean towel.

"Thanks," Trev had said hesitantly. He couldn't remember the last time the king had seemed happy with him.

"To see you take control of the situation with Joniss was excellent maneuvering. Joniss was the clear favorite with the people, and then you stepped in and put the attention back on yourself. Now the people see you as their strong, fearless champion. And tonight you'll seal it with a fairytale kiss between the royal lovers. I couldn't have planned it better myself."

Then the king had tightened his grip on Trev's shoulder, squeezing it uncomfortably as he leaned close and whispered, "You better be glad you didn't lose. You could have lost the election for us today."

"I knew I could win." Trev had met his father's eyes squarely and shrugged him off, careful to make the movement look accidental as he passed the towel over his arms.

Thinking back on the conversation now, Trev was alarmed by how cold and calculating his father could be. But was Trev much better? He'd had his own motives for entering the competition, and he wasn't proud of them. His reasons had nothing to do with Seran or the election and everything to do with keeping Joniss away from Renna.

"The kiss will be the finale of the evening," his father had said.

Trev wasn't looking forward to such a public display, but it was better than watching Joniss kiss Renna.

Even when he wasn't trying, his eyes always found her, like a magnet to metal. She stood across the courtyard with a group of men and, of course, Joniss was there, front and center. Each time Renna smiled up at him, Trev's stomach tensed. Surely she didn't see anything in him. But what if she did? He needed to warn her about him.

This was about friendship. It had nothing to do with jealousy. A good friend would warn her about somebody like Joniss—how he used people to get ahead and then tossed them aside when their usefulness expired.

Trev waited until she separated from the group to get a drink, then slowly made his way through the crowd to where she stood. It felt like forever since he'd had a decent conversation with her—since they'd joked on the training field.

He casually moved to her side, careful to keep his eyes on the dancing in front of them and not on Renna. "Miss Degray, are you enjoying the festival?" he asked.

Renna lowered her cup, eyeing him. "Yes, thank you."

Trev cleared his throat. "I'm glad." He noticed how her perfume lingered around him, and he secretly wondered what it would feel like to touch her.

Nope.

Never mind.

No touching, and no *thinking* about touching.

"I'm not going to dance with you," she said plainly, keeping her eyes straight ahead.

"I would be offended if you did," he quipped back.

"Well, I'd be offended if you asked me."

He raised his eyebrows at her. "I'm not going to."

"Good," she said, raising her chin.

"Good." He could see a playful gleam in her eyes and the way she bit back a smile.

They stood in silence for a moment, watching the people in front of them.

"Are *you* enjoying the party?" Renna asked, nodding toward his hiding spot behind the pillar. "Because you looked strange over there, watching everyone from the shadows."

"I was spying." He turned his head and widened his eyes

for dramatic effect. Renna snorted, giving him a rush of satisfaction. He loved to make her laugh.

"I've been thinking about the so-called spies," she said.

"Really?" That surprised him, and he turned to face her.

"Yes, really." She scrunched her nose at him. "Tolsten spies wouldn't be able to get information about your military unless someone high up told them what the plans were. I don't think your problem is spies. I think your problem is an informer."

"An informer." Trev let that sink in a moment. "You're right. I've been so blinded by everything else, but you are absolutely right. Thank you."

"You don't have to thank me. I could be wrong, you know."

"Well, if you're wrong and I make a fool of myself, I'll be sure to blame you." He nudged her with his elbow.

Oops.

No touching.

No flirting.

Trev quickly turned back to the crowd of dancing people in front of them.

"I guess congratulations are in order," she said. "I'm sure winning the tournament will help you with the election."

"I didn't do it for the election. I did it for the kiss."

"Oh." Her shoulders sank a little bit.

"No, not for the kiss," Trev stammered, trying to explain. "I meant, I did it, so Joniss wouldn't kiss yo—" He stopped himself, and their eyes met. He took a deep breath and swallowed back his real answer, replacing it with what he ought to say. "So he wouldn't kiss Seran."

Renna turned her gaze to the dancing, nodding her head dramatically. "Of course."

Trev stared at her for a moment, definitely *not* memorizing every curve of her face.

"I don't know what the big deal is between you and Joniss," she said.

Trev stiffened, reminded of the reason he was there. "That's what I wanted to talk to you about. I don't like Joniss."

"I can tell," she smirked. "You two look like you want to kill each other all the time."

"Maybe I do want to kill him." He laughed it off, hoping she sensed he was joking.

"He's not *that* bad," she said, rolling her eyes.

"You've spent a couple of hours with him. You couldn't possibly know the depths of his evilness."

"Evilness?" Her neck cocked back. "Good grief. That sounds serious."

"Why are you defending him so much?" His voice held irritation.

"He's been nice to me."

Now it was Trev's turn to roll his eyes. "None of that is genuine. He's using you. He's made you part of this stupid competition we have against each other."

Her eyebrows raised. "Is it impossible to believe that he might actually like me?"

"Trust me, I am very aware of how likable you are." He couldn't hide the bitterness in his voice. "But Joniss is trouble. I want you to stay away from him."

Renna gave a sardonic laugh. "*You* want me to stay away from him? You don't have a say in who I spend my time with."

"Renna, I'm trying to help you."

"I don't need your help," she snapped. "Instead, worry about your fiancée and what she needs."

His hand rubbed the back of his neck in frustration. That was his cue to leave.

Renna

RENNA'S ANGER flared as Trev walked away. Who did he think he was telling her who she could and couldn't spend time with? He had no claim on her. He had no say.

She took a deep breath and decided to go find Joniss. She needed his distraction.

She had thought about Trev more than once today, of course, but felt surprised by how often she had also thought about Joniss, of his flattering smile and the easy way his chest muscles tightened and relaxed as he moved so confidently in the arena. Maybe she just liked thinking about attractive men. Or maybe she had too much time on her hands to think. Either way, she couldn't deny that for the first time ever, she'd thought about Joniss in a romantic way.

She definitely found him attractive, but did she really like him? Or did she just like making Trev jealous? The answer was complicated and so was the fact that Joniss was challenging Trev for the crown. Renna didn't like aligning herself with the competition, but she wasn't going to marry Joniss. She just needed him to help pass the time in Albion.

Trev wasn't available, and Joniss was.

At least, he had been until now.

Now, Joniss completely ignored her.

It seemed like Joniss danced with every woman there except her. Renna stood in the crowd and watched as he offered his arm to a new girl each dance. And dance after dance, each girl smiled up at him like he lit the night. He walked toward Renna more than once, and her heart fluttered, expecting his wicked smile to fall on her, but each time he reached for someone else and walked away without a single glance in her direction.

She finally saw her chance as he broke from the dance floor to get a drink of water. Her stomach tingled with nerves as she thought about what to say. She wasn't good at flirting.

Just as she reached to tap his arm, he suddenly turned, accidentally colliding their bodies into one another. They shuffled awkwardly side to side as they tried to get out of each other's way.

"Is this your way of trying to dance with me?" Joniss raised an eyebrow.

She clasped her hands in front of her and nervously rocked on her toes. "I had to do something since you haven't asked me yet."

"So many women, so little time."

He winked at her, but Renna flinched at his patronizing tone. She felt a coolness from him, like he suddenly found her presence completely uninteresting. It was jarring compared to his earlier flirtation. Hadn't he said he wanted to kiss her?

Hoping to charm him into a better mood, Renna tried again, nudging him playfully. "You were really impressive in the arena today. I thought you did great."

"You can't win them all I suppose," he responded dryly, looking away from her.

She blinked. "But you *did* win. A lot. You swept all the preliminary rounds."

"*Preliminary* rounds." He scoffed. "Those mean nothing. But don't worry, the next time I go head to head with Ezra, I plan on winning."

Renna had no idea how to respond to that. She gazed up at him, his jaw set in a hard frown as he looked over the crowd and wondered where this cold Joniss had come from.

"The night is almost over, and I'm looking for more than just a dance." He glanced over her figure with a casual, assessing eye, then raised an eyebrow and smirked. "What are you offering?"

Renna swallowed. "I'm . . . only offering a dance."

"Is that all?" He leaned closer and trailed a finger down her arm, leaving goosebumps in his wake. "A dance is the beginning, Renna. What comes after?"

She stepped back, unnerved by the leering way he looked at her. "I don't know."

"Hmm." He straightened, his lips pursed together. "Other girls can offer me more than that."

Renna felt frozen to the spot, embarrassment washing over her. Something about this situation was totally unfair, but her thoughts buzzed so rapidly that she could hardly focus.

Joniss winked at her again, but this time with an edge of mockery. "I've wasted enough time today."

Jenica appeared at his side, her blonde hair draped over one shoulder. She pressed her body close to his with a coy smile.

"Officer Doman?" She curled her painted fingernails around his arm like a snake. "I know you want to dance with me."

Joniss looked down at her and smiled. He seemed interested enough in what *she* was offering. He glanced back at Renna and shrugged. "Like I said, so many women. What's a guy to do?" Then he let Jenica pull him away.

Rejection. Renna felt it in the core of her heart. She was alone, small, and insignificant. She folded her arms across her chest, wishing it wasn't the only means she had to hide herself.

A waste of time. That's how Joniss thought of her.

Where was the charming Joniss who had flirted and smoldered and made himself available whenever she needed a distraction from Trev? She needed Joniss to keep her thoughts away from unavailable princes, to firm her resolve. She was using Joniss selfishly, but that seemed inconsequential now that Jenica was wrapped in his arms.

Jenica pressed her body close and smiled up at Joniss through her lashes, seeming all too pleased to be in his arms.

Tonight, Renna had needed Joniss for a specific purpose and he had failed her.

But that wasn't even the worst part

The worst part was that Trev had been right.

The time came for the kiss. Trev and Seran stood across from each other at the front of the party. The tournament's headmaster raised Trev's arm victoriously, and the people cheered for their prince in appreciation.

Renna looked at the cheering people, at her mother and King Carver standing to the side of the couple with satisfied smiles, at Joniss with Jenica draped across his arm. Her heart squeezed painfully. The moment couldn't get much worse.

Trev bent his head and touched his lips to Seran's, lifting a hand to gently hold her face. It certainly could have been a longer kiss, but it also could have been much shorter; their lips stayed together for what seemed like an eternity to Renna.

The crowd loved it.

Renna had to look away.

Too many times, she had wondered what it would feel like to kiss Trev. Now she could ask Seran.

Trev dropped his hand, grazing the length of Seran's arm until his fingers interlocked with hers. His gentle caresses seemed *real* to Renna. Real enough to break her heart over and over again.

The couple raised their joined hands to the audience as if they had won a big prize. Or maybe *they* were the big prize.

King Carver stepped forward and hushed the crowd with his hands. "This is an important day for Albion and New Hope. For the unifying of these two great countries and the unifying of a young prince and princess. *When* you elect Prince Ezra as king in a few months, this powerful couple will lead Albion into a new age."

More cheers.

"Now, let's have more drinks and more dancing!"

Trev let go of Seran's hand and whispered something in her ear. She smiled at him shyly.

Renna turned to leave.

What was the point in staying?

24

The Informer

The dark alley stunk of garbage but was secluded from Albana's main streets, making it the perfect meeting place. Any minute now, the informer would hand off the letter to the Tolsten spy, knowing that once this information left his hands, there was little he could do to stop the consequences of its contents. So far, all the information he had handed over to Tolsten had been inconsequential. Where the Albion army planned to build a military fortress, what countries Albion was trading with, where the Albion army was stationed.

But this . . . this was different. This information would finally give Tolsten the excuse they needed to declare war against Albion.

The shadows of night hid him until the skunk appeared—the man with the white and black hair. Did he like having a thick, white stripe running through his long black hair? Did he know he looked like a skunk? These were questions he would never get answered. The man's shifty eyes and fierce expression said there would be no words between them. A simple passing of a letter. A nod of the head.

The skunk opened the letter, reading it silently.

He watched him read, tapping his toe on the dirt road

below him. He hoped the skunk would hurry so he could leave this filthy alleyway. He didn't want the smell seeping into him.

"This was all King Carver's idea?" he asked when he was done reading.

"Isn't that what the letter says?" There was a tinge of satisfaction laced between his lies.

"I just want to make sure I have the facts straight when I take this information back to King Adler."

"I haven't given you false information yet," he said, raising an eyebrow.

The man looked around before speaking again.

"We'll be in contact."

Then he disappeared in the same direction he had come from.

It was over. It would all be over soon. The thought brought a smile to his lips.

25

Renna

The front yard of the palace transformed overnight from the tournament festival into a field of games and entertainment. Activities like croquet, kickball, and tug-of-war were spread across the lawn. White chairs were placed throughout in semi-circles with tables on the edges for refreshments. Today the palace hosted children from the capital city. Renna liked this activity, a chance to run around with happy children and forget herself and her problems. It was precisely the kind of day she needed. Renna had woken up feeling depressed like there was nothing to look forward to in her life, but she refused to let that feeling take over her day. She needed to forget about herself and all her stupid *boy* problems and just focus on the children.

She waited at the steps of the palace for the children to arrive. Her mother was ahead of her with Cypress and a group of noblewomen. Renna didn't feel like joining their conversation. She looked to her left and saw Seran's friends laughing with some soldiers and other prominent young men. Luckily, Joniss wasn't among them. Renna didn't know if she could stand seeing him after last night's rejection.

"Good morning, Renna," Seran said, walking up to her

side. Her lavender dress was more casual today. The cotton fabric hung just below her knees, and she wore athletic shoes to play in.

"Good morning." Seran's genuine smile was a great reminder of why Renna needed to keep her distance from Trev.

The two women stood in silence until Renna couldn't stand it any longer and said something inappropriate.

"I saw your kiss with the prince."

Nice one.

"I think everyone did." Seran laughed. "I guess it's all part of the arranged marriage—part of the job."

"Is that what your relationship feels like to you? A job?" Renna tried to mask her hurt. Being with Trev wasn't a job or hard work. Everything between them felt easy and natural to her.

Seran met Renna's eyes and sighed. "It's difficult to feel otherwise when every moment I have with him is a public relations stunt. We've hardly had time alone together."

Renna nodded, hating the rush of relief she felt. Much as she hated to admit it, she needed things to go well between them. She needed Trev to fall madly in love with Seran, and she with him. It hurt, of course, but how else could Renna move on?

"I suppose things are going well," Seran continued. "Ezra has a lot of wonderful qualities that make us a fine match. But in other ways, I wonder if we are too different."

"How so?"

"Oh, he's silly when I'm serious, that sort of thing. But maybe that doesn't matter. Maybe our differences are a good thing." Seran shrugged. "Perhaps we will complement each other."

"Is that how it was with your parents?" Renna didn't have much experience with arranged marriages.

Seran laughed half-heartedly. "I could pretend that my

parents loved each other, but that would be a lie. They respectfully tolerated each other. I see that now that my father is with your mother. He loves Queen Mariele very much."

"I see it too," Renna admitted. "I don't think my mother loved my father the way she loves Bryant." A familiar pang of heartache pulsed inside her heart as she thought back to her father, desperately trying to win her mother's love.

"And your father?" Seran asked suddenly. "Do you think he ever loved your mother?"

"I think he did. He was kind to my mother. And patient." Renna swallowed her emotion. "I think he loved her as much as she allowed him to."

Seran smiled ruefully. "Then I suppose we should feel grateful that our parents finally found love with each other."

Grateful? Renna had never thought of it that way.

They lapsed into silence, watching a few servants in the field below battle a breeze as they set up a shade tent.

Seran was quiet for a moment, then said matter-of-factly, "I know my marriage isn't about love, but I still worry that I'll end up like your father and my mother—married to someone who will never love me back." Then, with detached emotion, she added, "The prince might even love someone else."

Renna's chest constricted. Did Seran suspect something? "I'm sure Prince Ezra isn't like that."

Seran shrugged. "I wouldn't know if he is or isn't. I barely know anything about him. But I hope you're right."

The palace door opened behind them and they both turned. Trev emerged, wearing fitted, black athletic pants and a blue t-shirt that made his eyes pop more than usual.

Seran greeted him with a full smile.

"Good morning, ladies," he said, glancing briefly at Renna before kissing Seran's cheek. Then he turned his attention on everywhere else but Renna. He was obviously trying to avoid her after the way they had left things last night.

The gates down the driveway opened up in front of them,

letting six palace transporters in. Little heads popped out the open windows as the children tried to get a better view of the palace. Against her better judgment, Renna stole a glance at Trev. He waved at the vehicles, showing his charming, boyish grin.

He was cute—obnoxiously and excruciatingly cute.

Trev

Bringing school children to the palace was another brilliant idea from somebody on his father's staff. Let the public see how excellent Princess Seran and Prince Ezra are with children. Real life at the palace wasn't really like this. Inside, men were brainstorming ways to attack the world's most threatening kingdom, while Trev was outside playing kickball. He hated missing those meetings. His father was pushing for revenge on Tolsten. Trev needed to be there to talk some sense into him, but he didn't have a choice. He was the host for the children's field trip.

Somehow Trev found himself in the middle of a game of tag. The kids loved trying to get him as he darted in and out, dodging little hands. Seran stood timidly on the sidelines, smiling and laughing at his antics. He was keenly aware of Renna across the lawn watching him as well, but he avoided her. Was she still mad at him for warning her about Joniss? He hated the way they had left things, but there was nothing he could do about it now. Now, his duty was to Seran.

"When I say go," he told a group of kids huddled around him, "I want everyone to run to Princess Seran and tickle her."

They nodded in excitement.

"Ready? Go!"

The children shrieked and burst toward her.

Seran squealed with wide eyes. She tried to jog away, but Trev was faster and quickly caught her around the waist.

"Tickle her!" he yelled.

The children descended in a mess of little bodies, fingers, and giggles. Trev let go of Seran and managed to wriggle out of the children's grasp as they focused on the princess. Seran dropped to her knees and tried to shield herself with her arms, laughing and begging for mercy. The children only tickled harder.

After a few seconds, Seran pointed desperately to Renna, who stood twenty feet from them, watching the spectacle. "It's Miss Degray's turn," she said. "Go get Miss Degray!"

Renna's eyes flew wide open. She started to back away, shaking her head comically. Laughing, the children broke away from Seran and charged toward Renna, tackling her until they all toppled to the ground. Renna laughed from the bottom of the pile.

"Oh dear." Seran chuckled, still on her knees. "You better go call them off."

Trev hesitated. He had purposely avoided Renna all morning. He offered his hand to help Seran stand. "I'm sure she doesn't need our help."

"Those kids will never release her, and it's my fault." Seran laughed, accepting his hand. She rose gracefully, then reached down to beat a few blades of grass from her skirt. "Go help her."

Trev nodded, reluctantly making his way to the pile of kids. "All right, all right. Give Miss Degray a break."

The children groaned, but dutifully scattered, leaving Renna sprawled out on the grass, her face flushed, her hair mussed, and a bright smile on her lips. She looked up at him, her green eyes glimmering in their playful way. "I think they won."

"It looks like it," was all Trev dared to say. He held his hand out to help her up, knowing that when her skin touched his, everything inside him would feel it. Their fingers touched, and their eyes locked, the spark between them bursting to life.

"You're good with them," she said through heavy breaths as she stood, not pulling her hand away immediately.

"I don't know about that." Trev shrugged. He let his fingers slowly slide over her palm as he released it.

He stared at her for one long moment, unsure what to say but *wanting* to say so much. He wanted to tell her he was sorry for upsetting her last night. He wanted to explain that the thought of her with Joniss tore him up inside. He wanted her to understand that she was the best thing that had ever happened to him—and the worst.

Renna broke the silence first. "I'm sorry I snapped at you last night."

"No." He shook his head apologetically. "I shouldn't have gotten involved in your personal life."

"True," Renna said, "but you were right about Joniss. He was just using me."

Trev couldn't hide his smile.

"Oh, don't look so happy about it." Renna rolled her eyes.

"I'm not!" But his laugh gave him away.

A little boy missing his two front teeth appeared at Renna's side and tugged her arm, breaking the moment. "Come play with me, Miss Renna," he begged.

"Colter," Renna smiled at the scrawny boy, "have you met Prince Ezra yet?"

"No, I don't care about the prince," the boy said, still tugging on Renna's arm as he looked up at Trev. "I just want to play with you."

Trev raised his eyebrows in amusement. "I know how you feel. I just want to play with Miss Renna too."

Renna dropped her eyes, alerting him to the fact that he shouldn't have said that. He tried to change the subject. "Where do you live, Colter?"

"My momma and papa live by the market square. They sell squash and zucchini and sometimes tomatoes if they aren't bad."

"When I was your age, my momma and papa sold vegetables too," Renna said, bending down so she matched his height.

Colter's eyes lit up. "They must've sold a lot of vegetables because now you live at the palace."

Renna laughed. "I don't live here. I'm just visiting."

"Like me!" Colter beamed.

"Just like you." Renna tousled his long brown hair.

"Do you wish you lived here?" the boy asked.

She shook her head, glancing up at Trev. "I don't belong here."

Trev hated the truth in her words.

Colter scrunched his nose. "Momma says I don't belong here either. I'm too dirty."

Renna frowned. "You look clean to me."

"My teacher scrubbed me clean so I could come, but Momma says it was a waste of time."

Trev caught the concerned look in Renna's eyes.

"Can we play now?" Colter tugged on her arm again.

"Yes." Renna smiled back at him and let the boy's small strength pull her away across the field to another game. Trev's eyes followed her retreating back as he breathed out one long, deep sigh.

Tearing his gaze from Renna, Trev turned to his right and his eyes locked with Queen Mariele's. She sat under a shade tent, methodically waving a small fan back and forth in front of her face to keep cool. But her eyes watched him.

Trev inclined his head respectfully, though his stomach twisted. How long had she been watching him? He thought back through his actions all morning: he had been with Seran, *played* with Seran, until the brief moment she had asked him to help Renna. He hadn't done anything wrong—at least not today—but the queen's gaze felt heavy with suspicion just the same.

He needed to find Seran.

With little searching, Trev found her kneeling under a tree, braiding a little girl's hair who looked no more than seven or eight-years-old. Her gray school dress was too big, hanging over her thin body and crisscrossed legs like a blanket.

"It's Prince Ezra!" The little girl squirmed excitedly as Trev approached. She tried to bow her head, but with her brown hair already in Seran's hands, she couldn't move much.

"Hello." He swept into a gallant bow. "What's your name?"

"Nalissy."

"What a beautiful name."

"That's exactly what I thought." Seran smiled at him. "I told Nalissy that I would do her hair like a princess today."

"Aren't I lucky?" Nalissy beamed.

"Very lucky." Trev looked past the girl to see if Queen Mariele was still watching him. She was.

He plopped down on the grass behind Seran. "Well, if Princess Seran gets to do your hair, then I should be able to do Princess Seran's hair."

Seran turned her dark eyes toward him. "I don't know if I can trust you. A princess must always look her best."

"Oh, please let Prince Ezra do your hair," Nalissy pleaded.

Seran leaned into the little girl. "How can I resist you? I suppose it's all right then."

Trev started combing his fingers through Seran's hair, noticing how the smooth strands were like silk against his fingers. The whole scene with Seran and the little girl surprised him. He hadn't pictured her playing with children. She seemed too refined for that.

"Am I invited to your wedding?" Nalissy asked.

Seran smiled at Trev, then answered, "I don't think so, but I promise we'll wave to you from the palace balcony afterward."

Trev twisted Seran's hair as if he knew what he was doing.

"The wedding is in three weeks. Can you believe it?" He tried to ignore the sick feeling in his stomach.

"It definitely feels surreal. Everyone has been talking about it for ten years. Now it's finally happening."

He let out a breath, hoping it didn't sound as heavy as he felt. "I know what you mean."

"I suppose we'll be busy the next few months with the election approaching. My advisors say we're going on a few city tours . . . to promote the alliance."

"That's the plan. If it's okay with you, of course." Trev had never asked Seran what she wanted to do after they were married.

"It's okay with me," Nalissy chirped, clapping her hands in front of her.

Seran reached forward and nudged the small girl. "If it is okay with Nalissy, then it's okay with me. I'm happy to do whatever is necessary for the election."

He bit his lip. "You know, there's a chance I won't win, even with you by my side. Joniss is extremely popular."

Seran worked a braid through Nalissy's hair. "I know. My father prepared me for that possibility."

"What does your father think if I lose? I'm guessing that would make me a disappointing choice in husband for his only daughter."

"It would be a bit of a shock, I'm sure. But, if you lost, we would go back to New Hope, establish a presence there, and then you or I could run for king or queen when my father's reign is up."

Trev didn't like that plan. How would he ever get over Renna if he had to live so near her?

Seran continued, clearly oblivious to the battle raging inside him. "The more I get to know you, the more I am convinced that you will win Albion's election. Joniss has some popularity, but he doesn't have my country backing him."

Trev released the hair twist, letting Seran's black hair fall onto her back. "That's what my father says."

"King Carver!" Nalissy interjected, picking up bits and pieces of their conversation.

"I believe in you," Seran said. "And I will stand by you. I'll help you win the election. And together, we'll rule the kingdom honorably."

He appreciated Seran's loyalty and unwavering support, but it came with a fresh dose of guilt centered around Renna. On paper, it all seemed so perfect. So easy. But nothing about Trev's situation felt easy.

He spent the next hour with Seran and Nalissy talking about silly things, laughing, and playing until the transporters arrived to take the children back into the city. Seran waved at the little arms and hands stretching out from the windows until they all disappeared down the royal drive and out the gates.

"That was fun," she said as they walked back across the lawn toward the palace, servants already bustling around them to collapse tents and gather up lawn games. "Usually I'm not fun in settings like these."

Trev shook his head. "I thought you did great."

Seran hesitated like she was trying to find the right words. "Sometimes I worry so much about being dignified that I don't connect well with people. I try so hard to be a princess that I forget to be a person."

"I think everyone struggles to be themselves in front of others."

"You don't seem to, and neither does Renna. She's always herself. You're very similar in that way, and I sometimes wonder if you would have been better suited marrying someone with a personality like hers."

Trev's stomach dropped. How was he supposed to respond to that? "Renna and I do get along well. She's easy to talk to, so we've become friends." At least, he was *trying* to put her in the friend category; he wasn't making much progress. "But if our friendship makes you feel uncomfortable, I can . . ." What? Try harder? Lock her in her room? Put a blindfold on whenever she was near, so he didn't notice the nuances of her facial expressions? There was no right answer.

"I can avoid her," he said finally.

I think.

"That won't be necessary." She pursed her lips together into a slight smile. "Renna is harmless."

He was starting to think she didn't know Renna that well because she definitely wasn't harmless. She was harming his thoughts, his sleep, his work—pretty much every aspect of his life.

Seran straightened. "I just hope that I can complement your life in the way you need me to."

Trev tried to offer a reassuring smile. "I hope to do the same for you."

Seran nodded before changing the subject. "Any word about the missing girls from Axville?" The concern in her eyes was apparent.

Trev shook his head. "Nothing yet. We sent a letter to King Adler last week, but it's still too soon to have received his response. I don't want to go to war with Tolsten. I just want to resolve this peacefully."

She gave him a reassuring smile. "I'm sure it will all work out."

They reached the palace courtyard, and Seran grabbed his hand, lacing her fingers through his. Besides the fake kiss, they had never touched this intimately before. Trev wanted to like the way her hand fit in his. He wanted to like the feel of her skin against his. He wanted to feel something, but the gesture felt forced.

Is this how the rest of his life would feel?

26

Renna

Renna craned her neck to see out the transporter window as the vehicle rolled to a stop.

"I'm so happy to get out of the palace!" Jenica said, fluffing her hair, preparing for their exit. "We've been cooped up in the palace for two days while Seran got to have all the fun."

"I don't think Seran would say visiting nearby estates for the past two days was fun," Lizanne said.

"But Prince Ezra accompanied her; I'm sure *something* fun happened. If you know what I mean." A guard opened the door and reached for Jenica's hand.

Patiently, Renna waited for her turn to exit the transporter so she could get a look at Albana's market day. Dying grass crunched below her shoes as she stepped out of the vehicle. Tables and stands were set up in rows with products skillfully displayed, enticing prospective customers over. Market peddlers lined the edges, their pushcarts full of goods and supplies. The sounds of buyers haggling over prices filled the square, adding to Renna's eagerness.

As a young girl, she'd loved going to market day in Vassel with her father. She would help him set up their booth and attractively align their crops so customers could see what they offered.

Today's market day was different. Renna had arrived in a transporter with the royal entourage, flanked by palace guards. There were no goods to sell or trade, no bottom line that her father had to earn to keep their household running through the winter. Instead, Renna would spend a few hours shopping at the market—just for the fun of it. The stark contrast with her old life sent a wave of guilt over her.

Renna slowed her steps, letting the group of girls walk ahead of her. The crowd around her was dense, forcing her to turn down the first aisle of goods. Ahead of her, Trev and Seran stopped at a vendor, rummaging through hats. Trev's back was to her, but everything about the ordinary moment paralyzed Renna. She couldn't move, only watch.

"How much for this hat?" Trev asked the seller, picking up a straw hat with a black ribbon.

"No!" Seran protested.

"Why? You'd look cute in it." He placed the hat atop Seran's head and nodded to himself.

Seran twisted her shoulder and dipped her chin in a brief pose.

"See," Trev said, slightly adjusting the hat. "You look amazing."

Something about the way Trev complimented Seran scraped Renna's heart like the ground skinned her knees whenever she fell as a child.

"I don't know. What do you think, Renna?" Seran looked past Trev right at her.

Trev turned around, his sapphire eyes showing something like embarrassment.

"I think," Renna said, swallowing the ache in her heart, "the hat suits you."

Seran shrugged at the vendor. "I suppose if Prince Ezra likes it, then I'll get it."

"Great." Trev forced a smile, handing the man some money for the hat.

"What about you, Renna?" Seran pointed to the table. "Would you like a hat? I'm sure Ezra won't mind."

Renna shook her head. "You don't need to buy me anything."

"I would love to buy you something," Trev said with intense eyes that awakened butterflies in Renna's stomach.

"What about a bracelet?" Seran offered, pointing to the table next to them.

She backed away from them. "Really, I'm good."

"I know what Renna needs." Trev's eyes lit up with excitement. "Follow me."

Renna followed hesitantly after him, partly to avoid being rude and partly out of curiosity. They stopped in front of trays of rolls and frosted bread lining a table. The sweet scent of fresh-baked dough wafted around her.

"Which one do you want?" Trev gestured to the table with a knowing smile.

"You really don't need to buy me anything." Renna hated how he knew her so well. Hated and loved it.

"Pick one!" Trev snapped playfully.

"Cinnamon!" Renna snapped, biting back her smile.

"See? That wasn't so hard." He turned to Seran. "Which one would you like?"

"Raisin, please," Seran said with perfect politeness.

The three of them continued down the row of vendors, Trev in the middle of the two women. They ate their rolls in a silence that nearly choked Renna. She needed to escape the royal couple before the anguish of her situation swallowed her whole. A pair of men walked toward them on the opposite side of the aisle, making it impossible for Renna to break away. A shove pushed her toward the men, putting her directly in their way. The men stumbled to a halt, visibly surprised by the woman who had so clumsily bumped into them.

Renna awkwardly shuffled around them. "I'm so sorry!" she said through a mouthful of bread as the men walked away, shaking their heads at her.

She looked at Trev, trying to figure out how she had ended up in front of the men in the first place.

"Wow," Trev said with a serious face. "You really need to watch where you're going."

Renna's face turned red with embarrassment. She wanted to slug him in the shoulder or push him back, but she was keenly aware of Seran standing next to him with a stunned expression.

Trev looked at the princess, a playful glimmer in his eyes. "Man, you can't take Renna anywhere. Is she always like this?"

Seran released a small laugh, almost too small to even be heard. She wrapped her fingers around Trev's forearm as she walked. "Poor Renna. You really shouldn't tease her like that."

"I don't know what you're talking about," Trev replied innocently.

Renna may not be able to punch him, but that didn't mean she couldn't get even another way. "You know, Seran, it's a shame your father didn't form an alliance with Appa," Renna said casually, hoping Seran picked up on her cues. "You could've been engaged to King Reddick instead."

"Yes, I hear he's very handsome," Seran said with a serious tone.

Trev scoffed. "Not more handsome than me."

Renna looked at him pointedly. "Definitely more handsome than you."

Trev's brows bent together in offense.

"What about King Davin in Enderlin?" Seran added, leaning around Trev to speak to Renna. "He's very attractive."

"He's like fifteen years older than you," Trev whined. "And married."

"Ah, yes," Renna teased. "He's old, wise, and good looking —a triple threat."

"I can't believe you guys," Trev pouted, throwing his hands into the air. "I'm clearly the best choice for a husband."

Renna pretended to look Trev over. He stopped walking, and slowly spun around in a circle, giving them a good look at every angle.

"I don't know, Seran. What do you think?"

Seran let out a heavy breath like she was disappointed. "I suppose he'll have to do."

"No way." He shook his head. "I'm the most eligible bachelor."

Then Trev started dancing in between them, moving his hips back and forth, waving his arms in the air. Renna glanced at the people around them, eyeing their prince like he was insane. Even Seran looked like she thought he was crazy.

"I bet King Reddick can't dance like this." He shimmied his shoulders in front of Renna. "We *know* King Davin can't dance like this."

"Because he's too old?" Renna asked, rolling her lips together to suppress a laugh.

"Exactly!" Trev stepped in front of a stranger, an older woman with a scarf tied on her head. He bowed in front of her, then grabbed her hands swinging her in and out, like they were dancing in a ballroom.

Seran gave Renna a sideways look, amusement brimming in her eyes. "Now we've really pushed him too far."

Trev put his arm around the woman's waist, dropping her backward into a dip. His free arm went into the air above his head forming a dramatic final pose. The audience around them clapped and cheered as Trev raised the woman up and kissed her hand.

He turned to Renna with his big smile and expressive eyes. "See? I'm a catch."

Renna's heart fluttered. She was totally falling for Trev,

even though she knew she would get burned in a crash landing. Then she saw the mischievous smile and wink he gave Seran and the flutters in her heart went up in flames. Suddenly she wished she was anywhere but here with the two of them. She was the third wheel. The friend.

She'd always known that would be her place, but the knowledge didn't make the reality hurt less.

She moved toward a booth selling pre-Desolation relics. This was Renna's chance to escape them. Her fingers grazed over several items: a cracked pair of sunglasses, a twisted aluminum can with the words *Diet Coke* written on the side, a rusted screwdriver.

"Miss Renna, you came to visit me!" a small voice said, bubbling with excitement.

Renna turned to see Colter and his toothless grin beaming at her. He was almost unrecognizable. His clean clothes were gone, replaced by torn brown rags. His sunken face was smeared with dirt and grime.

"Colter?" Renna looked around for his parents. "What are you doing here?"

"I told you. My papa sells vegetables."

"Hey, Colter!" Trev said, waving at the boy.

Colter rolled his eyes. "Why are you always with the prince?"

Renna exchanged an awkward glance with Seran.

"Because I'm the host." Trev's answer eased the tension in Renna's chest. "Have you met Princess Seran?"

Renna noticed the way his hand went to the small of Seran's back as he introduced her. A small gesture that left a big hole in her already aching heart.

Colter gazed at Seran. "You're pretty."

Even a seven-year-old was taken by Seran's beauty.

Seran smiled. "You're very handsome yourself."

Colter's eyes lit up at the compliment. "Do you want to see our booth?" His dirty hand grabbed Renna's. "Come on."

Renna let the boy weave them in and out of the crowd. At the end of the far row was a broken-down wood table with a stack of rotting vegetables scattered on top—vegetables that only a desperate person would eat.

"See!" Colter said proudly. "Here's our booth."

A short man with hollow cheekbones came out from behind a tattered curtain.

"This is my papa," Colter said.

"Hello." Trev gave a warm smile to the man.

"What's this about, boy?"

"Miss Renna came to see us, Papa. I told you she was like us. Her papa used to sell vegetables too." Colter smiled up at his father with childlike innocence.

The man looked Renna up and down with disgust. Her clean, mint green dress suddenly felt overdone and out of place.

"She ain't anything like us." The man spat a seed out of his mouth onto the ground by Renna's foot. It was all she could do not to jerk her foot back.

"And who are you?" The man nodded at Trev and Seran.

"He's the prince!" Colter said with pride.

Trev offered his hand to Colter's father. "Ezra Trevenna, and this is Seran Haslet."

The man licked his chapped lips, his eyes never leaving Trev's, but he didn't shake his hand. "He's not my prince. Ain't done nothing for me."

Trev's hand dropped along with his smile. "Well, I'm here now. How can I help?"

"Help, huh?" The man let out a rough laugh. "Just in time for the election." He held the curtain open and nodded at his son. "Get inside the house, boy."

Colter frowned but obeyed his father, walking into the small shack behind the booth. Renna could see a pile of kids sitting on the dirt ground behind the curtain watching them. *That* was their house? That small, wooden lean-to, blasted with holes and missing a wall? How could they possibly live there? Renna's own father sold crops for a living, but they never lived like this. Wellenbreck Farm looked like a palace compared to this shack.

"Bye, Miss Renna."

"Bye, Colter." Renna tried to smile. "It was nice to see you again."

"You all best be gettin' back to your privileged life. We don't want to get those fancy clothes of yours dirty in the real world."

"Perhaps we can buy some vegetables from you," Renna offered.

Colter's father gave a cynical laugh. "If you really want to do something," his eyes narrowed in on Trev, "start makin' things equal between the ruling class and the working class. There's a big gap in what's essential between your kind and mine."

"We all have the same basic essential needs," Trev said. "Perhaps you and I aren't that different."

"Food is essential to me. Not parties and colored clothes."

"Here's some money so you can buy food for your family." Trev pulled out several coins from his pocket and placed them on the table.

"What a good guy you are," the man sneered. "You've taken care of one family for a month. What about the rest of the working-class families like mine? Are you going to throw some coins at them too?"

"We'll try to help them however we can," Seran said while she pulled on Trev's arm to leave.

Renna took one last look at the haggard man, the hardships of life clearly carved into the creases on his face.

"What an awful man!" Seran said when they walked far enough away.

"I don't think he's awful," Renna argued. "I think he's hungry and tired of working so hard for nothing."

Seran smoothed her hair as she spoke. "Well, perhaps if he applied himself more, his family wouldn't be living in poverty."

Renna reared her head back. "How can you say that? Maybe he has no other options. Maybe he's doing all he can within a corrupt system. What's the Council of Essentials good for if it can't even guarantee food and decent shelter for everyone?"

Seran bristled. "The Council of Essentials can't be blamed for someone's poverty."

Renna shook her head. Seran would never understand. She had grown up in luxury, sheltered from the harsh realities of life. What about Trev? Could he see how messed up everything was?

She turned to him. "You're going to be king. Surely there is something you can do for families like that."

A sad expression crossed over his face. "There's poverty in every kingdom, Renna. It's been this way since . . . forever. I'm not sure how to fix it."

Renna let out a frustrated breath. "What's the point of being king if you can't even help people?"

Trev shrugged, and his lips turned down. He looked at her, holding her gaze. "I don't know."

Few things had ever left Renna as unsettled as the hopelessness written across Trev's face.

27

Queen Mariele

The pacing had to stop. Queen Mariele knew it the moment she looked down and saw the clear path she'd tread across the rug. What would the servants think when they saw it? Feeling embarrassed, she forced herself to sit at her desk and go over the treaty documents her advisors had sent for approval, but even that didn't seem to help.

She looked at the clock again. It was well past ten a.m. She'd sent Cypress out to fetch Mangum at least a half-hour ago. Where were they?

She wasn't sure that she wanted to hear what Mangum had to say, but she had to get to the bottom of this. Ever since she'd seen Renna talking with the prince on the night of the festival, Mariele's suspicions had deepened. She'd noticed a closeness between them, one that she couldn't easily dismiss, and it frightened her. Then with the children, and yesterday at the Albion market, it all seemed so obvious. Renna had feelings for the prince of Albion. But, did the prince have feelings for her?

Mariele's stomach churned at the thought. What would Bryant and the rest of New Hope think of their new queen if her daughter usurped the marriage alliance for herself? She needed Mangum to tell her that she had this all wrong. She desperately hoped he would.

A knock sounded at the door, interrupting her thoughts. It was the knock she had been waiting for. She rose from her chair and clasped her hands together to keep them from shaking.

Cypress entered and dipped into a low curtsey. "He's in the hallway, Your Majesty. Would you like me to send him in?"

"Thank you, Cypress."

Cypress nodded and disappeared back out the doorway. A moment later, she appeared again with Mangum beside her, his face drawn. He stepped forward and bowed as Cypress closed the door behind them.

"I want to ask you something, Mangum, and I demand your complete honesty," Mariele said.

"Of course, Your Majesty." He bowed again.

"The man you found with Renna by Wellenbreck Pond. Have you seen him here at the palace?"

He nodded.

"Who is he?"

The shame in his eyes gave it away before he spoke. "It was Prince Ezra."

Mariele had expected this, had tried to prepare herself, but hearing her suspicions confirmed sent a shock through her just the same. She gasped, letting go of a breath she didn't realize she'd been holding, and lowered herself back into her chair.

"And you didn't think to tell me?"

Mangum dipped his face down with guilt. "I didn't realize he was the prince until we arrived in Albion. I wanted to tell you, but Renna begged me not to. She said that her and the prince were just friends and that she knew her place. She didn't want to worry you."

A bright flare of anger shot through her. "You should have told me, Mangum. It's not your place to decide what I, *your queen*, should or should not worry about."

Mangum stood rigidly with his arms at his sides. "I made a serious mistake, Your Majesty. I have failed you."

"Who else knows about this? King Carver?"

"I don't believe King Carver suspects anything. But your daughter's maid . . ." He paused, looking in Cypress's direction.

"She's fine to hear whatever you have to say."

"Renna's maid told me that Renna received a note and a gift a few nights ago. I searched Renna's belongings when she went down to breakfast and found the note."

Mangum pulled a small, folded piece of paper from the inside of his jacket and handed it to Queen Mariele.

Shooting Cypress a worried look, Mariele unfolded the letter and began to read. With each word, her chest tightened, constricting the airflow to her lungs.

"The letter is signed by Tybolt. Not from the prince." Mariele looked up at Mangum questioningly.

"Mr. Tybolt wasn't at the palace that night. When Nora was coming down the hall, she saw Prince Ezra's personal assistant, Crosby, leave Renna's room. I believe the letter is from Prince Ezra; he was just smart enough not to sign his name."

Mariele's eyes scanned each word of the letter. *Normally, I would compliment you on how beautiful you looked tonight at dinner...I wished you were sitting next to me...I think about spending time with you again.* She grabbed at her throat as the meaning of the letter sank in. The room started spinning like she might faint.

Cypress rushed to her side. "My queen! Are you okay?"

"I . . . I . . . can't . . . breathe . . ." Her words were shallow.

Cypress knelt in front of her, forcing Mariele to look her in the eyes. "Breathe with me." Cypress sucked in slowly then pushed the air out of her lungs dramatically. "In and out."

The queen followed Cypress's every action until her breathing became a little steadier.

"Come, Your Majesty. You should lie down," Cypress said,

shooting a pointed look at Mangum. He sprang into action, assisting the queen to her bed.

"Perhaps we should finish this conversation later," he said as Cypress pulled the covers back and gently helped Mariele into the soft sheets.

"No. I need to . . . speak . . . to Renna." Each word was surrounded by deliberate, heavy breaths.

Mangum and Cypress exchanged a glance.

"I think you should rest awhile, Your Majesty," Cypress said softly.

"Renna. Get . . . Renna." There was no time. Renna was going to ruin the marriage alliance for New Hope. Bryant would never forgive her. She would lose him again. Didn't Cypress understand that?

No, she needed to talk to Renna now, even if she could barely find the breath to get the words out.

Mariele closed her eyes, trying to shut out her worry. It only felt like a few seconds, but when she opened her eyes again, Renna was there. She must have dozed off.

"Mother, are you ill?" Renna's face was full of concern as she knelt by the side of her bed.

Mariele brought her hands up from her sides and wrung them together distractedly. "I've had devastating news."

"What is it? Is everything all right?"

Mariele glanced at her nightstand where the letter sat unfolded and crumpled; Renna's eyes followed. Recognition washed over her face as she picked up the letter.

"You went through my things?" Renna's voice was small, sadness falling from every word.

Mariele propped herself up on her elbows, waving away Cypress's murmured protests. She needed strength to say this. She needed Renna to understand. "Prince Ezra will marry Seran."

Renna didn't reply, her eyes focused on the letter in her lap.

"This has to stop," Mariele said with all the authority she could muster.

"There's nothing to stop."

"That's what you said at Wellenbreck." She shook her head with frustration. "But now I find out you've spent time with him since we've been at the palace. Do you deny that?"

Her eyes flicked to the ground. "No."

Mariele let out a whimper as she collapsed back against the pillows. "This is bad, Renna! What if King Carver finds out? What if Seran finds out?" She grabbed Renna's arm and squeezed it urgently. "Seran will tell Bryant. They'll throw me out again. I can't face it. I can't do it again."

"What do you mean they'll throw you out *again*?" Renna questioned.

Mariele clamped her mouth shut. She had already said too much—more than she'd ever planned to.

"Mom, what do you mean they'll throw you out again? Who will throw you out?"

Perhaps it was time to tell Renna the truth. How else could she understand the consequences of falling for a prince?

Renna

THE WORDS WERE hanging on the tip of her mother's lips, but still the queen didn't speak. Renna placed her hand on her mother's arm as though she could prod the words out of her. "Mom, tell me what you're talking about. Tell me who threw you out."

Mariele gave a shuddered sigh. "My father was in government, and my family took up residence in the capital so that he could work under King Dayton."

Renna found herself leaning in, her interest piqued. She didn't know that her mother had once lived at the Government Center.

"I was only fifteen, and I was in awe of the New Hope

Government Center. The wealth, the parties, and especially . . ." Her eyes dropped. "Especially the prince. Bryant was eighteen at the time. We were young, stupid, and after two years of sneaking around, wildly in love."

Renna swallowed hard. Why had her mother never told her this before?

"Bryant was the younger brother. He wasn't supposed to be elected king. I was all that mattered to him."

Renna bit her lip, her nerves rising. She wanted to hear her mother's story. She wanted answers, but somehow she knew the truth would hurt.

Her mother continued. "Then things started to unravel. Bryant's older brother came down with a terrible fever. Within a few days, he was gone. King Dayton's thirty-year reign would be ending in the next few years and Bryant was now the only choice in their family to go after the crown. To help Bryant win the election, King Dayton entered into a marriage contract with the kingdom of Northland. Bryant was to marry Princess Isadora. The walls were closing in on us, and we were desperate. So we made our move and ran away together." She shook her head, scoffing. "We were so foolish. We had no money, nowhere to go, and no feasible plan."

So many questions gnawed at Renna, but she let her mother keep talking.

"We didn't get very far, of course. We didn't even make it out of the city before a group of guards found us and dragged us back to the Government Center."

Mariele paused, then spoke again in a quiet voice, as though the memory frightened her. "The king was furious. Bryant had almost ruined his chances in the election and had jeopardized the marriage contract between New Hope and Northland."

"We told the king how much we loved each other, begged him to let us be together, but he refused. Within a week, he fired my father from his government position and married me off to one of his soldiers."

"Kimball Degray," Renna said softly.

Mariele nodded. "To save the prince's reputation, King Dayton ordered us as far away from New Hope—and Bryant—as possible. The Degrays owned a small farm property on the east edge of the kingdom, and we were sent to live there. At Wellenbreck." Her eyes pooled with tears. "A couple of months later, Bryant married Isadora. I was devastated. Three years later, he was elected king."

This was a lot to take in, to process. Her mind spun, but Renna settled on a safe question. "Did you ever hear from Bryant again?"

"Yes. There were letters."

"What letters?"

"Cypress helped Bryant get letters to me." She flashed a small, grateful look at Cypress standing at the foot of the bed. "Bryant still loved me, but his brother had died. His family wanted him to be the next king, whether he liked it or not. We couldn't run away together. We were both married, and he was about to have a child."

Seran, Renna thought.

"So we wrote to each other, year after year, and hoped that one day we would be together again."

"Did Dad know about the letters?" Renna asked curtly.

"I believe he did," Mariele admitted. "But he never said anything to me about it."

"Why him?" Renna asked, her words clipped. "Did King Dayton just choose my father randomly from a regiment of soldiers?"

"Your father volunteered. Kimball insisted that it was an honor to serve his country this way."

"I don't understand." Renna shook her head, her voice rising slightly. "Why would he do that? Why would he sacrifice his entire life for you?"

"He . . ." Mariele faltered, tears slowly falling from her eyes. "He was Bryant's friend, and . . . and mine. He wanted to help us."

Renna's thoughts whirled. She thought back on her father, how she watched him care for her mother over the years, how he comforted and quieted her during her anxious fits and silently carried her responsibilities when she fell into gloom. Years of this, and all because he wanted to help?

There had to be more. "Was he in love with you?"

Mariele didn't answer, but the guilt in her eyes told Renna everything. Her father had married a woman he loved to save her, hoping she would love him one day, too. But she never had. Renna breathed in sharply as a stab of pain pierced her heart.

"Renna." Mariele shifted and reached for her hand, squeezing it earnestly. Renna let her but didn't squeeze back. "Your father was an incredible man. I appreciated him, I respected him—"

"But you didn't love him." A stray tear trickled down Renna's face—unnoticed and unwanted.

"I loved him with all I had left to give." Mariele squeezed Renna's hand again, pleading.

Renna pulled her hand away. "So I guess everything worked out nicely when Dad died." Renna couldn't keep the bitterness from her voice.

"That's not fair." Her mother's eyes flickered to hers.

Renna raised her eyebrows in skepticism.

Mariele's brows narrowed. "I don't expect you to forgive me for the way I treated your father, but you could try to see things from my perspective. I was heartbroken and miserable for years. I wasn't good enough for Bryant, I wasn't the wife your father hoped I would be, and I wasn't the mother you needed. I was never enough, and I had to face that every day."

"You don't have to tell me. My whole childhood revolved around your misery."

"Yes, I made a mess of things. I put my love for Bryant over everything else in my life, but my circumstances were difficult. I was devoted to Bryant for almost three years before they married me off to your father. How could I ever be expected to love Kimball?"

Renna stared blankly at her mother. Kimball Degray was the best man Renna had ever known. "He loved you," she whispered, feeling a piece of her sadness for her father drop with a tear. "Why did you treat him so badly? Why couldn't you love him back?"

"Your father knew what he was signing up for. He knew I loved Bryant." Mariele's voice was rising, her words coming out in heavy breaths. "You judge me, yet you are doing the exact same thing I did. Sneaking around with Prince Ezra behind everyone's backs. But what you're doing is worse. The prince is already promised to Seran."

"I'm not sneaking around with Prince Ezra," Renna said, her defenses rising.

"You're going to ruin everything!" her mother practically shouted in a haze of panic. "Seran will be furious. I'll lose Bryant again."

Cypress rushed to her side, a pill and a cup of water in her hands. "Here. Take this, my lady."

Mariele's shaky hand brought the cup to her mouth, letting the water wash the pill away. It wouldn't take long for the pill to work its magic, and Renna's mother would be lost to oblivion.

"They said I wasn't good enough for Bryant. They sent me away." Her mother's voice sounded thick like she had to dig the words from tar at the back of her throat. Her eyelids flopped closed. "You're not good enough for Prince Ezra. We need to send you away."

"Mom!" Renna wasn't done talking. "Mom!"

"Not good enough for the prince . . ." her mother whispered before finally letting the drug take her.

"Why did you give her that?" Renna snapped at Cypress.

Cypress glared at her. "Can't you see what your actions have done to her? She's having another one of her episodes, thanks to you! My job is to protect the queen. Her nerves needed to rest." Renna watched as Cypress dramatically threw a blanket over her mother. "You've gone too far this time, Renna, trying to get the prince to fall in love with you. You are just like your father, pining after something that isn't yours!"

So many emotions tumbled around inside of Renna, but anger presented itself first. "How dare you talk about my father. You think because you bring my mother her tea every day that you know all about my parents and their relationship, but you don't."

Renna stood, towering over Cypress's shrinking body.

"I don't have to answer to you for anything. If my mother wants to see me, she can find me when she wakes up. That is, if you ever stop drugging her." Renna slammed the door behind her as she left.

Her body slid against the door until it hit the ground. Tears fell freely as her head dropped between her knees. The pieces of her life fit together now, but it was no consolation. She cried for her father, for his hope of a love that was never returned. She cried for her mother's broken heart and her years of misery and loneliness. And she cried for herself—for the lies told to her and the lies she had told herself.

28

Renna

Applause echoed across the palace's Great Hall, jarring Renna from her thoughts as the audience stood from their chairs to pay respect to the evening's entertainment. Clapping her hands unconsciously, she looked around at the performers. They were bowing in appreciation. Renna had managed to zone out during the night's entire musical performance. Actually, she had zoned out during all of dinner as well.

Queen Mariele had missed dinner altogether. Renna made her excuses, telling the king her mother wasn't feeling well. Renna wondered what had upset her mother the most—the fact that she had feelings for Trev or that her mother had finally had to reveal her dirty secrets. Eventually, Renna would forgive her mother, but for now, she was grateful for her absence. She needed space and time to sort through her own feelings of betrayal and anger.

Renna's gaze wandered to Trev, the way it always did, but she only saw the side of his face and the strong outline of his jaw. He was turned toward Seran, giving her all of his attention. Things between her and Trev were changing, shifting, and it stabbed Renna in the heart. Earlier, King Carver had proudly announced to the royal table that the final negotiations of the marriage treaty were finished. The contract was done, ready to be signed. The wedding was two weeks away. None of that should have been a surprise. It had been the plan all along.

For the longest time, Renna held on to hope that she and Trev would somehow work out. She would never admit that out loud, but if she was honest with herself—honest with her heart—she had dared to hope. What a mistake.

After the performance was over, she found herself wandering outside. Fall nights were Renna's favorite. Her father always said that dusk was the most peaceful time, so she made her way to the flower garden to hopefully find some of that peace. Sadness had inched its way inside her heart tonight, loneliness tiptoeing not far behind.

Renna looked all around, making sure she was alone. Then she tilted her face heavenward as she walked, needing to talk to someone, needing to talk to her father.

"Everything is so messed up. I'm sure you're looking down on me wondering what I've gotten myself into." She shook her head. "I'm wondering that myself."

She hoisted herself up on a cement wall decorated with tiled mosaics, feeling the prick of branches against her back.

"I shouldn't have spoken that way to Mom. I feel terrible about it, but Dad, what were you thinking? How could you agree to marry someone that was in love with someone else?" She hung her head. "You really were the most honorable man, weren't you?" Memories of her parents' strained relationship filled her mind. The knowledge that her mother never loved her father weighed heavily in her chest. "How could Mom do that to you?" Renna whispered out loud. "I'd never do that to anyone." Tears burned at the corner of her eyes. "I was stupid to hold on to some make-believe relationship with Trev." She bit the side of her cheek, trying to keep her emotions under control. "He's just so . . ." she let out a breath, ". . . great. He's fun, happy, kind, smart, witty, caring." Her words quieted. "And so unavailable."

The moon's light glowed more powerfully, illuminating the sky as the last bits of sunlight faded behind the mountains. Faint stars appeared against the navy night sky. If she tried hard, she could almost feel her father's presence.

"Please help me, Dad. Help me find a way to forgive Mom and help me get over Trev."

The sound of crickets mixed with the trickling of water from a nearby fountain lulled her into a comfortable silence. She sat listening, letting the calmness wash over her.

"Well, aren't you a nice surprise?" Trev's voice startled her.

The outline of his body walked toward her until he came close enough for her to make out the features of his face. His tie was undone, lazily slung around his neck, and the top buttons of his plaid shirt were loosened.

"How did you find me?" she asked.

Mirth filled his eyes. "I wasn't looking for you."

She was glad he couldn't see her blush. "Of course not. I just—"

"Don't get me wrong. I'm happy to stumble upon you, but I was really just taking a walk. I do that sometimes when I need to think." He gracefully lifted his body next to hers on the ledge. "What about you? What brings you out here?"

"I was just missing my dad and wanted to talk to him." She smirked. "He's a great listener."

"I bet he is." Trev's expression was kind. "What was he like?"

She found herself wanting Trev to understand who her father was. "He was the best. Hardworking, honest, loyal, funny—he would do anything to make me laugh." Her mood lightened as she spoke about him. "I used to love the silly things he did. He would take a bite out of a banana when it wasn't even peeled yet. When he cooked spaghetti squash, he put the vegetable strands on top of his head like it was his hair. He had a ridiculous song for every occasion, and he told the same stupid jokes over and over, but I loved it. He used to dance with me in the kitchen. Read me fairytales late into the night. Explore Desolation ruins with me. He was my best friend."

"He sounds pretty amazing."

"He was." Renna looked into Trev's eyes, and it suddenly hit her why her heart hung on to him so tightly. "You're a lot like him."

"Me?" He shook his head. "Probably not, but I'll take the compliment." His mouth raised into a half-smile. "How did he die?"

She shrugged her shoulders. "He just got sick. It happened so fast that I barely noticed I was losing him, and then he was gone."

"I bet you miss him a lot."

Renna looked up at the sky and took a deep breath. "At first, the pain was suffocating, but I guess after so many years, I've just gotten used to it. Grief sticks with you—it changes and shifts as you grow, but it never leaves you."

He nodded his head slowly. "I like that description."

"Do you ever miss your mother?"

"I never knew her, but I miss the idea of her."

"What about Queen Avina? She died when you were young, right?"

"Yeah, I was only seven. I don't remember much. Sometimes I think I remember things, or maybe that's just my mind playing tricks on me because how could I really remember? I was so little when she died."

"What do you remember?"

Trev looked past her, as if far away for a moment. "Flying a kite in the palace courtyard. Sitting with her on a horse. Her tousling my hair. Simple things. Flashes of memories. But mostly, I just remember the feeling of being loved and how happy that made me. I haven't felt loved since the day Queen Avina died."

Renna's heart broke for him, and without thinking, she placed her hand over his. His face turned to hers, his blue eyes looking deep into her soul. They sat there silently—the air circulating so much between them.

Trev broke the silence. "I've been thinking a lot about what you said . . . about the purpose of being the king if I can't help anybody."

Renna sighed. "I shouldn't have said that. I was frustrated about Colter and his family. I'm sure you'll help a lot of people."

"No, you were right. I want to help people like Colter. I want to be better than my father. You make me want to be better. Sometimes . . ." He paused as if he was unsure of what he was about to say. "Sometimes I think about how things might have been different between us if I wasn't the prince."

"Or marrying Seran?" Renna raised her eyebrow, reminding him of the obvious.

"Yes, or marrying Seran." He said it in a respectful way.

"Aren't there any loopholes in this arranged marriage thing?" Renna laughed, trying to cover up how vulnerable that question made her feel. "I mean, if you're elected to royalty, and it's not a bloodline thing, why does marrying a princess even matter?"

Trev rubbed the top of her skin with his thumb. "It's more about *who* Seran is. Not *what.* She's the daughter of the king of New Hope. She's the link to a powerful alliance. The marriage isn't about a prince marrying a princess. It's about two powerful families and kingdoms coming together *through* marriage. The marriage will secure my future as king. It will help me win the election. It will protect Albion from Tolsten."

She nodded, already knowing why the arrangement had been made long ago. They sat in silence until she admitted,

"I've thought about it too—how things would have been if we were just two regular people."

The honesty about their situation felt good, natural even.

"What would've happened if we could've just continued what we started at Wellenbreck?" he said, his voice low.

"We probably would've gotten married and had a bunch of children," Renna said, her voice playful, belying the serious mood. "They would run around, be too loud, and be covered in mud. I would yell at them—"

He cut into her make-believe story. "And then I would yell at you for yelling at our children."

She laughed. "We'd fight all the time. You'd tell me I was acting crazy, and I'd throw a book at you."

"No, I would never say that. I like you best when you're crazy." He leaned in closer, and Renna could feel the warmth of his breath against her hair. "I would tell you every day how beautiful you were and how much I loved being with you."

It was all pretend, but she couldn't help but notice how he had said *I loved being with you,* and not *I love you.*

His words were quiet again, breaching her thoughts. "I would never take you for granted."

With each word, her feelings got more tangled up in him, knotting so tightly, she feared they might never be undone. The boundaries she placed carefully around her heart were getting smaller and smaller. She released his hand, hugging her knees close to her chest as if that would stop the ache swirling inside of her. She didn't care how unladylike the position made her look.

She dared a glance at him, the man who made her heart beat like it never had before. Everything with Trev had been red hot. The feelings came fast and forcefully. He was her friend. He was the man that constantly made her laugh. The man that said honest things to her.

"We would have been pretty amazing," she mused with a longing she couldn't hide.

"I think so." Sadness hung on his words. "I guess we'll never really know."

They stood at a crossroad, with Trev choosing to honor a promise made long ago—choosing a future of duty and righteous intentions.

And Renna had to let him. He was never meant to be hers. He was meant to be king. Meant to be Seran's. That had already been decided.

There was a new understanding between them. It was really over. Their relationship would no longer hide behind the guise of friendship.

"I guess I'll let you get back to your conversation with your dad." He scooted down to the ground. "Tell him I said hi." He smiled, but it didn't reach his eyes.

Renna watched until the darkness absorbed him, leaving her alone with her thoughts, her loneliness and the quiet aching of her desperate heart.

29

Trev

Trev lay awake, eyes wide as he stared up into the darkness of his room. He should be asleep, but he kept seeing Renna's face—seeing their future, their happiness, their love.

Love.

It was true; Trev hadn't felt loved since the day Queen Avina had died. His father had always shown him the opposite of love. Their entire relationship was based on how Trev could help him advance politically. His marriage to Seran would be based on the same thing.

Was it wrong to want love in his life? To want to love and be loved in return? He couldn't lose the last person in his life that made him feel loved.

His own words kept running through his mind. *The marriage isn't about a prince marrying a princess. It's about two powerful families and kingdoms coming together through marriage. The marriage will secure my future as king. It will help me win the election.* That was the reasoning behind marrying Seran, but couldn't all that be done with Renna too? Afterall, Renna's mother was the Queen of New Hope. Renna was a part of the royal family.

New Hope had *two* princesses, *two* royal daughters. Seran

was the only one with royal blood, of course, but did that really matter? The marriage was a physical representation of a political union. He just had to marry someone who represented New Hope. Couldn't that someone be Renna?

It all made sense in his mind. Perhaps there *was* a way they could be together.

He just needed to convince his father.

Trev passed a hand over his face, groaning. It wouldn't be easy. But he had to try.

He had never requested a private audience with the king and could see the shock on Gaines's face the next morning when he asked for one. Sweat gathered all over his body as he waited in his father's office. Was it hot, or was it just his nerves? He brought his hand to his mouth, fidgeting with his lower lip. He closed his eyes and let out a deep breath. The pressure of what he was about to ask weighed him down like a boulder in his heart. It was the conversation of his life.

His father entered the room, barely acknowledging him with a brusque glance. "Make this quick. I only have a few minutes."

Trev stood as Gaines shut the door, leaving him alone with his father. He didn't want anyone to overhear what he needed to say. The king sat at his desk and looked down at a stack of papers, giving him no attention.

Trev cleared his throat. "I don't want to marry Princess Seran."

His father calmly raised his eyes, keeping his chin down toward the desk. "You don't have a choice."

"I want to marry Renna," he said boldly.

His father's eye twitched, and Trev could tell he was starting to get annoyed. "Who?"

"Renna Degray, Queen Mariele's daughter." He shouldn't have to remind his father who Renna was.

The king laughed once, though clearly was not amused. "You're joking."

"No, I'm not joking. I want you to talk with Queen Mariele and tell her we still want to honor the marriage alliance, but with *her* daughter. Not Princess Seran."

Carver leaned back in his chair, his hands resting behind his head. If Trev didn't know the seriousness of the conversation, he would have guessed by his father's relaxed posture that they were talking about the weather.

"This alliance was devised between King Bryant and me. Queen Mariele is here on Bryant's behalf to approve the treaty, not to rewrite it."

"Then talk to King Bryant."

King Carver spoke slowly. "You want me to tell King Bryant that his daughter—his *only* daughter—who happens to be a beautiful princess, isn't good enough for my son?"

"She is good enough," Trev said firmly. "But I want Renna."

His father stared at him for a long, silent moment. Then he waved his hand casually. "Then have the girl. Just don't let anyone know. We can set her up with a house in the city." He looked satisfied, like he had just solved all the world's problems.

"No." Keep Renna as a mistress? Sickness stirred in his stomach. He could never do that to her. "No, I want to *marry* Renna. Her mother is the queen. She's part of the royal family too. She has the same connections as Seran, and the alliance with New Hope can stay the same. Just talk to Bryant. I'm sure he won't mind. Renna is his stepdaughter. He must have fond feelings for her too."

His father lowered his voice to a disgusted whisper. "The entire future of this country, not to mention your future as King of Albion, depends on the protection and connections that this alliance with New Hope provides." His voice grew louder. "How will it look to voters if you toss aside an attractive, well-connected princess for a *peasant* whose only claim to power is through her mother's pathetic second marriage to a king?" He scoffed. "They will say that you can't make up your mind, that you are fickle. You will lose *everything*, and Joniss Doman will stand ready to pick up the pieces. I will not speak to King Bryant. You will marry Princess Seran. End of discussion."

"No, we're not done here." Trev's heart beat faster, determination racing like fire through his veins. He'd never spoken to his father like this. A part of him wanted to shy away, afraid of his anger, but Trev refused to retreat. Not this time. Renna was worth it. "I'm not going to marry Seran. Talk to your advisors, come up with a plan, a new way to spin it."

"There's no new way to spin it. She's completely unsuitable to be queen. She's a liability!" the king yelled.

"You're wrong about her."

A loud knock sounded at the door just before Gaines pushed it open. "Your ten-o'clock meeting is here." Gaines held the door open as a group of three men entered the king's office.

The king lowered his voice so only Trev could hear. "I refuse to hear anything more about this. If you do *anything* to jeopardize this alliance or the election, I will see to it that both you and Miss Degray pay the price." Then he dismissed Trev with a flippant wave of his hand.

With Gaines and the other three men watching, Trev had no choice. He gave his father a stiff nod, then turned and stormed out the door. This wasn't over. He'd show his father that he could win the election and keep Renna. He had to.

30

Renna

Renna fidgeted with her peach dress under the dinner table, wishing she hadn't chosen a seat at the royal table. She thought she was a good daughter by sitting by her mother's side at dinner, even if they still weren't speaking. But her mother never showed up. Still sick, or at least that was what Renna told everyone when she didn't come down. Now Renna was alone, watching a room full of conversations take place around her.

"Miss Degray?" Renna's arm jerked, hitting the table with a loud thud. The king's intimidating voice continued, "What do you do?"

Renna looked to the other dinner guests at the royal table. Drake was in the middle of telling a story to Lizanne and Sheridan but paused when the king addressed Renna. A few high rulers down the table whipped their heads in her direction, and Trev's body tensed next to his father. It was as if everyone at the table was as surprised as she was that the king addressed her. He hadn't spoken a word to her since her arrival in Albion almost two weeks ago.

Unnerved by his attention and confused by the question, she replied tentatively, "Sire?"

King Carver leaned forward and laced his fingers together, eyes boring into her. "Princess Seran tells me that she spent much of her days back in Albion delving into politics, educating herself, and speaking with advisors, always hard at work learning to be a good ruler. What activities did you engage in?"

Renna blinked. "I studied with tutors . . . and I attended political functions with my mother and Princess Seran."

"And what else?" King Carver asked, his expression thick with judgment.

Renna's thoughts spun. Truthfully, she spent what free time she had by the ocean, but she was pretty sure that wasn't what the king wanted to hear. She tried to think of something else, but the look in his eyes seemed to choke out any other answer. Feebly, she responded, "Nothing else."

The king challenged her with a scowl. "You do nothing, Miss Degray?"

"I . . ." Renna's eyes flickered to Trev for help, but he looked disappointed with her answers, making everything worse. "Nothing. I do nothing."

The king's face twisted into an ugly frown. "Do you have talents? Accomplishments? Connections?"

Renna tried to speak, but her mind was blank. The king's glare ripped through her, making it impossible for her to think clearly. Everyone stared at her, waiting for an answer. "Uh . . . no, not really."

"Hm." He gave Trev a deliberate look before steering the conversation away from her.

Slowly, she reached for the glass in front of her and brought it to her lips. The cold liquid coated her dry throat, but it did nothing for her racing heart. She didn't know what game the king was playing, but she had lost. Of course, a thousand answers came to her mind now that the king's intimidating eyes weren't cutting into her.

She wasn't nothing.

Renna had talents and accomplishments. She knew how to work on a farm. How to prep soil, plant seeds, and harvest a crop. She knew how to sew. How to train a horse. How to fix a broken wagon wheel. She was a country girl—Kimball Degray's daughter. She was genuine, hardworking, kind, and thoughtful. She was passionate and witty. Bold and daring. She could sit around a fire with the working class or mingle with the ruling class in a fancy ballroom. She may not have *connections*, but she connected with ordinary people in a way that Seran never had.

It was too late for those answers now. Her chance to impress the king was gone.

When dinner was over, Renna hung back behind the dinner guests as they were being led out to the courtyard for a surprise.

"What did you do to make the king so upset?" Drake fell into a slow walk next to her, following behind the group.

"I have no idea." She shrugged as the cool evening air swept over her.

"He really hates you," Drake snickered.

Renna groaned. "I know." She leaned her forehead against the metal gate surrounding the courtyard. "He does hate me. I think he was contemplating whether or not he could have me killed at dinner right then and there." She lifted her head from the gate. "I just need to get out of this stupid kingdom."

Drake coughed back a laugh.

"What?" She didn't feel like playing games right now.

He pointed to her face. "You have a grease mark on your forehead from the gate."

Her hand flew to her head, trying to cover up the mark, but instead, grease smeared onto her fingers and across her forehead. Her eyes went wide with alarm.

"King Carver can't see me like this!" she said, panic filling her voice.

"It's fine. It's fine." Drake put his arm around her, ushering her through the crowd.

Her hand still covered her forehead as she ducked down. "I can't give the king any more reasons to hate me."

"Relax," Drake reassured her. "He's looking up."

An explosion of light and sound burst above them, making Renna jump. The crowd squealed with delight.

"What was that?" She looked up, forgetting to cover the grease.

"Fireworks," Drake said over the cheers.

"What?" Another explosion lit up the sky, causing her whole body to jump.

"You don't know what fireworks are?"

"I know what they are, but I've never seen them before. They aren't really deemed essential."

Drake's expression turned cold. "I don't think King Carver cares what's deemed essential."

"I'm beginning to see that," Renna said, walking slowly through the crowd as she looked up at the colorful sky.

Drake shoved her body to the right, avoiding a collision with an onlooker, but the move put her right in front of the king and Trev—both of them getting a good look at the grease mark on her forehead. The king shot Renna a deadly stare, and immediately her hand went back up.

"Excuse us," Drake said as he pushed past them. "She's not feeling well."

Inside the palace, they made their way to a side bathroom and locked the door. Renna gasped at the dark line across her skin.

"It's not that bad." Drake laughed.

"Not that bad? It's humiliating!" She grabbed a towel and started scrubbing.

Drake laughed harder as the black substance spread all over her skin with each scrub.

Who else in the world would lean against a gate and get

grease all over their forehead? *Only me*, Renna thought. It was an incredibly *Renna* thing to do.

"Stop laughing," she pleaded."It's not funny." She hit him with her towel but was already starting to laugh herself. "What is this stuff? It's not coming off!"

"Leave it. It looks good." He shrugged his shoulders like he was trying to convince himself.

"Grease marks look good?"

"No." He shook his head. "I was just trying to be nice."

Renna hit him with the towel again.

"Here, let me help." He dipped the corner of the towel in some water and then added soap and handed it back to her.

It took several rounds of scrubbing, but eventually, the grease was gone.

"There. Everything's perfect again," Drake said, inspecting her face.

Renna looked back at him. "Why are you being so nice to me? I thought you hated me too."

His brows bent together. "Why would you think that?"

"You've been avoiding me ever since the first night I arrived, and whenever Trev is by me, you look like you want to punch some sense into him."

"Am I that obvious?" He grimaced.

"Yes," she said. She leaned her back against the door and slid to the ground letting out a deep breath.

Drake sat down on the floor across from her, stretching his legs out next to hers.

"You really like Trev, don't you?"

She should lie to him again, tell him that he was wrong, but somewhere deep inside, the answer begged to be let out.

"I like him a lot. More than I've ever liked anyone in my whole life. And it's not because he's the prince. He constantly makes me laugh. He's not afraid to be silly just to make me smile, and in case you were wondering, I can't wipe the smile off my face when I'm with him. But it's more than just a good time. He's my friend. He's thoughtful. He actually tries to get to know me—to find out the things that make up who I am. I can't explain it. How do you explain—"

"Love?" Drake said knowingly.

Her face dropped into her hands partly from embarrassment and partly from agony. "I hate this. I hate acting like Trev's relationship with Seran isn't killing me when it is. I hate that I can't touch him or look at him or openly laugh at things he says. I hate that I can't be with him all the time," she dropped her voice, "because I want to be with him *all* the time." Her complete honesty left her feeling bare and exposed. "I shouldn't have told you all of that." Her head shook furiously. "I'm mortified I told you all of that."

"I'm glad you did." Drake's eyes were kind, easing her embarrassment. "The thing is, I want Trev to be the king of Albion for a lot of reasons—some of them honorable and some of them selfish. If my best friend becomes king, he will appoint me as commander of the Albion army, which I am more than qualified for. If Joniss becomes king, my future is uncertain. But the truth is, Trev would be an amazing king. The kind of king that inspires people to band together and be united in a great purpose. The kind of king who puts his people first and fights for them."

"And you think I stand in the way of him being elected king?"

"Yes," Drake sighed.

Renna's stomach dropped and she had to look away.

"I want him to be king, but I also want him to be happy, and if he loses you, I don't think he will ever truly be happy again." Drake paused, then added, "Maybe you should tell him how you feel so he has a choice."

"No! I couldn't do that to Seran. Besides, he told me the first day I met him that he doesn't believe in a one and only true love." She shrugged. "He doesn't even believe in love."

Drake shook his head. "What else would you say if you

had known since childhood that you would have to marry a stranger someday? Sometimes it's easier to pretend that love doesn't exist than to acknowledge that it *does* exist, but you aren't permitted to experience it."

Renna thought about the truth that might be lingering in his words.

"Tell him how you feel," Drake urged.

"What will he do?" She didn't want to end up even more hurt than she already was.

"He'll either choose you and lose everything or, if he's the man and leader that I think he is, he'll figure out a way to have you and still be elected king."

"What about King Carver?"

"He'll hate you even more than he does now. There will be no chance for reconciliation with him."

Renna took a deep breath.

Drake made it sound so simple. Tell Trev how she felt, and trust he would figure out a way to be with her and not ruin his life or the future of Albion. But what about her mother and Seran? Could Trev figure out a way that wouldn't destroy their lives in the process?

Outside, the sound of fireworks snapped and popped more furiously.

"You know, I've never been in a bathroom with a man before." She looked at the golden swirled tile beneath them.

"That's probably a good thing." Drake furrowed his brow.

"Probably." She smiled.

He rubbed the smooth surface of the ornate tile with his fingers. "I've never sat on a bathroom floor before."

"Really? I do it all the time," she confessed, not ashamed of how weird it sounded.

"All the time?" he clarified.

"Not all the time, but . . . sometimes it's the best place to be alone." Her eyes wandered as she recalled the times the bathroom floor had comforted her in her life, especially after her father had died. Some nights she had escaped to the downstairs bathroom so she could cry as loud as she wanted without waking her mother. Shaking herself out of her memories with a self-conscious laugh, Renna continued, "No one bothers you when you're in the bathroom."

"Thanks for the tip. I'll have to remember that the next time I'm trying to avoid Trev."

She wasn't sure if he was being sarcastic or not. "You're welcome."

The sound of fireworks faded into cheers.

"The show must be over." She stood, straightening her dress. "I better let you get back out there."

"Renna," his call stopped her, "I hope it all works out for you guys."

She hoped so too, but she didn't dare say it out loud. Not yet.

31

Trev

His father's office was empty, but the king would be there any minute. His father always stopped by his office before retiring to his room for the night. Trev walked the edges anxiously. How was he going to handle his father? What would he say to convince him that being with Renna wouldn't ruin his chances of being elected king?

What if he couldn't convince him? Was he prepared to go against his father? He had always been a loyal son—a loyal subject of Albion—adhering to what was right. But none of this felt right.

His fingers grazed the back of his father's brown leather chair. Trev could smell the richness of the leather from where he stood behind his father's desk. He'd always thought this chair would be his someday.

This mantle.

This responsibility.

Being the future king had governed his every move as far back as he could remember. He sat down in his father's chair and tried to picture himself as the leader of Albion. The thought was overwhelming, but the rightness of it sank deep into his soul. Could loving Renna really take all of that away from him?

Trev didn't want to see it. He refused to consider it, but in the farthest corners of his mind, his father's words gnawed at him. He picked up a stack of papers on the desk in front of him. His thumb flipped through a few of the pages until one paper in particular stopped him.

One word.

Confidential.

Wildly, his eyes scanned the document. He couldn't read it fast enough. Details, dates, and times of the assassination plot against King Adler were described throughout. The words pelted his mind one by one as if he was caught in a massive hailstorm. No wonder his father hadn't fought back during the high ruler's meeting. He was going to go ahead with the assassination without their approval.

Secretly.

"The answer is no." King Carver breezed through the door, heading straight for the side table where his liquor was stored. "You will not marry that girl. Did you see her tonight at dinner? She can't answer a simple question, and don't even get me started on the spectacle she made of herself during the fireworks."

"What's this?" Trev held the paper up for his father to see.

His father paused, staring at the paper only for a moment before continuing to pour his drink.

"You can't do this." He could only hope his father could see reason. "The high rulers voted. The assassination plan was never supposed to happen."

His father casually took a seat by the fireplace. The sound of leather squished beneath him as he sat. "I'm the king. I have the final say."

"That's not how this works, and you know it. You need the high rulers' permission to take any action against a foreign nation."

"What are they going to do, depose me? My service is over in two months anyway."

"But Father, this is more than just an overreach of power. This is corrupt and brutal! The Council of Essentials will arrest you for instigating violence against a fellow nation. You'll get the death sentence and I will lose the election because of my connection to you."

"No one will find out! Tolsten will believe that their own insurgents committed the killing. And in the chaos of the power vacuum it creates, no one will have time to investigate."

Trev waved the paper through the air. "How can you say no one will find out? You've left a paper trail just sitting on top of your desk. I found it within one minute of entering your office."

The king rolled his eyes. "No one is allowed in here except you and Gaines."

"This is suicidal, and I won't let you do this."

"And how are you going to stop me? I'm afraid we can't go back on our plans now. The pieces are already in place." His father spoke in mock disappointment.

"I'll expose you and your plan to everyone," Trev threatened, waving his finger accusingly at the king.

"I'll tell everyone you knew about it too. If I go down, you go down with me."

"You would never do that," Trev argued. "You want me elected king."

His father sighed. "The order has already been given. Men have already left to carry it out. I'm the only one who can stop it now."

"Then I demand you stop it!" Trev stood, thrusting his hands on the desk in front of him.

"You demand I stop it?" His father's devilish smile had returned. "And what will you do for me in return?"

"What do you want?" Trev straightened his back.

A small smirk formed on his father's lips. "I want you to

marry Princess Seran. I hate Tolsten and King Adler, but I can put those feelings aside as long as you are elected king. That princess is your ticket to winning the election."

The marriage was the only thing Trev could bargain with, and his father knew it. It was the only thing that could stop the assassination and the unimaginable consequences of what it would bring.

"I want the assassination of King Adler called off," Trev said, his voice full of determination.

"I wish everyone could see the value in my plan. Killing Adler would open up an enormous amount of power for us, but if you're king, we can revisit this topic again later."

As if Trev would ever consider killing King Adler.

"It would set the standard that anybody could kill any leader for no reason or wage war on any kingdom for no reason." How did his father not see this?

"I have my reasons!" Carver's face turned red with anger.

Trev remained calm. "Your reasons aren't good enough. No reason is good enough for *murder*."

"You'll never make a good king if you aren't willing to get your hands dirty. But that'll be on you. The situation with Tolsten will be on you. As long as you are elected king." His father swirled the last bits of liquid in his cup. "I'll stop the assassination. In return, you will marry Princess Seran and stay away from the other girl."

The other girl. Trev hated how flippant his father was. The moment felt big and final. Once he agreed, he could never go back on his word. Ten years ago, when the alliance was struck with King Bryant, someone else had made the promises. Someone else had chosen for him. But today—at this moment—he was the one making the promise. He was the one making the choice.

He *had* to do this. There was no other way to stop his father and no other way to end the assassination. He had to protect Albion from the wrath of Tolsten.

Trev swallowed his dreams. "Fine. I'll marry Seran."

There it was—his loyalty, his honor, his morality—it had all manifested itself in a single sentence.

His father's evil eyes glared at him. "I'll have Commander Pryer send the orders to stop the assassination first thing in the morning," his father muttered.

Trev walked to the door. "I want to be there. I don't trust you to do it without me watching."

32

Renna

Maybe. It was a cruel word that had tortured Renna ever since she'd left Drake alone on the bathroom floor earlier that evening. *Maybe* kept her hopes alive when they probably shouldn't be. It was Drake's fault. His words kept playing over and over in her mind, like a young girl practicing her piano piece for a recital.

You should tell him how you feel . . . he'll figure out a way to have you and still be elected king.

Was Renna really contemplating having the most vulnerable conversation of her life? Contemplating devastating her mother and Seran? Despite every blockade Renna had put up, she had fallen in love with Trev. It was that realization that had brought her outside of Trev's office. She loved him, and now she was going to tell him. She took a deep breath and knocked on the door.

Please don't answer. Please don't answer.

Crosby opened the door.

"I'm sorry," Renna said, stunned. "I was looking for Prince Ezra."

"I believe he has retired to the royal living room." He

spoke in a formal, businesslike way. "May I help you with something?"

"Oh. I suppose it can wait until tomorrow."

Crosby looked down the hall in both directions, then lowered his voice. "The king is not with him. I believe Prince Ezra is alone."

She smiled timidly back at him. Did this short, serious man know why Renna had come at such a late hour to the prince's office? Did he know that she was about to confess her undying love? To say 'you have my heart, so take it and don't hurt me'? The thought was enough to carry her feet to the royal living room as she tried to work out the words.

Each heartbeat thudded distinctly against her chest until she saw Trev through the small crack in the door. His curls were pushed back slightly like he had been combing his fingers through his hair all night. The top of his shirt was unbuttoned, and somewhere along the line, he had ditched his suit jacket and tie. He looked ridiculously appealing as he leaned against the open balcony door, hands in his pockets.

The palms of her hands pushed against the wooden door, slowly opening it beyond a crack. Everything froze when she saw Seran coming in from the balcony, smiling warmly at Trev. Her slender arms wrapped around Trev's waist, hugging him to her. Renna's breath caught in the back of her throat. She should leave, but it felt like she was wearing concrete shoes. The ache inside grew as Trev's hand slowly lifted out of his pocket and tucked Seran's shiny, black hair behind her ear. His fingers made a trail down the side of her neck—the way they always had with Renna.

"I'm glad you invited me here tonight." Seran's voice was impossibly sweet, but it held a sultry undercurrent. Renna had never heard Seran speak that way.

"I'm glad I did too," Trev said quietly. "You're my only future."

His words knocked the air out of Renna in one swoop.

Renna couldn't see his face. She couldn't see if his eyes looked at Seran with the same intensity they had when he looked at her. But then his head started to move toward Seran. The final few millimeters between their lips were the longest, most agonizing nanoseconds of Renna's life. The moment Trev's lips gently fell onto Seran's, her heart shattered into a million pieces, ricocheting off every bone inside her, cutting back into the center of her chest. She couldn't breathe. She literally couldn't breathe as their lips slowly moved in synchronized motion. Her feet shuffled backward, refusing to let her watch.

She was such a fool, thinking that maybe he loved her too. She would not cry in the hallway of this stupid palace. She would wait until she made it to her bed. She rushed down the hall, her body in autopilot until she reached her room.

Renna shut her bedroom door behind her, leaning her back against it. Thankfully Nora wasn't there. The room was dark.

"What do you want with my son?"

She jumped with fear, a small scream escaping as she quickly turned toward the voice. Even in the dim light of her room, she could see the intimidating form of the king's body, leaning against the wall.

"Your Majesty." She let out a deep breath, flipping on the light. Every alarm went off in her body and the uneasiness in her stomach made her nauseous. What was he doing in her room, waiting for her in the dark?

His gaze narrowed. His words were slower and more deliberate as he spoke again. "What do you want with my son?"

She shifted her weight nervously. "I don't know what you mean."

But she did know, and so did the king. The entire world was caving in on her—one mountain crashing down on her at a time.

"I underestimated you." He crossed the room to her dresser. His fingers skimmed over her makeup, left out carelessly by Nora. "Actually, I didn't even notice you. There was nothing about you worth noticing."

She watched his reflection through the mirror. There was no reason to impress him or his son. She hated them. "If I'm so unnoticeable, why are you in my room?"

His lips curled up into one of his sickly smiles. "You have interfered with things you shouldn't have."

"I haven't done anything." She felt defiant, strong even.

"Are you sure about that? You jeopardized the entire alliance between Albion and New Hope." Keeping his eyes on her, he grabbed a small glass bottle of perfume and brought it up to his nose to smell, then placed it back on the dresser before turning to face her. "But rest assured, it's all under control now."

Renna hardly had time to consider what he meant by that when the king suddenly moved toward her, his steps slow like a predator stalking his prey. She reached behind her back, searching for the door handle and a quick escape, but it wasn't there. Before she could move another inch, King Carver stood over her, his body uncomfortably close and his face leering.

"My son was willing to destroy everything just to be with you." Gently, he reached up to stroke her cheek. She turned her head away from him, squeezing her eyes shut. Each touch of his fingers caused her chest to tighten with dread. "What's so great about you that makes a man want to ruin his entire future to be with you?"

He reached behind her head and grasped the hair at her neck, forcing her to look up at him. Her breath caught at the pain. Any second she was sure her hair would be clumped around her feet. There was no way it could still be attached to her head; he was pulling too hard.

He breathed, "Maybe you need to show me what you've

shown him, so I won't feel so upset about what I lost tonight. What I had to give up."

Terror raced through Renna, forcing bile to the back of her throat. She had no idea what King Carver was capable of, and she didn't want to find out.

"Tell me, what was your aim when you targeted my son? The alliance? Or was it something more? A vendetta against King Bryant and his daughter, perhaps?"

His face was close, but she didn't let her eyes drop from his. "I didn't target your son."

"You would have me believe you're just so charming he couldn't help himself? I don't believe that." He tightened his hold on her hair. She let out a small yelp of pain—letting him know he was winning.

"You're just like your mother. Did she tell you how to entrap a prince? Did she tell you how you could someday become queen?" His tone mocked her.

Moisture gathered at the corners of her eyes. "Leave my mother out of this."

"Yes, she's much too fragile for a scandal like this." He leaned in closer; Renna wasn't sure how it was even possible. The scent of alcohol burned her nostrils. "Stay away from him," he said, his voice dark and nasty. "He may believe he would've been happy with you. You may even believe it, too, but I know the truth. I know that you would've ruined his future. He will never become king with you by his side, and one day he would have resented you for it." He released her hair, thrusting her head back into the door with a loud thud. It took all her strength not to rub the back of her scalp furiously.

"You're an embarrassment." His insult came with a touch of laughter.

A rogue tear dropped from her eye.

The king towered over her, sinking her back into the wall. She was sure his next words rumbled through the walls the way they rumbled through her.

"You are a liability."

He flung open her door and slammed it behind him. She stared at the door for a moment, frozen in fear, but his words hung in the air. How could one sentence hurt so much? They were just words, after all.

Renna locked her bedroom door then walked across the room. She checked under the bed as if somehow the king could still be lurking in the shadows, tormenting her. She kicked off her shoes and reached for the zipper on the back of her dress but suddenly, she didn't feel safe enough to be without the extra fabric. She didn't feel safe anywhere. Her body folded into the soft bed and pillows. She pulled the blanket up over her head and let the sobs come freely.

33

Trev

The memory of the kiss with Seran tasted bland on Trev's lips. There was no excitement. No heat. No longing. No tension. Those weren't the feelings he wanted to feel. Even the delicious food at breakfast the next morning couldn't get rid of the aftertaste of disappointment. But he'd made a deal with his father and couldn't go back on it.

One hour ago, he had watched his father write the letter to call off the assassination, then watched him give it to the messenger, an officer that Trev had chosen. He watched the man drive away, finally satisfied that the plans were going to be stopped.

He had done the noble thing, but that didn't prevent him from feeling depressed.

Renna appeared in front of him on the stairs, and his mood immediately lifted. Somehow everything seemed better when she was around. He couldn't control his smile or the racing in his heart as he stopped to greet her in the middle of the giant staircase.

"You missed the fireworks last night."

"I saw them." Her words were clipped, full of an emotion he didn't understand.

Her curtness took him by surprise. "Oh. I thought I saw you leave with Drake."

He wanted to see the different shades of color in her green eyes, but she refused to look at him.

Something was wrong.

"I did leave the fireworks display." She folded her arms tightly across her chest, finally letting her eyes rest on him. "But I saw the ones later that night."

The coldness in her voice confused him. "What fireworks? I don't understand."

"You know, the ones between you and Seran in the royal living room."

"What are you talking about?" Tension filled his shoulders as he furrowed his brow.

"Your kiss with Seran," Renna clarified.

Heat rushed to his face in embarrassment. "You saw that?"

"I wasn't spying. I just wanted to tell you something, but you were . . . busy." A tight smile spread across her lips. "I didn't want to interrupt your intimate moment."

"It wasn't an intimate moment." Not to Trev, at least.

"It looked pretty intimate to me," she said, hurt evident in her eyes. But then she looked up, the hurt replaced with a coldness that pierced Trev's heart. "Anyways, I'm happy for you both." She slipped past him and continued down the stairs.

"Renna?" He tried to reach for her, but she pulled away.

"I'm really busy. I have to go."

His fingers scraped through the curls at his forehead, pushing them back. "I'm trying here. I'm trying to be what everyone wants and needs. I'm trying to be with Seran. You know I have to be with her, but yet you accuse me like I've intentionally hurt you."

"I'm not hurt," she said with a smile that looked too big to be real. "Like I said, I'm happy for you." She took the stairs two at a time, distancing herself from him.

How was it even possible that she made him feel *everything*?

Trev couldn't help but think about how much he missed seeing the playful sparkle in her eyes. How he wanted to know what she thought about the fireworks show. How he was dying to find out how the grease had gotten on her forehead so he could tease her about it. How her skin glowed with a touch of yesterday's sun. How the citrus of her scent would stay with him the rest of the day.

Why did his heart have to betray him so completely? Why couldn't he just let her go?

34

Renna

"I don't think you should do this, my lady. It will be social suicide." Nora shook her head vigorously as she sat on the edge of Renna's bed, looking at the drawing Renna had made of the strapless dress she saw in the magazine.

"But could you do it?" Renna asked.

"Make you a new dress?" Nora looked over at the already finished piece hanging in Renna's closet, fresh from the palace seamstress. The blue gown was conservative and flowing—perfectly befitting of a young woman, or rather, what everyone *said* was befitting of a young woman.

But Renna didn't want to fit in tonight.

"Yes." She nodded at her maid.

"The ball is in twelve hours," Nora said anxiously. "And this dress doesn't exactly fit the modesty rules."

"But can you do it?" Renna pressed.

Nora started shaking her head again.

"Please!" Renna begged. "I'll even help, if you need me."

Nora folded her hands in her lap. "Not until you tell me *why* you want to do this."

Of course Nora would want to know why. Renna was

asking her to do something risky. To do something that could get her fired.

Renna sat next to her on the bed, still towering over her even while sitting. She started speaking, the words coming out fast and full of condemnation. “We all pretend that the Council of Essentials, that the rulers, are making decisions based on what’s best for us, but they’re not. They only do what’s best for them. Working-class people are starving. They don’t even have the basic essentials in life, but the Council isn’t worried about that. No, they’re worried about rules! Why do a few people get to decide what everyone else can and can’t do? Huh? It’s stupid! I’m sick of them telling me who I have to be, how to behave, what I can wear, how much skin I can show, what color my clothes need to be. Before Desolation, women used to be in charge of things; they ran huge corporations, even countries. There hasn’t been a woman elected queen for more than one hundred years. The Council is slowly removing us. Women are inessential unless we are lucky enough to have the right connections.” She hesitated, unsure how much she wanted to reveal, but decided to continue anyway. “I’m sick of the Council telling me who I can or can’t love. I’m sick of arranged marriages and negotiations.” She looked at Nora. “When did we all lose so much control of our own lives?”

Nora shrugged her tiny shoulders. “And what does any of that have to do with a new dress?”

“It’s about taking control. I’m wearing what I want to wear. It’s only a dress, I know. It won’t solve starvation or elect a queen, but things will never change if someone doesn’t do *something*. That’s why I want a new dress.” Renna didn’t know if it was a good enough reason, but it was all she had. That, and an unyielding certainty that if she had to walk away from Trev forever, she would do it on her own terms. And she wouldn’t be forgotten.

“That’s what my father always says,” Nora said, sitting up

a little taller. "*Things will never change if someone doesn't do something.*"

"So you'll help me?" Renna smiled. "I promise I'll tell everybody that I did it on my own. I'll leave you out of it, so you won't get in trouble."

Renna must have said something right because Nora nodded. "Okay. I'll help you."

She leaned over, hugging the girl's small body to her chest.

Changing her dress was just one of the many crazy things Renna had thought of since witnessing Trev's kiss with Seran, since King Carver's visit, since running into Trev on the stairs. The memories were vicious; every cutting word, every heartbreaking moment, none of it had been lost. Instead, the memories had taken up residence in the front of her mind. It was all there, the highlights on repeat, wreaking havoc on her self-esteem.

You're just like your mother . . . you're an embarrassment.

And her favorite.

You're a liability.

There was no way to escape the diseased thoughts. Instead, she let them become her excuse—her reasoning—for wanting to challenge societal rules.

Renna spent the rest of the day working on her new dress with Nora. It was a good distraction from her broken heart.

At seven p.m., Cypress opened the door in a rush. Renna glanced at her through the mirror as Nora worked on her makeup.

"Renna, why aren't you ready? The queen is waiting for you in the hall." Her words were filled with displeasure.

"Tell my mother not to wait for me." She smiled sweetly—too sweetly. "I lost track of time. I'll be down to the ball in a minute."

Her mother would be fine going ahead without her. They still weren't speaking.

Renna's dress wasn't going to help their strained situation, but the dress had nothing to do with the queen. Eventually, her mother would get over it.

Eventually . . . when they were back in New Hope and no one knew about it.

Cypress seemed upset, but that was nothing new. "Very well."

A dramatic entrance—that's what Renna was after. She was going to demand everyone's attention, especially Trev's and King Carver's. Nora finished arranging Renna's hair exactly how she had asked; she had even shown her the picture of how it was supposed to look. It was twisted in a pile on top of her head with wispy bangs sweeping across her forehead. Her makeup was done a bit thicker than usual with bright red lipstick as the finishing touch. Renna didn't want to miss a single detail.

Now it was time for the dress.

What Renna stepped into was anything but conservative. She and Nora had worked for hours recreating the red dress from the magazine. The one Trev had shown her during the tour of the palace. Nora and Renna had even run back to the artifact room several times to figure out how to replicate it. After hours of measuring, cutting, and sewing, the dress looked exactly like the one pictured. They'd had to get creative with Renna's undergarments, unsure how women used to keep their breasts in place in dresses like these. She'd also had to practice sitting down carefully because the slit came up so high on her thigh.

Wearing the dress, Renna would show more skin than she ever had in her life—more skin than she had ever seen anyone else show, either. A dress like this was borderline criminal in conservative New Hope. It was even pushing the limits in Albion, but the modesty rules were stupid. The Council of Essentials didn't follow their own rules, so why should Renna follow the modesty one? That was the whole point, wasn't it?

To remind the Council they weren't the only ones who could exercise a little bit of will power.

She took a deep breath as she looked at herself in the mirror. This was what crazy looked like, but she liked knowing she was doing something for herself.

"Are you sure you want to do this?" Nora had a worried look on her face, making her look older than her twenty-one years. "We could still put you in the blue dress, and no one would ever have to know."

This was the first step Renna needed to take to prove to herself she was in control of her own life. "I'm sure."

"Well, the dress is stunning." Nora squeezed Renna's shoulders from behind, the way an adoring mother would. "You look stunning!"

"Thanks, Nora. And thank you for all your hard work today. I couldn't have done it without you."

Music floated upward from the great hall below. Renna steadied herself on the railing at the top of the stairs—her confidence going head-to-head with her self-doubt.

A hard swallow. A countdown.

One. Two. Three.

Renna's red, high-heeled shoe took the first step down the stairs.

No one noticed her.

Another step. Then another.

One head turned. A couple more, until a sea of eyes took in her dress and her body. All the pleasant party sounds muted into hushed whispers. Renna even swore the musicians faltered for a moment. She scanned the crowd as she slowly moved down the last few steps, not missing her mother's shocked expression, Seran's embarrassed grimace, King Carver's angry glare, and the gaze she anticipated the most: the jaw-dropped expression on Prince Ezra's face. She had stopped him midsentence.

Seran and Jenica got to her first at the bottom of the stairs. "Your dress is outrageous!" Jenica's words came out in a high-pitched whisper.

"I thought I would try out a new style," Renna said innocently. "Do you like it?"

"No, I don't like it! Go upstairs and change this instant!" Jenica's face contorted into a pout.

Renna raised her eyebrows at the obnoxious girl. "Oh, I'm sorry. Am I taking too much attention away from you?"

Jenica's eyes went wide as she stuck out her bottom lip. "I'm not worried about me. This night is supposed to be about Seran. How could you do this to *her*?"

Renna looked at Seran as guilt expanded in her chest. She had guessed Seran would be upset, and rightfully so, but Seran was a gorgeous princess; nothing would ever take the attention away from her completely.

Renna braced herself for Seran's anger, but whatever the princess felt, she masked. She raised her chin. "There are modesty rules in place for a reason, Renna. I think it is important to obey the rules."

"Not every rule should be obeyed." Renna shrugged and pushed past Jenica and Seran and nearly collided with the queen.

Her mother's tight grip stopped her feet. The queen's long, painted nails dug into her forearm like the claws of an eagle. She looked like she was going to have a heart attack. Probably fall dead on the floor. Renna wouldn't even be able to help her, with the way the tight fabric of her dress trapped her legs and torso, keeping them from bending. The dress was that ridiculous; her mobility was a complete hostage to it.

"Renna, what has gotten into you?" Her voice was laced with panic. "Go upstairs and put something appropriate on."

"Who says this dress isn't appropriate? The Council of Essentials? They don't even follow their own rules." She tried to make her voice sound kind, easing her mother off the ledge. There were too many people around for her mother to make a big scene.

Renna wriggled her arm free from her mother's grasp and continued through the crowd. With each stare, look, and nod, she grew bolder and bolder until her feet were taking her past the king.

"You're testing my patience, girl." The king's fangy teeth were barred. He looked like a wolf ready to devour her.

"Like you said, I'm a liability." She returned his gaze with a fierce look of her own. "I can't help it."

Was he going to rip off her dress like the evil stepsisters in the pre-Desolation Cinderella fairytale? That would draw too much attention, but the look in his eyes suggested he was contemplating it. His boney, sharp chin jutted out, but then his body turned from her, and he walked away.

The breath she had been holding escaped.

There was one last person to confront.

Trev stood in the middle of the ballroom with Drake. Both men hadn't taken their eyes off her since she'd descended the stairs.

Despite Trev's good looks, his elegant suit and the glittering gold crown on his head, right now, Renna knew she looked better.

Trev

THE FIRST THING Trev saw was Renna's smooth, lean leg as it gracefully kicked out from the slit in her dress as she walked down the stairs into the great hall. The sight rattled his insides like nothing ever had before. To say he was speechless would be an understatement.

Drake was mid-drink when he saw her and practically choked.

All Trev could do was stand there and stare at Renna in that red dress.

"It's the dress from the magazine," Drake somehow got out.

"I . . ." Trev couldn't locate his voice. It was caught somewhere in his throat or caught up in Renna. "She . . . she . . . looks way better than the woman in the magazine. How did she . . ." Trev's words trailed off as Renna approached, her bare skin affecting every nerve in his entire body.

"Good evening, gentlemen." She bent down in a slight curtsey. Trev's eyes followed a little too closely, and judging by the smug smile on her face, she knew exactly where he had looked. He hadn't done a good job hiding it this time.

She paused for a moment in front of them, and then walked away, lost in the crowd. All that remained was her perfume floating in the air.

Drake slapped him on the back. "You're in big trouble tonight."

Trev had to peel his eyes away from Renna's smooth shoulder, from the stretch of her neck, the lengths of her bare arms.

He couldn't just stare. Oh, but what he would give to just stare.

"There you are." Seran's sleek hand wrapped around his forearm, startling him. "The king said you were looking for me."

Trev glanced at his father and knew what the king's stern expression meant.

"He said you wanted to dance with me." She smiled in her flirtatious way, raising her right shoulder in the process. Apparently, she had been unphased by Renna and her red dress.

This was the agreement he had made—the life he had

chosen. From the outside looking in, it was the most straightforward trade-off ever.

Marry a beautiful princess and stop the murder of King Adler.

Trev could imagine people rolling their eyes at his pain.

"Yes, he's right." He gestured to the dance floor. "Let's dance."

The crowd parted, letting the royal couple through to the center of the ballroom. Trev nodded at all the admiring faces as he took Seran in his arms. They were the perfect couple—the ideal future for Albion.

They swirled around the floor in coordinated grace until his eye caught on something he couldn't look away from. *Renna*.

One of his officers held her close as they swayed to the music, his face nuzzling into her bare neck. Trev stumbled a bit, stepping on Seran's toes, making her squeal in pain. Their bodies awkwardly bumped into each other as they tried to get back to their graceful steps again. Everyone's eyes were on them, and his face heated with embarrassment. Did everyone in the room know he had been tripped up by Renna?

The song ended, prompting him to part from Seran. "Sorry. I'm usually better at this."

Seran smiled tersely but pulled him to her as another song started. "Let's just do it better this time. Everyone's watching." Her smile widened as she looked at their audience. Trev spun them around, positioning her so that her back was to Renna, giving him the perfect angle to watch her. She was dancing with a new officer now, laughing and leaning her body into the young man's, making him pull her closer.

Slow song after slow song played. Who were these musicians? They were all fired. Forever.

As Trev held Seran in his arms—Renna in the arms of everyone else—he realized with sickening clarity that none of the other men could ever possibly feel as much for her as he did.

Renna

The line of men wanting to dance was a bit overwhelming. Officer after officer grabbed Renna's hand and kept her out on the dance floor. Her feet were sore, and she was so hungry, but King Carver was somewhere across the room, so she kept dancing, kept acting like she was having the time of her life, like a corrupt king couldn't control her.

At the beginning of a new song, Mr. Tybolt grabbed her arm, his sweaty palms sticky against her skin. "I have been waiting for this moment all night."

Instinctively she leaned away. "Where's your lovely wife tonight?"

He licked his perpetually chapped lips. "She's not here."

Where was all the luck in the world?

Tybolt wrapped his arm around her possessively, turning her to him. She was trapped.

"Tybolt." A new voice broke in. "You'll have to excuse me, but I'm going to steal Miss Renna from you." Renna's eyes went wide in surprise.

"Officer Doman." Tybolt coughed nervously, obviously not wanting to let go of his turn. "I'm afraid you'll have to wait until we're done."

"I'm done with waiting," Joniss said, pulling Renna free from Tybolt's grip. He wore a dark purple suit, and his brown hair was slicked back away from his face. "My apologies, sir."

Tybolt looked stunned, but what could he do? Joniss Doman was intimidating in the most charming, charismatic way.

"I'm surprised you even remember my name," Renna said sarcastically as they started to dance. "It's been so long since we've talked."

"That was clearly a mistake on my part." He scanned her body with his eyes.

Renna had wanted attention tonight. She wouldn't have worn the dress if she hadn't wanted to be noticed, but she hadn't thought about how it would make her feel to have guy after guy drooling over her. Or drooling over her body, at least. *That* wasn't the kind of attention she wanted. She wanted to prove she had a mind of her own. She wanted to challenge the rules of society.

Joniss led her to the center of the dance floor. The music had already begun playing. Renna dared a glance at Trev, and, as if on cue, Joniss put his arm around her waist.

Trev was definitely paying attention.

"So tell me, why the dress? Obviously, I'm a fan, but it does seem a bit . . . unlike you."

Renna's words were short. "How would you know what is or isn't *like* me?"

Joniss laughed. "You're flashing attitude tonight. I like it." He pulled her closer.

Renna rolled her eyes. The last thing she needed was another arrogant man in her life.

"Is he watching?" Joniss asked, nodding his head toward Trev.

Renna clamped her mouth shut. She wasn't about to give anything away to the irritable man; he already seemed to know too much.

"Don't pretend like you don't know what I'm talking about. I'm excellent at reading people," he boasted.

Her mouth remained shut.

"We can help each other, you know." He tilted his head so he could see her better. "We both want the same thing—for Ezra to suffer."

Renna kept her face expressionless. Was that what she wanted? For Trev to suffer? She had hoped he'd notice her in the dress. Hoped he'd feel a small part of the hurt that had torn through her yesterday like a tornado. But to hear it come from Joniss's mouth like that, like they were plotting some big scheme? It all sounded so callous. The truth was, despite her broken heart, she wanted Trev to be happy. She wanted happiness for Seran and her mother too. Fighting over a love that was never meant to be hers was the most foolish thing she had ever done.

Renna stiffened when Joniss's hand slid farther down her back—lower than any other man had dared that night. The audacity of this guy was astonishing. She reached around her back and pulled his hand up until it was at a more respectable level.

"My hand placement was strictly strategic, I assure you." Joniss gave her an innocent smirk. "I'm only trying to help you with Ezra."

"How considerate of you." She gave him a warning look, but it didn't seem to faze him. "But I don't need any help with Prince Ezra. I'm afraid you're not as good at reading people as you think. Nothing is going on between Prince Ezra and me."

The song ended, and Renna stepped back.

"I'm going to need proof that I'm wrong about you two. Proof that I'm not good at reading people," Joniss said.

"What?"

"Prove it," he challenged.

Before Renna could say anything else, Joniss grabbed her hand and led her through the crowd toward Trev.

Trev

"EZRA! I THOUGHT it was time you danced with your soon-to-be sister-in-law," Joniss said, pulling Renna toward the royal table where he sat with Seran, the king, and a few high rulers.

Hate was a strong word, but after tonight, Trev could definitely say he *hated* Joniss.

Renna shook her head in protest. "I . . . I . . . think he

should dance with Seran." Her pleading eyes looked back at Joniss.

"Yes, I agree. Ezra should dance with the princess." His father weighed in on the matter a little too quickly.

Trev stood. "Sorry to disappoint you, Joniss, but I promised Seran we would dance again." Trev stretched his hand out in front of Seran, willing her to take him up on it.

"I'm actually a little tired." Seran's expression was guarded.

Trev felt desperate. He couldn't dance with Renna. Not tonight.

"Perfect! Renna can keep Ezra company while you rest. You don't mind, Princess, do you?" Joniss raised one cunning eyebrow.

"Of course not. Why would I mind?" Seran flashed a calculated smile at Joniss.

Trev remembered Seran's words. She'd said Renna was harmless, but he wasn't sure Seran genuinely believed that. Was this a test?

"Actually, Ezra should be getting ready for the signing of the treaty." His father stood abruptly. The desperation in his father's voice added to Trev's panic.

Maxwell Doman, still sitting at the table, began to laugh. "What are you going to do, Your Majesty, go fetch the pens? I'm sure Gaines has everything prepared already."

"He's right," Levi Karda added. "Let the boy enjoy himself."

"I apologize." Renna looked to the king and the group of men around the table, pretty much anywhere but at Trev. "I'm a little thirsty. I think I'll sit this next song out."

"Renna, it's just a dance." Joniss gave her a pointed look before turning to Trev. "Unless, Ezra, you can think of some reason why you two *shouldn't* dance."

Joniss was manipulating him, and there was nothing he could do about it.

"Of course not."

"Then dance with her." His manipulation turned into a challenge.

Trev swallowed hard, reaching for Renna's hand. "My lady?"

She nodded, cautiously putting her feather-like fingers on his.

They walked across the swirled marble in silence, bodies tense. The song had already begun—another slow song, of course. Trev swung her around to face him, their eyes meeting. She looked as scared as he felt. He placed his arm around her, his hand on her bare back. The feel of her skin burned into his touch. Their movements were guarded and stiff, both of them trying to keep the tension between them in check. They didn't speak, just glided through the crowded dance floor robotically. Other couples swayed close by, not knowing the agony inside of Trev. For surely, this was agony. To have Renna in his arms, but not be able to truly hold her, feel her.

An accidental bump from a couple nearby forced him to step closer to her.

"Excuse us, Your Highness," the man chirped before steering his partner away.

Renna's breath caught, and she leaned in just a fraction, as if momentarily forgetting that distance between them was their only means of self-preservation. Trev briefly closed his eyes and breathed in her perfume, a light citrus scent that was now his favorite smell. Her head melted into the closeness of his cheek, allowing him to whisper in her ear, "You look beautiful tonight."

She didn't pull away.

He tightened his arm around her back in a more intimate way. The movement closed the gap between them even more.

She sucked in the air around her.

"I've wondered all night what it would feel like to dance

with you, to hold you." He could feel strands of her hair on his lips as he whispered in her ear.

"Please," she whimpered, shying away from his touch.

"Sorry." He remembered himself and the room full of people.

They spun around the dance floor in a choking silence until finally, Trev laughed to himself. "I've never wanted to hold or hug something so bad in my life. I feel actual pain in my chest as real as any gunshot wound—a tangible, physical pain."

"Stop saying things like that." Renna pulled away even more, the space like a cold breeze against his skin.

"I just think it's crazy. Don't you? To feel physical pain because I can't hug you or touch you." He turned his head toward hers, the tip of his nose barely touching her cheek. "Do you feel the pain too?"

There was an audible swallow before she inched her face away from his.

"That was a stupid question," he continued. "I know you feel pain. I know I hurt you."

Renna breathed heavily against him. "I can't—"

"I need to explain about the other night."

Her body stiffened even more.

He hated to be the reason for her distress. "I just want you to know that I never—"

"I can't do this." She pulled away from his grasp like she was desperate to escape. If the look in her eyes was any indication, she *was* desperate to escape.

35

Renna

Renna couldn't breathe. The tight dress suffocated and squeezed her. Feelings for Trev exploded within, her skin the only thing holding them inside. She hurried for the stairs, Trev's stunned expression in her wake.

Joniss grabbed her arm, stopping her. "I think you just proved me right."

She yanked out of his grasp, climbing the stairs as fast as her stupid dress would allow. Someone scrambled behind her, following. Picking up her pace, she made it to the top of the stairs and headed for the second-floor sitting room.

"Renna!" Trev called down the hall, piercing her heart. She kept moving.

"Renna!" he begged again behind her.

She pushed open the wooden doors to the sitting room, quickly making her way to the window. She needed air to help her heaving chest. Furiously, she fidgeted with the lock on the window, but it wouldn't budge. Tears already streamed down her cheeks when she heard Trev enter the room behind her.

"Renna?" She could sense he was coming toward her—slowly, cautiously.

She stood with her back to him, swiping at her tear-filled

eyes. "Please just go back downstairs. People will notice you're gone."

"I can't. Not until I know you're okay." His warm fingers gently wrapped around her shoulders, sending chills everywhere, forcing her to turn her body to look at him.

His blue eyes were stormy with sadness and regret. She wanted nothing more than to sink into his arms and let him console her broken heart, even though he was the one who had broken it.

"I'm so sorry. I'm sorry that I've hurt you." His voice was low and genuine. "I never wanted to hurt you."

His sincerity prompted the fall of another one of her tears. His hands sweetly cupped her face allowing his thumb to wipe the tear away; the intimate touch all but completely melted her willpower.

"You mean too much to me. I hate myself for hurting you." His eyes were so concerned, twisting her heart like a wet rag. "Last night with Seran—"

"You don't have to explain." Renna tried to be brave. She stepped back from him, trying to wiggle out of his perfect grasp. The wall and the velvet curtains were against her back, but somehow he was still just as close—*too* close.

"I need to explain." He reached out, his fingers gently playing with the tips of her own fingers. "Seran and I have never—"

Renna placed her hand on his chest to stop his talking, to stop him from getting closer, which he seemed to be doing effortlessly. His chest moved up and down and his heart raced against her palm. "It's none of my business," she said weakly.

"You need to know." His voice was as soft as the velvety fabric behind her. "Besides the festival, that was the first time Seran and I have kissed."

The way his fingers gently grazed her skin, the way his heart spoke to her, the way his blue eyes seemed to know her, made her entire soul ache with the pain he'd mentioned earlier. It really was a piercing, physical pain.

She wanted him.

Needed him.

"You're everything to me," he whispered. "When I found you, everything changed. My heart changed. You made love real, not just an illusion. And I don't want to kiss Seran for the rest of my life." An intense emotion radiated from his eyes, an emotion she immediately recognized in herself. "What I really want," his eyes dropped to her lips, "is to kiss you."

She wanted that too.

What would it feel like to be in his arms, to feel his chest against hers? What would his lips feel like? Taste like? What would his touch do to her skin? She had wondered these things a thousand times.

The desire in his eyes matched her own. She could see the moment he'd made up his mind—the moment he gave in.

His face slowly inched toward hers. In the seconds before his lips touched Renna's, he scanned her eyes for permission, and she gave it. Wholly. Completely.

His lips skimmed the top of hers.

Quietly.

With restraint.

It was sweet and sensual, gentle and explosive all at once. Trev's warm fingertips brushed over her cheeks just as gently as the movement of his lips. There was so much behind his kiss. So much between them that couldn't be said.

For a brief moment, they only *felt*.

And Renna felt it all—the longing, the attraction, the friendship, the chemistry, the passion stirring within. It was all in his gentle kiss.

Trev broke the kiss for a moment, searching her eyes again. They both knew what was coming next by the way they looked at each other—by the heavy breaths between them.

In a fiery instant, their lips crashed together once more.

This time it was different. At first, Renna couldn't even breathe—couldn't keep up with the hungry demand of Trev's kiss.

His body pressed against hers, but there was nowhere for her to go. The wall at her back forced her to blend into him. His wild hands clung to the fabric of her dress, grazing over her bare skin, pulling her body impossibly close.

She wrapped her arms around his neck, digging her fingers through his curls the way she had always wanted to. By kissing, they had crossed a line. Renna didn't know who had pushed who over it, but neither of them seemed to care.

The kiss went on, eager, passionate, endless. Her heart raced, charging her body with explosive fire. Everything intensified. Her desire. His desire.

Surely, no kiss had ever felt like this before.

"Prince Ezra." Her mother's confident voice sounded from across the room, interrupting them.

Trev and Renna broke apart, slowly untangling their limbs as they turned to face Queen Mariele.

"We are expecting you downstairs. They are about to sign the marriage treaty." Her mother spoke smoothly, seemingly unconcerned that she had just found them in each other's arms. She didn't even seem surprised, really.

Trev cleared his throat. "Of course." He pulled his suit jacket down and repositioned the gold crown on his head. The burning fire that had been in his eyes moments ago had turned to embarrassment. Or was it regret? He exited without a glance in Renna's direction.

Renna dared a look at her mother. She couldn't read the expression on her face. Was it pity?

"You are done for the night," her mother said authoritatively. Mangum appeared behind the queen's shoulder, his face solemn as if he knew exactly what she and the prince had been caught doing. Shame and guilt hung around Renna like a halo.

"Mangum will escort you to your room, and you will remain there until I say you can come out. All of your food will be brought to you and Nora can get books or anything else you require."

Renna didn't say a word, not of acknowledgement, nor of protest.

She followed Mangum to her empty room.

He hesitated by the door before leaving, like he wanted to say something to her, but he didn't.

Kicking off her heels, Renna dropped into bed, covering herself and the dress with her bedspread. She imagined nobody at the ball would have guessed that the girl in the red dress was upstairs above them, crying herself to sleep.

36

Trev

Queen Mariele hadn't been exaggerating.

His father and Seran were on the dais in the great hall, ready to sign the treaty. An ornate table had been brought in with colorful flowers in a glass vase sitting on each end. Two extravagant pens with feathers poking out the back were placed on each side of the treaty. The only thing missing was Trev.

Everyone watched him. They had all seen him chase after a woman that was not his fiancée. He could only imagine what they were thinking now. The heaviness of their stares and the sounds of their hushed whispers made his heart race with a panging guilt.

Trev cleared his throat as he approached them, praying his lips weren't swollen from the kiss. He swiped a hand at the beads of sweat forming on his hairline and stepped onto the dais.

"Ezra," Joniss sneered behind him, "you've kept an entire ballroom waiting, chasing after Renna like that."

Seran came to him with a smile, and all the blood drained from his face and rushed to his beating heart. She clasped her hands around his, dropping something inside his palm then pulled back.

"Did you find my engagement ring?" Seran asked, raising her eyebrows as if prompting him. She turned to the guests gathered around the dais, smiling in her calm way. "I asked Miss Degray to hold my engagement ring, and then she left the ball, not feeling well."

Trev wrapped his fingers around the small circular object in his palm.

A ring.

He looked at Seran with her flawless smile, but her eyes gave her true feelings away.

Seran knew.

She knew, and she was helping him anyway.

Trev swallowed hard. He had never hated himself so much.

"Yes!" he said, a little too energetically. He opened his palm to the crowd. "I caught up to Miss Degray just in time."

A murmur rippled through the crowd and the tension loosened in the room. Seran's actions had deflected their suspicions. They believed her.

Queen Mariele stepped onto the dais as Trev slipped the ring onto Seran's finger. Her expression was guarded, but he could see disappointment behind the brown swirls in her eyes.

"Are you ready to sign the treaty?" Seran asked, leaning into him.

Trev plastered on a smile. "Of course."

He picked up the feathered-pen and nodded at Seran. She bent over the document and signed her name. Then it was his turn. A heaviness rested on his shoulders. His heart protested that this was wrong, but then his mind reminded him of his kiss with Renna.

That was wrong.

He scrawled his name across the paper as if the very act could somehow take away his sins.

The great hall cheered as King Carver held up the signed document. Then a procession of people came to shake his hand, congratulating him on a job well done.

Trev didn't deserve their respect. He didn't deserve anything.

The guests started thinning, and the servants rushed around, picking up glasses and plates.

"I'm going to retire for the night," Seran said as she passed him.

"Wait," Trev said, leaving the group of men he was talking with. "Can I walk with you?" He needed to face up to what he'd done, unsure as he was of what the consequences would be.

She nodded, and he followed her out of the great hall.

Neither one of them spoke as they walked to her room. She paused just before her door and turned to him expectantly. Trev rubbed his sweaty palms on the sides of his suit.

"Seran, I'm sorry." His words held so much shame.

She took a deep breath like she was gathering her own courage. "For chasing after Renna, or for something more?"

He wanted to hang his head, but he didn't. He looked straight into her dark eyes. "For something more."

Seran let out a harsh laugh. "I guess I shouldn't be surprised." She folded her arms across her chest. "But I thought you were different. I thought you were going to actually try to make this marriage work."

"I do want to make this marriage work."

Her dark eyes glossed over. "So then, am I to blame Renna?"

"No! It's not Renna's fault. It was all me." He raked a hand through his hair. "Let me explain what happened. It's not what you think."

"Ignorance is bliss," she whispered as she bit her bottom lip. "My mother was married to a man who loved somebody else, but she never confronted him about it. I remember her saying that what she didn't know couldn't hurt her." Seran puffed out a small laugh. "I used to think that made her weak, but I understand now. I don't want to know any details about you and Renna. I don't want them hanging over our relationship the rest of our lives. I just want to know if you can let her go."

Trev had wondered that same thing a hundred times. "I can let her go."

Her jaw set. "You're going to have to because I won't cover for you again."

"Why did you cover for me in the first place?"

She laughed her harsh laugh again. "Because I was hoping it was a misunderstanding, but I can see that I was wrong."

"Seran, I'm so sorry." His voice was raspy and thick as he tried to hold back his growing emotion. "I betrayed your trust and I don't blame you for being angry. I promise nothing like this will ever happen again. I know my promises don't mean much right now, but hopefully someday you can trust me again."

She placed her hand on the doorknob. "Then there's nothing else to talk about." For the first time, she didn't look like a dignified princess. Just a young girl trying to be brave. He'd been so consumed with his own feelings of not wanting to be forced into marriage; he hadn't considered Seran's.

She opened the door to her room. "I'll see you in the morning." Then she was gone, and somehow Trev felt worse than he had before.

THE NEXT MORNING, Trev sat in his office, staring blankly out the window. He wasn't hiding out. At least that's what he told himself.

It was just a kiss.

Just a kiss.

Now wasn't the best time for his excellent attention to detail to surface, but it did anyway. His memory recalled every moment with Renna, every touch, and exactly how it made him feel.

It made him feel *hot*.

He had been a sweaty mess since the kiss—loosening his tie, squirming out of his suit jacket, tossing the covers off last night. This was a persistent heat he couldn't turn off, and he hated himself for it.

"I think I will pay a visit to the province of Axville." He spun in his chair, so he faced his assistant. "How soon can we be ready to go?"

Crosby's brows creased. "Sir, the wedding is in less than two weeks. What about the preparations?"

"Princess Seran has all of that covered."

"What about your father? He won't like you leaving so soon before the wedding."

Trev thought about Renna. "I don't think my father will mind."

"What about the guests? They will be starting to arrive soon."

"Crosby, are you trying to talk me out of leaving?"

Crosby dropped his chin in embarrassment. "No, sir. It just seems like odd timing to be leaving town. That's all."

It was odd timing, Trev knew that, but he didn't care. Nothing was happening at the palace that he couldn't miss, and he needed to get over Renna. He couldn't do that if they were under the same roof.

"Not really," he argued. "They still haven't found the missing girls. I think it's time somebody from the royal family visits their families and shows some support."

"It sounds like an excellent political plan, sir. I will get things arranged for a departure in a couple of hours."

37

The Informer

The night was quiet. Not even the echo of voices filled the city. The buildings lining the streets cast shadows one on top of the other, creating shapes in the dirt below him. He studied them for a minute, lost in thought as he waited in the secluded alley. A shadow emerged from the shapes; the skunk had finally come.

"You're late," the informer said, pushing his body off the wall he leaned against.

"So?" the skunk replied sharply.

"So, I don't like waiting." His eyes flicked over the brusque man and his white streak of hair. He wasn't intimidated by the skunk or his brooding eyes. No, he was repulsed by his filth.

"Are you scared of the dark or something?" the skunk asked.

He lifted his nose in disgust. "No. I just don't enjoy fraternizing with the riff-raff." He waved the man closer. "Do you have what I asked for?"

The skunk shoved an envelope into his hand. He eyed him as he flipped through the stack of money inside.

"It's all there," the skunk sneered. "Or don't you trust me?"

He gave the skunk a wry smile. "I don't trust you at all. But I do trust King Adler. Here." He opened his suit jacket, pulled out a file, glanced over his shoulder, and made sure no one was around before passing it to the man. "I'm sure this will make for some very interesting reading. All the information is there, everything that Adler needs to do and say to pull this scheme off. If he does his job right, the plan will succeed." He couldn't help but be proud of the plot he had come up with against King Carver and Ezra. "And in return, Adler better turn those pretty little missiles away from Albion when I'm king."

The skunk grabbed the file and turned to go.

"Hey!" He grabbed the skunk by the shirt collar and pulled him close, whispering into his dirty face. "This plan puts the Trevenna family on a platter. Tell Adler not to screw this up. My entire future depends on it." He released his grasp and roughly shoved him away.

The man glared back at him but didn't comment before disappearing around the corner.

Joniss crossed the street, making his way to the waiting transporter.

"Is it done?" Maxwell Doman asked once Joniss had climbed inside.

"Have I ever let you down?" Joniss raised an eyebrow at his father then motioned to the driver to pull away. "Are you sure everyone believes you were strongly against the assassination plan? I wouldn't want anything to be linked to us because you didn't do your part."

"Yes, I'm sure. I've said it to Karda, Folly, Pryer, everyone. I said it during the high ruler's meeting to the king himself. I may have planted the seed, but I made sure everyone knew I was wrong for suggesting it and was against it. This can't be traced back to us."

Joniss pulled out the envelope from his suit jacket and flung it at his father.

"That was the final piece in bringing down the Trevenna family," Maxwell said, showing a satisfied smile as he peeked inside at the money.

"Not entirely." Joniss smirked. "There's one more thing I need to do to secure the throne. Every future king needs to save the day."

38

Renna

Renna had been lying in bed for two days. Hours passed in a blur. The sting of loss had taken over her entire soul, seeping into every crack and crevice.

Occasionally, she drowned herself in memories of Trev—memories of his lips on hers, his gentle touch, his playful banter. It all invaded her weak heart. She read his note about not flirting, tracing over the curves of his handwriting. It was a terrible game to play, but she'd always had a flair for the dramatics.

Renna lay half asleep. An autumn breeze floated through the open window wrapping around her, cradling her in her depression. Her eyes opened to listen as voices got louder and louder until her door flung open.

"She looks awful!" Cypress twisted her face into an ugly grimace then looked at Nora. "Bathe her and take her downstairs to Mangum. He's waiting by a transporter for her."

"A transporter? Where are we going?" Renna was annoyed by Cypress's intrusion.

"Mangum wants to take you to explore some ruins." She could tell Cypress didn't approve. "And for some reason, your mother said yes. Nora is going to try and make you look presentable." Cypress nodded at Nora then quickly left as fast as she had come.

Once Renna was dressed, the anxiety of possibly seeing Trev plagued her as she looked down both directions of the hall.

Nora must have read her thoughts. "Don't worry, miss. The prince is not here. He left yesterday afternoon to Axville for a few days."

Renna's heart squeezed. He left? Without saying anything to her?

"I only say that because I heard the queen and Mangum talking," Nora added. "It sounded like his absence was a big deal."

Did Nora know about her and the prince?

"He's checking on the girls taken by those awful Tolsten soldiers. It's so thoughtful of him to think of those poor girls. I'm sure their families will be delighted to see him and his kind eyes after such a terrible ordeal. It's mighty good of the prince. He's just such a sweet . . ." Nora clamped her mouth shut when Renna rolled her eyes. "Sorry, miss," she said. "I won't talk about the prince anymore."

Oh, Nora definitely knew *something*.

Outside, Renna found Mangum waiting by an open transporter door.

"It's good to see you out of your room, Miss Renna."

She climbed past him into the soft leather seat. "I was only allowed out of my room because Prince Ezra is gone."

Mangum climbed in after her. "That may be true, but it's still good to see you out."

"Where are you taking me? Cypress said something about ruins."

"I know how much you enjoy things from Pre-Desolation. There are a few acres of ruins about an hour away." His lips curved into a half-smile. "I thought it might cheer you up."

Mangum had thought about her—planned something for

her? His kindness prompted a cautious smile—the first one in days.

The drive was a much-needed change from the last few days. They were headed east of the palace, a direction she hadn't been yet. At first there were towns with houses and shops that zoomed by her window, but the scenery eventually changed to open, green fields with the occasional farmhouse. The mountains surrounding them had changed too. In some places, there weren't any mountains at all. In other places, the mountains were brown and desert-looking instead of stacked with pine trees. Eventually, Renna could see the ruins off in the distance. A few dilapidated buildings scattered the skyline beyond.

"It must have been a city," she said as she slammed the transporter door behind her.

Mangum looked around at the scene. "Yes, a small one, I think."

Renna ran toward the rubble, calling behind her as she went, "It's amazing!"

For more than an hour, she climbed through the area, touching structures, examining parts of buildings, imagining people coming and going. It was the most significant area with the tallest fragments of buildings she had ever seen. Ruins were commonplace, but not like this, not this much in one area. Mangum was always close behind her, warning her to be careful, telling her not to climb on that, telling her things were unstable, or too sharp to touch. She had to laugh at his fatherly ways.

She sat atop stairs that were still intact, like a bird perched on a tree branch. The remains of the rundown city square sprawled across the land around her. Behind her, decaying pillars threatened to tumble over from years of neglect. A diamond and the words *Bank of Colorado* were etched into what was left of the building.

Desolation—so much emptiness and destruction. The last

few days had been her own personal desolation. She was empty, hollow, and ruined everywhere. She thought about the pre-Desolation world and its people. They'd had it all, and then everything had come crumbling down. They'd lost everything. Renna had been like that pre-Desolation world. She'd had everything she could ever want with Trev. Then he had been ripped away by external forces, and there was nothing she could do about it.

She wondered about the Desolation survivors. Would she ever be able to rebuild again like they did, to start completely over with nothing? There would always be fragments of Trev that remained—cutting into her mind and heart like the jagged pieces of metal and concrete that jutted out of the ground before her. He was a part of her story now, but he wouldn't be the only chapter. She knew, sitting there, that she couldn't let this experience cripple her. She was a survivor. She had already lost somebody she loved once before. Nothing would ever hurt as much as losing her father had, and she had survived that. She would survive this too. She would rebuild again. Her unconquerable spirit would see her through.

A soft breeze blew through her hair, cool enough to remind her that summer was over. The warmth would soon fade, allowing room for something new. She would miss Trev like she missed summertime when in the depths of winter, but winter ice eventually thawed into a beautiful spring, a new beginning. She just needed to figure out what her new beginning would be.

"Miss Renna? Are you ready to go?" Mangum asked from the steps below.

She looked at Mangum. For the past four years, he had been steady, helping her, coaxing her along in her new life at the Government Center—always trying to keep her safe. And yet, she didn't know anything about him.

"Mangum, have you ever been in love?" She hoped her question didn't sound too personal.

He seemed surprised but answered anyway. "Once." He climbed the steps, so he was right in front of her.

"Who was she? What happened?"

"Jarie Swire." Slowly, he lowered his body, sitting down next to Renna. "And I married her."

"I didn't know you were married. Where is your wife now?" Renna wanted all the details.

Mangum rested his elbows on his knees. "There's a lot about me you don't know."

Renna watched him patiently, hoping he would tell a piece of his story to her.

"There's not much to tell. We were in love, got married. I left King Bryant's service to go and work on the Swire Farm. We were happy." His voice trailed off as if his mind was lost in another time.

"What happened?" Renna pressed.

"We had a baby. A beautiful little girl named Paulette." Mangum looked at Renna, his eyes full of lost love. "She would have been just a little older than you. The cutest little thing, but she didn't live long. She was born with a crooked back, and who knows what else. So we just loved her. Made her comfortable. We had three good years with Paulette." His eyes filled with tears. "They were my best three years."

Renna's heart broke just looking at him. Sometimes she felt like she was the only one who went through hard things but talking to Mangum made her realize that everyone had heartache. All you had to do was ask.

"We tried to move on after Paulette passed, but Jarie and I saw things differently. Grief consumed her, and there was no consolation. After a few years, we decided it would be best if I left and went back to King Bryant's guard. She stayed at the farm."

"Is she still there?"

"Yes." His voice grew stronger like he was over the worst

part of the story. "I visited her a year ago. We're still married—but it's not the same."

Renna put her hand on his arm. "I'm sorry."

Mangum shrugged. "Sometimes, life comes from behind and scares you so badly that it takes your breath away." He patted her hand, leaving his on top. "But don't worry. You will breathe again."

Renna leaned her head against his shoulder, missing her own father more than ever. She was grateful for Mangum—grateful for his comfort and words of advice. He wasn't Kimball Degray, but he didn't need to be. He filled a void in her heart, and his assistance couldn't have come at a better time.

She was ready to breathe again.

39

Trev

Smoke swirled and faded into the orange sunrise hovering above the Axville camp. Albion soldiers circled around fires savoring the heat against the chilly morning air. Two miles away, at the enemy's camp, Trev could see similar patches of smoke dancing upward, most likely warming Tolsten soldiers. Albion had been fighting for the last few weeks, pushing back Tolsten soldiers who crossed the border, trying to take residence in Axville.

The town was unrecognizable. Houses and factories were partially burned. Roofs were scorched. Windows were broken, leaving a spray of glass everywhere. But none of that even compared to the tragedy of the missing girls, taken by a group of Tolsten soldiers. Eight teenage girls were missing. They had been gathered together by the riverbank, friends chatting after a long day of work in the factory. The soldiers had watched them, waiting to make a move. The girls hadn't stood a chance. And now, there were still no answers to their whereabouts. King Adler denied Tolsten's involvement, claiming the girls could have been taken by anyone, but Trev knew better.

"It's mighty good of you to come, Your Highness." A skinny-to-the-bone woman squeezed Trev's hand, pulling him out of his own thoughts. "We've been scared out of our wits for our young girls."

"I'm scared too," Trev admitted. "But we're doing everything we can to find them."

A tall man spoke up. He was balding, hanging on to his last pieces of hair, spreading them across his scalp like sprawled out fingers. "What'dya think Tolsten meant by it? Kidnapping our girls like that. Do they want war?"

Concerned murmurs rippled through the crowd of villagers.

"I want to promise that Tolsten can't hurt you, but I can't do that. Your village knows how relentless Tolsten can be. You had to live through their invasion a few weeks ago. You had to see your young girls dragged away."

Trev's eyes swept across the people listening intently to his voice, hanging on every last word. From the bottom of his heart, he wanted to help them, to find their daughters, to give them hope of a better future. "What I can promise is that you won't be alone. Our soldiers will stay here and help protect you while we get things straightened out so you can have your land and your homes back. I can also promise we are doing everything in our power back at the palace to keep the peace between Tolsten and Albion so that this doesn't end in a war."

"What about the election? Your father is out in a couple of months," a young man shouted from the crowd.

"Yeah! Who will protect us then?" another man stepped forward.

This was the perfect moment to make an election pitch, to say something energizing like, *Rah, rah! Vote for me!* That's what his father would do, what his father would *want* Trev to do. But that's not what these people needed. They needed something they could hold on to and believe in. They needed confidence in their government and the Council of Essentials.

"Axville matters to me. Your families, your jobs, your lives all matter to me. As long as I have a say, your village will be protected," Trev replied.

"You have our vote, my lord!" the crowd cheered.

"Don't worry about that right now." Trev didn't want this visit to be anything about the campaign. He truly was concerned about the welfare of these people. "We have set up a tent with supplies. Please visit the officers over there for anything that you may need. If we don't have something, let them know. I'm sure we can send for more supplies if necessary."

He spent the afternoon among the people. Trev and his men helped rebuild parts of homes and barns that had been damaged by Tolsten soldiers. It felt good to work, to get his hands dirty, to think of others before himself. When he laid his head down later that night, his body tired from heavy labor, he was sure he would fall right to sleep, but rest wouldn't come, not with thoughts of Renna filling his head.

The weight of his marriage and his future were like a ton of bricks on his chest. He rolled to his side, trying to ease the suffocating feeling, but nothing worked. When he had promised Seran he would let go of Renna, he'd meant it. But the inescapable ache inside his heart made Trev wonder if he had what it took.

Forgetting her should have been easier than this.

40

Renna

Renna sat with Seran's friends in the dressmaker's room, waiting for Seran to appear in her wedding gown. Fluffy pink couches had been brought in and positioned in a semi-circle around the long mirror. In front of the sofas, trays of food had been laid out for the women to snack on.

"Oh, this is so much fun!" Lizanne's excitement bubbled out of her like an overdrawn bath. "I can't wait to see Seran's dress. I know it's going to be exquisite."

Jenica plopped a strawberry in her mouth but still managed to get an insult out. "Would you calm down? It's not your wedding."

Lizanne's voice was timid. "I know. I'm just happy for my friend."

Renna gave Lizanne an encouraging smile, admiring how Lizanne's beautiful red hair stood out against her pale skin.

Sheridan leaned forward, taking some grapes. "Did you know they had the fabric for her dress brought in from the kingdom of Cristole?"

"We were all there when she told us that," Jenica sneered.

Queen Mariele popped her head around the curtain. "Okay, ladies. Are you ready for the big reveal?"

There was genuine excitement in her mother's voice—something that had never been present for Renna. It was strange watching her mother act like that for someone else. The curtains were pulled aside, and Seran gracefully stepped in front of them.

The room of women, including Renna, all gasped in unison. Seran looked beautiful in her simple, yet elegant wedding gown. White silk hugged her body, coming up high to the base of her neck then squaring off across her collarbone and shoulders. Billowing sleeves ended just below her elbows. Her tiny waist was accentuated as if it had been cinched together by the dress itself. Silk fabric fell straight to the floor barely above her toes in front, but in the back, it trailed long behind her. Pearls and crystals lined the edges of the dress in a classic way. Seran's black hair was slicked back at her forehead, the veil resting on top. The rest of her glossy, straight hair rested neatly around her shoulders and chest, the coal-black contrasting perfectly against the white dress.

Renna always thought it was odd that a culture that attached so much emphasis and prestige to color would choose to wear a white wedding dress. It was one of the pre-Desolation traditions that had stuck all these years later.

Her friends jumped to their feet, gathering around her, gushing over every detail. Renna slowly followed behind. She stared with admiration at Seran until her mother caught her eye. There was the pity look again. Renna put on her best smile to reassure her mother. She didn't want to ruin this moment for her mother or Seran.

"You look stunning," Renna said from the back of the crowd.

Seran glanced at Renna, a timid look in her eyes. "Do you think he'll like it?"

Why was Seran asking *her*?

"How could he not?"

It was true. How could Trev not think she was the most beautiful woman alive when she walked down the aisle toward him? The thought of that moment flashing through her mind made Renna realize something; she didn't want to be there. There was no need for her to be at the wedding—no need for her to see how the story would end. Her father had told her enough fairy tales for her to know that *they would live happily ever after.* At this point, she was only a distraction—a hurdle in the way of Seran's happily-ever-after.

The luncheon was cleaned up. The dress taken off. The room cleared out, except for Renna. She remained on the fluffy couch, planning her future.

"There you are. I thought you had gone to your room." Her mother walked toward the couch, sitting on the edge next to Renna. They had fallen into a polite routine since the night of the ball. They hadn't spoken of the kiss or any of the other problems between them, but here her mother was. She had come back for her. That was more than Trev had done.

Renna stared at Queen Mariele, the woman who had held so many secrets and heartaches for years. Renna used to pray that her mother would let her guard down. Pray that she could understand what was going on in her mind. Now she did. She was more like her mother than she had ever thought. Mariele was the one person who could understand her pain. The one person who knew what it was like to love a prince and give him up. The realization flooded her with heavy emotion. Her nose tingled as her eyes welled up with tears.

"I'm sorry, Mom," she said, her voice ragged.

"Oh, Renna." Her mother grasped her shoulders, pulling her close. "Don't cry."

But it was too late. Tears rushed down her cheeks, rolling onto her neck, wetting her mother's hair and shoulder.

"I know how much you're hurting right now, but all is not lost. You will find happiness again."

Renna shook her head against her mother's neck. "It took you a long time."

Mariele stroked the back of her hair as she spoke. "You have your father's strength inside you. You're much stronger than I ever was, and you'll be okay."

Renna pulled back and wiped at her eyes. "I want to ask you something."

Her mother nodded for her to continue.

"I'd like to move back to Wellenbreck Farm. I own it, after all. Father left it to me."

Mariele looked perplexed. "Why would you want to do that? The Government Center is so much more comfortable than Wellenbreck. And . . . you'd be all alone."

"I wouldn't be alone. I'd have Nellie and Preetis with me." Renna swiped at her cheeks again, brushing away the last remnants of her tears.

Her mother shook her head. "No. No, we couldn't possibly do that. The next few months are going to be difficult for you. You should be surrounded by people that love you."

"I've never felt like I fit in in New Hope and I can't bear to be there when Trev and Seran come to visit for the Council of Essentials in January. I can't do it. I belong at Wellenbreck now more than ever. Please, let me go home."

Her mother let out a sigh. "I suppose you living at Wellenbreck for a little while wouldn't hurt."

Renna lurched forward, giving her mother another hug. "Thank you!"

"Don't get too excited. This isn't permanent."

"I know, but I'm still excited."

Her mother pulled away but kept her hands resting on top of Renna's. "Would you like to leave before the wedding?"

Renna bit her lip as fresh tears pooled in her eyes.

Her mother swallowed back her own emotion. "I couldn't have watched Bryant marry Isadora."

"I don't think I can do it either," Renna admitted, fighting to keep the tears in her eyes.

"I'll arrange everything," her mother said, squeezing her hand. "Don't you worry about a thing."

41

Renna

The week of the wedding had arrived, despite the groom's absence. Renna had no complaints, though. His absence gave her the space to breathe freely, and to roam around the palace.

Guests were beginning to arrive. The palace staff was busy preparing rooms, decorating for the wedding, and cooking lavish meals. The feeling throughout the place was electric. Renna even found herself getting caught up in the buzz. It was easy without Trev around. Easy to pretend this wasn't his wedding. Just Seran's.

"Your Majesty." Mangum bowed excitedly before the queen. The New Hope women were gathered in the royal sitting room after a lovely Sunday brunch with some of the wedding guests. "A New Hope rider just arrived. King Bryant will arrive shortly."

Mariele clapped her hands in joy. "Oh!" She looked at Seran with the happiest of smiles. "He's here! We must go greet him." The queen jumped to her feet. "Did you notify King Carver of his arrival?"

Mangum nodded. "Yes, they are preparing for him now."

"Cypress!" the queen shouted excitedly. "Help me freshen up before he arrives. I want to look my best."

"Certainly, Your Majesty." Cypress quickly followed the queen out the door.

The courtyard was lined with people much like it had been the day Renna had arrived so many weeks ago. So much had happened since then. It was a lifetime ago, but Renna could still remember her feelings, the shock and disappointment she'd felt when she'd discovered who Trev really was, when the ground had dropped out from underneath her.

The New Hope transporter rolled to a stop in front of the palace steps, and Mangum rushed forward to open the door. King Bryant stepped out, and his brown eyes immediately found Mariele. His smile widened as he took her in. Then he glanced at Seran, the same happy smile touching his lips. Mangum ushered him to King Carver.

Everyone watched in silence as the two kings greeted each other. Renna couldn't help but notice their differences. King Bryant was a little bit shorter and held more weight around his midsection and shoulders. His brown hair hadn't yet faded to gray like Carver's had, and his wrinkles weren't as prominent—a small sign that Bryant was a few years younger.

It was all her mother could do to stand properly next to King Carver and not run to Bryant, but she stayed put through all the introductions. And so did Seran. Then Bryant turned to the queen, his hand gently caressing the side of her face. Her eyes closed as she melted into his touch.

"You get more exquisite every day," Bryant said. "How is that possible?"

A young Prince Bryant and a young Mariele flashed before Renna's eyes. She could picture them in love, sneaking around the Government Center. Her heart clenched. It was a vision all too familiar to Renna.

"And you," he turned to Seran, "there's never been a more beautiful bride."

Both women beamed at Bryant's attention.

"Renna, it's good to see you," he said, nodding at her.

Renna curtseyed in front of him. "It's good to see you too, Your Majesty."

"Have you been enjoying your time in Albion?"

She glanced at her mother. "Of course, thank you."

Once the formal introductions were done and the crowd started to disperse, Mariele and Seran flanked both sides of the king. Bryant's arms draped across their shoulders, hugging the two women closer to his sides.

Renna trailed awkwardly behind, just like she always did.

42

Trev

Seran's joyous laughter echoed from the royal sitting room. Trev hadn't seen her since the morning after the ball, and he wondered if she would be happy to see him again or if her happy laughter would fade at the sight of him. He found her on the couch with a man twice her age, holding hands and smiling.

"Ezra!" She hopped up, dragging the man up with her.

Trev had never seen that kind of unrestrained movement from Seran before.

"I want to introduce you to my father." She beamed from ear to ear. "King Bryant."

Trev bowed. "Your Majesty. It is an honor to meet you. I'm so sorry I missed your arrival yesterday. We were desperately trying to get back."

That wasn't true. Trev had desperately been trying to stall his arrival as long as he possibly could.

King Bryant reached his hand out to shake Trev's. "No apologies are necessary. I understand the hectic schedule of a ruling family. He looked Trev up and down before turning to Seran. "So this is the man who will marry my daughter."

Seran smiled with pride. Trev could see the similarities in

them. They had the same thin nose, the same high cheekbones, but everyone that knew Queen Isadora said Seran looked exactly like her.

"I trust you are good enough for her," the king said.

It was like he had thrown a knife right into Trev's heart. He laughed his guilt off. "I doubt anyone is good enough for your daughter, but I will try every day to be worthy of her."

"That's what I want to hear." The king slapped Trev on the back. "Besides, if you don't treat her well, I have an entire army that I'll send after you."

The king laughed, but for some reason, Trev didn't feel like it was a joke. His eye caught Seran's. She looked uncomfortable.

"Let's go down to dinner," Seran said, clutching her father's arm, practically dragging him out of the room.

43

Renna

Renna sat as far away from the royal table as she could. She was alone at her table so far, but whoever came to sit by her would be a better dining companion than King Carver.

Chills went to the back of her neck as someone whispered in her ear. "You don't know how much I've missed you."

She turned slightly, seeing Joniss out of the corner of her eye. "That's funny. I haven't missed you at all."

Joniss laughed her insult off, taking the seat beside her. Maybe the royal table would have been better than this. "Are you sure you want to sit by me?" she asked. "I'm kind of a lot to handle."

"Lucky for you, I'm good at handling things."

She rolled her eyes.

"You look ravishing tonight in blue."

"This old thing? It was supposed to be the dress I wore to the ball last week."

"Really?" His eyebrows raised in interest. "Honestly, I prefer the red dress. Do you still have it? So I can take it off you later?" His smile was steamy and wicked.

She glared at him, trying to decide if Joniss was refreshingly fun or if she wanted to punch him in his handsome face.

"Now that we have a groom, we can finally get this wedding out of the way. I was beginning to worry Ezra wasn't coming back."

Renna choked on her drink a little bit.

"Ahhh," Joniss said annoyingly. "You didn't know he was back?"

She cleared her voice. "Why would I know anything about the prince?"

"Don't worry. I'll help you get over Ezra." Joniss winked at her. "I'm really good at what I do."

Renna didn't dare ask what, exactly, it was that he was really good at.

The trumpets sounded, turning all eyes to the stairs, except Renna's. She focused on the table, her napkin, the ground, anything but the royal family.

Everyone took their seats, and King Carver motioned for dinner to begin.

Maxwell Doman and a few other prominent men Renna recognized joined Joniss at their table. There was a lot of political discussion, making it easy for Renna to hardly ever speak. Overall, she considered it a very successful dinner. Now she just needed to get out of there before she ran into Trev.

"Leaving so early?" Joniss asked as she scooted her chair back to go.

"Yes." She didn't plan on staying a minute longer than she had to.

He stood with a smirk. "I'll join you." Renna placed her hand on his chest to stop him. He raised an eyebrow at her intimate touch. "Is that an invitation?"

Quickly her hand shot to her side. "Not in the least. I'm leaving alone tonight."

"I'm up for a challenge." He cocked an eyebrow.

I'm sure you are.

She turned to leave, but behind her, a familiar voice almost stopped her in her tracks. He was still a distance away, but she recognized Trev instantly. Her hands began to shake, nausea swelling in her stomach.

After all the convincing she had done in her head, he still made the world shake, still made her heart race. She moved through the crowd in the opposite direction as fast as she could, but she heard Joniss behind her.

"Ezra, what kind of man abandons his fiancée right before their wedding?" Joniss said loudly.

"I was in Axville helping the people," Trev bit back.

"Did you find the missing girls?"

"No."

Renna heard Joniss's response before slipping out the side door. "Perhaps I'll visit Axville as well. See what *I* can do to help."

A SOFT KNOCK tapped on Renna's door. The dinner party had long since ended, and Renna was getting ready for bed. Nora opened the door.

"May I speak with Miss Renna?" Mangum's voice was timid, quiet.

Renna sat up in bed, nodding to Nora to let him in.

He stepped into the dim room. "Forgive me if I woke you."

"Not at all. What's the matter?"

"Nothing. I just wanted to tell you that I'm coming to Wellenbreck with you to live. I'm sure you don't want a babysitter, but I agree with your mother that you shouldn't go alone, even though Nellie and Preetis are there. You are still part of the royal family, and you should be protected."

Renna processed his words. "You're going to come to Wellenbreck Farm with me?"

He nodded. "Is that okay?"

She couldn't help it; she jumped out of bed and threw her arms around Mangum's neck.

Ever since the ruins, things had been different with Mangum. There was a tenderness in the way Mangum looked at her. Renna's father used to look at her like that—like she was the most special girl in the world. "I would love for you to come to Wellenbreck!"

Mangum laughed freely, awkwardly hugging her back. "I can work too, you know. I used to work on the Swire Farm."

Renna stepped back to see him. "Just as long as you don't tell my mother everything I do there."

He laughed a full, hearty laugh. "Some things are best kept just between us."

44

Trev

Every hour it seemed like another distinguished guest arrived. The prince of Cristole, the queen mother of Enderlin, and now King Adler of Tolsten walked toward the palace's front steps where Trev stood with his father.

Adler was tall and big, with straight black hair slicked back. His olive skin added to his already striking looks. The resemblance between him and his older sister, the late Queen Avina, was evident. Adler was twenty when Avina had moved to Albion to marry King Carver. Trev had sometimes wondered if Adler knew how much Avina's stepson loved her. If Adler knew how Trev locked himself on the roof of the palace and cried for hours after her funeral.

If Adler knew all that, would he still hate Albion so much?

"Are you surprised to see me, Carver?" King Adler spoke with an edge of anger as he greeted him.

"Not particularly." King Carver's brows furrowed. "We invited you to the wedding, and you accepted our invitation. We've been expecting you."

Adler laughed his answer off. "Was that before or after you tried to have me killed?"

King Carver froze. "Excuse me?"

"Enough with the games, Carver. You sent someone to my room at the Dawsey Inn the other night to have me killed. What did you do? Pay off the hotel staff?" Adler asked.

Trev looked at his father, who seemed just as confused as he was. Trev was there when his father had written the note to call off the assassination. He had personally chosen the soldier sent to deliver the letter. The man had reported back that the message had been delivered. What had gone wrong?

"I applaud your efforts. It was a seemingly good plan. Invite me to the wedding then use the element of surprise to get me when I would least expect it. The only problem with your plan was that you underestimated my men. And me." Adler smiled smugly.

"King Adler," Carver shifted his weight nervously, "if there was an attempt on your life within our kingdom, I will do everything in my power to identify and punish the guilty. And we are, of course, deeply relieved that you escaped unharmed. But we had nothing to do with any attempt on your life."

Adler laughed. "Of course you would deny it."

"There are many people who could have done this. Why would *we* try to"—King Carver leaned in close so nobody could hear their conversation—"kill you? We are in the middle of a wedding."

"I wondered that same thing myself." Adler lowered his icy gaze on King Carver. "But then again, you never planned on me surviving and showing up here to confront you. It's like you *want* to start a war between our two kingdoms. First, you accuse me of kidnapping those girls by the border and now *this.*" He leaned in closer between Trev and his father, whispering so only they could hear. "If I were you, I'd play nice. There are rumors that I have sophisticated weapons back in Tolsten. I'm dying to try them out."

King Adler's laugh was cruel and wicked, making the hairs on the back of Trev's neck rise.

"What did you do?" Trev asked an hour later as he paced the king's office.

"I didn't do anything." His father looked to Commander Pryer for help. "I called off the assassination. You both saw me."

Trev wanted to believe him. "Then explain to me why Adler is accusing us of attempted murder."

"I . . . I . . . honestly don't know." For the first time, his father seemed speechless.

"He's not just accusing us. He knew the details, how we were targeting him at the Dawsey Inn. How could he know that unless it was true? Unless one of our men tried to carry out the plan." Commander Pryer swore under his breath. "This is a disaster! And now he's here." His arms flew into the air. "How can I protect Albion from Adler when he's here?"

Trev pointed at his father. "If I find out that you two are lying to me, that you two went behind my back on this plan, I swear I will—"

"We didn't," his father said, interrupting him. "Something is wrong. Pryer, bring the man to me who was sent to deliver the letter. I want to question him personally. And find the men that were stationed at the hotel, the ones that were going to carry out the mission. I want to question them all." His father was beginning to yell. "I want to know who attempted to kill Adler against my express orders!"

Commander Pryer scrambled out of the room.

Trev looked at his father in a severe way. "You promised, if I married Seran, you would call off the assassination. You gave me your word."

His father rubbed his hand on his face before raking it

through his graying hair. He looked older today than he ever had before.

"I didn't do this."

Trev shook his head. "I don't know if I can trust you anymore."

"Don't do anything foolish with the wedding. Let me figure out how this happened." The king's voice sounded desperate.

"You need to tell King Bryant about this. He needs to know."

"No, not yet." His father shook his head.

Trev threatened, "If you don't tell him, I will."

"Just give me more time." The pleading on his father's face should have made him feel something, but it didn't.

"Tell him before dinner tonight, or I will." Trev slammed the office door behind him as he left and walked down the hall. He turned the corner and nearly collided with Joniss.

"Ezra!"

"What do you want, Joniss?" How was the man so annoyingly *everywhere*?

"Oh, nothing. I just arrived early for the dinner tonight. Is everything all right? Things seemed kind of tense with King Adler out in the courtyard." Joniss seemed to be enjoying Trev's distress.

Trev masked his fear and kept walking. "You know King Adler; he can be difficult."

"I hope everything is okay," Joniss called after him. "I would hate to have something ruin your wedding."

I'm sure you would.

"Do YOU THINK your father is lying?" Drake asked. They stood in the corner of the great hall so they could talk freely.

Around them, guests finished dinner, laughing and drinking, unaware of the political tension in the air.

Trev took a drink. "I don't know. He seems completely distraught by everything, but I can't tell if that's because he doesn't know what's going on or because he got caught." He eyed King Adler cautiously. His fine, mint green suit stood out across the room, a cloud of smoke billowing around him as he puffed on a cigar. Cigars weren't essential. They were illegal, but Adler had the audacity to smoke one in front of all the other leaders in the room.

"Does King Bryant know?" Drake asked.

"Yes, my father told him just before dinner. He's not happy about any of it."

Drake rubbed his chin. "But does he believe your father?"

"He seems to." Trev shrugged.

Drake folded his arms across his chest. "So if King Carver didn't do it, then who did? An informer?"

"I've thought about it, but it doesn't make sense." Trev had gone over it in his mind a hundred times. "Spies or even an inside informer would know what we're planning, and might give away our secrets, but they wouldn't carry out our plans."

"True." Drake nodded.

"What about Joniss and his father? The idea to kill Adler originally came from Maxwell. Do you think they are trying to frame us to win the election?"

"Possibly, but that seems risky. Wouldn't they be worried about Adler coming after Joniss and Albion once he was king?"

Trev scratched the back of his neck, trying to sort his thoughts out. "Maybe."

Drake lowered his voice even more. "What about Commander Pryer? He was the only one who knew that the assassination plan had been put together and then called off again. He was for the assassination, and I'm sure he didn't like your father calling it off because of you."

"That's what my gut is saying too, but my father would never hear it. They've been together for thirty years. Why would Pryer turn on us now?"

Drake raised his shoulders. "Maybe he thought he was doing the right thing. He probably thought the mission would be successful, and King Adler would be dead. He could never have foreseen the plan not working and Adler showing up here like he did."

"You're right." Trev put his glass down on the table in front of him. "I need to go question Pryer."

Drake pulled his arm. "Let me do it. It would be best if you didn't leave the party. It will look bad. Besides, Fenton Pryer doesn't like you. We might get more information if I question him."

Trev agreed, letting Drake take the lead on this one.

He joined his father on the dais, taking the throne seat next to him.

Carver fidgeted nervously with the end of his tie. "Let's hope the worst is over."

"What about Commander Pryer?" Trev asked. "Is it possible that he betrayed us? Carried on with the mission without your knowledge?"

His father shot him a look. "No."

"Well, I know it wasn't me. You claim it wasn't you. That only leaves one man that could have given the order." He looked at his father, hoping he saw the logic behind what he said.

King Carver slammed his hands on the thick arms of his chair, then pushed himself up.

Trev should have known better. His father never saw the logic.

"We'll know more tomorrow," the king said. "It's late. I'm going to bed."

Trev sat alone on the dais. The seriousness of the situation weighed him further into his chair. King Adler had consumed his thoughts for hours. He would never say the situation was a *nice* distraction, but it was a distraction, nonetheless. Now, in the quiet, he allowed his mind to drift. Seran had gone up already, saying she had packing to do for the honeymoon, and he'd lost track of Renna long ago.

45

Renna

The next morning, Renna knocked on the door, hearing Seran's soft voice in the room beyond. Her maid answered the door, giving Renna a slight curtsey.

"Come in," Seran said from behind her maid.

"I wanted to talk to you." Renna stepped into the room and paused, looking at the pile of dresses sprawled across Seran's bed. "Unless you're too busy."

"We're just packing for the honeymoon." Seran looked at her maid as if she understood the headache of it all. "The first few days we'll spend in the mountains at the Trevenna family lodge. Summer is over and up in the mountains, it's going to be chilly." She pointed at a stack of colorful dresses with long sleeves. Next to them were bright jackets. "I have to be prepared for cooler temperatures, but then after that, we're traveling around to several cities. The king thinks that showing the happily married couple will help with the election. So I have to have dresses that work for those occasions and temperatures." She shook her head in annoyance. "There's just so much to think about."

Renna tried not to let the word *honeymoon* bother her. It was the first time she had heard Seran speak about what would happen after the wedding. The wedding ceremony had always been the culminating event—the final moment that loomed over her like death to the terminally ill. She hadn't put much thought into Trev and Seran's immediate future, into their *honeymoon.*

"So yes, I am busy, but not with anything I can't do while talking." Seran's words pulled Renna out of her own head. "What do you need?"

Renna took a few more steps into the room. It was exquisite. The marble floor was covered with plush, striped rugs. Deep purple sofa chairs surrounded a large marble fireplace, the mantel molded and carved on the sides into ornate designs. Three French doors led to a spacious balcony that overlooked the city. Seran had all three sets of doors open, letting in the soft morning sunlight and the first evidences of Fall.

"I like your room," Renna said.

Seran looked around while she continued to fold clothes. "I like it too, but I won't be in it much longer. When we get back, I'll move into Ezra's chambers, and then after the election, I suppose I'll have the queen's suite attached to the king's."

More things Renna hadn't thought about.

Things she didn't *want* to think about.

"I'm leaving tomorrow," she blurted. "I'm going to live at Wellenbreck Farm."

"Oh?" Seran paused her folding, giving her full attention to Renna.

"I'm leaving before the ceremony." Renna talked fast, the same way she always did when she was nervous. "I just wanted you to know, so you didn't wonder where I was. Not that you would even think about me on your wedding day." Renna frowned. Why did her words sound so weird? "I just . . . thought you should know."

Seran set the dress in her hands down on the bed, then

turned to her maid. "Vivian, will you give us some privacy, please?"

The maid curtseyed once then left the room.

"It seems strange that you're leaving before the ceremony," Seran said.

Renna's voice came out a little too high. "Does it?"

"Well, yes." Seran seemed a bit put out. "It will look bad if you're not there. Like we had a falling out or like I *asked* you not to come."

"No one will even notice that I'm gone."

"Ezra will." Seran's lips tugged further downward. "He notices everything about you."

Renna's stomach began to churn, and suddenly it was hard to breathe.

"You know, sometimes I watch him watch you." Seran gracefully sank onto the edge of her bed, squishing a pile of undergarments in the process. "His eyes always find you, but the look on his face is the most interesting part. Everything about him brightens."

Renna swallowed back the rising bile in her throat. How long had Seran known about them? "Seran, I—"

She put her hand up, stopping Renna. "At first, I was angry with you. You're not chained to a marriage alliance. You can fall in love with and marry whomever you want. Why did you choose the *only* man I can be with?"

"I . . ." Renna shook her head. Her chest tightened and it was hard to find her voice. She swallowed. "I didn't choose him. I would never intentionally do that to you."

Seran nodded. "Do you want to know the worst part?"

Renna didn't dare answer.

"The worst part is none of us will truly ever be happy. No one wins in a situation like this."

Emotion crept its way up Renna's throat, but she refused to let it out, refused to let her own pain diminish the significance of Seran's. She swallowed back the lump forming in her throat, willing herself to stay strong.

"I feel awful," she managed to get out. "What can I do to fix this?"

Seran's lips lifted into a small smile, but it didn't reach her eyes. "There's nothing to fix. You'll go away, and I'll pray that Ezra forgets you someday."

Renna felt numb.

"I'm scared to marry him. Not just because he has feelings for you, but because I *don't* have feelings for him," Seran admitted. "I know that's probably the last thing you want to hear me say, to complain about marrying a man you'd give anything to be with."

Renna had thought she would give anything to be with Trev but seeing the hurt in Seran's eyes ripped her heart wide open. Seran was right; no one won. "I wish you were free to do what you want with your life."

"I do too." Seran's eyes dropped to her hands. "And what about you?" She abruptly stood. "Will you be happy?"

Renna nodded her head, not daring to speak, afraid if she did she might crumble to pieces right there on Seran's floor.

"Well," Seran pulled her into a hug, "good luck, Renna."

This was another goodbye. If Renna was going to cut Trev out of her life, she had to cut Seran out too. She was the closest thing to a sister Renna had ever had. Even though they were different, Renna was going to miss her.

There were probably a hundred things Renna should say to Seran, but all that mattered now was that Seran and Trev found happiness. "Take care of each other."

"We'll try," Seran said, giving her one last hug.

RENNA WAS ALL packed and ready for Wellenbreck—it wasn't as complicated as Seran's *honeymoon* packing—so she decided to spend some time on the roof. She had only discovered the roof last week. With lots of time on her hands, she had followed a staircase in the west corner of the palace, finding it led to the roof. It wasn't the entire roof, more like a little section above the west tower, but it was secluded and had picturesque views of the city and the changing leaves on the mountains. Renna wished she had known about it earlier. She could imagine hours of stargazing from this spot.

She pushed open the steel door and walked through, letting it slam behind her. The late afternoon sunlight was blinding, but her eyes still made out the outline of Trev. He sat on a cooling unit with his elbows on his knees, staring out across the kingdom, his back to her. The door slammed shut behind Renna, causing him to flip his head around.

There was nowhere to run.

Nowhere to hide.

There they were, face to face for the first time since he'd kissed her. He looked somber, but handsome as ever.

There was a slight hint of stubble on his face like he'd forgotten to shave that morning. His clothes were casual—a green t-shirt and black athletic pants. And his blue eyes, Renna had forgotten how blue his beautiful eyes were. She would have to forget that again. The realization made her sad.

"I'm sorry. I didn't know you were up here." Her words came out rushed, and she turned to go.

"Wait!" He scooted off the green unit. "I've been avoiding you. Now here you are."

Slowly she turned around. "I thought I was the one avoiding you."

He chuckled, just a soft laugh, the kind you give more out of courtesy than anything. "How have you been?" he asked.

Renna's brows bent as she thought back over the last week and a half. The loneliness. The heartache.

Her face must've given something away, because he

quickly added, "That was a stupid question. Don't answer that." He shoved his hands in his pockets, obviously nervous.

She tried to ease both their anxiety. "How was Axville?"

"Frustrating. Sad. Disappointing. I just wish I could do more for the people. I repaired some damaged homes. They probably won't invite me back." He shrugged. "I'm not that great with tools."

Not knowing what else to do, she looked to the sky. "It's a beautiful day."

He twisted his body to look upward. "Isn't it? The weather couldn't be any more perfect."

"They say it's going to get cold soon," she added.

It's going to get cold soon?

He must have felt the ridiculousness of their conversation as well. "I can't believe we've resorted to talking about the weather."

She smiled. "Yeah, it's pretty bad."

He smiled too, the big smile that she loved, the smile that gave hints he was about to say something charming. "First of all, I'd like to apologize."

"For what?" He was going to bring up the kiss.

"For not locking the door behind me the night of the ball." He smiled, but it didn't hide everything; it didn't hide his shame. "They make locks specifically for reasons like that. Specifically, so that your future mother-in-law doesn't walk in on you kissing somebody other than the bride."

Renna raised her eyebrows. "They make locks specifically for moments like that?"

"Mm-hmm." He nodded. "Can't you picture the lock makers sitting around a table, discussing the worst possible things a human can do? Things you wouldn't want anyone else to see?" His laugh was cynical. "Kissing your fiancée's stepsister has to be top of their list."

She longed to ease his guilt—guilt she was all too familiar

with herself. "There are probably a few other things that are worse."

A hint of playfulness touched his eyes. "Well, maybe a few." He took his seat back on top of the unit, casting his eyes across the land. She didn't dare sit by him. Instead, she kept close to the door. It was always good to have an exit strategy.

"There are so many people at the palace right now. I had to get away for a minute. Clear my mind," he explained.

"Me too." That wasn't entirely true. She'd come to the roof not to escape, but as a way to say goodbye to the city that had been her home for the past month. She wasn't going to tell him she was leaving. He wouldn't try to stop her, and him not stopping her would hurt more than everything else combined. So she wouldn't tell him; she wouldn't test him that way. She'd go on pretending that if he knew, he would surely make her stay.

The corners of his mouth lifted into a slight smile. "Actually, you came up here because you knew I was here. You've been following me, waiting for a moment when I was alone so you could"—he slowed his speech dramatically—"*kill* me."

"Kill you?" She balked at his choice of a storyline, but she was grateful for something light-hearted to talk about. Everything else between them felt so heavy.

"Yes, you came up here to push me off the roof," he said matter-of-factly.

She smirked. "For not locking the door?"

"Exactly."

Renna questioned his plan. "Why wouldn't I have just poisoned you at dinner?"

His head wiggled back and forth. "Too hard."

"Or shot you from across the room?"

"Too messy." His mouth contorted into a grimace.

"Or strangled you while you were asleep in your bed?" she argued.

He raised his eyebrows. "Too intimate."

She finally laughed, and it caught her off guard. "Okay. So now what happens?"

"Well, I overpower you and push you off the roof instead. It's a surprise ending."

Her face twisted in disgust. "What a gruesome story."

His hands raised out in front of him. "I know, right? It took an evil turn somewhere, and I just had to go with it."

They fell into an uncomfortable silence, the only sound the soft hum of the cooling unit. Neither one of them had planned on seeing the other, let alone talking to each other. Beyond make-believe, what real things could they even talk about?

She decided to leave. "I better go get ready for the wedding dinner."

"Renna?" Trev hopped to his feet again, staring at her for a moment. "Thank you."

She shrugged her shoulders. "For what?"

"For teaching me what it feels like to have a broken heart."

A familiar sorrow coiled around Renna like an old friend keeping her company. "I don't think that's a good thing," she whispered, trying to keep her emotions in check. She completely loved him, and yet, *he* had a broken heart.

They both did.

"I'll take anything I can get from you, even if it's only a broken heart." His eyes were defeated, adding to the canyon of heartache inside her. "I've never been so miserable in my life," he said, half laughing. "This misery has changed me. It has taught me about myself and . . ." His words got quieter. "About love."

Renna had to look away.

She couldn't handle the seriousness of it all. She couldn't handle the use of the word *love,* especially when he would never be hers. She swallowed hard. "I'm afraid you'll never be satisfied again," she said with an air of sarcastic haughtiness.

"Obviously," he whispered.

"Obviously," she whispered back.

Renna didn't need to look at him. She knew from the sound of his voice what smile he gave—the sad one, full of longing.

But she did look at him.

One last time.

His blue eyes were glossed over with moisture, contradicting his charming smile. He stood there, hands in his pockets, staring back at her. Every fiber of her being swore she was meant to look at him for the rest of her life and beyond, but somehow this was goodbye.

She loved him enough to let him go.

She turned to leave, letting their story end one last time.

46

Trev

Later that night, everyone gathered in the great hall for the pre-wedding dinner. Glasses clanked together after each toast and each shout of, *'to the happy couple!'* Trev's jaw ached from all the smiling he was doing. The pretense of happiness was exhausting. Of course, nobody used the word *love* in their speech. This was an arranged marriage, a political move. Instead, they said things like, *'they make a charming couple,' 'Albion's future is bright with the two of them,'* or Trev's personal favorite, *'there's never been two people more perfect for each other.'*

As if any of these well-wishers knew anything about what was perfect for Trev. What was perfect for Trev was sitting eight tables away, wearing a shiny silver dress. Her hair was down and impossibly straight—Trev had never seen it that straight before. She was sitting next to a young soldier, who seemed to be leaning into her just for the fun of it.

"To the happy couple!" Alba Folley said, finishing his speech. Trev raised his glass to Seran's again. More cheers. More clanking glasses.

King Adler stood, making tensions rise. Nothing had been solved yet. Drake had tried to question Commander Pryer, but he was already gone; he had left to find the men stationed at the Dawsey Inn to bring them back for questioning. Still, Pryer's absence seemed extremely convenient.

Adler raised his glass. "To Prince Ezra, Princess Seran, and the unity of two great kingdoms. May their marriage lead to happiness, not war."

"Hear, hear!" shouted the crowd. Trev took a drink, not missing the knowing look from Drake.

King Carver stood, raising his glass. "Thank you all for coming. King Bryant and I are honored that you would all travel so far to celebrate this joyous occasion with us. King Adler is right. Tomorrow marks the joining of two great kingdoms." Trev held his breath. He would have preferred his father not mention Adler. "And, in a few months, this happy couple will rule Albion together, uniting us all, making Albion stronger than ever." Even from where Trev was sitting, he could see the snickers pass through Joniss, Maxwell, and their friends. If they had their way, Joniss would be the one ruling Albion in a few months. "Again, thank you all for coming. We'll see you all tomorrow at the wedding ceremony."

The crowd applauded.

Trev and Seran stood. Hand in hand, they smiled and nodded at the crowd applauding them until enough time had passed, and they exited the great hall together, waving like idiots.

"I'm glad that's over," Trev said as they walked down the hall.

Seran removed the long gloves covering her arms. "I didn't think it was that bad. Besides, anytime we can be in the spotlight right now is good. It only helps with the election." She sighed. "It's all part of the job."

Trev looked at the beautiful, intelligent woman walking beside him. "What would you do with your life if you weren't marrying me?"

She laughed his question away. "I am marrying you, so it doesn't really matter."

He stopped walking. "It matters to me."

Her steps slowed, and she looked up and down the hallway as if making sure no one else was around. "I suppose I . . . I would love to be an educator, teach history and politics."

Trev smiled. "You would be amazing at that."

For the first time since he had known her, Seran got embarrassed. Her cheeks reddened, and she turned away. "I would ask what you would do if you weren't marrying me, but I think I already know the answer."

The truth behind her words hurt. "Am I that predictable?"

Her eyes softened as she looked at him. "I guess neither of us is free to do what we want with our lives."

He grabbed her hand. "At least we have that in common."

"It's a start."

Trev leaned his body into the cement railing of his balcony. City lights shone like stars below him, radiating a soft glow into the night sky. He would have considered the moment peaceful if it weren't for the anxious feelings inside him. The gravity of it all—Adler, Renna, Seran, the election—pulled him down.

Relentlessly sinking him.

Drowning him.

He had been dropping into this darkness for a while, desperately trying to claw his way out. It was easier when he thought he was saving Albion, saving Adler from the assassination, but now, he didn't even have that. His grip had slipped, and he never thought he could fall so low.

47

Renna

Overnight, the palace's great hall was transformed for the wedding ceremony. Pale yellow silk billowed across the ceiling, covering the expansive roof like an airy tent, making it seem more intimate than usual. Flower garlands were strung above, decoratively stretching across the fabric. Rows and rows of yellow chairs lined each side of the room with flowers fastened to the ends, pink ribbon dangling from the sides to the floor. Even more colorful flowers dripped from the walls, sweeping up and down like waves in the sea. The dais sat at the front of the room with large floor vases on either side, full of the most exquisite flowers Renna had ever seen. The room smelled like a garden on a chilly spring day. Everything was colorful, bright, and happy—just the way it was supposed to be.

But Renna was leaving.

Her mother's shoes clicked on the marble as she walked in the room. "There you are."

Renna smiled at her mother and King Bryant. "I just wanted to see the decorations before I left."

"Are you sure you're going to be okay?"

Her mother was asking about her heart. Would her heart

be okay since the man she loved was marrying someone else today?

Renna pretended her mother was referring to Wellenbreck.

"I'll be fine. Mangum will be with me. He'll keep me out of trouble. Won't you, Mangum?"

Mangum stood outside the doors to the great hall. "Certainly, my lady."

King Bryant took Renna by both hands. "Please know that you're always welcome at the Government Center if you ever want to come back."

"I know," she said, not believing that she would ever want that.

"And if there is anything you need, anything at all, don't hesitate to ask."

"I won't," Renna said, wondering if her mother had told Bryant about her and Trev. If Bryant knew, would he still want his daughter to marry the prince? Or would he want Trev to marry her instead? She shook her head. None of that mattered because Renna knew her mother and knew that she would never tell Bryant about what had happened.

King Bryant stepped aside, so Renna's mother had room to say goodbye. "I don't think I'm strong enough for this. My nerves can't handle it." Her mother wrung her hands together.

"Your nerves will probably do better when I'm gone," Renna teased.

Mariele pulled her into a hug, her heavy breathing rising and falling against Renna as she held her.

"I'm so sorry, Renna," her mother whispered into her ear. "This is exactly like the day King Dayton sent me away to Wellenbreck Farm. I wish there was something I could do. I wish you could be with Ezra."

Renna tightened her grip around her mother, refusing to let her see how much leaving this place, leaving Trev, was crushing her. "Nobody is sending me away. I'm choosing to go."

Mariele took a deep breath and pulled away. "You're right, and you'll be better for it."

They gave each other one last squeeze, and then Renna followed Mangum out to the waiting transporter.

"Are you ready, Miss Renna?" Mangum said, holding the door open for her.

She hesitated for just a moment, turning back for one last look. Her eyes swept over the grand palace, and the balcony she knew belonged to Trev.

There was no one there.

She took a deep breath, got inside the transporter, and didn't look back again.

48

Joniss

Joniss watched his father put the finishing touches on to his formal wear. His father stepped in front of him, ready to go down to the waiting transporter. "This is a big day for us."

"Very big, indeed." Joniss felt giddy. The first part of his perfect plan had already been set in motion the day Adler had arrived. The man deserved an award for his acting skills. He almost had Joniss convinced about the assassination attempt.

Joniss gave a crooked smile as he thought out loud. "Carver and Ezra are still trying to figure out who attempted to kill King Adler."

"I'm sure they'll blame Commander Pryer for it." Maxwell snickered. "He'll be hanged for something that never even happened."

Joniss looked at himself in the mirror one last time. "Yes, I suppose he will." Satisfied with his appearance, they followed each other out the door.

JONISS WHISTLED AS he walked into the great hall with his father.

His eyes scanned the lavish decorations. "They sure went all out on this wedding. Didn't they?"

"What a waste of money," Maxwell said bitterly.

"I don't know about that. I think the decorations will add to the drama today."

"True. It should be rather entertaining."

"By next week, this kingdom will look to you for their future." His father's voice was smug. "And in a few months, you'll be the one sitting at that dais."

He felt a tinge of excitement. He had been feeling that way all morning, like a kid who had been anxiously waiting for his birthday present. It was a big day. The day that would secure his future.

"I better go make the rounds," his father said, leaving him all alone.

Across the room, Adler caught his eye. Both men nodded in silent, subtle acknowledgment of their secret plan.

49

Trev

"It'll be over soon," Drake said as he shifted in his chair, crossing his leg over his knee. "Then you can go back to how things were before."

Trev sat quietly, unmoving.

A hard knock at the door shattered the silence.

Drake stood to answer it. "It must be time to go down."

Crosby rushed into the room. "Your Highness, Commander Pryer is back. He just arrived in the training hall."

Trev jumped to his feet, anxious for answers about Adler. "We need to interrogate him."

Drake stopped him before he could leave the room. "You can't go now. The ceremony is starting any minute."

Drake was right, but still, Trev felt desperate. "I need to question him and the other men from the hotel. It can't wait!"

"I'm afraid there aren't any men from the hotel with him," Crosby said. "All the other men that were involved are dead."

Trev and Drake exchanged looks. "That's convenient. So there's nobody left to rat him out for his betrayal." Trev's words were laced with anger.

"We don't know that," Drake said, trying to calm him down. "Adler's men could have killed them all."

"Oh, come on! Pryer is behind all of this with Adler. This is just further proof of his guilt. I just don't know what part my father played in it as well." He shook his head in frustration.

"Your Highness? It's time." Gaines waited by the door, expectantly.

Drake placed a hand on his shoulder. "We'll deal with Fenton Pryer after the ceremony. Let's get through the next hour, and then we can make a plan."

Trev nodded. Everything was converging all at once. He smoothed his black tie and tugged on the jacket of his black, fitted suit. Drake handed him his gold crown. The last time he wore it, he'd held Renna in his arms. Trev swallowed, trying not to think about her and that night. There was nothing he could do but follow Gaines out of the room.

From his place on the dais, Trev could see everyone seated in the aisles, all of them counting on him. Everyone but Renna, he noticed. He scanned the faces for hers but came up with nothing.

King Carver stood next to Trev in the middle. As the ruling king, he would be the one performing the marriage ceremony.

"Did you hear Pryer was back?" his father leaned over and whispered while they waited.

"Alone. Everyone that could testify of Pryer's guilt is dead."

"Oh, get over it!" His father's voice was hushed but stern. "So what if Pryer did this? I wanted him to do it. If you hadn't intervened, Adler would probably be dead now, and we wouldn't have to worry. You've ruined everything. This is your fault."

No matter what Trev did, nothing was good enough for his father. Even now, he stood ready to marry the woman his father had chosen, to shackle his life to unhappiness, and his father *still* found a way to be disappointed in him.

A musician started playing the harp softly. The crowd stood and quieted as they turned. At the top of the grand staircase, Seran and King Bryant magically appeared. She wore a tasteful, sleek, white gown with a glittering tiara on her head, while the king wore a navy suit with purple and yellow ropes draped around his neck, signifying the kingdom of New Hope. Cellos and violins joined the harp, adding to the beautiful sound as they began to descend the stairs, Seran's white train blanketing the steps behind her.

Trev's heart raced, but not in a good way. He wiped at the sweat forming above his brow. His eyes scanned the crowd again. All heads were turned to the stunning bride, but one. Queen Mariele glanced at him, sadness written across her face. Trev's eyes questioned her. Where was Renna?

She shook her head slightly.

She wasn't there.

The music seemed to pick up intensity, matching his feelings inside. Seran was at the beginning of the aisle now, a mere sixty feet from Trev. He had sixty feet to make up his mind.

Fifty-nine.

Fifty-eight.

He wiped his sweaty palms on the sides of his pants, sucked in all the air around him, and pushed it back out again. His heart continued to thump to the rhythm of the music. It was like the orchestra couldn't keep up with its furious beats. He looked at the ground, weighing the consequences in his mind. He dared to look at Seran, who had somehow made it to the dais by his side. His father already thought he had ruined everything. At this point, what did it matter if Trev ruined the alliance too?

Then Seran's own words played back in his head.

Neither of us is free to do what we want with our lives.

What did he want to do with his life?

He pictured growing old with Renna. That's what he wanted to do with his life.

He loved Renna.

He always would.

The music stopped. Everyone took their seats, and his father opened his mouth to speak.

"There's something I'd like to say." Trev's voice sounded loud against the silence. He took Seran by the hands and whispered so only she could hear. "I'm sorry. I hope you can forgive me someday, but I want to set you *free*. Set us both free."

Her eyes filled up with tears, but not the angry kind he'd been expecting. She looked more relieved than anything.

He quickly glanced at his father who tried to warn him through panic-stricken eyes. He glanced at Drake who didn't seem surprised. He looked at Queen Mariele, tears streaming down her face, and the confused King Bryant next to her.

"Before we start, I just wanted to say . . ."

Trev turned his body to the audience, letting go of one of Seran's hands. They all looked stunned, waiting on the edge of their seats for the next words out of his mouth. He tried to gather his thoughts, but something caught his eye. A small movement in between the stillness of the statue-like people. The kind of movement that a trained soldier would notice. But what he couldn't understand, what he couldn't register fast enough, was the gun in the hand of the man with white and black hair. Or why the gun was pointed directly at Seran.

Trev lunged, throwing his body in front of Seran's as shots blasted off. A bullet stung his arm instantly as he and Seran tumbled to the ground. There seemed to be a lot of blood. And screaming from all the guests.

There was a lot of screaming.

He wrangled his body on top of Seran's to protect her. Another round of shots broke out while guards surrounded them, dragging King Carver away, pulling at him and Seran.

"Ez . . . ra . . ." Seran choked from underneath him.

Trev lifted his body enough to see the crimson blood spilling out of her chest.

He tried to stem the wound with his hand, her blood spilling between his fingers. "Help us!"

"Ez . . ." Her frightened eyes looked at him to save her.

Strong arms tried to lift his body away.

"She's hurt!" he yelled.

More men came and pulled him off her, filling the wound with their hands, dragging him away from her.

Amidst the chaos, he remembered the man with the white and black hair.

"The shooter! Get the shooter!" Trev tried to twist his body back around to see, but they continued to yank him toward the exit.

"Officer Vestry has him," a guard spoke through breathless pants.

They turned a corner, leaving the pandemonium of the great hall behind. The men ahead of him rushed down the hall with Seran's seemingly lifeless body—her white train, dyed a crimson red, trailing behind them. Farther ahead, his father, King Bryant, and Queen Mariele ran, surrounded by a group of guards tugging at their arms to keep them moving.

"You've been hit," the guard said as they burst through the door of the closest safe room.

"I'm fine! Help the princess!" Trev's voice was loud, matching the yells of everyone else in the room.

He tried to get to where they had lain her body on a table, but there were guards everywhere surrounding her.

The guard who dragged him there pushed him back, away from Seran. "We need to look at your arm."

Trev yelled at him, "Let me help her!" He covered his wound with his other hand.

"There's nothing you can do for her right now." The guard tried to reason with him as he pushed him down into a chair and pulled off Trev's suit jacket. He rolled his sleeve up to look at the wound. "It's clear. The bullet nicked the side of your arm and went clean out," he said, ripping his shirt fabric and tying it around Trev's arm.

Clean out and into Seran's chest.

The shock started to set in as the crowd of people worked furiously around Seran, cutting her dress, trying to reach where the bullet had entered.

The palace doctors appeared with a new team of people to help. Queen Mariele cried into King Bryant's shoulder, who seemed crippled by his daughter's injuries. King Carver paced nearby, emphatically giving orders to his guards.

"We need to get her to the medic hall!" One of the doctors shouted above the commotion.

"Is it safe to move her?" King Bryant asked, putting his hand to his chest.

"We have no choice. She'll die here if we don't operate." The doctor didn't wait for a response. Instead, he shouted instructions for how they were going to move her to the medic room.

Trev stood abruptly to follow but was stopped by one of the medics. "We have to see to your arm." The fabric the guard had tied around his arm was already stained with blood.

Trev reluctantly sat down again. A dull pain ached through his arm with each thread of the medic's needle. He couldn't get over the fact that the bullet that had gone through his arm was now lodged somewhere in Seran's chest.

"Is everyone okay?" Drake asked, entering the room in haste.

King Bryant's voice was solemn. "They just took Seran to the medic hall. She needs surgery."

Queen Mariele let out a yelp before burying her head into the king's chest once again.

"What's going on out there?" King Carver's voice was panicked. He didn't even try to act concerned for Seran.

Drake put his hands up in front of everyone as if attempting to calm them down. "I took down the shooter. The other guards have the hall surrounded, and everyone is being questioned." He looked at Trev. "If you hadn't noticed the shooter first, I wouldn't have known where the shots were coming from. I saw you look at him before you jumped in front of Seran."

"I didn't know what else to do," Trev stammered. "I didn't have my gun on me." His stomach dropped, thinking back to that moment. Why would he think to put a gun in his boot on his wedding day?

"What you did was enough," Drake said reassuringly. "Is she going to be okay?"

Bryant shook his head like he was trying to keep his growing distress in check. "We don't know."

"Do we know anything about the shooter and why he did this?" His father looked to Drake, wanting more answers.

"I shot him, and he didn't make it. I did a quick check of his pockets, and there wasn't anything there to identify him. He isn't anyone that I recognize from the palace or city. I would have remembered hair like that."

"I'm sure Adler is behind this," King Carver said, fury in his voice. "Who else would do such a thing?"

50

Joniss

Wedding guests were everywhere. After the guards released them, people ran down the halls to get to their rooms. Others were in the palace courtyard, yelling at servants for a transporter to be brought around. Servants worked hard to clean up the blood. This much, Joniss had figured would happen, but what he didn't count on was something to go wrong, which it had.

Something had gone very wrong.

Guards were positioned outside Adler's door. As Joniss approached, both men pointed their guns directly at him.

"Step away from the door!" one of them shouted.

Joniss put his hands up in innocence. "Calm down! I'm unarmed. I just want to talk to King Adler."

The two men looked at each other, a silent conversation between them.

"I don't think he'll mind. Tell him it's Joniss Doman."

One of the guards slowly backed up to the door and knocked. An assistant opened the door, and the guard spoke in hushed tones then the door shut again. A moment later, it was flung open.

"Search him," the assistant barked.

Joniss laughed. "I think we both know I am not your enemy here." But he raised his arms again, letting the guards search for weapons.

"All clear," the guard said. Joniss pushed past the man and into Adler's room.

Adler lay casually on his bed, legs crossed, pillows propped up around him. Nobody would have ever guessed that thirty minutes ago, Adler had been a part of a shooting.

"Can I help you?" Adler said coolly.

"What was that downstairs?" Joniss tried not to let his anger ruin the conversation.

"What do you mean?" Adler played stupid.

"Your man didn't follow my plan." Joniss wasn't in the mood for any games right now.

"Your plan?" Adler finally stood. "Your plan was weak and only served your interests. You wanted me to do your dirty work for you. To kill Prince Ezra so that you could easily take the crown. I didn't like that plan, but I did like the idea of a dramatic wedding shooting. That was good stuff."

"Killing Ezra would have helped you. I would've won the election and would be your ally." Why couldn't Adler see that?

"I don't need allies." His eyes had all the confidence of an illegal arsenal behind them.

Joniss shook his head. "What was the point of targeting Princess Seran? It makes no sense."

"It makes complete sense. Prince Ezra is not a threat. My biggest threat is New Hope and Albion joining forces. Their alliance is my biggest threat. That's something I can't have. Now there's no marriage treaty. King Bryant won't want anything to do with Albion once his daughter dies here. The alliance will be off."

"We had a deal," Joniss said, desperation surging in his chest.

"Yes, you gave me information, and I paid you for it," Adler said plainly.

"You were supposed to carry out my plan in exchange for that information."

"Didn't I?" Adler looked around the room at his assistant and guards. "I pretended that Carver tried to kill me. I pretended to be angry about it. I had one of my men, who is dead now, stop the wedding by shooting a member of the royal family. I think I did my part."

Joniss clenched his fists, grinding his teeth together. "My plan was to kill Ezra."

"I don't carry out anybody's plans except for my own. Now, if you could leave me, I have to get ready for a long journey back to Tolsten."

The air escaped Joniss. "I can expose you, you know."

"No, you can't." Adler's lips curled up. "Then everyone will know you and your father were the lying backstabbers behind it all. You'll never become the king because you'll be hanged for treason."

He was right. Adler had backed him into a corner, and there was nothing he could do about it. The old saying was true; don't play with fire or you'll get burned.

51

Trev

Gaines entered the king's office, whispering something in King Carver's ear that made his father's face twist downward.

Trev stood abruptly. Was there news about Seran? It had been a little over an hour since the shooting. Since then, they had taken Seran away to the medic hall and released the royal family from the safe room. Trev couldn't stop worrying. Couldn't stop seeing her pained face. Hearing her cry for help.

"Bring him in," his father said to Gaines, and then he turned to the rest of the men. "Adler's here."

Adler walked in the room, bringing a thick tension that covered the room like fog on a winter's night.

"I came to say goodbye and offer my condolences," Adler said, seemingly unaffected by their accusing glares.

"Condolences? She's not dead." King Bryant flared red with anger.

"Of course. My apologies." But Adler didn't seem apologetic at all.

"Leaving so soon?" Trev hated the disgusting man.

"Can you blame me?" Adler coughed out a laugh.

"I can blame you for a lot of things," Trev said.

Drake gave his arm a warning squeeze.

Adler raised a cocky eyebrow. "As I can blame you."

"What's that supposed to mean?" King Carver scoffed.

"Only that I believe Albion, more importantly, King Carver, is behind the shooting today." Adler looked at King Bryant as he spoke. "It wouldn't be the first time this week that Albion has tried to kill someone from another kingdom. I would know."

"That's ridiculous." King Carver's arms flew out in front of him as if pushing the awful truth away. "Why would I try to kill my future daughter-in-law?"

Adler shrugged. "I don't know. Maybe we should ask my sister, Queen Avina, your wife." Adler glared at him. "Oh, but she's dead, and you killed her."

King Carver stood, every muscle taut, his face and ears tipped with red. "You know I didn't kill Avina. She killed herself!"

Adler spoke to Bryant. "There's a pattern here. All of us keep sending our loved ones to Albion to make great alliances, and what happens? They die. King Carver doesn't care about them. He didn't care about my sister, and he certainly doesn't care about Princess Seran. I would've never considered an alliance with Albion for my own daughter. I wouldn't want Myka to die."

Trev tensed. Adler was doing this on purpose, trying to stir up a fight between Albion and New Hope.

His father's face was near purple with fury. "How dare you accuse us of—"

Adler interrupted. "I'm just stating the facts."

"You did this! You're behind the shooting, and I'm going to prove it!"

Trev and Drake stepped forward, flanking the king and holding him back. A fight now would only escalate into a war later. Maybe they were already headed for war.

The thought made Trev sick.

King Carver's anger only seemed to satisfy Adler more. "I'm not sure how you would even prove something like that. I heard the shooter's dead, his secrets dead with him. It's a shame we'll never know who was really behind it."

"If I were you, I'd be nervous," Trev said. "I'd be very nervous because one of these days, we'll prove that it was you, and when we do, there will be no stopping us from turning every kingdom against you."

Adler breathed out a laugh. "Empty threats from the next boy king."

Trev hoped it wasn't an empty threat. He hoped that he could prove Adler's guilt one way or another.

"Well, I must be going." Adler looked at King Bryant. "I hope the princess makes a full recovery." He turned to exit, stopping briefly to add, "And a word of advice? I would rethink New Hope's so-called alliance with Albion. You can't possibly trust your daughter with them now. I know I wouldn't." With that final word, King Adler left.

THE CLOCK TICKED each second on, it's rhythmic pattern the only sound in Trev's office. He didn't know where his father was. King Bryant was upstairs with his wife. The queen of New Hope had been hysterical, crying, and heaving uncontrollably. Her maid and a guard had to practically carry her to her room.

There were so many things running through Trev's mind. His thoughts bounced to the ceremony, to Seran walking down the aisle, and the words Trev had almost said. He was tormented with guilt even though he thought he'd seen a glimpse of gratitude in Seran's eyes.

Would things have been different if he hadn't stopped the ceremony? He thought about Renna, and how glad he was that she hadn't been in any danger.

Where was she now?

Was she with her mother, consoling her?

Thoughts of Renna sprung up fresh guilt from somewhere inside him. He shouldn't be thinking about Renna when Seran was fighting for her life. Only a terrible person would do that.

"Your Highness?" Crosby peeked his head into his office. "The doctor is out of surgery and is going to address everyone in the royal sitting room."

Trev prayed the entire way to the sitting room that Seran would be okay. He promised God that if he would just let Seran be okay, he would marry her and never think about Renna again.

He was the last of the family to arrive. A fire blazed in the fireplace, its glow lighting up the concerned faces on the couch. He took a seat in the open chair across from his father. Nobody spoke. They just stared at the dancing flames before them.

Doctor Von, a middle-aged man with a mustache and half-moon glasses, entered the room with Gaines. His clothes were stained with blood, and his eyes were defeated. Everyone turned to face him. He bowed before the two families nervously as if he preferred to take up as little room as possible around people.

Nobody moved as they listened to Doctor Von. "Princess Seran received a gunshot wound to the chest. When we began operating, we hoped that the bullet missed her vital organs. However, when we opened her up, we discovered the bullet had damaged part of her aorta, causing a lot of internal bleeding. We were able to locate the tear in her aorta and thought that we could stop the bleeding. We spent hours trying to repair the major artery. Her heart was under a lot of stress. Unfortunately, we didn't fix the damage in time. She lost too much blood and didn't survive."

"No, that can't be right." King Bryant leaned forward, his expression heavy.

Doctor Von dropped his tired eyes to the floor.

"No. No." King Bryant shook his head as Queen Mariele melted into him, sobbing. "Surely, she survived."

The doctor met King Bryant's tear-filled eyes. "I'm sorry. We did all that we could do."

The agony on King Bryant's face dragged up a suffering in Trev he had never experienced in his whole life. The regal pair, the royalty of New Hope, hugged each other in the most intimate and sorrowful way. They clung to each other for support, with fresh tears pouring down their faces. They held each other, rocking back and forth as they wept—their heartache raw and real.

Trev had to look away. It seemed too personal and too private a moment to witness. His cheeks dampened with tears as he listened to their sorrowful wailing.

Seran was dead.

The kind-hearted, intelligent, classy woman he had been engaged to was gone. How could that be? How could Trev not have protected her?

All his training and work as a soldier was for nothing. When it mattered—when Seran's life was in danger—he hadn't saved her. None of this would have happened if Pryer hadn't attempted the assassination, bringing the wrath of Tolsten on Albion.

Trev couldn't sit still any longer. His anger carried him out of the room.

Drake followed quickly behind him. "Trev? Where are you going?"

"To give Pryer a thorough beating." He thought Drake would talk him out of it. Instead, he followed him to the commander's room.

Trev threw open the door, startling Pryer; he almost fell out of his chair with surprise.

"Are you happy with yourself? Is this what you wanted?" Trev grabbed him by the collar of his shirt and pushed him up against the wall. Drake was at his side, ready to intervene if Trev went too far. But how far was too far with scum like Fenton Pryer? Trev didn't know.

Pryer grabbed at Trev's wrists in self-defense. "What's going on?"

"She's dead." Trev slammed his back against the wall again. "And you're the one who killed her."

"I told you, I didn't do anything!" Pryer fought back.

"None of this would have happened if you hadn't continued with the assassination!" Trev's hands moved from Pryer's shirt collar to his neck, his fingers wrapping around his skin.

"I swear!" Pryer coughed between strangled breaths.

Drake's strong hands pulled Trev away, separating him from Pryer and his neck. He gasped for air, leaning over, coughing.

"There's no one else who could have done it. Seran's blood is on your hands."

"Maxwell," Pryer said between coughs.

"What?"

"Maxwell and Joniss Doman. I told them." Pryer straightened his body, leaning against the wall for support. "I told them that King Carver still wanted the assassination. Maxwell asked if he would go through with it without the high ruler's approval, and I said that Carver wanted to, but had changed his mind. Joniss asked how he would have carried it out. I told Joniss about the plan. I shouldn't have, but at the time, it seemed harmless because we had called the whole thing off."

"Why didn't you tell us this before?" Drake asked.

"When Adler first arrived, accusing us, I was caught off guard and angry. I focused in on the men stationed at the inn, thinking that they somehow hadn't gotten the message to stop the plans. The king sent me immediately to find them. It wasn't until I was on the road that I remembered my conversation with the Domans."

Trev shook his head. "Why didn't you say something as soon as you returned this morning?"

"I tried." Pryer looked at him with desperate eyes. "Right before the wedding, I started to tell your father, but Gaines came in saying the ceremony was about to start. There wasn't enough time to have the conversation."

Trev dropped his head. He'd had suspicions about Joniss and Maxwell but hadn't given it enough thought. Everything happening with the wedding had clouded his mind.

"Think about it," Pryer said. "The entire assassination plan was Maxwell's idea. He wanted to frame you and the king all along."

Drake pointed his finger at the commander. "If you're lying about the Domans, I will personally kill you."

"I'm not. Besides the men who were going to carry out the assassination, Maxwell and Joniss Doman are the only other people who knew the details of the plan."

Drake glanced at Trev. "Do you think the Domans sent their own men to kill King Adler, hoping to pin it on you and your father?"

"I don't know," Trev admitted. "But I'm going to find out."

52

Renna

Preetis stepped around the front of the house as soon as the transporter pulled up in front of the farmhouse. His sleeves were rolled up, and dirt was on his hands and pants. His smile widened when Renna stepped out of the vehicle.

"Come here! Let me get you dirty with a hug." His arms stretched out, beckoning her to him. Renna gladly fell into him, savoring the familiarity of it all. "That fancy wedding over already?"

The ache in her heart flickered alive again—Preetis's words giving it a new breath of life. "Yes." She pulled apart from him. "They were married yesterday at noon."

"Yesterday? How in the jimmy-dickens did you get here so fast?"

Renna busied herself with her bags, noticing Mangum's watchful eye. "We actually left before the wedding."

"Before the wedding?" Preetis rubbed at the stubble on his chin but didn't say anything more. Preetis always knew when to leave a subject alone. Renna liked that about him.

"When's the queen coming?"

"I'm not sure." She carried a bag into the house, Mangum trailing not far behind.

"Is that my girl?" Nellie came running from the kitchen, bumping into the sides of furniture on her way. Her body slammed into Renna's in a tight hug. "We've been waiting for you to come back to us." She let go of Renna as suddenly as she had grabbed her. "Let me get you some food, child. You too, Mr. Mangum."

They shuffled into the kitchen, taking a seat at the table.

"Where's that little maid of yours?" Nellie peeked around them. "She's a wispy little thing. Needs some more fat on her if you ask me. Let's get her some food too."

"Nora didn't come with me this time. It's just going to be Mangum and me."

"I won't complain about that." Nellie grabbed a pan and lit the stove. "How long do I get you this time before you have to go back?"

"Well," Renna sat up a little taller, "if you don't mind, I'd like to stay. Indefinitely."

Preetis and Nellie exchanged looks. "Child, of course we don't mind." She gathered Renna up into another hug. "This place is yours. You belong here."

That's exactly what Renna needed right now—somewhere to belong.

Renna's hair was wet from a warm bath, and it hung around her back and shoulders, dampening her nightgown. Nellie's soft fingers combed through the strands, just like they had when she was a child. The crackling of the fire soothed Renna's soul. She lay on her side against the worn-out pillows of her old bed, feeling the comfort of home wash over her.

"What happened in Albion?" Nellie asked quietly. "Why did you leave before the wedding?"

Renna thought about lying. It would have been easier that way, but her heart longed to be comforted.

"I fell in love with the prince. That's what happened in Albion."

Nellie's fingers paused for a moment, no doubt from the shock of Renna's confession. "Oh, child!" She patted Renna's head like a toddler and then continued combing through her hair. "Tell me all of it."

Renna had held it all in until now. As soon as she started, the floodgates opened, the words pouring out of her, begging to be told. Nellie listened quietly as Renna told her about Wellenbreck pond and the fake drowning. About meeting Trev there the next day. She told her how easily her feelings for him had come, how he made her feel light and tied up in knots all at the same time. She told her how they had almost kissed at the pond and how he had promised to see her again in Albion. Nellie gasped at the part where Renna found out he was the prince and endured the horrible first dinner at the palace. She talked about all the times they had tried to convince each other they were just friends. The ways they had justified their relationship so they could be near each other. She told her about the deep sadness she felt when she saw Trev with Seran and how King Carver had threatened her in her room. Nellie laughed about the red dress and sighed deeply when Renna told her about their kiss. She explained how she had managed to avoid speaking to Trev until the day before the wedding. How she had wanted him to say the wedding was called off, even though he couldn't. Finally, she told her how she had wished he'd been in the courtyard, stopping her from leaving, telling her he loved her.

"My, my, my," Nellie clucked, shaking her head. "You poor dear." Nellie hugged the back of Renna's shoulders, her warm hands squeezing all the disappointment and sadness out of her until Renna found herself sobbing uncontrollably in Nellie's soft arms. "Let it go, child. Let it go." Nellie stroked the back of her hair deep into the night until there were no more tears to cry, and sleep swept Renna away.

53

Trev

Trev stood on the dais in the great hall next to the casket holding Seran's body. A line of people from the nearby villages came to pay their respects to their almost-queen. Tomorrow, King Bryant and Queen Mariele would leave for New Hope with Seran's body so they could have a proper funeral and bury her near her mother, Queen Isadora, at the New Hope Government Center. Most of the viewing, Trev nodded graciously at strangers and thanked them for coming. Occasionally there was someone he knew coming to give their condolences. Seran's friends cried and cried in front of him, leaning over her casket, hugging the king and queen, and telling him how sorry they were. That was a tough one. He should be telling them how sorry he was. Not the other way around.

Joniss stepped up next. Everything inside Trev turned cold. He'd known for a few days that Joniss was the informer. Drake had done some investigating but couldn't find anything concrete to prove it beyond the words of Commander Pryer. There wasn't a single trace of evidence tying him to Tolsten, but Trev wasn't worried. They would prove it eventually; it was all about timing.

"Ezra, I'm sorry for your loss," Joniss said a bit too smugly to really be sorry.

From the corner of his eye, Trev saw Drake coming across the room to them. He must have thought Trev wouldn't be able to control his temper. He was probably right.

Joniss looked at Seran's casket covered in an elaborate bouquet of flowers. "Well, this all ended up very tidy for you, didn't it?"

"How's that?" Trev said, unable to hide his disgust.

"Just that Seran is conveniently out of the way now, opening the door for you to run after Renna."

Trev's fingers tightened into a fist.

"I wouldn't be surprised if you planned the shooting yourself as an easy way to get rid of her."

Trev's fist went flying through the air, landing on Joniss's jaw, knocking him to the ground. A crowd of people around them gasped.

Joniss grabbed his jaw while a few men reached to help him up. Everyone in the room watched them now.

"I know this is a hard time for you, Prince Ezra." Joniss spoke the words loud enough for the watching people to hear. "And I don't hold you accountable for your actions today. You're grieving."

Trev struggled against Drake's grasp. He wanted to kill Joniss and his fake persona.

"Let him go," Drake said in his ear. "He's not worth it."

Trev relaxed in Drake's arms. Everyone around them had gone silent, still watching the drama in front of them.

Trev couldn't do this anymore. He turned and left the viewing without another word.

54

Renna

Renna bent over a row of cucumbers, knife in hand. She examined each vine, cutting the large vegetables at the stem and throwing them into a nearby basket. She had been at Wellenbreck almost a week and was starting to settle into a nice routine—waking early in the morning to feed the animals with Preetis, working hard in the fields all day, and laughing with Mangum, Nellie, and Preetis at night until she was too tired to even think.

Each day she spent time at her father's grave. She had forgiven both her parents for the past. She didn't blame them for the choices they had made. She understood now more than ever the difficulties they had faced and why they had done what they did. Forgiveness—especially when it came to her mother—brought a new sense of peace into her heart, and Renna liked the way it felt. She hoped someday she could feel that kind of peace about Trev.

A sleek, black PT zoomed toward the front of the house, pulling her from her work. She struggled to her feet, wiping her hands on her pants. By the time she came around the corner, a guard was off the machine and walking toward the door.

He stopped when he saw her. "Miss Renna, this is for you." He held out a letter.

She recognized the man from King Bryant's royal guard. She took the letter, and the soldier turned to go. "Won't you come in for a drink or a bite to eat?"

"No, M'lady," he said, swinging his leg over his PT. "That's very kind of you, but I'm headed to New Hope with an urgent message."

Before she could say anything else, he turned his machine on and sped away.

"What was that about?" Mangum asked. He had a horse by its reins and was leading it out to the field.

Renna held up the paper as he passed by. "I got a letter." She quickly added, "I'm sure it's from my mother." She didn't want Mangum thinking she still held out hope for Trev. She tore through the paper and began reading to herself.

Renna,

I don't know where to even begin. Our hearts are broken. Seran is dead. There was a shooting at the wedding. Ezra tried to save her. He jumped in front of her, but the bullet scraped the side of his arm and hit Seran in the chest. Officer Vestry was able to take down the shooter before anyone else was hurt. Seran was rushed to surgery, but they couldn't save her. We are utterly devastated. Bryant believes the shooting is somehow tied to Tolsten and King Adler. I don't know what will happen with that. We are leaving Albion tomorrow with Seran's body and will stop at Wellenbreck Farm on our way. I'm assuming you'd like to be there for Seran's funeral and burial. I'd like you there. With the election coming up and everything going on right now, we all thought it best that Ezra stay in Albion and not travel the long distance to Seran's funeral. As you can probably guess, I'm having a very difficult time dealing with all of this. I'm trying to be strong for Bryant, but I am afraid my nerves are not cooperating. Cypress is taking good care of me and assures me that once I return to New

Hope, I will be able to function much better. I hope she's right. I'm sure you have a lot more questions. We all do. We'll get through this terrible time together.

Your loving mother,
Queen Mariele

Renna didn't know when she had put her hand to her mouth, but it was there. She reread parts of the letter to be sure she'd understood it correctly.

Mangum returned from taking the horse to the field. He placed his hand on her shoulder. "Everything okay?"

"Seran's dead," Renna whispered, handing him the letter.

"What?" Mangum scanned the paper. "This is crazy," he muttered under his breath as he continued to read.

"I'm going for a walk." Renna headed for the hill behind the house.

"Do you want me to come with you? Maybe you shouldn't be alone right now," Mangum said, his concern apparent.

She shook her head furiously and kept walking—practically running—until she collapsed at her father's grave. The tears had already been falling, soaking her neck and chest as they fell.

Seran was dead.

It didn't seem real.

Renna could remember the first time they met when she and her mother had arrived at the New Hope Government Center. Seran stood there as her father explained that he was going to marry Mariele. She didn't cry or protest. She took the news with grace, hugging Renna and her mother, welcoming them to New Hope to their *family*.

Then there was the time Seran had taught Renna how to do one of the latest dances. There were plenty of people at the Government Center that could have taught her, but Seran had taken the time to do it personally. At the next ball, Seran had made sure to dance next to Renna so that she could follow her lead if she forgot any of the steps.

The beautiful woman Renna had envied the last four years was gone, even after Trev had jumped in front of a bullet to save her. He'd almost died *for her*. A new wave of tears spilled down Renna's face. She thought of King Bryant losing his only child and cried some more. She thought of her own father's death and a fresh sting of loss stabbed at her. Then a very human part of her thought of Trev—now available. She hated herself for thinking that. How unfeeling could she be? The tears kept coming until night was upon her, and she needed to go back to the house.

Tomorrow she would pack for Seran's funeral.

55

Trev

A line of servants and a few remaining wedding guests bordered the sides of the courtyard, quietly watching the waiting transporters. New Hope flags were attached to each vehicle, flapping freely in the wind. Seran would leave Albion much in the same way she had arrived, heralded by all the fanfare a princess deserved. Except this time, she was in a casket.

Trev's grief and guilt had prevented him from sleeping the night before. He should have treated Seran better. He deserved the bullet, not her.

"Thank you for everything," Queen Mariele barely managed to say before all her fragile strength was gone.

Trev bowed in silence. What was there to say? Mariele knew the truth, knew what kind of a liar he really was.

King Bryant spoke to his father first. "We'll be in contact about the next move with our alliance and Tolsten."

The two kings shook hands.

King Bryant stopped in front of him. Trev wanted to say a million things to him, but all that came out was, "I'm sorry."

Bryant put his hands on Trev's shoulders, and that's when

Trev lost it, when his tears started to come heavily. "I'm sorry," Trev said again through his sobs.

Bryant folded him into a fatherly hug, the way his own father never had. They stood there, hugging, crying, not caring who was watching.

"It's not your fault." Bryant's words were soft and comforting. "You did all you could."

"I didn't deserve her," Trev cried.

"Yes, you did." He pulled Trev back, forcing him to look in his eyes. "When you jumped in front of her," Bryant fought to speak between stifled sobs, "when you risked your own life to protect her, I knew you were a good man. I knew you deserved her."

Trev wiped at the tears that wouldn't stop coming, wishing he could believe him. "I should be coming with you to New Hope for the funeral."

"No." King Bryant shook his head. "Things are uncertain with Tolsten, and with an election around the corner, you need to be in Albion right now."

King Bryant was right, but it felt cruel to watch Seran's body leave in a transporter without him.

56

Joniss

The blackness of night felt thick around Joniss. Even the narrow sliver of moon glinting in the night sky seemed darker than usual. He whipped his head around, making sure he wasn't followed, but there was nothing but a canopy of pine trees behind him. Joniss wasn't usually this jumpy, but ever since the wedding ceremony a month ago, he'd been watching his back, half expecting King Adler to be lurking in every shadow.

Joniss quickened his steps, pointing his hand light into the dirt in front of him. Through the rays of light, he could see his breath puff out like a cloud of smoke in the chilly air.

He was almost to the cave.

Joniss had sent a note earlier in the week, letting his men know he would be visiting Axville as part of his campaign. His men knew the plan and what was supposed to happen during his visit.

He looked back one more time before ducking under the rocky ridge that led to the opening of the cave. He crouched to avoid hitting his head as he slowly walked through the narrow tunnel. The flicker of firelight danced ahead of him and there was a panic of frantic movement.

"Calm down. It's just me!" Joniss called out to his men.

"He's here," someone shouted to another. "Get the blindfolds ready."

The passageway opened up into a large alcove. Joniss straightened, the rocks finally high enough for him to fully stand. He stopped at the opening, careful to stay in the shadows. He didn't want to be heard or recognized. So far, his men had done all of the dirty work for him.

Parson stepped in front of him, a long gun slung over his shoulder. He was dressed in all black with clunky black mountain boots that almost went up to his knees. Firelight danced off his bald head and face, making his teeth look more yellow than they already were.

"Is everything ready?" Joniss whispered.

"Dundy and Fike are finishing with the ropes and blindfolds." Parson gestured behind him to where the men worked.

Joniss shone his hand light to the far corner of the cave, watching until his men were done. He walked toward his prisoners, examining them. A purple bruise stretched across the first one's face.

"I thought I told you not to hurt them." Joniss looked directly at Fike.

Fike's mouth twitched, and his gray eyes flashed with fear. "Well, that one there causes trouble."

Joniss looked at the older man, and without any notice, struck him across his cheek the way he imagined the prisoner had been hit. Fike stumbled back, grasping his face.

"Did that hurt?" Joniss asked calmly.

"No, boss," Fike replied, still holding his cheek.

Joniss looked back at the prisoner. "Then, I suppose it didn't hurt her either." He shone his light on the rest of the prisoners. Despite the blindfold over their eyes, they turned their faces from the bright light. Their hair was tangled and matted, their gray working dresses dirty and ripped in places, but they all seemed fine.

The missing daughters of Axville had been relatively compliant prisoners.

It was a brilliant plan, and in the end, Joniss would be the hero. It would be him, not Ezra, that found the girls and returned them home, laying the blame for their capture firmly at the feet of the Tolsten soldiers.

He glanced at Dundy, a tall man with muscular arms and long brown hair. "Gather them up, and let's go."

Dundy nodded, pulling on the rope that tied the eight girls together, preventing them from escaping.

"Watch your head," Dundy said, as he pushed down each girl's head. "It gets low here."

Everyone followed Joniss down the passageway. In a few hours, he would save the day.

Joniss ducked under the last ridge then stood. He waited for the rest of the group to exit the cave before moving.

When cold metal pushed against his neck—metal from the barrel of a gun—he froze.

"Hello, Joniss," an icy voice said behind him.

The blood drained from Joniss's face.

From the corner of his eyes, Ezra emerged from the darkness.

Trev

"You're finished, Joniss," Trev said, digging the gun further into his neck.

A bald man behind Joniss pointed his gun at Trev. "Not so fast."

"I wouldn't do that if I were you," Drake said from up above the ridge, pointing his own gun at the bald man. "You're surrounded."

Two dozen Albion soldiers with guns appeared from the trees and circled around them.

"You all should be thanking me," Joniss sneered. "Not pointing guns at me."

"Why would we thank you?" Drake asked.

"Because my men found the missing girls."

Trev scoffed. "Your men kidnapped them."

"Prove it!" Joniss huffed.

"Oh, we can," Drake replied. "We've been following you for a month. Tracking your every move. We can prove you kidnapped these girls and that you've been leaking government information to Tolsten."

Two Albion soldiers stepped forward, taking the rope from the tall man, and ushered the girls away from their captors. The girls sobbed as the soldiers untied them and removed their blindfolds. Trev had to cough to keep his own emotion in check.

For months, he had been looking for these girls, worrying that they had been killed. Trev had felt helpless and defeated. Now, they were standing in front of him, crying and hugging each other. He'd finally found them.

"Why kidnap innocent girls?" Drake asked, still pointing his gun at them. "Were you trying to start a war with Tolsten?"

"Why would I want to start a war with Tolsten?" Joniss spat.

"You tell us," Trev said. He pressed the barrel of the gun deeper into Joniss's neck, making him wince. "You're the one who tried to assassinate King Adler."

"You both think you're so smart." Joniss laughed. "You think you have it all figured out."

"Don't we?" Drake raised an eyebrow.

"Hardly," Joniss muttered. "I didn't try to kill Adler. I was working with him. Up until the time he double-crossed me."

Drake and Trev exchanged glances.

"Adler was supposed to kill *you* at the wedding." Joniss looked right at Trev. "And if he had followed the plan, I would be returning these girls to Axville and would look like a hero right now. The crown would have been mine. Instead, Adler took matters into his own hands and killed Seran."

Trev felt like he'd been hit with a bullet again. He was supposed to die. Not Seran. Guilt emerged like a companion —reliable and constant.

"We can work together, Ezra," Joniss said. "If you spare me, I can work for you. Gather information about Tolsten from King Adler. We can get revenge for Seran's death."

Trev gave a rough laugh. "I'm not interested in revenge. But I am interested in justice. Joniss Doman, you're under arrest and will be tried before the king and high rulers for kidnapping, attempted murder, and treason against the kingdom of Albion."

57

Renna

Snow flurries floated to the ground outside, dusting over the fields and trees. That was about as much snow as Wellenbreck ever got, but Renna made the most of the small winter magic. She pulled out an old blanket Nellie had made years ago. The seams were opening in places, and some of the stuffing was coming out where the blanket had been snagged on something sharp. She sank into her father's favorite chair, the one that had been worn into the shape of him, and read from her favorite book of fairytales.

Renna had only been back at Wellenbreck Farm one week. After Seran's funeral, it felt wrong to leave the Government Center so soon, so she'd stayed for a few weeks, helping her mother and King Bryant adjust to the loss and their new normal without Seran.

Nellie, Preetis, and Mangum talked about winter preparations and what crops they might want to try next spring while Renna stared blankly at her book.

Remorse and guilt hung in the back of Renna's mind, awakening at night when her head hit the pillow—when there was nothing to think about but Trev and Seran. Her mind always drifted to the last conversation she'd had with Seran. That conversation would forever haunt her. The last words they'd spoken to each other were about Renna's feelings for Trev—feelings she never should have had. They should have been talking about Seran, her wedding, her future. That's what a good sister would have done.

"I think I'll go take a bath," Renna said, throwing the book to the side.

"That's a fine idea, child." Nellie nodded. "I'm just going to soak some beans for tomorrow's soup. Then we'll go to bed too."

Renna started to climb the stairs to her room, then remembered she still had her apron on. She turned back around to go hang it up in the pantry. She'd be sorry at breakfast if it wasn't there.

Nellie's usually loud voice was lowered into a hushed whisper, slowing Renna's steps. "All I'm saying is it's been almost three months. What's taking the man so long? Why hasn't he sent even a letter to the poor child?"

Mangum whispered back, "I'm sure he's under a lot of pressure. From the fallout of the wedding to the election, he's had a lot going on. Not to mention everything with Tolsten."

"I just thought he would have reached out to her by now. Are you sure he loved her?" Nellie asked.

"I thought so, but maybe I was wrong." Mangum paused before admitting, "I thought he would have come for her by now too."

Renna pulled her hands to her chest, hoping it would somehow make her heart feel better.

"Well then, he's a fool!" Nellie spat.

Renna tiptoed back to the stairs. The apron could wait.

Apparently, she wasn't the only one who thought Trev would've written by now.

She was pathetic.

Why did she even want him to write? It's not like they could be together, not after everything that had happened to Seran.

58

Trev

"I heard you were back from your campaign tour," Drake said, walking into Trev's office. He casually sat down in the seat across the desk from Trev. "How was it?"

Trev looked up from the paper in his hands, the most recent report from Axville. "Good. Really good, actually. I spent a lot of time with the people, learning about their ways of life, finding out their needs. It's given me a lot of ideas for the Council of Essentials." He shrugged his shoulders. "Assuming I'm the one going to the Council of Essentials."

"I think it's safe to assume you're going. The high rulers have reviewed Joniss and his father's case. They'll be executed in a few weeks."

Joniss's life as payment for Seran's hardly seemed like justice. She was so young and so ready to give her life to serve a kingdom that was new to her. Joniss was cunning and despicable.

"So . . . did you . . . hear from anyone while you were gone? Write any letters?"

Trev rolled his eyes. Drake was clearly being coy. It didn't suit him. "Just ask what you want to ask."

"Have you written to Renna, or has she written to you?"

"No." Trev went back to looking at the paper in his hand.

"Why not?"

Drake could be so annoying when he wanted to be.

"Why would I?" It seemed absurd to contact Renna. He was still grieving Seran. Even though he hadn't loved Seran, he still felt an incredible amount of pain at how her life had ended, how he hadn't saved her.

Drake persisted. "I don't know, maybe because you love her? I'm just taking a stab in the dark here, but that's my best guess."

Trev set the paper down and rubbed his forehead. Drake gave him a headache. "There's no chance for us now. We can't be together after everything that's happened. I couldn't do that to Seran."

"What do you mean you couldn't do that to Seran?"

"You know what I mean. I can't dishonor Seran's memory by running off to Renna. I already dishonored her when she was alive."

Drake's eyes softened. "You need to forgive yourself."

"What about King Bryant?" Had Drake even thought about him? Because Trev had every day. "I can't do that to him. He doesn't deserve it."

"King Bryant doesn't expect you to be single your whole life."

"I agreed to marry Seran, and in all honesty, I wasn't even going to do that. I won't disgrace their family further by being with Renna. He's a good man who's just lost his daughter. I don't want to complicate things more."

Drake stood. "I hope you change your mind. I know you miss Renna, and I hate to see you so unhappy."

Trev shrugged. He wasn't going to change his mind no matter how much he missed Renna, even if it was every second of every day.

When Trev didn't answer, Drake stood to leave. "You should write to her."

Trev tossed and turned in his bed that night. So many things had happened in the last few months. *Big* things he wished he could talk to Renna about, but he couldn't. There was no future for them. Trev's guilt, his shame, his errors would always be in the way. But none of that stopped his mind from racing with words he'd never get the chance to say. All those words had been keeping him up night after night.

He threw off his covers and pulled out a piece of paper and a pen from his drawer. He would write a letter.

Renna would never read it because he would never send it, but maybe the writing of it would be enough.

To the lovely Renna,

I've thought for weeks about what I would say to you if I saw you. The words take up space in my mind, making it hard for me to think or even sleep. There are so many things I want to tell you. I've decided to keep a list of all the things I would say if you were here, if I could talk to you every day.

1. I miss you.
2. I feel like I killed Seran.
3. Tybolt shaved his beard. Shocking, I know!
4. Transportation. You were right. Every working-class person I've asked wants an easier way to get around. Bicycles, transporters, you name it. They just want to be able to go places quicker.
5. Dara, the horse, misses you. I miss you.
6. While I was on the campaign tour, someone locked the door to the roof of the palace, and no one can seem to find the key to open it for me. I'm livid.
7. The wedding ceremony.
8. Joniss was the informer. How did I not see that sooner?

9. Joniss kidnapped those girls from Axville. I don't even know what to say about that. I'm just glad they're back home.
10. There's snow on top of the mountains. You would love it.
11. Your mom and King Bryant really love each other. When Seran died, I found myself envying them—how they had each other to lean on. I'll always be jealous of anyone that gets to be with the person they love.

Trev's eyes started to get heavy. It felt good to get some of his thoughts out on paper, so they didn't run a marathon in his mind all night long. He climbed into bed and eased into a heavy sleep for the first time in months.

Writing to Renna became a ritual on the nights Trev couldn't sleep. Sometimes even during the day, he would think about what he was going to add to his list that night.

12. I'm sick of only the ruling class wearing colored clothes. It's stupid.
13. It's freezing outside. I've never been so cold in my life.
14. I had a wedding present for Seran. It was silly, a figurine that Crosby picked out. I'm not sure what to do with it now. It's on my dresser, taunting me.
15. Yesterday I went to the artifact room to look at the magazine picture of the girl in the red dress. I may or may not have used my thumb to cover her face so I could picture you. I know. I'm pathetic.
16. My father is in a terrible mood (more than usual). I think he's throwing a tantrum because he's about to lose his role as king.
17. Sometimes I daydream about all of your different expressions. I think my favorite one is the look you get on your face when you are nervous—when I make you nervous because I've come too close.
18. I beat Drake in a fight a couple of days ago for real. At least

I think I beat him. On second thought, he probably let me win like he always does.
19. I got a new suit for the election. Blue, of course.
20. I moved Colter's family into a real house with more land. Now they can plant better crops and live off of that money. Don't worry, though, I'll still check in on them.
21. I feel bad that I didn't attend Seran's funeral. Somehow, that doesn't seem very kind of me, even though everyone told me I needed to stay in Albion.
22. Drake keeps mentioning Lizanne in conversations—casually as if I wouldn't notice he keeps bringing her up. Did you know there was a connection there? I didn't.
23. Crosby wants to start planning my "victory party" for after I win the election. It seems a little presumptuous, don't you think? Especially after everything that has happened.
24. You would be scared if you knew how much you were on my mind—borderline stalker-ish.

59

Trev

25. I won the election. Not really a big surprise since Joniss, the only other candidate, is in prison.
26. I'm thinking of changing my name. King Ezra sounds weird.
27. Our kiss . . . can we just talk for a minute about how mind-blowing it was? My heart still races when I think about it.
28. Are you somewhere missing me too?
29. Do you think I would have beat Joniss in the election? I'll never know, and that bugs me.
30. I was sworn in as king today. Crosby's kind of a big deal now. I'll try not to let it go to his head.
31. It's weird. I always pictured myself getting sworn in with Seran by my side. She was a faceless person when I thought about it before I knew her. I felt sad today when I stood there all alone. She should have been by my side.
32. Tybolt is growing his beard back out again. Probably a good choice.
33. You don't know this, but I chose you. I was going to leave this all behind for you. The words were about to roll off my tongue when everything . . .

34. Joniss and his father were executed today. I thought I would be happy, thought I wanted justice, but instead, I feel empty.
35. I just ate ten chocolates. I feel sick. I must be depressed.
36. New Year's Eve . . . the loneliest night of the year.
37. I cried the other night. Did you know I cry sometimes? Only manly tears, of course.
38. I made my father move out to the Trevenna lodge in the mountains. It was a huge fight, and I can't believe he actually left. I guess I really am in charge now. It's kind of great to have him gone.
39. No one ever thinks about the meetings. Being king means going to a lot of meetings.
40. Will it ever be warm again? I'm starting to doubt it.
41. I think you are the most beautiful woman I have ever seen. Do you think I'm good looking?
42. Drake wants to come to New Hope with me for the Council of Essentials. He says it's not to see Lizanne. Sounds suspicious.
43. I've been growing my hair out. I think you'd like it. Who doesn't like more curls?
44. Packing for the Council of Essentials. Should I go with the red or yellow tie?
45. I ate a cinnamon roll today and thought of you. The roll was delicious in case you were wondering.
46. I can't sleep. We drove past Wellenbreck Farm, and I didn't stop. I told them not to stop. I hate myself.
47. It's getting warmer the closer we get to the New Hope Government Center. Why do I live in the mountains?
48. I just saw a cactus. I've never seen one before. I made them stop the transporter so I could get out and see it.
49. The Government Center is plainer than I expected. It just shows how vain and non-essential Albion has become. It's not fair. I have to fix this somehow.
50. Cypress. How have we not talked about her yet? She terrifies me.
51. I had a servant take me on a little tour. We just happened to

pass by your room. I can picture you there. I might've taken a bottle of your perfume.
52. How does King Bryant not hate me? I hate me after everything with Seran, but he still wants to be aligned with Albion, with me. I'm not sure I deserve his friendship.
53. This place seems absent without Seran. Without you.
54. I wish you were here.
55. My first Council of Essentials meeting was today. Ahhh, there is so much I want to tell you with this one. I wore the red tie in case you were wondering.
56. King Adler didn't come to the Council of Essentials. Not a big surprise there. He doesn't follow the Council of Essentials rules anyway, so why would he even bother coming? He sent some advisors, though. They were annoying.
57. I really like King Davin of Enderlin. King Bryant introduced us formally, and I think there's a lot of good we can do with Enderlin as far as transportation and trading goes.
58. Do you really think King Reddick is better looking than me? You were joking, right?
59. I got public transportation approved for everyone! My first essential item as king. You are the first person I wanted to tell. I think you'd be happy about it.
60. I miss you so much it hurts.
61. Have you found a good-looking guy from Vassel to keep you company these past few months? I hope not.
62. There's a lot of political dinners and parties and a lot of political men trying to throw their daughters at me. I'm not saying that to make you jealous. I'm just saying it.
63. Can you believe it has been 166 days since you pretended to drown, and I pulled you out of the water? It has also been 132 days since I last saw you, but who's counting? Definitely not me.
64. The king of Cristole proposed that clothing dyes should be essential for everyone. I voted for it. I already told you I thought the distinction of color was stupid. It passed.
65. Your mother and I mostly avoid each other. I think she's

worried I'll ask her about you and I'm worried she'll bring up our kiss. Avoidance is much easier.
66. Drake is in love with Lizanne. He denies it, but I know.
67. I wonder how long this list will get. I wonder if I will ever stop thinking about you.
68. I don't like Jenica. Is that okay to say?
69. I just realized, if we got married, your name would be Renna Trevenna. That's awful! You would need to go with Renna Degray Trevenna, just to break it up a little bit.
70. This is the last week of the Council of Essentials. I've learned so much from the other leaders. I think the world is in good hands. Well mostly—we've still got King Adler and Tolsten to deal with.
71. King Bryant and I have had some side conversations with other leaders. Everyone wants to avoid a war with Tolsten. We're going to hold tight for now. There are rumors that Tolsten rebels are challenging King Adler on his own soil. Adler won't have time for a war with Albion if he is trying to keep his throne from the rebels.
72. I wish you had been here in New Hope this past month. You promised to show me around.
73. I had a dream about you last night. You were swinging on a tree swing, which was weird since I've never seen you on a swing, and you're not five years old, but I'm not complaining. You looked beautiful with your hair blowing back and forth. I can't seem to get you out of my head.

King Bryant poured Trev a drink as the two men sat in the king's office. The room wasn't anything extravagant. It was painted a light cream that almost looked yellow, and there were a few pieces of art hung on the walls. Two leather chairs sat in front of his wooden desk, and a black sofa leaned against the wall under a window. It was all very modest compared to King Carver's office, which was now Trev's office.

The last official meeting for the Council of Essentials ended yesterday, and all the rulers were preparing to go home.

"I'm glad I got you alone before you leave tomorrow," Bryant said, handing him his glass.

"Oh yeah?" Trev took a sip of the tangy liquid, letting it tingle down his throat.

"I want to talk to you about Renna." Bryant sat on the couch, his leg resting across his knee.

Trev looked at his glass, not knowing what to say. He had almost made it an entire month in New Hope without having to talk to Bryant about her.

"Mariele told me a few weeks ago about you and Renna, and I can only guess what you were going to say when you stopped the wedding ceremony."

If there ever was a man Trev didn't want to disappoint, it was Bryant. Even more so than his own father.

His eyes dropped to the floor. "I'm sorry. I didn't mean for any of it to happen. Seran deserved better from me, and I let you both down. I'm so ashamed." The weight of guilt dragged him down again. Would it ever go away? "I hope you can forgive me."

"I was angry at first. Livid, in fact. You're right. My daughter deserved better than that." Trev braced himself for the king's wrath. "But my anger made me a hypocrite, and that realization was very confusing. I was enraged for Seran, but at the same time, I felt sorry for you."

Trev let out the breath he'd been holding, startled by the king's words. "Why would you ever feel sorry for me? This was all my fault."

"For the last ten years, I've put politics over my daughter. I never should have made the marriage alliance." Bryant shook his head with regret. "You might not know this, but many years ago I was in your same shoes. I loved a woman I wasn't supposed to and was forced to marry another—a princess."

Trev eased back into his chair, listening intently, hoping King Bryant's words could somehow make him feel better.

"I know what Seran's future with you would have looked like because I lived it with Queen Isadora. I was never able to love Isadora the way I loved Mariele, and it was an empty, sad marriage. I wouldn't have wanted that kind of life for my daughter."

"I didn't want that for Seran either." Trev could feel the emotion rising in his chest.

"I know." King Bryant's eyes were kind. "You made the choice that I myself was not brave enough to make so many years ago. And because of my own cowardice, I hurt the people closest to me."

Trev sat forward slightly. "But you chose your country. New Hope would have suffered if you hadn't."

The king waved his hand. "New Hope would have been fine. My country didn't need a marriage, it needed the benefits that the marriage provided. But we could have renegotiated our agreement with Northland and removed the wedding altogether. It might have been awkward, but with time I believe everything would have resolved itself."

"I just hate that the last words Seran heard were the beginnings of me breaking off the marriage."

"You need to forgive yourself for that. It takes a lot of courage to do what you were going to do, and it shows me that you're strong and that you fight for what you believe in. Those are qualities a good king must have. I should have done what you were about to do. And now you have the chance to see it through to the end. "

Trev shook his head. "I can't. It wouldn't be appropriate."

"Do you still love Renna?"

Trev hadn't told anyone out loud how he felt. There was a long list of people who could easily guess his feelings, but he had never said it out loud. He had been writing her that list for months, but that was something he did to make himself feel better. Those were words he never planned to send her.

"I love her," Trev finally admitted.

King Bryant smiled. "Then there is nothing left to talk about."

"I'm not sure it's that simple."

"Ezra, it's within your power to love your country *and* to love Renna. A good king doesn't need to choose. He can do both." King Bryant stood, walking over to where he sat. He extended his hand to Trev. "Let everything else go."

King Bryant's words attached themselves to Trev. He couldn't shake them off even if he wanted to. They were exactly what he needed to hear—the final key that unlocked the floodgates. Trev shook King Bryant's hand then pulled the man into a hug.

60

Renna

It was unusually warm for the first of March, but Renna wasn't complaining. The good weather made it easier to get things done around the farm. Today they were repairing the stone wall in front of the house. Mangum brought new rocks in by the wagon full. Renna sorted them, finding the perfect fit for the damaged areas. Preetis and Nellie worked to cement them into the wall. It was a job Renna had wanted to get done ever since she had arrived. The wall was the first thing people saw when they came to Wellenbreck Farm. Renna wanted to make a good impression.

"What in the jimmy-dickens is that?" Preetis held the palm of his hand up to his eyes, shading the sun.

They all turned to look at the row of transporters headed toward them.

"I suspect it's the queen," Nellie said.

It wasn't her mother. Renna recognized those transporters.

"They're from Albion." Mangum's eyebrows rose as he shot a glance at Renna.

Renna's breath caught in the back of her throat.

The four of them watched in silence as the vehicles rolled

to a stop. The door of the middle transporter opened, making Renna's heart jump.

Trev stood, his hands on the door, and his lips curled into a timid smile. She thought she had toughened up, had gotten over him, but it was amazing what the heart remembered. It was amazing how just one look at him could bring her right back to where she had been all those months ago. Actually, it *wasn't* amazing. It was annoying what the heart remembered.

Trev pushed the door closed and slowly walked toward her. His hair was long, and dark curls bounced freely with each of his footsteps. He had navy suit pants on, and a white button-up shirt, but the shirt gave his casualness away. It was rolled at the sleeves, the buttons loosened at the neck, the way it had always been in Albion at the end of the day.

"Oh child, he's handsome," Nellie said under her breath.

Renna swatted her hand in Nellie's direction, shushing her.

"I thought I had the entire walk up to the door to work out what I wanted to say." Trev's voice was deep and full of nervousness. "I guess I better think quick."

Renna couldn't think of anything to say herself. All she could think about was how fast her heart was racing.

"You look so beautiful." Trev paused, smiling as he glanced over her. "And stronger. Farm life has been good to you." He nodded at Preetis, Nellie, and Mangum. "Hello."

The trio returned the greeting in perfect unison.

"We have work out back we need to get done," Mangum said, shuffling Preetis and Nellie around the side of the house.

That wasn't obvious at all.

"I'm sorry to stop your work," Trev called after them. He looked around at the stone wall they were repairing, then at the house and the farm. "It's incredible, Renna. You're incredible."

The line of transporters behind him was like a procession of black ants. "I see you brought everyone," she said.

He shrugged in his easy way. "They come with the job. Don't worry, though. I told them all to stay in the transporters."

"Congratulations on being king." Renna didn't mean the words to sound so negative, but they did.

He laughed it off. "There was no one else who wanted the job, so I got it by default . . . literally."

Renna bent down and started picking up rocks again. "Well, thanks for stopping by to say hi, but we've got to get back to work."

Trev shook his head, smiling, amusement in his eyes. "I didn't come to just say hi, and I think you know that."

"I don't know what you came for. I haven't heard from you or seen you in months. Why would I have any clue what you are here for?" She tried to hide the bitterness she felt inside but was pretty confident she wasn't doing a good job.

"I'm sorry I didn't write. Things were so crazy after the shooting, and I was just trying to figure everything out."

"It's understandable. Your wife had just died and—"

He sighed. "She wasn't my wife. Not yet, at least."

"Well, she was about to be, but who needs to argue about a few minutes here or there?" Renna gave a tight smile.

"I can see you're upset with me, and rightfully so, but I'm just so happy to see you right now."

She didn't want to be upset with him, but she couldn't help it. Her anger was her only defense mechanism, a way to protect her heart from getting hurt again.

She raised her chin. "So why did you come?"

He took a step forward, obviously nervous. "To tell you I love you. To tell you that you belong with me. To tell you that I want to spend the rest of my life with you. That you're the only one for me."

"Well." She raised her shoulders. "*The only one for you* now that Seran is gone."

Trev threw his head back in obvious frustration. "Why do you have to make everything so difficult?"

"What did you expect me to say?" She folded her arms across her chest, standing her ground.

"I don't know, that you love me too?" He shrugged. "Would that be so hard?"

"Now you love me? Now that you're the king and your fiancée is dead, and no one can be mad at you for being with me? That's when you decide you love me?"

"I loved you all along. Ask anyone!" His toe kicked the dirt in front of him. "You seem to be the only person who didn't know. And you weren't at the wedding. You don't know that I wasn't going to marry Seran."

Renna straightened, trying to make sense of his words.

"Before all the chaos happened, I was about to call it off. I was choosing you. I wanted to marry you."

Tears gathered in the corner of her eyes, but she blinked them back. Why hadn't her mother told her that?

"Not that you'll believe me now." Trev let out another frustrated breath.

"If that's true, why didn't you write to me or come for me? It's been almost six months." She struggled to control her emotion, hoping he didn't see how hurt she was.

"I wanted to." He bit his lip. There was a vulnerable honesty in his eyes that made her want to hug him. "I didn't know how to balance my feelings for you with everything that happened with Seran. I felt like being with you would somehow betray her."

Renna sighed, knowing exactly how he felt. "Why now? What makes you think we can be together now?"

"King Bryant. He's the reason I'm here. His forgiveness and blessing were enough to make me realize *we* deserve to be happy."

Renna wanted to be happy with Trev, but she'd spent the last six months convincing herself of why they could never be together. "Even if we put everything with Seran aside, we still would never work. I can't be the queen of Albion, and you can't be a farmer. I would never fit in your world, and you would always be trying to get me to. It just wouldn't work."

"You'd be a great queen of Albion," he said, the sincerity in his voice saying he really believed it.

"I don't know the first thing about being queen."

"Yes, you do! You're strong. You don't let people get away with things just because that's how it's always been done. You fight for what you believe in, even if it isn't popular. You care about the working-class people and bring so much perspective to those who don't understand what it's really like out there. You're kind, compassionate, and full of ideas. I would be proud to have you by my side."

Renna couldn't believe he saw all that in *her*.

"Besides," he gestured to all the transporters behind him, "there are a thousand people who will happily tell you what to do and say every minute of your life."

She shook her head, not knowing how to get past her insecurities, doubts, and fears.

"Can we just start over?" Trev asked, throwing his hands out to the side.

"It's a little too late to pretend like we're just meeting for the first time."

"No, just start *this* conversation over. I'm going to go back to the transporter and get out again, and you're going to respond differently this time. You're going to tell me how you really feel."

"This *is* how I really feel." At least a part of it, anyway. She was upset with him, but underneath it all, of course she loved him.

"No, it's not." He called her bluff.

"Yes, it is." She meant to hold her ground.

"That was the anger and logic talking. It's good we got it

off your chest." He smiled. "Did it feel good to say all those things to me?"

She bit back her own smile. "Yes."

"Are there any other angry things you want to say to me?" He stood tall like he could take whatever beating she wanted to give him.

Renna opened her mouth to speak then shut it dramatically. She didn't want to rehash all the pain and heartache. Trev was here, and he wanted to build a future with her. It was her turn to let go of the past. "I guess not."

"Okay, then." He took a quick breath. "I'm going back to the transporter, and we'll redo the entire conversation—with you being happy to hear that I love you and excited that the love of your life has arrived." He started jogging back to the vehicle. "And depending on how you respond," he turned, walking backward so she could easily see his adorable face, "we'll see if I get enough courage to ask you to marry me. Okay?"

The butterflies were back, stirring inside her. "Okay."

"All right, Trev loves Renna, take two," he said as he opened the transporter door, ducking inside, then shutting the door.

Trev

Trev sat against the black leather seat of the transporter and took a deep breath.

"How's it going out there?" Drake asked from across the seat.

Trev looked at his friend. "It could be going better."

"That's what I gathered." Drake laughed.

"Okay." Trev pumped himself up. "Here I go again." He swung the door open and stood like he had when he'd first arrived. She took his breath away again, just like she had the first time he saw her. She wore gray pants, but they actually fit her this time, making her long legs look incredible. Her shirt was loose, but every once in a while, the breeze would push it against her torso, chest, and arms in the best way. Her hair was coiled around the top of her head into a loose bun, and her skin was a golden color that accentuated the light color of her hair. He smiled again, just looking at her.

Trev slammed the door behind him and walked toward her with purpose so she was only an arm's length away. She didn't seem as stunned as the first time or as angry. That was a good sign.

"It's so good to see you." He smiled as he looked into her green eyes. "I've missed you in every way possible, every single day."

She raised her eyebrows at the ridiculousness of it all.

He cupped his hands around his mouth and whispered to her, "Take two. Remember?"

Her head shook. "It's good to see you too." She half mumbled the words, but it was better than nothing.

"I'm sorry it took me so long to get here. I was scared, but now the only thing I'm scared of is losing you. I've been miserable without you." He reached into his pocket and pulled out a folded paper. "I even started keeping a list of things I wished I could talk to you about." He smiled big at her. "Proof that I was thinking about you." He unwrapped the paper and began reading from its lines. "Tybolt shaved his beard. I beat Drake in a fight." His eyes scanned down the page. "I got a new suit. King Ezra sounds weird." He tugged at his hair. "I'm growing my hair out. I saw a cactus. Drake loves Lizanne." He looked up at Renna to see her reaction on that one. Then he suddenly felt self-conscious and tucked the paper back in his pocket. "Well, it's all there. You can read it later if you want."

Her brows furrowed. "Did Tybolt really shave his beard?"

Trev knew she'd love that one. "Yeah, right off. Somehow, he looked uglier without it."

She laughed, and he felt whole again.

For months he had been empty; even just her laugh was enough to put his heart back together.

His voice grew soft and serious. "Renna, I love you. I should have told you that the day we sat on the edge of the dock at Wellenbreck Pond because somehow, I knew it then. Or when we were in the artifact room or shooting guns or dancing or when we kissed. I should have told you I loved you when we kissed.

"We spend so much time thinking about and deciding what is essential. The last two months, that's all I've done. I've spent all my time worrying about what is essential for everyone else. You . . ." He took a step closer, his hand reaching out to touch her face. Her skin was warm and smooth, and just like he knew it would, a surge of energy flew through his body.

"You are essential to me," he said softly.

Trev thought he heard someone sigh. His eyes flickered to the side of the house. The plump woman seemed embarrassed she had been caught eavesdropping and quickly hid behind the stone.

She wasn't the woman he was trying to impress with his undying love, but at least someone thought he sounded good.

He looked back at Renna, hoping his words had melted her heart as much as they had her friend's. "So?" he asked expectantly.

A slow smile spread across her lips as if she liked stringing him along. "So what?"

He slipped his hand behind Renna's neck and pulled her closer, so their foreheads were touching. "So, do you love me too?"

He had never been so vulnerable in his life.

Her head bobbed up and down against his forehead. "I love you too," she whispered.

"Whew!" He threw his head back. "That is a relief!" He

pulled her into a hug, her body fitting perfectly under his arms. "I was worried after the disastrous take one."

Her body laughed against his.

"You should've been worried." She backed out of the hug to look at him. "I wasn't sure this was going to end well for you."

"I know, but I really think I nailed it in take two," he said with mock seriousness. "Don't you?"

She raised an eyebrow. "It was all right, I guess."

"All right?" He called out to the older woman who was watching them again. "You thought I did good, right?"

She ducked her head behind the house again, but Trev heard her loudly and clearly say, "Yes, sir! Pretty darn near perfect."

Renna spoke over her shoulder. "Don't say too much, Nellie, or it will all go to his head."

"Never!" he said sarcastically.

She looked up at him, a glimmer in her deep green eyes. "It's been so long, how did you know I wasn't completely in love with someone else by now?"

"I thought about that but knew no one else could stand a chance against me."

"How could you be sure?" she asked. "Maybe he's the most attractive man I've ever seen. Maybe he writes poetry and bakes . . ." She stuttered, obviously searching her mind for something to say. "Bread."

Trev nodded, keeping a straight face. "Yes, because the *most* attractive men always bake homemade bread."

"Don't forget about the poetry," she added.

"He doesn't write poetry. That was just the bread recipe."

Her laughter escaped in the most adorable way.

Trev pulled her into him. "Since we know the bread-making poet doesn't exist, and we know you love me . . ."

She nodded, agreeing with everything he said.

"Can we kiss now? I've been here like, twenty minutes, and we haven't kissed yet. It's torture."

She raised her chin up, and that was all the answer he needed to bring his lips down to hers. He kissed her slowly, pouring all his feelings of love into each movement of his lips. He wanted her to feel how much she meant to him. To feel how much he needed her in his life.

The kiss solidified everything.

Trev hugged her tightly again. "Are you going to marry me or not?"

"Are you going to ask me?" she quipped back.

Trev grabbed her by the hand and knelt down on one knee.

"Renna Degray, will you agree to rhyme your name with mine?"

"What?" Her face was confused. That was clearly not the proposal she was expecting. Perhaps he should have gone with something more traditional.

Trev grimaced. "Did you know your name will be Renna Trevenna?"

"I . . . hadn't thought about it." Her eyebrows puckered.

He quickly added, "Well, don't. Especially if it's going to make you answer negatively."

"Renna Trevenna?" she questioned, looking around, obviously mulling it over in her mind. "That's awful!"

He nodded to the transporters. "I'll get my advisors on it. They'll know what to do."

She puffed out a little laugh.

Trev laced his fingers through hers, searching her green eyes. She was the best woman he had ever known. She had the most amazing mind, her wit alone kept him constantly entertained, her happiness made him a better man, and her beauty took his breath away. She was everything to him. "Renna." He smiled up at her, so sure of how he felt. "Will you marry me?"

She nodded first before answering. "Yes." It wasn't too loud or crazy. Just subtle and perfect.

That was all Trev needed to gather her into his arms and kiss her again. Renna pulled back as his kiss deepened.

His lips tried to follow after her. "What just happened?"

She looked around nervously, ducking her head like a turtle trying to hide in its shell. "I feel like everyone is watching us."

He looked back at the transporters. "That's because they are. I'm sure their heads are pressed against the windows as we speak."

"Well, I'm not that kind of girl," she said frankly.

He raised his eyebrows. "What do you mean?"

"I mean," she gestured around them, "I'm not going to kiss you, *really* kiss you when the whole world is watching."

Trev immediately grabbed her hand, pulling her toward the house.

"Where are we going?" Renna stumbled behind him, trying to keep up.

"To find some privacy." He opened the front door. "Is there anyone in this house I should know about?"

"Nobody." She smiled back at him and he nearly came undone.

Trev closed the space between them, pressing her back against the closed door. "I've been waiting six months to kiss you again, to kiss you like that night at the ball."

"You might be disappointed." Her green eyes sparkled, taunting him as he inched closer. "Too much buildup," she whispered between them.

"I doubt it," he breathed against her lips.

Then he kissed her the way he really wanted to.

They kissed until they had been kissing so long, Drake came knocking.

Epilogue

RENNA

The Kingdom of Albion
Six Months Later

"You know, kidnapping is very unattractive." Renna reached for the blindfold covering her eyes but stopped when Trev tsked at her from across the transporter. She was annoyed with his surprise, only because she hated not knowing where he was taking her. "I mean, it is probably the *least* attractive thing you could do."

"You think this is the least attractive thing I could do?" Trev said skeptically.

She couldn't see his face but could tell he was poking fun at her.

"I can think of twenty things that should be more *un*attractive."

Her fake annoyance increased as he started rattling off ideas. "Throw up is more unattractive. No, I take that back, vomit coming out of my nose is extremely unattractive."

She put her palm up to stop him. "I don't need you to list things."

It was too late. Trev was already continuing. "Don't even

get me started on other bodily fluids . . . the kind that should only be found in bathrooms."

"Stop!" she giggled out, putting her hands lightly over her ears.

"*Those things* should be top on your list of the least attractive things about me. Trust me, I know."

"Okay, you proved your point." Her head shook as she pretended not to hear him.

"Are you sure?" he asked. "Because I could keep going."

"No! Please just stop now." The transporter rolled over a bump jostling her body against the door. "Are we almost there? I feel like we have been driving for a while."

"You're kind of whiny when you're blindfolded. Did you know that?" The tone of voice said he was kidding, even though she was, in fact, being whiny. "You're in luck though; we're here."

The transporter slowed to a stop, and Renna instinctively reached for her blindfold.

"Not so fast!" Trev grabbed her hands. "I'll tell you when you can take it off."

Trev helped her out of the transporter. Her heart pounded with excitement at every slow step and pull from him. Renna still had no clue where they were or what they were doing. Everything sounded like typical outside noises.

"Now I'm *sure* this is where you're going to kill me," she said as her foot shuffled cautiously ahead.

"Do you think the killing thing will be an ongoing theme throughout the rest of our lives, or do you think there will come a time when you don't think I'm trying to kill you? I'm just trying to mentally prepare for the future."

She raised her eyebrows, making the blindfold shift a little. "*If* there is a future."

"I can assure you there's a future." Trev stopped pulling her forward, shifting her sideways a tiny step. "Right here," Trev said gently.

Renna smiled in giddy anticipation. This surprise had been going on for hours. It had started that morning. She woke up to Trev sitting on the side of her bed with a dozen pink roses. There was a split second where she thought she might have been dreaming. Even though she had been living at the Albion Ruler's Palace for months, she was still getting used to the fact that this was her new home—her new life. Trev's charming smile was definitely the best thing she had ever woken up to, but she hadn't really enjoyed it because her thoughts had immediately gone to her bedhead and bad breath. Trev had practically shoved breakfast down her throat before making her put on the stupid blind fold. That's when Nora had arrived to get her ready. Renna wasn't allowed to see what she wore or what she looked like. She could tell her dress was lacy. That seemed a little fancy for a day dress, adding to her suspicion. Nora wasn't even helpful—tight-lipped about the entire surprise. Every once in a while, Trev popped his head in the room, annoyingly reminding her not to peek. But now they had finally arrived. Things were about to get exciting.

"Okay, you can take it off," he said with a nervousness she hadn't sensed in Trev in months.

Renna pulled at the fabric covering her eyes and blinked at the overpowering light now blinding her. Trev was across from her, dressed in a handsome black suit she'd never seen him wear.

It was crazy how just one look at him could get her heart going.

She gasped as she recognized King Bryant and her mother standing off to the side. Renna lurched forward into her mother's arms. "I can't believe you're here." Her mother's soft hands brushed over her hair as they hugged.

"I've missed you so much," her mother said, hugging her tighter.

Their relationship wasn't perfect. Levels of hurt, mistrust, and guilt still needed repair. Renna might never understand her mother's motives for her actions, but at least they were both trying. It was a good start.

King Bryant's strong hands wrapped around them both. "It's so good to see you." His voice was kind and full of love.

Renna pulled away from them, noticing Drake, smiling at her like an idiot, and Nellie, Preetis, and Mangum. She quickly took in her surroundings. They were in the mountains. Tall pines circled them, making the majestic mountain views even more breathtaking. Two wooden posts were behind King Bryant, decorated with white netting and cream-colored flowers. She looked down at her dress—beautiful white lace with flowing sleeves and a seersucker waist. Her smile widened. She knew what this was.

It was her wedding.

An excited laugh rolled off her lips. "Did my 'Save the Date' get lost in the mail or something?"

Trev smiled at her in the most adoring way. "I hope you don't mind, but I went ahead and planned our wedding." He grabbed her hands, intertwining his fingers with hers. "It's more intimate than my last wedding." He looked at King Bryant and her mother. "We all agreed that big weddings give us anxiety now."

Renna looked around at everybody she loved. "I . . . can't believe this." She looked back at Trev, amazed by him. "I actually don't mind at all. It's absolutely perfect." Happy tears gathered in her eyes as she hugged him. "Wait. There's someone missing."

Trev pulled back. "Who? Tybolt? You've really got to get over him."

She rolled her eyes. "No, where's your father?"

"Oh, him. We all decided he shouldn't be invited. He's kind of a despicable person."

"Yes, I've seen that side of him." Renna shuddered, thinking back to the night he came to her room.

"So, are we going to do this?" Drake asked.

Trev turned to him. "Are you in some kind of a hurry?"

Drake colored, clearly a little embarrassed by the question. "No, I just want to get to the good part."

Trev smiled at Renna. "What he means by that is he wants to see Lizanne. She traveled with Bryant and your mother from New Hope."

"Ohhh," Renna said, dragging the word out. "I'm sorry my wedding is such an inconvenience to you," she joked.

"It's not . . . I'm going to shut up now." Drake smacked his lips together dramatically, proving he would be silent from now on.

"Where is she? You could have invited her." Renna looked between him and Trev.

"He's fine." Trev looked at his friend. "He'll see her back at the palace."

Renna nodded, and everybody stepped in closer as if they all knew it was time. Her heart thumped against her chest, not because she was nervous, but because she was so happy. For the first time in her life, everything was just as she always hoped it could be. She looked at the faces of the people she loved most, each of them important to her in a different way. Each of them having shaped her into who she was at that moment.

The sun broke through the clouds, lighting her features, warming her face. Renna closed her eyes, and for one peaceful moment, her father was there with her, giving his blessing. Giving his love.

"Are you ready?" Trev's hands squeezed hers.

She bobbed her head up and down and studied his striking blue eyes.

Trev was everything she had hoped she would find someday. Every dream that she had ever had about love was coming true because of him.

King Bryant stepped between them. "I am honored to

marry you both, and I know Seran would be happy about it too."

Renna was astonished at King Bryant's kindness and support. Trev had shared with her that Bryant was the reason he finally felt okay about being with her. There was something beautiful about Bryant wanting them to be happy despite Seran's death; hearing that Bryant thought Seran would be happy for them too was a big relief. In the last few months, Renna had thought about Seran and felt guilty. Guilty that she was marrying Trev. Guilty that she was alive, and Seran wasn't. Trev felt it too. It was a sadness they both carried with them. But it many ways, it had brought them closer together because it was something only the two of them understood. There would always be a part of Renna's heart that wondered about Seran, but in this moment, she felt peace.

Bryant was right. Seran was happy wherever she was.

Trev gave her a knowing look.

Such a big moment came with so many big emotions. Renna wrapped her fingers tighter around Trev's as Bryant began the simple words to the ceremony. Her breathing picked up intensity, keeping pace with the swirling excitement in her chest. She wanted to cry. She wanted to laugh. She wanted to break out into a little dance or start singing a ridiculous song from the top of her lungs.

This was what happiness felt like.

THE NEXT MORNING, Trev and Renna lay in bed at the Trevenna family cabin, surrounded by the mountains of Albion. A fluffy gold comforter was draped over them, their bodies meshed together, curving into each other.

"I can't believe you kicked your dad out of his home for an entire week." Renna turned her cheek toward him as she spoke.

"Would you have preferred he stay here with us on our honeymoon?"

"No." She shook her head.

"Well, then, you're welcome." He pulled her closer, snuggling against her body.

"He's just going to hate me even more." Renna was a little scared of how her relationship with Carver would work out the rest of her life.

"I guess you have a lifetime to figure it out," he mused.

"And what are you going to spend your lifetime figuring out while I'm doing that?"

Trev sighed. "I'll probably spend a lifetime trying to figure out how to keep Albion safe from Tolsten."

"Oh."

Trev leaned his head up, noticing the disappointment in her voice. "What? You didn't like that answer?"

Renna stumbled over her words. "No . . . I did. I just . . . thought you were going to say something cheesy and cute like, *I'll spend a lifetime trying to make you happy.*"

"Ah, yes. Cheesy honeymoon talk," he said, letting his head fall back onto his pillow.

"Cheesy honeymoon talk? Is that a thing?"

"It is now." He switched to his baby voice. "My sweet tender muffin."

Renna let out a harsh laugh. "On second thought, I don't think I'm the type of girl that likes cheesy honeymoon talk."

"Whatever you want." He nuzzled his face into her neck. For a moment, the only sound was the rhythm of their breaths.

"Sometimes I wonder," she said, breaking the silence, "if I am the only person in the history of the entire population who has ever lain in this position."

"What? Like next to a king?" he asked. "I thought you didn't like cheesy?"

"No, like this." She jostled her arm a bit, prompting Trev

to reach his head up again so he could see the position she was lying in.

She had her left arm straightened out under her pillow with her head leaning on top of it, and her right arm formed a triangle, resting her fingertips comfortably below her chin.

Trev started laughing. "You think you are the only person who has ever lain like that?"

"No." She defended herself. "Not logically. I'm just saying, what if I was? It's such a comfortable position; what if everyone else in the world didn't know about it?"

He wrinkled his brow as if to consider her question. "Yes, I can picture it even from the beginning of time. Adam and Eve not knowing what to do when they lay down to rest—not being able to figure out how to get comfortable. If only they knew they could stretch one of their arms out and use it as a pillow to lean on." The sarcasm in his voice betrayed any chance of sincerity.

"Seriously." She nudged him with her right elbow. "What if I was the first person to discover this position?"

"Then you must patent it," he said. "It would be your patented position."

"What does that mean?"

"It means no one else would ever be able to lie like that again without your permission or without paying you. It was something they used to do before Desolation."

"Thank you," she said.

"For teaching you about patents?" His arms hugged her body tighter.

"No, for letting me talk about stupid things. For letting me be me." She bit her lip as she spoke, a little shy about her vulnerability.

"I wouldn't want to talk about stupid things with anybody else. That reminds me," he threw back the covers on his side and climbed out of bed, letting a rush of cold air snake up the back of her nightgown. "I have a wedding present for you."

His bare feet tiptoed around the bed. "It's freezing! Why is it so cold in the mountains?" he complained.

"Well, maybe if you put on more than just undershorts, you wouldn't be so cold." She leaned up on her elbow, watching him.

Trev stopped dead in his tracks and looked at her with a mischievous smile. "Why would I put on more clothes?" He started flexing his stomach and arm muscles as he danced around the foot of the bed. "You can't resist my super, amazing abs."

Renna laughed at his outrageous dance moves.

"I know you love my body," he said. "You were checking me out the second day we met." He continued to dance in front of her. "When I was swimming in the pond."

"I did not check you out!" she said, throwing a pillow at him. "I remember covering my eyes, like a good girl."

"You were peeking." He danced over to the cherry armoire and pulled out a wrapped gift, then he danced his way back to her.

She threw another pillow at him just to be dramatic, but he swatted it away, jumping onto the bed next to her.

"Open it," he said excitedly.

She tore through the wrapping paper and box. Inside were four frames, each with a wrinkled paper guarded inside the glass. Renna smiled, recognizing Trev's scribbled handwriting.

Trev pointed to the frame on top. "It's the list I wrote you —all the things I wanted to talk to you about when you lived at Wellenbreck."

She nodded, loving that he was giving this to her. She had asked to read it several times, but he'd always acted like he had lost it.

"If we ever run out of things to say to each other or stupid things to talk about, we can consult the list." He held the frame up in front of him, scanning the paper with his eyes.

Renna kissed his cheek. "I love the list, but I don't think we'll ever run out of things to say to each other."

Trev tucked a piece of hair behind her ear, trickling his fingers down her neck on the way. "I don't think we will either. After all, we'll always have Tybolt."

THE END

I hope you enjoyed Trev and Renna's story. If you did, please consider leaving me a review. I love hearing what people liked about the book.

If you would like to learn about future books, read sneak peeks, and find out about sales, join my newsletter and receive a deleted scene from The Promised Prince. You can connect with me and join my newsletter at www.kortneykeisel.com. Or find me on Instagram, Facebook, and Pinterest.

Read the next book in the series:

Also by Kortney Keisel

The Desolation Series (Dystopian Royal Romance)

The Rejected King

The Promised Prince

The Stolen Princess

The Forgotten Queen

The Desolate World

Famously In Love (Romantic Comedy)

Why Trey Let Me Get Away

How Jenna Became My Dilemma

The Sweet Rom "Com" Series

Commit

Compared

Complex

Complete

Christmas Books (Romantic Comedy)

Later On We'll Conspire

The Holiday Stand-In

Acknowledgments

I've always loved acknowledgments after I finish a book. Now, I can't believe I'm actually writing one of these things. When I first set out writing this book, I never imagined how many people it would take to make this dream become a reality. I am so thrilled to give a shout out to all of the people who "Support Kort."

I have to start by thanking my niece, Erin. She was the first person to read my halfway-finished manuscript and my partner in crime when it came to editing. I'm so grateful for the hours and hours you spent making this book what it is. I loved all of our phone conversations, our back-and-forth texts, our Google Doc threads, and our side conversations at family parties. You made me a better writer, and you added so much to the development of the plot. I will forever be grateful for the work you put in. You have a real talent, and I can't wait to see what the future brings for you.

To my very first beta readers: Stacy, McKenna, Kaylen, Sidney, Michelle, Chelsea, Jen, and Laura, you guys read this book when it was a hot mess. Thank you for all of your honest suggestions and the time you spent reading and thinking about how the book could be better, especially Stacy, McKenna, and Kaylen. I will NEVER forget the hilarious comments and threads on that first document. I can look back through this book and specifically name parts that each of you added. You three make up the dream team when it comes to beta readers.

Thank you to all of my other beta readers. There are too

many of you to name individually, but I appreciate all the time it took to read and send me feedback. Mostly, you gave me confidence that maybe this book didn't suck.

Another person who made this book so much better was my editor, Jenny Proctor. You taught me so much about writing and helped strengthen everything from my word choice to my confidence. I loved your helpful tips about publishing and how you made me feel like we had been friends for years. Thank you!

I owe a huge thank you to Tasha, @the_clean_read_-book_club. Not only is she the best bookstagrammer out there, but she held my hand, answered all my stupid questions, and promoted this book like crazy. You are my first official fan. Thank you for loving this book as much as I do and for helping me get it in front of so many people.

I have the best group of girlfriends. You girls are the first people I admitted to that I was writing a book. It took me four years to complete it, but I always appreciated the enthusiasm, the laughs, and the encouragement. You girls are my biggest fans, and you truly know how to "Support Kort." I look forward to many more years of monthly dinners and peeing my pants from laughing so hard. Each of you has blessed my life, and I am grateful for the years of friendship we've had.

Thank you to my family and Kurt's family. I'm pretty sure me writing a book came out of nowhere for most of you, but thanks for indulging my whims and supporting me anyway. Even my cute dad joined in on all the "book talk." He's the best. And a big thank you to my nephew, Austin, for building my website.

To my sisters, Stacy, you have been my biggest cheerleader since day one. Shelly, thank you for proofreading...twice. Kendra, thanks for all of the emotional encouragement. This just might be the first fiction book you read. I look up to each of you so much! Not having Mom here to share this book with me has been hard, but I'm so grateful for how you three have rallied around me to fill her void. It means so much.

Speaking of my angel mom, I feel like I need to publicly state that Trev's list at the end of the book came from her. I can still remember the moment the idea popped in my head, and I remember the distinct feeling that she was adding her bits-and-pieces from heaven. This book is for you, Mom.

A huge thank you to my amazing five children. Finding the balance between writing and being a mom has been difficult, but they still cheer me on despite all the times I've been distracted or there hasn't been anything to eat for dinner. In all honesty, their excitement made me want to finish the book and publish it. I love you all, and am so lucky to be your mom.

To Kurt, my extremely handsome husband, you make it easy to write about love. There will be pieces of you in each romantic hero I write. Thanks for making me laugh every day, for coming up with the Council of Essentials, for loving me and all my crazy, and for laughing out loud when you read my book. You make life so much more fun, and I love you.

Finally, I would feel very ungrateful if I didn't thank my Heavenly Father and His Son, Jesus Christ. I have been so blessed, and I know that every blessing I have comes from them, especially when it comes to writing and publishing this book.

About the Author

Kortney loves all things romance. Her devotion to romance was first apparent at three-years-old when her family caught her kissing the walls (she attributes this embarrassing part of her life to her mother's affinity for watching soap operas like Days of Our Lives). Luckily, Kortney has outgrown that phase and now only kisses her husband. Most days, Kortney is your typical stay at home mom. She has five kids that keep her busy cleaning, carpooling, and cooking.

Writing books was never part of Kortney's plan. She graduated from the University of Utah with an English degree and spent a few years before motherhood teaching 7th and 8th graders how to write a book report, among other things. But after a reading slump, where no plots seemed to satisfy, Kortney pulled out her laptop and started writing the "perfect" love story...or at least she tried. Her debut novel, The Promised Prince, took four years to write, mostly because she never worked on it and didn't plan on doing anything with it.

Kortney loves warm chocolate chip cookies, clever song lyrics, the perfect romance movie, analyzing and talking about the perfect romance movie, playing card games, traveling with her family, and laughing with her husband.